G... Mulrooney,

was born in 1952. She took a degree in English at the
University of Ulster and lived for a few years in Dublin
working as a hospital cleaner, a plastics riveter (fitting
together Guinness signs) and teaching English. She then
came to England to teach, before taking up social work.

  Gretta Mulrooney's first novel, *Araby*, was published by
Flamingo in 1998. *Marble Heart* is her second novel.

From the reviews of *Araby*:

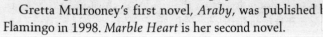

'What is admirable about Mulrooney's writing is the way she manages to keep the tone buoyant, while alluding to many heartbreaking strands of family history. For both Kitty and Rory, this is a story of gallant survival.'　*Independent*

'I loved it. Such a sweet story without being in the least bit sentimental, and very moving without being harrowing. There are moments when the reader is absolutely *there*, so acute is this novelist's eye and ear.'　MARGARET FORSTER

'A wonderfully funny view of Irish motherhood, but Mulrooney also evokes powerful emotions as Rory comes to appreciate quite how much his infuriating but irreplaceable mother means to him. Highly recommended.'
Literary Review

MARBLE HEART

GRETTA MULROONEY

Flamingo
An Imprint of HarperCollins*Publishers*

Flamingo
An Imprint of HarperCollinsPublishers
77–85 Fulham Palace Road,
Hammersmith, London W6 8JB

www.**fire**and**water**.com

Flamingo is a registered trademark of
HarperCollins Publishers Limited

Published by Flamingo 2000

9 8 7 6 5 4 3 2 1

First published in Great Britain by
Flamingo 2000

Copyright © Gretta Mulrooney 2000

Gretta Mulrooney asserts the moral right to be
identified as the author of this work

ISBN 0 00 655182 3

Set in Aldus

Printed and bound in Great Britain by
Clays Ltd, St Ives plc

FOR EVE AND ALAN

1

JOAN

Alice Ainsley once told Joan that she always got a feeling in her bones when something was about to go wrong for her. It was like a dull ache, she said. She could sense in the morning if she was facing one of those days when the world was aiming to slide out of kilter. She felt like that the day her husband announced he was leaving and when her son rang to tell her he'd been arrested for possession of Ecstasy. Alice's people had been tenant farmers in Somerset for generations. That was where she reckoned she got the knowledge in her bones from; it was inherited. Folk who worked the land needed a feel for all kinds of things. They had to be in touch with the world around them, the weather, their animals and crops. Her grandfather could tell if a cow was sickening from the feel of its ears and could forecast thunder, snow or drought. Alice had a habit of raising her nose and sniffing the air as if she were standing in a field, scenting rain.

Joan's bones didn't signal any warnings to her the morning she met Nina Rawle, but then she wasn't from country stock. Her mother's parents had worked in a garment factory in Bromley and her father's family were street traders in Canning Town. No hairs stood up on the back of her neck as she parked the car outside Nina's flat. She didn't spot any black cats or magpies presaging disaster, there was no ominous rush of goose pimples on her skin. She walked in with a smile on her face, ready to do a good job. 'Take people as you find them' had always been among Joan's numerous aphorisms, one of the many commonsense dictums she had heard from her Bromley grandmother. On that April day with the tart sap of spring in the air she saw in front of her a very sick woman who obviously needed help.

Alice was Joan's employer and her friend, a combination that wouldn't work in many situations but fitted the two women well. Joan had been on the books of the Alice Ainsley bureau for six years and knew the business thoroughly enough to run it on the rare occasions when Alice was unwell or took a quick break. They often had a glass of Martini in a little wine bar near the bureau, sweet red with lemonade for Joan, dry white with soda water and ice for Alice. Sipping slowly, they would discuss contrary clients and their problems with men, the major difficulty being the lack of them.

Maybe if Alice had met Nina, instead of just taking her phonecall, things would have turned out differently. If Nina had made her way slowly up the stairs to Alice's office, leaning on her sticks, her hair swinging, Alice's nostrils might have twitched. Detecting trouble, perhaps she would have told Nina that Joan's schedule was full and offered her another assistant. Maybe, if, perhaps. Nina didn't visit the office; she made a phonecall and Alice simply heard a cultured voice putting business her way.

Joan's grandmother used to sing while she did the washing, a forties' number: 'If I'd known then what I know now I'd be a different girl'. She sang roughly but tunefully, tapping out a rhythm with her little nailbrush on the shirt collars as she worked carbolic soap into a lather. Nina reminded Joan of her gran, perhaps that was why she warmed to her so quickly. There was something about the no-nonsense way that Nina talked, her strong chin and firm lips, that summoned up Gran's face. And of course there was the Lily of the Valley perfume; it was so unusual, so surprising to find a younger woman wearing it. It had been many years since Joan had sniffed that fragrance. The scent of it was strong the first morning she met Nina, calling up clear, happy memories.

Joan was feeling particularly well on the sunny Wednesday morning when Alice offered her a new client. She'd had blonde highlights done the previous day and her hair had a lovely shine. The locum doctor had given her a new prescription for sleeping tablets and he'd said, with an air of surprise that told her he wasn't just trying to make her feel better, that she didn't look forty. When the alarm rang at seven-thirty she realised that she'd had a good night's sleep. That was always a bonus, like an unexpected present. Her face in the mirror was smooth, her eyes clear; anyone could see why a young man had given her a genuine compliment. She cleaned her little flat before she left for work, finishing with the kitchen floor. No good keeping other people's places ship-shape if your own's a mess, she always said.

She was full of energy as she ran up the steps to Alice's office above the dry cleaner's. Alice referred to it as the nerve centre. Joan had never understood how she managed to organise so many people from that tiny space. She supposed that Alice was just a natural although she did suffer: her voice was often scratchy with tiredness. Her nails were bitten ragged and she always looked a mess, her clothes thrown on any old how. It was just as well she didn't often get to meet the public, dressed in her shapeless skirts and limp cardigans. Sometimes Joan used to think she lived in that office. She'd had calls from her at all hours of the day and evening. Alice derived huge enjoyment from creating rotas, writing in capitals with a black, thick-nibbed marker on the wipe-clean board which she divided up into weekly grids. She spent hours puzzling out the most cost-efficient use of staff time. That was her true talent, they'd often agreed. If Napoleon had had you, Alice, Joan would joke, he wouldn't have lost Waterloo. Joan was a people person with a liking for hands-on contact and could always find a way of getting around even the most awkward of clients. They made a complementary duo and Alice's acknowledgment of this was evidenced in the post of deputy manager she had created for Joan and the regular, albeit small, wage increases.

The office held one large desk and a sturdy metal filing cabinet with a phone and fax machine on top. There was a microwave, a kettle and a toaster perched on a shelf next to telephone directories. Alice was eating toast spread with jam and dragging a comb through her flyaway hair when Joan arrived. She saw a hair land on the dark jam and shivered; that kind of thing made her skin creep.

Alice didn't have to soft soap her friend the way Joan knew she did with other staff, to get them to take on cantankerous old dears with more money than sense. She could depend on Joan, especially in a crisis. Some of the staff she employed were here today, gone tomorrow, leaving her in the lurch. A certain number of them just didn't take to the work, others found something better paid. Joan prided herself on doing a thorough, efficient job. She had never had a day's sickness, not even when the old dreams made her restless. She would arrive for work feeling heavy-eyed when she'd have liked nothing better than to burrow back under the bedclothes. It was important to her not to let people down. Rich said that she had the kind of face that made you want to trust her. When she tried to get him to explain what he meant he laughed, saying that she was just fishing for compliments. Alice appreciated her dependability. Joan had stepped in at the last minute quite a few times to pull the irons out of the fire; she was the only one willing to look after a boy with AIDS while his parents took a holiday. She had an album full of thank you notes from people she'd helped: the man with the broken pelvis, the couple who had the car smash, the girl with ME, to name but a few.

Working for the bureau was more than simply a job for Joan. Before she was taken on by Alice she had been employed by Mrs Jacobs, a widow in her late sixties whose first name Joan had never known, in an old-fashioned ladies' clothes shop in Forest Gate. It was one of those places that the years seem to have ignored, a narrow-fronted shop with tangerine-tinted plastic taped inside the window to protect the stock from the sun. Buxom dummies displayed corsets, well-upholstered brassieres, pastel-coloured cardigans and shirtwaister dresses in man-made fabrics. The wooden drawers held a supply of support stockings in a shade of brown that reminded Joan of oxtail soup. By the till was a notice stating, PLEASE DO NOT ASK FOR CREDIT AS REFUSAL EMBARRASSES. Mornings were punctuated by Mrs Jacobs' steaming Bovril at eleven and in the afternoons the malty odour of her hot milk drink hung over the acrylic jumpers. Joan measured customers' bosoms and hips and discussed the qualities of triple-panel girdles while her employer wrote out price tags and talked on the phone to members of her Bowls club.

There had never been a great amount of custom and once the ageing female clientele started to die the doorbell rang less and less. Mrs Jacobs hinted that she didn't need help any more so Joan took to scanning the job centre window.

The forced move had been a blessing in disguise. Living

on her own, the evenings used to drag when she worked from nine to five. Alice paid more and Joan liked knowing that she would be out in other people's houses some week-nights instead of sitting in with a glass of sweet vermouth, keeping the TV on for company while she worked one of her tapestries. Of course, since she'd got to know Rich she wasn't available on Sundays any more. She had told Alice about the plans she and Rich had made for when they could be together. Alice was the only person she had confided in about their situation. Joan knew that she was discreet and broad-minded. Her own son had been in trouble a couple of times so she lent a sympathetic ear. Back then, Joan would have said that people who had suffered in life were more understanding; that was certainly true of Alice. But after-wards, when everything had fallen apart, she wasn't sure of anything.

'I've got a new lady for you,' Alice said that morning, munching. 'You'll have to watch your Ps and Qs from the sound of her.'

If someone else had made that remark Joan would have taken offence but she was used to her employer's sense of humour and knew that Alice appreciated all the times she'd put up with vulgarity and rudeness. The old boys were the worst, exposing themselves, pretending they couldn't man-age their underpants. Some of the old women were no better though; the ones who were losing their minds could be ter-ribly crude. It was just as well that Joan's attitude was one of live and let live.

Alice leaned forward with the details she'd written down. 'She sounded very top drawer on the phone, not quite our usual customer. Her name's Nina Rawle, aged forty-six. She needs someone every day.'

'What's up with her?'

'She didn't want to go into it when she rang, said she'd

discuss things with you. She asked for you in particular, by the way, said someone recommended you.'

Alice gave her a satisfied smile. Word of mouth wasn't unusual; quite a few clients came the way of the agency through the grapevine, especially people who'd had Joan working for them. Joan liked it when this fact was acknowledged, although she would always be quick to add that she wasn't one to blow her own trumpet. When she saw Nina Rawle's Crouch End address she decided that it was probably the woman who'd needed help with the baby a couple of months ago who had put her on to the bureau.

After she'd finished the usual formalities with Alice, Joan headed off to Crouch End. Before she started the car she pulled on her work tabard. Alice was rightly proud of it. She had designed it herself, in apricot polycotton with a cream trimming. It had AA on the front, in fancy gold lettering, which often brought a smile to clients' faces.

The address Alice had given her turned out to be a big Edwardian house in a leafy street. It was divided into flats and Nina Rawle's name was on the ground floor bell. Joan rang and waited. There was one of those spy holes in the door so she made sure she placed herself dead in front of it with the AA of her tabard showing. After some time the door opened slowly and a woman with grey shoulder-length hair and the biggest eyes Joan had ever seen was standing there, supporting herself on two sticks.

'Good morning, I'm Joan Douglas from the Alice Ainsley bureau. Are you Mrs Rawle?'

The woman nodded and gestured with her head, already turning back into the house. 'Close the door, will you,' she said in a firm voice, the kind that Joan always thought of as BBC.

She stepped into a beautiful hallway, wide with polished floorboards and a huge gilt-edged mirror along one wall.

The wallpaper was dark green, patterned with tiny red flowers, the kind that she guessed cost a day's wages per roll. Classy, she thought; you'd need a bob or two to buy a place here. She followed Nina Rawle along the hall and through her own front door. Nina walked slowly, head bent, leading Joan to a long, high-ceilinged living room. The walls were freshly painted in pale cream but completely bare. There was a leather two-seater sofa, a recliner easy chair, stacks of boxes and at least two dozen plants in china bowls. The floor featured the same polished boards as in the hall, with one soft Persian rug covering the centre. A small table had one coffee cup and a lap-top computer on it. There was a slightly empty, impermanent feel to the room. Mrs Rawle might be moving in or out, it was hard to tell.

Nina lowered herself into the recliner chair, gesturing Joan to the sofa. The way she fussily settled her sticks next to her leg reminded Joan of an old woman and that was when she realised that this new client resembled her grandmother. She was wearing a dark blue tracksuit that obscured her shape but her body looked thin. Her face was pale; her cheeks marked with pink blotches, the skin stretched so finely that it seemed as if layers had been stripped away. Her neck was scrawny, her big eyes dull. You're a poorly creature, Joan thought, but she said how lovely the carpet was because she liked to start on a positive note with all her clients.

'Yes, I think so too,' Mrs Rawle said, propping her arms on the sides of her chair. Her voice was the strongest thing about her. 'It's good of you to come so promptly. I'm sorry I can't offer you tea but it would take me ages to get it. Maybe you'd like to make us both a cup in a minute.'

'Of course,' Joan said, 'I suppose that's why I'm here.'

'You're not bothered about routines, are you?'

'Some like them and some don't,' she replied, guessing what was on Mrs Rawle's mind. 'My older clients prefer them but with younger people it's different. Basically, I'm here to do whatever you ask.'

Mrs Rawle looked at her coolly. 'Then could you take off that horrible apron? The colour reminds me of vomit.'

She stared, taken aback. 'People tend to find it reassuring,' she said.

'I'm sure, but I'm not "people". Really, it's nasty, I can't sit and look at it. Reminds me of hospitals, of officious busy-bodies.'

Joan undid the side ties and pulled it over her head, thinking she had a real nit-picker here. But as Alice never tired of saying, the customer's always right. Over the years Joan had had a few classy clients like Mrs Rawle. They all shared the same tremendous confidence about coming straight out with what they wanted. Her gran used to say that toffs got their own way through sheer brass neck.

'There,' she said, 'I shan't wear it here again, I'll leave it in the car.'

Her client positioned a cushion and sat back. 'I'd like some tea now. Earl Grey for me with no milk. Please help yourself to whatever you want. I think there are biscuits in the tin. The kitchen's through there.' She switched on the portable CD player that was clipped to her waist, hoisting the head set draped around her neck up to her ears.

The kitchen was narrow, no bigger than Joan's but beautifully fitted out in light oak with marble worktops. It was what Joan called slubbery: littered with bits of food, dirty crockery and saucepans. The tiled floor was tacky and the built-in hob had tomato sauce spilled on it. Her fingers itched to get cracking. Nothing pleased her more than to transform mess and clutter into sparkling order. A side door led from the kitchen to a good-sized sunny conservatory where there was a small pine dining table and four chairs covered in bits and pieces; candlesticks, glasses, papers, more boxes with china and a tea service. Around the floor stood a jumble of tall plants and by the far window a desk littered with folders and magazines. In spite of the mess the place had that under-stated, expensive sheen that meant the quality spoke through the grime. Joan's poky flat was homely but she could only afford white melamine cupboards and a thin floor covering in her kitchen. If she let it get the slightest bit untidy it quickly took on a down-at-heel air.

She was about to take a look at the bathroom when the kettle clicked. She had never made Earl Grey before. The tea bag exuded a sickly perfume. She was looking to make a cup of coffee for herself but Mrs Rawle didn't have any decent instant, just coffee beans so she settled for an ordinary tea bag which came from a Fortnum and Mason box. All the crockery matched, lovely white bone china with a blue flower but it was sticky to the touch and Joan thought that living in this mess must have been depressing for her new client. Then she said to herself that if anyone came into her home and found it in this state she'd be mortified, even if it had got that way because she was ill. But that was your middle-class confi-dence for you again. She searched for white sugar but there wasn't any, just brown crystals that would taste of toffee. She remembered that she had a box of sweeteners in her bag.

Mrs Rawle was reading the newspaper but she put it down and switched off her CD player when she saw Joan.

'Did you find everything?' she asked.

'No problem. I'm used to getting my bearings in other people's houses.'

'Of course.'

Mrs Rawle's hair fell from a side parting, just skimming her shoulders. Joan thought it had probably been a dark brown before she went grey. In her opinion long hair didn't suit middle-aged women, especially if it had faded. She had worn her hair long until she was twenty-eight; then she had it cut and layered and people remarked that she looked eighteen again. Mrs Rawle's needed a good styling and a colour, one with a touch of bronze or mahogany to give her a lift.

Joan sipped her strong tea and asked her client if she had a garden. She replied that yes, the garden was hers, it went with this flat. She'd only moved in a month ago, that was why things were still disorganised.

'I overestimated what I could do,' she explained. 'That's partly why I've had to call you in. This is new to me, having paid help. What do your clients usually tell you on the first visit?'

'Well, a bit about themselves and what they want me to do. If they've got a medical condition, they let me know if there's anything I should be aware of.' Joan preferred to say 'medical condition' rather than illness, especially with someone younger like Mrs Rawle. She thought it added a touch of dignity.

Mrs Rawle propped her chin on one hand. 'I haven't always looked like this, I didn't have a collection of tracksuits because they're easy to put on until fairly recently. I became ill three years ago; my tissues started fighting each other. I've got worse in the past six months. Most days I can do very little. That about sums it up. I want you to come in the mornings and get me some breakfast and any shopping I need, then again in the evenings to prepare supper. I need you to help me unpack all this stuff, get organised. I might like to go out once a week if I feel up to it. Does that sound negotiable?'

The way she listed it all, fast and crisp, she might have been asking Joan to be her secretary. She was a cool customer all right. Her big hazel eyes were very direct, almost uncomfortably so. It was only her body that was frail, Joan decided; there was a firm will inside that thin frame.

'What about lunchtimes?'

She shook her head. 'I want to have to fend for myself some of the day; can't be going soft.'

Joan wondered where her family were. Maybe she's like me, she thought, pretty much alone. There was no wedding ring on her finger but Joan could see a faint white strip there, as if she'd removed one in the recent past. She and her husband must be separated or divorced, Joan decided, unless he'd died. But widows didn't usually get rid of their wedding rings, they clung to them. Mrs Waverley had been distraught because she couldn't find her ring when her Harry dropped dead. Joan had searched high and low for it to no avail and in the end had lent her an ordinary signet ring she had been wearing.

'That all sounds fine,' Joan said. 'I can't do Sundays.'

'Weekends are covered, this is a Monday-to-Friday arrangement.'

'Have you had breakfast today?' It was just on eleven.

Nina Rawle hesitated, then said no. She smiled at Joan, the first smile she'd given, as if she could relax now they had agreed terms. She'd like an egg, she said, and toast.

Joan got her what she wanted, wondering what her talk about her tissues amounted to; maybe she had cancer but couldn't say it. People came out with all kinds of expressions to disguise illness; a man she had helped who had lung cancer always referred to his dodgy chest. She wiped things over as she waited for the egg to boil and made the toast nice, cutting off the crusts and slicing it into triangular shapes. When you're ill, she thought, the little touches make a difference. She had noticed a patio rose planted in a tub in the conservatory, a bushy variety with orange-red blossoms. She nipped out and cut a single flower, putting it beside Mrs Rawle's plate on the tray.

'Oh,' she said when she saw it, 'how lovely! I'm not used to this kind of luxury.'

'When I'm helping someone I like to attend to the details,' Joan told her. 'Now, tuck in before it cools down. Something tasty and hot is just the ticket when you're not feeling too chipper.'

Mrs Rawle looked taken aback but she laughed. 'Thank you, I will. Have you been doing this kind of work long?'

'Six years, just on.' Joan moved a plant which had tilted over on top of another.

'And do you like it?'

'Oh, yes, I love it. There's always something new and I like meeting people.'

'Some of them must be difficult, though – demanding.'

'Well, sometimes. But I try to see the best side of people. You have to, and most clients are decent when you get to know them.'

'Do you live near here?'

Joan chuckled. 'Oh, I couldn't afford this area. I've got a place in Leyton.'

'Leyton.' Mrs Rawle looked puzzled. 'I don't think I've been there.'

'It's okay, the only drawback is there's no tube near but I've got Bessie – that's what I call my car – so I'm not dependent on public transport. Now, shall I pop and tidy the kitchen while you're eating?'

'Please do. And could you see to the bathroom, too? I make quite a mess when I'm showering.'

There was an archway at the end of the kitchen, leading to a small tiled hallway. The bedroom was to the right, the bathroom on the left. It had a shower unit with a fitted seat, a bath, bidet and washbasin, all in the green of mint-flavoured chewing gum.

Quite a mess was an understatement. The floor was greasy with water and hair, toothpaste and soap clogged the basin. There was a perfume in the air that Joan recognised immediately. She lifted a bar of creamy soap and sniffed. Lily of the Valley. She could see that Nina Rawle had talc, deodorant and an atomiser, all from Selfridges. She used to buy Gran a tin of Lily of the Valley talcum powder from the Co-op for every birthday and Christmas. On the front of the yellow tin was a spray of dark green leaves with drooping delicate white flowers. Joan had thought it was the height of classiness. Gran's name was Lily and she used to pull the front of her dress forward and shake the talc down her chest, saying, 'Lily by name and Lily by smell!' Then she'd tell Joan that she would be the most perfumed lady at the opera which would set her granddaughter giggling as Gran never went anywhere except to the whist drive. When Gran died and Joan was sorting her clothes, drifts of the snowy powder crept from the seams of her dresses and the perfume was all around her. Inhaling the scent of the soap took her right back to their dark little bedroom in Bromley with the gentleman's oak wardrobe and the commode disguised as a chair. If Joan thought that she detected any omens that day, finding the Lily of the Valley seemed a good one. Then she gave herself a shake; she wasn't being paid to stand and daydream.

She spent a good hour cleaning without even touching the conservatory. By then it was getting near the time she had to be at Mr Warren's, so she washed up Mrs Rawle's dishes and arranged to come back at six-thirty to cook supper.

'There's food in the fridge for tonight,' Nina Rawle said. 'I prefer light meals, soups and soufflés, snacks on toast, that kind of thing. I'd like some fruit. Could you possibly pick up a cantaloupe for this evening?'

Joan had never heard of a cantaloupe but she supposed they would have one in the supermarket. As Nina Rawle gave her the money she yawned, eyes watering. 'Do excuse me,' she said, 'I don't sleep well at night so I snatch naps during the day. I'm ready for one now.'

'I sleep badly sometimes,' Joan told her, 'I have worrying dreams. Have you tried sleeping tablets?'

Nina looked uneasy. 'Yes, but I don't like taking them. Maybe I'm anxious that I won't wake up.'

Joan didn't believe in encouraging that kind of talk. 'You're just a bit down,' she told Nina. 'Try and get some rest and things will look brighter. Meeting someone new takes it out of you.'

Mrs Rawle gave another, fainter smile. 'Oh, you haven't tired me. I think we'll get on, don't you?'

Joan picked up her bag. 'I speak as I find, and I think we can rub along very well, Mrs Rawle.'

'We won't stand on ceremony,' came the reply. 'You must call me Nina.'

'Then you call me Joan.'

Nina Rawle was making her way carefully to the sofa as Joan left, leaning on her sticks, old before her time. She wore soft, Chinese-style slippers and the plastic soles made the lightest of taps on the floorboards, like a cat's paws. There were only six years between them but there could have been twenty. Count your blessings, Joan told herself, heading for Bessie; you've got a good job and a neat little flat and Rich. She took a quick peek at the photo she kept inside her purse before starting the engine. Mr Marshall had kindly taken a snap of her and Rich with her own Instamatic. When Alice saw it she said they looked like peas in a pod because they both had round faces and Rich's hair was the same shape, square-cut and layered. He came out quite blond in the photo although when you saw him in person there was a tiny bit of grey at the sides. Joan had warned him, as soon as she had her hands on him she'd tint that out. Mr Marshall laughed when he heard that and said could Joan pop in and do his for him sometime?

Sitting there outside Nina Rawle's flat Joan thought that you met some good people in this world: Mr Marshall had been kind to Rich and of course Alice had been a brick about the whole thing. On the other hand, Mr Warren, the client she was about to see, was a real moaner; never a please or thank you but always quick to criticise if everything wasn't just so. She gave Rich a kiss and tucked him away. There were another three days to go before she'd see him again but one of the advantages of having such involving work was that it made time fly.

2

JOAN

Joan spent the first week with Nina Rawle helping her to get her flat organised. Nina didn't want to be taken out anywhere; she said she'd rather concentrate on ridding the place of the stacked cardboard boxes. She could do very little herself. The least exertion tired her. By the time Joan arrived each morning at nine she'd showered but the energy she had expended left her exhausted for an hour afterwards. Her hair never looked quite clean and at times Joan could see a sticky crust of lather on the crown of her head. Joan wondered about offering to help her in the bathroom but Nina had a reserve that made her think better of it.

While Nina sat reading the paper or listening to music or the radio Joan prepared her breakfast. She liked a small bowl of muesli or a poached egg on toast and fresh fruit; a segment of melon or a peeled orange or grapes. Joan had never come across this eating fruit for breakfast before; to her, fruit was for puddings or for when she was watching her weight and then she ate apples. For evening meals Nina requested blended home-made soups, pieces of chicken or fish with steamed vegetables or cheese or tomato soufflé followed by more fruit. She liked two glasses of wine in the evenings, French or Australian red from the rack in the kitchen. She invited Joan to have a glass, too, but it wasn't to her liking. If Joan drank wine she chose a sparkling sweet variety; Lambrusco was her favourite: those bubbles tingling on her tongue spelled luxury.

At first, Joan found the shopping nerve-wracking. Nina's list sent her searching for star fruit, lychees, artichokes, smoked applewood and goat's cheeses, Greek olives, red snapper and lemongrass. Joan had never taken much interest in cooking and, as most of her clients were old, they liked the kinds of dishes her gran had preferred: tinned steak-and-kidney pies with mushy peas, jellied eels, liver and bacon with a thick cornflour gravy, sausage and mash and shepherd's pie. They were meals she could make with her eyes closed.

She felt anxious for the first few days, examining the produce at the delicatessen counter in the supermarket, but there was a kind, motherly woman there who helped her out. Joan explained that she wasn't used to this sort of shopping; with me, she said, it's a quick whip-round for a jar of coffee, a couple of ready dinners, a boxed pizza and a packet of frozen peas. The assistant laughed, tucking a straying hair under her cap and told Joan that she could hardly keep up herself with the new lines they were always introducing. They had to have what was called familiarisation, she revealed; sessions with the section manager where they learned about the product and how to pronounce its name. When she was a young housewife you bought either Cheddar or Leicester cheese. Now it was Italian this and Norwegian that, soft and hard, pasteurised and unpasteurised and were we any the better off for it? Joan was reassured that she wasn't the only one who'd never come across some of these alien foodstuffs.

It was years since she had been to a proper fishmonger's. She used to go to the one in the High Street with Gran on Friday mornings to buy slabs of the waxy yellow haddock that she then poached in milk. Gran had stomach ulcers and ate a lot of what she called slop food: junkets, custards and milky sauces. One of her favourite dishes was fresh white bread squares sprinkled with sugar and steeped in warm milk with an egg whipped in. Nourishing, she called it. She used to feed that to Eddie, Joan's brother, when his chest was bad but she never made it again after he'd gone. Joan couldn't imagine what Nina Rawle would make of such a concoction. She specified the fish shop where she wanted Joan to buy the red snapper, salmon and trout she liked. The raw smell of the place made Joan gag; give me a boil-in-the-bag kipper any day, she thought, avoiding the staring cod eyes. The assistant who served her had wet chilled hands and his eyes bulged too. The right one had a cast, the pupil pale as if it had been bleached. She hurried in and out of there.

Nina took it for granted that Joan was familiar with all these foods and although this unnerved her it also afforded her a certain pride; she liked to think that she could keep her end up in any situation. When Nina handed her the shopping list Joan glanced at it and nodded. Out in the car she would sit and read through. Unfamiliar items such as Jarlsberg or Prosciutto made her frown but then she headed for the woman on the delicatessen and all was explained. Nina also gave exact instructions about how she wanted things cooked, which was just as well as Joan wouldn't have known one end of an artichoke from another. She had never come across some of the kitchen utensils but she was quick off the mark with anything practical and worked out how to operate the asparagus steamer and the chicken brick. As she grilled monkfish or turned bean sprouts in a wok moistened with sesame oil she thought that she would serve some of these dishes to Rich and impress him. He'd grown up by the coast in Frinton so she imagined that he might be partial to seafood. He complained about the muck he'd had to eat over the years; there was never enough and it was tasteless, worse than school dinners. Joan wouldn't try him with the fruit, though. She knew he liked what he called proper puddings: jam roly-polys and treacle sponges with thick custard.

After Nina had eaten her breakfast they got on with the boxes. Joan knelt on the floor and Nina sat by her in her chair, sneezing now and again as dust rose. If there was a spring chill in the air she pulled her old woollen shawl around her shoulders, plaiting the fringes over her knuckles. Sometimes Nina wore dark glasses when the light was particularly bright. She had them attached to a silver chain and they dangled on her chest when she took them off.

She had worked out ways of saving energy and keeping things to hand: there was the CD player clipped to her waist and the headphones around her neck. She also had a leather belt of the kind that Joan had seen carpenters store their tools in where she kept her tablets, eye drops, glucose sweets, tissues, a hip flask and a slim volume of Keats. She sucked glucose constantly, saying that it bucked her up. When Joan mentioned that the sweets might rot her teeth, she said flippantly that she didn't think she was going to need teeth for that many more years. Joan was shocked, especially by the casual way Nina came out with it. She felt herself colouring up and said something about it being a warm day.

The boxes were mainly full of books, dozens of novels. Some of them were old, creased paperbacks with dark green and orange covers. Two boxloads were in French. Joan recognised the actor with the big nose on the front of one.

'Goodness,' she said to Nina, 'have you really read all of these?'

'Yes, most of them more than once.'

Joan flicked through one, glancing at the strange words. 'I'm not much of a reader, although I like a magazine story. The best are those ones with a twist at the end. What language is this?'

'Italian. I was a university lecturer in languages, French and Italian, for twenty years.'

'Did you have to give up work because of your illness?'

Nina nodded. 'These are just a fraction of the books I used to own. I got rid of a load of stuff before I moved here.'

'I try to read,' Joan told her, 'but I can never settle for long. I always notice a bit of dusting that's needed or a cushion cover that wants mending.'

Nina raised an eyebrow. 'I don't think I've ever mended a cushion cover.'

'There's real satisfaction in doing a neat job on a seam.' Joan rubbed a book jacket with the duster. 'I suppose I'd better watch my grammar, now that I know I'm around a teacher,' she said, laughing. 'You know, no dropping my aitches.'

'I've just realised, I've put the cart before the horse here,' Nina said. 'I need bookshelves for all these volumes you're unpacking.'

This fact had crossed Joan's mind already but she had assumed that Nina had something organised on that front. 'Those alcoves would fit shelves very nicely,' she suggested. 'We could get free-standing ones at the DIY place or if you want fitted I could do it, but I'd have to borrow a drill.'

Nina shrugged. 'No, I can't be bothered with drilling, that sounds too permanent. Where did you learn to put up shelves?'

'I taught myself out of a book when I got my flat.'

'You live on your own?'

'That's right, I'm a single gal.' Not for much longer though, she thought; just three months to go. She and Rich would need a bigger place to live eventually but her little nest would be fine to start with. Now that it was all beginning to seem more real, she had started to imagine how it would be in the evenings, the two of them watching TV over a takeaway or deciding to catch a film. Sometimes she pictured him there on the sofa and chatted to him, telling him her plans.

'Let's go to the DIY place then,' Nina said suddenly. 'I'll just get a jacket. You have time, do you?'

'You're my only client today.' Mrs Cousins, who she usually visited on Tuesdays had died two nights previously but she wouldn't mention that, of course. She found a tape measure and sized up the alcoves while Nina went to the bathroom. When she returned she smelled of Lily of the Valley.

Joan told her it was the perfume her grandmother had used. 'Funny how a scent can bring a person and lots of little things about them back to you, isn't it?' she said.

Nina buttoned her jacket up, even though the day was warm. Her poor circulation meant that she felt chilly when other people were taking a layer of clothing off. She nodded agreement but offhandedly, as if she wasn't paying attention. Joan hoped that she hadn't thought she was being compared to an old lady and taken offence.

The superstore was only ten minutes away and the mid-morning traffic flowed lightly.

'You're a good driver,' Nina observed, 'very confident.'

'Ten out of ten?' Joan asked.

'Well, nine and a half. It's always important to leave a margin for improvement, give a student something to aim for.'

Joan was getting used to her dry way of talking. She could just see her at the front of a class. She'd have been the kind not to take any nonsense, although Joan supposed that university students didn't misbehave.

'Did you like teaching?' she asked.

'Oh, yes. But it all seems a long time ago. It's only a year since I gave up work and yet I feel as if I haven't stood in front of a group of students for much longer. I'd be frightened to now, I've lost the knack.' She laughed. 'It was hard going for my colleagues at my leaving party, they didn't know what to say. It was difficult for them to wish me a happy retirement, after all. People generally don't like illness, it makes them uneasy, reminds them their own lives are fragile.'

'That makes me think of a little verse I know,' Joan said: '"We only know that each day bears, Joys and sorrows, sometimes tears." Do you know Grace Ashley's poems? I love them, I cut them out of magazines and put them on my fridge; I always carry a few in my bag.'

'No, I don't think I've come across her.'

'They're only a couple of lines, each one, but they make you pause. She really sums things up in a nutshell. I find them comforting.'

'I think I'll stick to a glass of good wine for comfort. Which reminds me, I'd like to stock up at the off-licence later.'

When they parked Nina handed Joan her sticks, then pulled herself out of the seat, holding onto the door frame. Her fingers were long and bony. Joan heard her knuckles crack as she put her weight on them. Her nails looked at odds with the puckered skin around them; they were oval, beautifully shaped with perfect half-moons at the cuticles.

They walked slowly into the store and made for the shelving section. Nina went straight to the pine and selected what she wanted within minutes, a golden Scandinavian wood. The two sets of shelves came to four hundred pounds. Joan thought it must be nice to go for the best without hesitating. Maybe once Rich was in a job they would be able to rip out the chipboard in her living room and have pine. *If* he was able to get a job; no, she wasn't going to think negative thoughts, she was going to put her best foot forward.

That evening Joan assembled the flat-pack shelves in the alcoves and cooked turkey with baby sweetcorn and broccoli for Nina's meal. When she carried it through on a tray Nina was pouring a glass of wine for her, a sparkling white.

'Here,' she said. 'I bought a couple of bottles of the stuff you like. Tastes like lemonade to me, but each to her own. Cheers!'

She looked exhausted after her outing. Mauveish smudges ringed her eyes and Joan noticed her hands trembling on her sticks. She was terribly touched by the wine.

'You'd no need to buy this for me,' she said, sipping.

'It's nothing, it humours me. Where are we up to with the books? The Ms?'

Joan was lining them up on the shelves in alphabetical order. 'Alberto Morave next,' she said. 'Is he interesting?'

'*Moravia*. I think so. The turkey is delicious. What do you have in the evenings? Do you visit family?'

'No, I've nobody close, they've passed on. I usually eat on my own, a pizza or a chop, something quick. I quite like those low-calorie, ready-made meals. You can pop them in the microwave and they're done in a couple of minutes. It's not much fun, cooking for one.'

'No. I used to find it a bore before I got married. The university had a staff restaurant which was excellent so I ate in there most days.'

'Are you divorced then?'

'Separated. Have you ever been married?'

'Yes, only for a year, in my twenties. It didn't work out. I don't like living alone. I pretend to; you have to, don't you?

It's like what you said about illness. People get embarrassed if you admit you're lonely. I didn't think Mr Right would ever show up but he has and we're marrying soon.' She heard Rich's voice telling her it wouldn't be long now. They planned to go to the registry office the week after he came out. Joan would have married him and waited for him – she knew other women in a similar position did – but Rich insisted that he wanted to be a free man before they tied the knot. Joan wasn't going to explain any of that to Nina, though. There were certain things you didn't confide to clients if you valued your job.

Nina gave a pained smile. 'Sometimes it doesn't work out even when you do meet the right person. It's all a gamble, it can tear you apart.'

'You're tired, I reckon,' Joan said, thinking she sounded low. Her voice was flat and there was a slide in it. 'You've done too much today. A good night's sleep will put a smile back on your face.'

Nina lowered her head and finished her turkey. She dozed for a while, the tray still on her lap. Joan didn't move it for fear of waking her. She carried on quietly with the books, wondering how anyone could read this lot, thinking of all the hours of sitting still it would mean. Like her, Rich wasn't a reader, which was a shame because it would have been a way of passing those long hours he complained about. Joan had to be on the go, doing something; a tapestry, some mending, cleaning windows, stripping the cooker. She was just like Gran that way, always up and active. She had never seen Gran sitting for long: 'I'm as busy as a hen with one chicken,' she used to say, zipping from room to room. The day before she died she was turning a mattress. Joan thought of Nina, alone here at night with just her books for company and little else to look forward to. It made a sad picture. She chatted to Rich inside her head, telling him that she was going to get on with decorating the living room when she got home. The whole place was going to be revamped before he arrived; she'd drawn up a timetable. The last time she had been to see him she'd taken colour charts and they'd chosen the emulsion. Rich suggested that she should wait until he was out and he'd help her but she said no, she wanted the place just so from their very first day together.

Joan and her brother Eddie went to live with their widowed grandmother in Bromley when she was three and he was eleven. Their father had died of a heart attack just before Joan's birth and their mother was felled by cancer when Joan turned three. Gran had a two-bedroomed terraced house. She and Joan slept in the front bedroom, Eddie in the smaller back one. Gran worked long hours in the rag trade but she ran a tight ship at home and they all had their domestic jobs. Gran couldn't stand even a speck of dust in the house. When the coalman came to shunt his sacks into the bin outside she covered the floors and furniture in the back room with sheets of newspaper. She craved an end-of-terrace house so that he could take his filthy, blackened hessian bags up the side alley but none ever came up for rent. She'd hover around him, warning him not to touch anything, monitoring his mucky boots. Sometimes, to annoy her, he'd pretend to lose his balance and her hands would fly to her face in silent agony.

The house was chilly during the day but on a winter's evening, with the coal fire well stoked, there was nowhere cosier. When Gran arrived back from work they would make pilchards on toast and she'd tell them how she'd machined twenty skirts that day, or stitched three dozen collars. Sometimes she brought back clothes she'd got cheap because they were seconds. Joan was the first girl in the street to have a pair of loon pants and Eddie cut a dash in hipster trousers when they were just reaching the shops.

Joan was fifteen when Eddie disappeared. By then he had rented a tiny flat in Islington but he often stayed with them on a Friday or Saturday night and his room was kept ready for him. Gran would put a hot water bottle between his sheets on winter weekends to make sure that they were properly aired. His chest, weakened by bouts of childhood asthma, was easily affected by damp.

After they heard the terrible news Gran insisted on maintaining his room just as it was on the last Sunday morning they had seen him. She literally wasted away in front of Joan's eyes, worn out with grieving for him. Joan would hear her crying in the night, deep sobs against the pillow in her bed by the window, sobs that went on month after month. Joan stopped crying after a couple of weeks. She seemed to have used up all her tears. She felt dry and tight inside and remote, as if nothing much would ever matter again. She didn't know how to comfort her gran. She was a young fifteen, tongue-tied and awkward. What could she find to say to a woman of sixty-six who had raised two families and outlived a child and grandchild?

Her grandmother died when Joan was eighteen. She was alone in the world then apart from an aunt who'd rowed with Gran and kept her distance and a couple of cousins who'd moved out to Essex, shaking the dust of the inner city from their feet. They had never been one of those close cockney families who were supposed to inhabit London. Joan would wonder if those families ever truly existed – she had never met any of them. At times it occurred to her that she had been handed a raw deal, orphaned and then deprived of the two people closest to her. The sight of her single plate and cup on the kitchen table could make her heart knock.

Gran left her exactly one hundred pounds. Joan put it in a building society and carried on renting the house. She had left school at sixteen with four O-levels. The teachers said that she was good enough to stay on and do secretarial training, maybe head to college eventually. Eddie had been of that opinion too; he'd said that when the time came he'd help her choose a course. But then he'd gone, everything changed and Joan couldn't see herself as college material. She didn't have much self-confidence to start with and what had happened to Eddie made her inclined to keep her head down. The world seemed an unpredictable place. She preferred to tackle the small, domestic issues of life, move in a familiar groove where there were certainties. That was why the agency work suited her so well; things had to be done on set days at set times and this pattern rarely varied. The wider scene – politics, the environment, world problems, the chaos resulting from wars and famine – she ignored; other people were welcome to worry about and deal with those problems. She never bought a newspaper and watched only variety shows, soap operas and films on TV.

When she left school she went to work in a bakery, then in the ladies' clothes shop where she stayed until she moved to Alice's agency. At twenty-two she married Bernard Douglas, who had been in her class at school and turned up at her door now and again when he wasn't driving long-distance lorries. It hadn't lasted long and she had felt relief tinged with only a shade of melancholy when he had written from Düsseldorf to say he'd got a job based there and he wanted a divorce. She had married him because of panic, seeing that other women of her age were setting up home, choosing curtains and carpets. His motives were unclear. His absences had pervaded the house and even when he was there he imposed so little of himself on it that he left no vacuum when he took off for a trip to the continent. He was capable in a slow, unwitting way, good at practical tasks and she had confused this with dependability, ignoring the evidence that a man who chose to let his work regularly take him far from home might not have domestic interests at heart. The divorce left her with mended window latches, a new drain pipe and guttering. Occasionally she would recall the stale plastic-and-oil smell of his lorry cab and the duty-free brandy fumes he breathed on her as he came through the door.

Resolutely she put her mistake behind her, saved regular amounts and eventually had enough for the deposit on her flat in Leyton. It was on the first floor of a three-storey fifties block, one-bedroomed with no garden but she'd loved it the moment she had set eyes on it. There was a Grace Ashley verse that said:

> Give me a room
> And I will paint it with love's loving colours,
> Cushion it with heart's ease
> And it will be our cherished home.

Joan had worked those lines into a tapestry when she moved to her flat. It hung in its frame on the living-room wall. She went and read it over to herself on that night when Nina had appeared depressed about her marriage. It meant even more now that she was preparing a home for herself and Rich. The paint for the living room was standing ready inside the front door. They had selected white with a hint of butter-cup for the walls and deep yellow gloss for the skirting board and radiator. Joan had spent the previous weekend stripping off the old wallpaper and putting up lining paper. When she told Alice what she was doing, her friend had offered to come and give her a hand with the painting. She was lonely herself, that was why she spent so much time at work. Joan understood that her business had replaced her family, who had abandoned her. Her one son had become a drug user, then joined a road protest group and was living up a tree somewhere. Her husband had taken off with his optician years ago, clearing out their joint bank account the day he left. According to Alice, all that had remained of fifteen years of marriage were his golf clubs and a stack of pornographic magazines stashed in the back of the wardrobe. It was generous of her to root so strongly for Joan and Rich, advising that they should grab whatever happiness came their way. Some people's scars made them resentful of their friends' good fortune.

Alice arrived promptly at eight that evening, dressed in overalls. She had brought her own roller and tray so that they could do two walls each.

'How are you getting on with that new woman, Nina Rawle?' she asked as they worked.

'Okay. I thought she was a bit stand-offish to start with but it's just her manner. She's very weak physically. It must be terrible to be able to do so little when you're comparatively young.'

'What's the matter with her?'

'Something wrong with her tissues, that's all she's said so far. She moves like an old woman. I think she's quite depressed.'

'You'll be good for her then, Joan, you'll chivvy her along. We're survivors, you and me, aren't we? Get on and make the best of things.'

'You have to, don't you?'

'Suppose so. Any vermouth going?'

Joan poured two glasses and they took a quick breather while they sipped.

'It's a lovely colour,' Alice said. 'Warm. I hope Rich appreciates all this. I'll be having words with him if he doesn't.'

'I don't think you need worry about that. He's a smashing man, Alice, he really is. Will you be a witness when we get married? His brother's agreed to be the other one.'

Alice raised her glass. ''Course I will. It will be a pleasure, as long as you promise me you won't want to do anything daft like give up your job.'

'No chance. I love the job. Anyway, we'll need the money.'

They carried on painting, finishing by ten-thirty. Alice washed out the rollers while Joan wiped splashes off the skirting board.

'That Nina Rawle,' Alice said, 'did she tell you who recommended you?'

'No. It was probably Jenny Crisp, the young woman with the baby in Crouch End.'

Alice shook her head. 'That's what I'd assumed, but it wasn't her. I know because she rang today and she said she hadn't mentioned us to anyone. I'm sure we haven't any other customers from Crouch End.'

'I don't know then. I must be more famous than I thought!'

Alice was sniffing the air. 'There's a very scented smell in this kitchen, sort of musky. What is it, some kind of air freshener?'

Joan pointed to the cantaloupe sitting on top of the fridge. 'It's that melon. Strong, isn't it? They were on a special offer, I thought I'd try one.'

They had another vermouth as a nightcap and Alice left. Joan knew she wouldn't be going straight home, though; she'd be calling at the office to check the answer-phone. She couldn't wait to introduce Alice to Rich; she knew that they'd like each other. Her life felt good. For the first time in many years, everything was coming together. She raised her glass to Rich's photo in the kitchen and said goodnight, sleep tight to him, as she always did.

3

NINA

'*C**ara* Majella,

'I wonder if you are asleep now in your dormitory, breathing in dry Ethiopian air? I have no idea of time-zone differences between our respective continents. You're probably toiling in the daylight, helping with irrigation or holding a health class. You used to refer to sleep as "John O' Dreams". It was a name you'd got from your mother, one of those comforting childhood sayings that adults cleave to. "I'm ready for John O'Dreams," you would yawn at the end of a long evening in the students' union bar, shaking your hair out. When I was bleary-eyed after listening to one of Finn's lengthy position papers on Irish capitalism you would say that John O'Dreams was after me. He would steal gently into a room, unnoticed, relaxing tired muscles, softly closing the eyes. My mother used to warn me that the Sandman was on his way. When I was reluctant to settle down, she would say that she could hear his footsteps on the stairs. He was as bold as John O'Dreams was self-effacing, a threat-

ening figure in my childhood imagination who threw stinging dust under the eyelids.

'"Sleep offers us escape from grinding reality. It says,
'that was then, this is now". A balance evolves through
sleep, an acknowledgement of the need for order. People say
"sleep on it" when they mean that you need time to consider
something, put a shape to it. That's the kind of truism my
new acquaintance Joan Douglas would utter: "sleep on it,
things always seem different in the morning". I'm sure that
for most people, those with everyday anxieties, it does happen; they wake and smile, realising that in the light of day,
things aren't so bad after all.

'Depriving someone of sleep is a form of punishment or
torture; apart from the physical effects, it disorders their
world and makes them crazy. But then we both knew that
back in 1970; do you recall that we demonstrated outside
an RUC barracks, protesting about the harsh treatment of
political prisoners? We sprayed the reinforced concrete wall
with yellow paint to signify police cowardice and ran before
they could catch us.

'I woke at two o'clock this morning and I immediately
thought, some of us punish ourselves and some of us punish
others. My father punished himself for losing his job by
drinking his way to an early death. My mother punished
him for never being the husband she aspired to by criticising
every move he made. You punished yourself for what we
did by becoming an exiled voluntary worker. I have delivered
punishment on two fronts, pursuing retribution against
myself for what I did with you and against Martin for loving
me when I didn't deserve to be loved.

'One form of my punishment has been to wake at two
every morning since the day I got married fifteen years ago.
As my eyes open I look at the clock face and there it is,

exactly two, as surely as if I had set the alarm. John O'Dreams and the Sandman linked arms and vanished from my life without warning on my wedding night. It is as if I knew that I wasn't supposed to have the comfort and pleasure that Martin wanted to give me. The memory that lies always just beneath the surface was rising up in the silence of the night. Why should you sleep, it asked, why should you know warmth and companionship? So instead of the sanctuary I had hoped for, my marriage delivered me to bleak stretches of the night when I would lie and watch Martin sleeping. Contemplating another person sleep while you ache with tiredness becomes a kind of torture. There he was sailing a balmy sea of dreams while I stood shivering on a desolate shore. I knew all the little noises Martin made, the snuffles and sighs; I counted the number of times he turned in an hour and the pattern of his movements on the mattress. I tried copying his breathing, wondering if I could catch on to the shirt tails of his sleep and join it.

'I could never make the night my friend. It pressed down on me, a heavy, alien blanket. I had intimate knowledge of all the phases of wakefulness. I could have written a thesis on them. First the sudden, dry-throated exit from sleep, eyes heavy but watchful, then the awareness of a rapid heartbeat, the twitch of tired limbs, the efforts to find a magic position that would lure slumbers back; left side, stomach, back, right side, foetal curl, left side again. As the minutes slid into hours there would be unsuccessful attempts to clear the mind, the random racing and crashing together of thoughts. Often in the thick darkness I would see you, your hair misty with smoke from the turf fire, jazzing on Finn's grand piano or playing duets with him. Snatches of the songs you used to sing echoed in my head, particularly that rousing chorus from Brecht:

''So left, two three,
So left, two three,
To the task that we must do;
March on in the Workers' United Front
For you are a worker too.''

'I could hear the thump of your ankle boot as you kept time on the ancient carpet, dislodging years of dust: *left, two three, left, two three.* The march would go on and on, resounding along the years.

'Sometimes I would be awake for three hours, sometimes four; on a very bad night, five. I learned the different qualities of darkness, from the impenetrable blackness of two AM through the thinning greyness that preceded dawn and finally the pale, lemony light that illuminated the striped curtains. In the summer months I regularly heard the day stealing in. A feeling of panic would take over as the first birds whistled or a milk float whined along the street; another episode of my life was about to begin and I had had no respite from the previous one. All order, all balance had vanished. Then I might cry from sheer frustration, tears of tension and self-pity, but very quiet tears so that Martin wouldn't wake. My poor Martin. God knows what he made of it all, watching me mutate into a semi-zombie. He must have thought the woman he'd married was cursed with a schizoid personality.

'On campus each day I would lock my office door at lunchtime and doze in my chair, the kind of sleep where you are half alert to voices and noises, where you twitch and jitter. My watch alarm would warn me when my time was up and I would come to, dazed and hot, eyes pricking. I took to not eating in the middle of the day because food made me more sluggish. My afternoons were spent sleep walking. I delivered lectures through an obscuring haze. It was as if I was inside a tank and my students were sitting on the other side of the scummy glass. I have no idea how I managed to keep going for so long. The students were kind and long-suffering. It is just as well that I had to resign when I did. No doubt in these days of mission statements and quality monitoring one of them would eventually have complained about me and I would have been inspected and found wanting, perhaps dismissed.

'I have separated from Martin. I left him some months ago. I was mistaken if I hoped that giving him up would mean that I could sleep again. Deep down I believed that if I denied myself my husband, made a conscious sacrifice, some pity might be afforded me. My gesture of self-denial might be taken into account, weighed on unseen scales and go some way towards restoring the order I had helped to disrupt. But of course there is no unseen dispenser or order and justice – the responsibility for that lies within ourselves. And so I continue to wake at two. I suppose that the habit of fifteen years is hard to break. Returning to a single, friend-less bed made no difference. It simply meant that I had no one to watch but myself, no breathing to listen to but my own.

'I lied to the woman you will hear more about, Joan Doug-las. She asked if I had tried sleeping tablets and I said I had. I knew that if I told the truth she would have encouraged me to get some; I would have had to listen to advice about breaking the pattern of insomnia. I'm sure that at some point she would have said, "You won't know yourself once you've had a couple of unbroken nights". Joan is one of those people who needs to think that every problem has a solution. I won't allow myself sleeping tablets because I don't deserve them. I deserve to lie awake and contemplate shadowy demons.

'As the clock ticked this morning I imagined Joan lying

asleep in her bed, snugly lulled by her own medication. She confessed that she is sometimes wakeful. Any wakefulness you experience will have skulking in its depths our shared memory, that icy hammer that shatters the warm layers of unconsciousness. I have no idea how the passage of time might have assisted you in reshaping that memory. I know that when I turn on my computer I will find exactly what I committed to it previously but the mind shifts and trans-forms, illuminating the past with the light of present experi-ence. I only know that I can describe what happened in a certain place at a certain time.

'We last saw each other in 1972. The annual letters we have exchanged since then have been paltry things, lists of domestic trivia. We have been unable to let each other go but we never allude to what we did. Our short notes have summarised the passing years; my teaching and marriage, my ill health, your involvement in crop planning and health promotion. Neither of us ever mentioned Finn until 1994 when you wrote that you'd heard from a cousin that he had been shot with two other men by a Protestant paramilitary. It was a pub shooting and that phenomenon all too familiar in Northern Ireland, a case of mistaken identity, the drinkers taken for IRA activists. That was all; one stark sentence sandwiched between paragraphs about the orphanage you were working in. "Peter said he was sure he heard the name Butler on the radio report." When I read it I felt a gentle lift of the heart; he had, after all, been the instigator of what we did. He had presented us with the idea, urged us on, set up the plan. Then, as I re-read the news I thought, that deals with him, that settles part of the account. Now, what about us? His going was like a crack of light entering a dark room; the knowledge that he was dead allowed me seriously to consider what I should do to resolve my own unchallenged guilt. And so I pondered and recognised that no amount of charitable work or self punishment would do. I came to the decision that has prompted this letter and will unravel the past.

'Joan, my new paid helper, will maintain me while I marshal my energy to write. She will be here again in the morning with her exhaustingly breezy manner and skirt that is just a little too short, making her plump knees look oddly naked. She will say how nice the bookshelves are looking now or aren't the roses in the conservatory coming on a treat or I'll feel better once I've got a nice breakfast down me. I will smile at her and when she's bustled to the kitchen I will sink my head onto my chest and breathe deeply.

'When she arrived the first time, wearing an awful apron, I was amazed at what I had let myself in for. I hid my feelings behind a businesslike mask. Cowardly, I almost told her that I had changed my mind or that we wouldn't suit each other. I nearly cried out when she said that she'd have to be careful with her grammar now that she knew that I had been a teacher. Joan is the kind of person I would normally avoid, one of life's surface optimists and lover of shallow wisdoms. When she touches her cheek and says that she speaks as she finds or you have to put your best foot forward, I want to run and hide.

'But I won't run, because I need Joan, I am no longer able to function alone. The days are too onerous without someone to do all those time-consuming tasks that can easily take hours when one moves at a snail's speed. I am willing to endure recitals of the dreadful poet she likes, one Grace Ashley. Joan informed me that she has six teddy bears on her bed and in the early hours of today I pictured them watching her, open-eyed, just as I used to watch Martin. Then I reached into the drawer under my bed and took out this lap-top computer, a leaving present from my fellow lecturers. It wasn't a surprise gift, I had told the head of languages what I wanted. As the parcel was handed to me I surveyed the uneasy figures in the room, standing awkwardly with their paper cups of cheap wine. I thought how horror-struck they would be if they had an inkling of the story that was going to be typed on their token of farewell, how their embarrassed sympathy would turn to outrage. An echo of the kinds of comments often uttered to reporters when a neighbour has been discovered in a crime came to me: ''She always seemed a nice, quiet sort of person, kept herself to herself. Nobody round here would have thought she'd been involved in anything like that.''

'As I waited for the blue glow of my computer screen to appear I propped my pillows higher, then took a couple of sips of brandy from my flask. It doesn't stop the constant ache in my joints but it helps me bear it. Since this illness took hold I am always hot when I wake at night, chilled during the day. I had left the window open as usual and I turned my head towards the sharp air before I started writing.

'The record that I am confiding to this screen, this long, painful series of letters, will serve several purposes. It is primarily for you, Majella. I want, I need you to have my account, my version of what happened. I want to say those things that could not be said then, when life raced away with us and words had to be so carefully chosen. Martin will receive his own personally tailored copy, a coward's gift. I can summon up courage for many things but not for him; his reproachful eyes sear me. This is also a general confession for a wider audience, a purging of shadows and demons, a mapping of a blight that fell from the Belfast air. My frailty means that it will be in instalments but I will wait until I have completed it to send it to you, a small package bearing love and agony in equal proportions.

'I am convinced that you confessed to a priest somewhere

in Africa. You made a point of writing that you had returned to the church. I pictured you in a simple confession box in a tin-roofed chapel, a dusty village of thin people and animals around you. An ebony-skinned priest or perhaps a sandy-haired Irish missionary would have listened, his shocked breath freezing despite the heat before he raised his hand to bless you. What penance could he have given? What would the tariff be? I envied you your confession, your unburdening. My jealousy of it has grown with time. I wished that I could believe in a God who listened and forgave through human mediums. I have had to find another way of unburdening, lacking divine channels.

'I find that I have addressed you in Italian, the language that we both excelled in, that we often talked in, that Finn didn't speak and that first brought us together on an October morning in 1969.

'You are going to have to forgive me, Majella, for the plan I am going to execute. I have taken a decision to clear the decks. I feel like a person who has been meaning to sort out a cluttered attic for years and finally gets down to it. Your mother didn't like Finn, she thought he was a bad influence on you. I think that one of the reasons she was so kind to me was that she saw me as a polite, well-brought-up girl who would counteract Finn's dogmatism. She once said to me in the cow shed that Finn was a cold, unfeeling character, that he had a marble heart. You will recall that I used to wear my emotions on my sleeve; when I loved I loved without reservation, hungry for affection. The cold clutch of guilt has made me guarded and watchful. Over the years it has frozen my spontaneity, slowly icing over my feelings. I have fashioned myself a marble heart in order to effect my plan. I have deliberately reduced my life to a small flat and a single purpose, abandoning Martin in order to concentrate on my task. Finn would have applauded my single-mindedness: "There is only one goal, comrades," was his constant refrain.

'I realise that I am addressing a Majella from another time. I don't know the woman who inhabits an Ethiopian hostel and who has written that her skin is parched by the sun. I was familiar with a fresh, milky complexion, one that glowed with a rich bloom when you became fervent, which was often. That is how I visualise you, untouched by the years, no wrinkles or crow's feet. You would joke that you'd have preferred the faded, wan look that was popular in the late sixties but your mother had given you too much butter-milk during childhood. The person you are now may hardly recognise the young woman then. When I glance back and see myself I feel an anguished fondness for the needy, uncertain person I was. That Nina bears little resemblance to the woman I am now, a grey-haired, crab-like creature. Finn would have been amazed at my apparent confidence in middle age and the certainty with which I run my days. "Nina Town Mouse" he used to call me in that teasing blend of comradeship and affection, or "Nina-mina-mina-mo". My own secret name for myself now, stemming from my illness, is Wolf-woman. Finn would have had little time for my sticks and physical weakness. He was intolerant of sickness. When you had tonsillitis he bullied you from bed, saying that it was a question of mind over matter. He prescribed a long walk or a strenuous swim as antidotes for any ailment.

'You see, Majella, I'm determined to say Finn's name, to bring him in to this story at the earliest opportunity. We have been so coy about him over the years, leaving his name out but he is there, always a presence around us. Sometimes he used to stand between us and place a hand on our heads as if he was anointing us. I can still feel his palm with the chewed nails resting on my skull.

'What is it you Catholics say when you enter the confessional? "Bless me Father, for I have sinned." I think I remember you telling me that the first autumn we met. You were an atheist at the time and you were explaining the superstitious rituals of the church to me, its rigid dogma and controls, the way priests ordered the lives of women, subjugating them. Finn came in as you were speaking and lightly ran his finger over the back of your hand. You turned to him with that eager love he always drew from you. He was holding a leather-bound copy of Trotsky's writings to his chest. He looked like our very own cleric that day, dressed as he often was in a grey polo neck and black jacket. He may even have read an improving paragraph of Leon's thoughts to us in your kitchen, a homily for the true believers.

'I clearly recall the first time I saw you. I walked into the lecture theatre on an October Tuesday in 1969 and there was a woman in a frilly, fussy smock bending down from her seat. Your red hair foamed around your dipped head, tendrils spreading across the floor as you retrieved the pen you'd dropped. I had been paralysed with nerves since arriving in Belfast the previous week. My only image of Ireland was the one I'd seen on a flickering TV screen. News bulletins delivered pictures of a savage, reckless place where blood flowed and neighbours freely murdered each other because of complex and, to the English, baffling ancient divisions. I was convinced that I could be shot or blown up at any time, especially if I opened my mouth revealing a home counties accent. I'd hardly spoken because of my fears; it seemed to me that my tongue was becoming swollen and dry, pressing against my teeth. I'd heard somewhere that a shock to the nervous system could cause muteness and I was genuinely fearful that next time I tried to speak, no sound would issue. I had sat alone in my room, looking at the bags I couldn't bring myself to unpack and listening to the thud of feet in the corridors outside. From my window I saw students hurrying to join societies and heard them calling to each other. Even their accents, harsh and unfamiliar, unnerved me. The sounds they made were like snarls. I'd had difficulty understanding people in the few words of conversation I had been forced to exchange. I would have turned and fled, heading for home but there was little to go back to. I knew that my mother would already have stripped my bed and aired my room, shutting the door firmly, relieved that I would only return for brief holidays.

'I had steeled myself to attend that first lecture in Italian. I held my books against my chest for security and to conceal my trembling arms. My legs were weak from lack of food. You swept up the pen and threw your hair back as you settled in your seat. I was aware of bows at your shoulders and down the front of your smock. I thought you looked like a sturdy countrywoman in an eighteenth-century painting, fresh from milking or hay-stacking.

'You watched me hovering and pointed at the empty chair next to you. "D'you want this?" you asked. "You look as if you're going to faint."

'I sank down next to you, overwhelmed with gratitude because I had been able to understand you. Your speech was slower and more measured than the other accents I had struggled with. You introduced yourself as Majella O'Hare and I told you my name.

'"Nina," you said, "that's attractive, musical. I hate my name. I think it sounds like a sweet preserve: 'a full-fruit Majella confiture flavoured with cognac'."

'I thought of marmellata, the Italian for jam. "I've never heard it before," I confessed. It sounded exotic to me.

'"That's because you're a Brit and your unfamiliarity with it is refreshing. My name doesn't tell you what it would shout at someone from Ulster; that I'm a Taig, a papist, a

left-footer, a Fenian and a feckless member of an underclass."
You gave me a friendly smile as you offered me my first
lesson in the intricacies of Irish identity.

'You asked me if I'd read the set text and I said that I
had. In the original or in translation? you enquired. The
original, I said, replying in Italian. Then you asked in Italian
where I was from and I told you Maidstone, becoming articu-
late in the shared language and accent that provided us with
a mutual territory. You hailed from a place called Pettigoe,
which you added sounded like a skin disease.

'"I've not seen you around," you said. "Did you arrive
late?" There was something about you that made me feel
less fearful. Your voice was rich and amused, your eyes
sparked with interest.

'"I've been in hiding," I admitted, "starving in my room
because I was frightened at being in Belfast. I've been living
on a scant supply of chocolate bars and canned drinks. I feel
sick but starving."

'"God almighty," you laughed, "no wonder you look like
a wraith."

'After the lecture you took me to the canteen and we ate
huge plates of spaghetti. Why, you asked, had I come to
Belfast if the place was so terrifying? I'd not got the exam
grades I needed, I said; this course had been offered through
clearing, they were being kind because it was a new degree.

'"Why did you do so badly in your exams? You don't
strike me as thick."

'"My father died last spring. I lost my concentration."

'"That's tough all right," you said. "It's not so awful
here, you know, we get a bad press."

'Strange that you should have used that phrase during
our first meeting, "a bad press". That type of press, the one
we considered prejudiced, was our motivation and justifica-
tion for what we did on that other October day when the

rain fell and kept falling until dawn. But on that afternoon in
the canteen, with the autumn sun still warm, the comforting
clatter of dishes and my famished stomach contented, I was
reassured by your presence. I was like a lost child bonding
with the first person to offer affection. In saying that, I am
not trying to diminish our friendship. I simply wish to record
it honestly. I was always a moth to your candle, Majella.
You didn't set out to have me fluttering around you, but
that is what happened.

'I was fascinated by you as I sped through my spaghetti.
Your clothes were crumpled and none too clean; under the
blue smock you wore several bright vests in mustards and
purples, teamed with one of those layered and fringed Indian
cotton skirts that had glass beads sewn into the seams. You
ate carelessly, gesturing as you talked, unaware of tomato
sauce spattering your chest. On your feet you wore clumpy
ankle boots. I never saw you in any other footwear, not even
in high summer. You were big boned without seeming heavy
and you had a clarity that I was attracted to. A strong tobacco
aroma clung to you, especially noticeable when you shook
your hair and I was puzzled because you didn't seem to be
a smoker. When I met Finn I realised that it was the odour
of his French cigarettes that adhered to you like an invisible
gauze. I was entranced by your easy laugh and the way you
accepted me. As weeks went by I flourished in the affection
you offered, an easy friendship that was new and wonderful.
And your family romanced me with their noise and boister-
ousness. They eased the memory of the formality and chill
silences I had been used to in my home. I envied you the
wholesome, happy childhood I heard tales of when I visited
Pettigoe, the kind I had only read about. In my imagination
I made it mine, too; the lambings, the shared labours of
potato harvesting, the battles to protect the hens from
marauding foxes. I pictured lush, bucolic scenes, placing

myself in them, filching glimpses of your past contentment for myself.

'When I met you I emerged from a long, bleak hibernation. In your glow I uncurled, stretched, and stepped into a new life. I grew to see you and the straightforward, honest people you came from as my bedrock. Lacking strong ties and beliefs of my own, I believed in you. When your glow dimmed and I was deprived of your affection I suffered terribly. For some years I hated Finn more for sundering our friendship than for the path down which he led us. Of course, in my blinkered enthusiasm for our cause I didn't see that our transgression would inevitably mean our losing each other. I was too naive and inexperienced to understand that there are no pure actions in life, that everything has consequences and pay-offs. I don't think I saw or understood anything. When we set out in the car that night to carry out our mission as comrades we might as well have been wearing blindfolds, so completely oblivious were we to humanity.'

4

NINA

'*C*ara Majella,
            'Before I go any further, sifting through memories and years, I must tell you about the letter cards. The first one arrived a fortnight ago, the second this morning. I have them in front of me now. If I hadn't already made the decision to open up the past they would frighten me more. Even so, they are alarming enough. I feel as if I'm being watched, my reactions monitored. When I received the first I sat frozen in my chair most of the day. As the sun faded I stared into the shadows and saw myself standing in a country lane, my feet mired in mud.

'The cards are glossy productions, the kind that you fold over and seal. The photographs on the front feature views of phoney azure skies and intense landscape colours that rarely occur in Ireland. The peaceful rural scenes and wide stretches of picturesque strand flanked by hazy blue hills contrast oddly with the information inside. Both cards are a little creased because they have been typed. The first depicts

panoramas of County Cork and I have read it so many times
I could repeat it from memory:

*'I am stretched on your grave and you'll find me there
always; if I had the bounty of your arms I should never
leave you. It is time for me to lie with you; there is the cold
smell of the clay on me, the tan of the sun and the wind.'*

*It is no wonder that there are so many Irish laments and
elegies, that so much keening has gone on here. You find it
impossible to escape the past in Ireland. Everywhere you
turn it surrounds you. You see it in the very shape of the
country. You cannot go far here without stumbling over
ruins and graves from previous times. Burial sites from
pre-history stand silently on hills, watching the solitary
walker. Graves hide under the vast boglands, waiting to
be discovered by turfcutters. Passage graves, cairns, gallery
graves, dolmens, wedge graves, killeens, court graves, portal
graves, entrance graves, famine burials in cemeteries or
under grass by the side of the road; the land is etched with
random and ritual burials. The whole country is a series of
catacombs. In the midst of life we are in death; that senti-
ment rings particularly true in this land where the dead
keep close company with the living.*

*So many secretive graves, concealing the bones of those
who died natural deaths as well as the many who were
finished off by hunger or their foes.*

*In the view of Cork harbour, the second photograph, you
can see Curraghbinny. It is a hill-top cairn, probably bronze-
age. A clay platform inside it would have cradled the
deceased but the body had disintegrated by the time the
cairn was excavated. High up here, under a steely sky, it
seems that the breeze carries cries of grief from that other
time.*

'Can you imagine, Majella, how I felt when I picked up that first card? I was puzzled before I opened it and read the message. I know no one in Ireland these days; I could only think that one of my ex-colleagues was taking a holiday there. That line, *you find it impossible to escape the past in Ireland* resonated in my thoughts all day. An ambiguous *you* which could be interpreted both generally and specifically. I knew which way to take it, I repeated it to myself, over and over.

'The card that came this morning was equally disturbing. Joan brought it in with the post when she arrived. I read it while she cleaned the kitchen. She sings while she works; verses from "Raindrops Keep Falling on my Head", "Tea for Two" and other such jaunty numbers. This card is from Limerick and the first photograph shows Lough Gur, calm and sparkling in brilliant sunshine:

Megalithic tombs were built of huge stones and usually contained collective rather than individual burials. Bodies were buried singly, though, and you will still stumble on a lonely place where solitary bones have lain for centuries. Inhumation or interment of the corpse was usual although evidence of cremations has been found. Sometimes, with inhumations, bodies were exposed until the flesh had rotted and the skeleton was then buried.

The wedge grave was the first all-Irish grave form and you can see a fine example of one near the shore of Lough Gur. A couple of cremated bodies were found here but remains of twelve inhumations lay in the main gallery. The buried were surrounded by fragments of some of the good-quality eating vessels placed with them. Even now it is common to bury a loved one with some treasured possession. It is a way of soothing grief, imagining the departed helped on their way by familiar objects. The bereaved take comfort from it, feeling that they have established a link between the worlds of the living and dead. In a nearby churchyard today a musician being lowered in his coffin had his fiddle tucked in beside him. His wife stood by the grave, eyes brimming, lost in her sadness. She knows where her love lies, she will come back to hold vigil over him: 'I would be a shelter from the wind for you and protection from the rain for you; and oh, keen sorrow to my heart that you are under the earth!'

'I knew that I had been waiting for this second card. I know that there will be others. As Joan sang, "I'm gonna wash that man right outta my hair" I understood that my correspondent is determined to unlock my heart. Without warning, I felt that I might break down and release the swell of secrecy that I had harboured for so long. My eyes were scalded with tears but I heard Joan approaching and I composed myself, knowing that I mustn't give in just yet.

'In the early hours of this morning I have lain awake, wondering who is sending the cards. Whoever it is seems to be on the move, visiting chosen sites. I was always sure that only you, myself and Finn knew about our plan but now I've been imagining that one of the others found out or that you or Finn confessed to a comrade. There could have been a lonely hour, particularly after you split up, when one of you became desperate to share the guilt. Perhaps it was disclosed during pillow talk or maybe you told one of your brothers during a visit home, unburdening yourself while cleaning the hen house. But why would the confidant wait all this time to declare their knowledge? I have heard nothing about the comrades for years, with the exception of Declan. He was mentioned to me at a party and the unexpected confrontation with the past was extraordinary. I trembled as if a warning bell had clanged brutally in my ear. I've always assumed that our fellow revolutionaries became respectable middle-class professionals, much as comrades in England did, as I did myself; occasionally they might mention their madcap student days to one of their children or at a jolly supper, shaking their heads, smiling at memories of youthful radicalism. I recall reading that the leaders of the '68 Paris rebellion are now bankers, lawyers and TV executives. They featured in a Sunday colour supplement, sleek looking in soft chairs.

'Then, as a cat yowled in the street at four AM I thought that perhaps your news of Finn's death had been a mistake. Your cousin could have been confused and it would be easy to muddle facts long distance. What if there was a killing spree but Finn was only injured or he escaped the sprayed bullets and is now announcing himself? It's the kind of thing he might do, don't you agree, and a close brush with death can alter perspectives, make one look at priorities anew. My own illness has played no small part in my current actions. And Finn did so much love mystery and the rich weave of conspiracy, especially when they gave him the advantage. The typing points to him; he always typed, joking that everything about him favoured the left, including being left-handed but his handwriting was illegible through being forced to use his right hand at his boarding school. You would complain that his portable typewriter was like a prosthetic, often tucked beneath one arm. His clattering on the keys used to drag you from sleep early in the morning as he set about another day's crusade. He is the only person I ever knew who would carry his typewriter to the bathroom, balancing it on his lap as he sat on the toilet.

'I pictured him, perched in hotel rooms in Cork and Limerick, typing, still smoking untipped cigarettes. You may well have had cards too. I've no idea how he would have obtained our addresses but Finn was always an excellent information gatherer. Perhaps he is down on his luck and looking for a helping hand from old friends; he'd run through a fair part of his inheritance during the years when we knew him and he had expensive tastes despite his professed solidarity with the proletariat. His public face may have been in harmony with them but when he brought the shopping home he'd always bought the best lean steak and his claret was the finest in the wine rack. Or maybe he simply wants to talk about the past and being Finn, is coming in at a tangent, testing the ground. All these ideas might just be the wild products of a tired brain. I can only wait and surmise, see where the next card comes from. Living with uncertainty is hardly new to me.

'You introduced me to Finn the day after I met you. "Come and listen to traditional music," you said, "meet some interesting people." It was the first time I heard the word *craic*; "*the craic's great at Mulligan's*" you explained as we headed through the dingy streets. I already knew then that I wanted to get as close to you as possible. You were sporting a fringed shawl and I touched one of the swinging tassels as we walked. I can still feel its warm, rough texture. I didn't tell you I had never been in a pub, embarrassed by the extreme narrowness of the world I had inhabited. I remarked on the shabbiness around us, gesturing at boarded-up shops and broken glass in doorways. The contrast to leafy, prosperous Maidstone was shocking. I don't think you ever fully understood how subdued and genteel my childhood had been. You had never visited England, had no way of knowing the culture gap I was experiencing. You replied that it was people, not buildings that mattered; come the revolution, when the proletariat triumphed, all these streets would take on new life and purpose and the equal distribution of wealth would mean that the populace had an investment in their surroundings. I was impressed by your certainty and the apparent imminence of the revolution. We passed an army patrol at a street corner, squaddies no older than ourselves with blackened faces and camouflage jackets that looked out of place in an urban setting. The first soldier said hallo civilly enough and instinctively I nodded back. The second quickly followed with a cockier, "hiya, darlings, wotcha doin' tonight?" and you snarled back, "fuck off, you bastard shits." I felt a quiver of fear mingled with excitement as he spat on the pavement. "Nothing to write home about anyway, lads," one of them mocked behind us.

'"Didn't people welcome them with cups of tea and cake when they arrived?" I asked. I had seen photos in my mother's *Daily Telegraph*; little boys perched on squaddies' knees, fingering their guns while aproned women ferried teapots.

'"A gut reaction of relief," you said. "Now the military are exposed in their true colours, tools of the fascist state."

'In the pub you introduced me to people whose names and faces I no longer recall and we sat in a blue haze of cigarette smoke, listening to jigs and the roar of conversation. I was stunned by the chat which flowed seamlessly; people in England don't talk to each other the way the Irish do, enjoying the flavour of words on the tongue. Despite the plain floorboards and cracked window glass the pub seemed exotic. I drank in the atmosphere along with my lager. I recounted the story of hiding in my room and described the other women surrounding me in the hall of residence. There were five of them, plump pasty-faced Protestant girls from local townlands I'd never heard of. Union Jacks and banners stating "No Surrender!" had been pinned to their doors. They dressed in white nylon blouses and dark pleated skirts, wore brown barrettes in their hair and plain, flat lace-up school shoes, the uniform of fervent Evangelists. Within days of arriving they had put hand-written notices in the communal bathrooms: "Please Remove Your Hairs From The Plug Holes" – I think it was the sight of pubic hairs that caused specific offence – and "Remember, No one Wants To Bathe In Your Tide Mark!" Perhaps the college accommodation service had thought that coming from England, I would be more comfortable situated amongst a group of students who were loyal to the crown. Early in the mornings they visited each other's rooms to pray and sing fierce-sounding hymns in their rural Ulster voices:

"Awnwerd Crustyen So-o-oul-dye-erz!
Marchin' az tuy wur,
Wuth the crawz of Jeezuz
Goin' awn beefurr . . ."

'I was sure I had detected a tambourine but there was no danger of "Mr Tambourine Man" drifting through the thin walls. I heard myself being witty as I described them. I had never before been the centre of attention in a group of people, never talked so much and so freely; I didn't know you could become intoxicated with language. There are times when, clawing my way through a typically constipated English conversation, I find myself craving some of that old, easy jawing.

'You talked and laughed that night but you were distracted and when Finn came in and you relaxed I understood that your tension had been that of a waiting lover. He was wearing dark clothes and a black beret. A pack of papers was stashed under his arm and he was in a foul mood. That testiness, that air that nothing ever quite pleased him was part of his attraction. Sales had been poor, he said, and Vinny hadn't turned up to help him. He laid the papers on the table and I saw that they were thin bulletins, printed on a duplicating machine and that his fingers were smudged with dark ink. *Workers' Struggle, The Paper of Red Dawn,* I read as I craned my neck and you told Finn my name. He nodded a brief hallo and went to get a drink.

'"Is Finn your boyfriend?" I asked.

'"My lover and comrade," you corrected.

'I gazed at you and then at Finn's long back, impressed by this mysterious world I was glimpsing and experiencing a twinge of envy that you were involved with such an interesting-looking man.

'Did I fall in love with Finn a little myself that night? I think I must have done, otherwise why would I have come to dislike him so intensely? He was dark and sure of himself; even his irascibility fitted a certain brooding stereotype and I had, like many another teenage girl, immersed myself in the Brontës and Du Maurier. When he came back with his drink he sat next to me and asked me questions about how I was finding Ireland. He tipped mixed nuts from a bag into his palm and offered them to me, saying I should pick out the almonds, they were the best. When the nuts had vanished he licked his salty hand as carefully as a cat licks its plate clean, running his tongue between his fingers. As he spoke to me he was examining my face. Although his eyes were a soft brown they had a directness that made me feel nothing would escape his attention. And nothing did, Majella, nothing did; he was watchful and always at the end of the road before we had turned the corner.'

Nina sighed and opened a new document, naming it 'Martin'. She typed quickly, her eyes a little blurred.

'You are beginning to understand that I left you not just because I am ill or contrary. If you are bewildered by me, well, that makes two of us. When you harbour a knowledge that cannot be revealed you feel set apart from the rest of humanity. There were times in the long nights when I longed to wake you, confess to you, beg your help. But I had no right to taint you.

'Can you picture me in that pub? My hair was long and wild and sometimes I used to colour it so that it took on a hue like ripe red gooseberries. I wore pale pink nail varnish until Finn remarked that it looked cheap; he was a puritan about make-up although I expect he would have approved of the type of products you can buy now, recipes originating from far-flung populations of the third world.

'That was a magic night in Mulligans; the kind of vivid experience you always remember with completeness: the sounds, the colours, the voices, the feelings engendered. On that night when I met Finn I started to feel a release of energy, a thrilling giddiness. It seemed to me that I had spent my days up to my eighteenth year in a timid stasis, waiting for something to happen. My mother's message to me was enshrined in her stock phrase, "no fuss please, darling," and my father's self-effacement and premature death left a void.

'In my mother's shaded drawing room, behind ruched curtains, I had watched television pictures of Soviet tanks in Prague and rioting in the streets of London and Paris; demonstrations against the Vietnam War in Washington, civil rights marchers from Belfast with blood streaming down their faces, the reality barely impinging on me as I went about the discreet life lived in English suburbia, preparing to go to the tennis court or the library. I was dimly aware of Joan Baez singing "We Shall Overcome" and of the student power that was setting European streets ablaze. The only cold war I was familiar with was the one my mother had waged for years against my father, a series of frosty skirmishes that left me stranded in no-man's land, unsure of who I should offer my loyalty to in any particular week. There were plenty of occasions when they communicated by leaving notes for me and I ran back and forth like a messenger between the trenches. My mother's dugout was the drawing room, my father's the potting shed. The events of 1968 took place while I was attempting and failing to broker peace somewhere between these camps, carrying communications written in codes which the two sides were doomed to misinterpret. If I paid any attention to them, it was with feelings of distaste and anxiety at such breakdown of order; locked as I was in the long disintegration of a marriage, I couldn't face combat in the outside world.

'In Mulligan's bar I grew inebriated on the yeasty tang of stout and the fumes of golden hot whiskies in which cloves bobbed like tadpoles. I tried my first plate of boxty, the publican's speciality, a dish that I became addicted to. It was hot, peppery and buttery and when someone said it was the food of the gods I agreed. A student who I later learned was Declan, the treasurer of Red Dawn, leaned across and asked teasingly if I'd heard that old rhyme:

"Boxty on the griddle
Boxty on the pan
If you don't eat Boxty
You'll never get a man!"

'I smiled at him, registering that he had deep blue eyes but Majella reproved him, saying that we didn't want to hear any of that old sexist claptrap. Finn took a spoonful from my plate without asking permission and declared that boxty was good, humble peasant food, the backbone of Ireland, the kind of dish that had its equivalent amongst working people in all cultures. A man stood up and sang a traditional ballad that brought tears to my eyes, a song about loss of land and family. Then Majella rapped the table and launched into a song that spoke of present injustice. She sang with such passion that I bit my gum through the boxty:

"Armoured cars and tanks and guns
Came to take away our sons
But every man will stand behind
The men behind the wire.

"Through the little streets of Belfast
In the dark of early morn
British soldiers came marauding,
Wrecking little homes with scorn;
Heedless of the crying children,
Dragging fathers from their beds,
Beating sons while helpless mothers
Watch the blood pour from their heads.
Round the world the truth will echo
Cromwell's men are here again,
Britain's name forever sullied
In the eyes of honest men."

'Afterwards, I asked her in a whisper if that was really happening and she said yes, nightly; men taken away and never charged, never given the chance of a fair hearing, their families left devastated. We were living in a tyranny but Bob Dylan was right, these were times of upheaval and change; this system of injustice couldn't last, the people's blood was up.

'I understood that night that life had been racketing around elsewhere while I quietly occupied my little corner, mediating my parents' antagonism and avoiding my mother's censorious eye. In our tidy bungalow tucked away in a cul de sac it was a crime to leave an unwashed cup on the table, draw the curtains back untidily or spill a drop of liquid on the furniture. The background orchestration to my childhood had been the tight hissing from my mother's lips as she heaped blame on my father or found fault with me. Now I was in a city where people opened their mouths wide to bellow their opinions and were willing to suffer terrible wounds, even death, for their beliefs. A sense of sheer animation, an impetuosity I would never have guessed at, was pulsing in me. I saw it reflected in Majella's eyes, heard it echoed in her voice. The urge of something to aim for, something to risk everything for, that was what I wanted. The deliciousness of the boxty was giving me a taste for more flavours. I was ready for tumultuous change. I was ripe for falling in love and I did, with the scarred warring city and Majella and Finn.

'When you are judging me, when you finally weigh up what you have learned, remember that the impulse was to do good, to create, to make a positive mark on the world. I fell far short of my own aspirations but I did possess them, and that remains some comfort to me.'

5

MARTIN

He looked in the bathroom mirror the evening Nina told him their life together was over and saw that he had a puzzled expression, like a child who doesn't understand what it's done wrong or a dog that suspects its owner is displeased. Then he did something he used to do as a child when he wanted to ease his troubles. He breathed on the mirror, wrote NINA in the condensation, then rubbed her name away hard with a flannel, making sure that none of the letters reappeared in the humid air. There, he thought angrily, morosely, self-pityingly; if that's the way you want it, you can have it.

The next day he felt numb, as if his limbs had been shot full of Novocain. He prodded his arm; nothing. When he picked his hand up and let it drop it rested on his knee; someone else might have left it there. On the way home from work he stopped and had his right ear pierced in three places. The slap of the gun and the mild stinging helped him back into himself as did the burning antiseptic he had to bathe it in later. Nina didn't notice, she was looking through him but when he fingered the tiny punctures and wiped the spots of blood he knew that he was real.

During the following weeks he stayed strangely calm. Maybe, he thought, he'd been expecting Nina's decision for some time. She had always eluded him. Before she became ill she was light on her feet, fast moving. There she would be on the periphery of his vision, vanishing through a door or up the stairs. He would hear the car ignition and realise that she had left the house with no warning. She would come back hours later, cheeks flushed, or yawning, with puffy eyes. When he asked where she'd been she would reply for a walk or a visit to a museum or just sleeping in the car. The first time she said that, 'just sleeping', he was convinced that he was being made a fool of and she was seeing someone else. Yet it was only a few months into their marriage and he couldn't detect an air of deceit; she looked at him full in the face and spoke with such simple frankness, he had to believe her. She had driven up to the Heath, she'd say, parked near the pub on Spaniard's Hill and drifted off. When he asked why, if there was something wrong, she shook her head, saying that there was no explanation she could give.

He followed her once, feeling craven, a sneak. He was annoyed that she was the one taking off, behaving oddly, and yet he was acting as if he was the guilty partner, trailing her covertly. His hands were damp at the possibility that she might spot him but she didn't, driving just over the speed limit. She headed down by the River Lea near Tottenham Hale and pulled up at a fishing area. Then she reclined the seat, folded her arms and tucked her chin down. He waited there for an hour, feeling ridiculous, spying on his wife sleeping and wondered what he had done to cause her to flee from him.

Before he and Nina married they had known each other

for just over a year, living together for six months prior to the wedding. During those months she had never, as far as he was aware, felt the need for solitary outings. She was often a little touchy about her own possessions and her books but he understood that; they had both lived on their own and it was difficult adjusting to an invasion of territory. It seemed that, as soon as they were married, she found the need to put spaces between them, spaces that grew, broadening, deepening. He was alarmed, thinking of those people who discovered that the charms of their partner quickly waned once they had formalised the relationship but when he asked Nina – and he asked her often, more often than he wanted to – if she was happy she would smile and say yes, of course, he mustn't mind her strange foibles. Mystified, he would put his arms around her, sniffing the brackish odour of the river or polish from a museum bench in her clothes and hair.

She was rushing past him the first day he noticed her at the university. He had been appointed manager of personnel a month before and was still finding his feet. A person flashed by him, sweeping him into her slipstream rather as a tornado sucks up objects from the ground. He sought out that small, slim figure with the huge brown leather satchel that banged against her hip as she blew around the corridors. It was her lightness, a kind of sprite-like quality, that attracted him and held his interest. He would have to put his hand on her arm to secure her attention and keep her still. Her students, he discovered, called her 'The Exocet'. She was a popular lecturer, admired for her zest and wit. Her singing voice was surprisingly strong for someone so slight and she occasionally entertained her colleagues or students with Italian and French songs. Her talent for mimicry was well known; she did a convincing Edith Piaf and Shirley Bassey.

He sat opposite her in the buffet one day and introduced

himself, explaining that he'd seen her whirling along a corridor. Ah yes, she said she'd noticed his name in the university newsletter. Her head was neat, her glossy brown hair cut like a cap, glinting where the sun was illuminating it from behind. He found out that she had spent the summer in Italy which accounted for her lightly tanned complexion, the same honey shade as the melba toast she was crunching, and the deeper, caramel scatter of freckles across the bridge of her nose. He recounted his own fortnight spent on a walking tour of Tuscany and they swapped stories of Florence and Siena. She pushed her plate away and rested her chin on linked knuckles. He saw that she bit her nails and guessed that her confident air was overstated. He wanted to reach out and cradle her head, which to him seemed terribly vulnerable, between his hands. When she laughed she ran her fingers through her feathery hair so that strands stuck out. He liked the way she didn't care, wasn't bothered about her image. She reminded him of one of the wood pixies in an illustrated plate in one of his favourite childhood books, a hardback volume called *Tales of the Forest Folk*. The pixies were nimble and busy, collecting berries and honey, bandaging the wounded paws of squirrels and badgers. As she talked she played with an empty sugar sachet, folding and smoothing it with narrow fingers, shaping it into a star. Even when she was sitting she appeared active, her arms moving, shifting in her chair.

He used to joke that if he'd known he was going to fall for someone so energetic, he'd have taken up fitness training. Their relationship grew as they walked and cycled. He had to buy a bike, not having owned one since he was sixteen. At weekends they caught the tube and tramped around Epping or Theydon Bois or drove down to Sussex and walked on the Downs. Their cycle routes took them through Hampstead Heath or south of the river, following the Thames. It was autumn when they met and the air was growing misty. Yellowing leaves dived under their wheels and an edge of cold nipped their fingers. Their conversations rose and fell with dips in the road, paced to the rhythms of their booted feet and clicking gears. He found some of the longer walks, the ten-mile ones, hard going but the intensity of a new love buoyed him up, willing his legs on.

She was unlike any other woman he had come across. The two serious relationships he had been involved in before now seemed pleasant but arid affairs. Neither Helen nor Suzy would have made him stop on a road, pushing his head towards a bush and urging him to sniff deeply the pungent leaves. Nina knew the names of trees, plants and wild flowers; she would bend and scoop rainwater from a blossom with a quick flick of her tongue or deftly pick berries and cram them into his mouth so that his lips were purple stained and he would taste the tang of wild fruit for the rest of the day. She told him the best places to find small sweet plums in August and took him to a bridle path where blackcurrants massed, so heavily clustered that they bent to the ground. Her small garden was a riot of carefully tended plants and tubs brimming with greenery. Often, when he arrived, he found her crouching, hands buried in a bag of compost or taking cuttings. Herbs grew everywhere, on window ledges throughout her flat and in a special trough just outside the back door so that it seemed that there was no dividing line between inside and out. She gave bunches of herbs away at the university; dill, sage or marjoram frequently trailed from her satchel, scenting the pages of marked essays as she stood in corridors, advising on their use in cooking or in medicinal drinks. Sometimes she would slip from bed in between love making, returning with a handful of lemon balm which she would massage onto his skin. They rolled on the leaves, crushing them on the sheet as they slipped down a tunnel of fragrance.

One warm morning, when he had stayed the night with her, she took him onto the patch of lawn outside her garden flat and got him to lie face down with her on the damp grass, one ear to the ground. If you listened quietly you could hear all of London moving, she said; the tramp of thousands of feet, the rolling of buses and trains, the surging of boats on the Thames. Concentrating, eyes closed, he thought he could; there seemed to be a humming under the soil.

'This is my favourite season,' he said, freewheeling near Richmond. 'The colours are soft.'

'Yes, but the tastes are tart and many of the berries are inedible or poisonous. It's a deceptive time of year; the golds and russets make you want to linger when you should be on your way home, securing your winter nest.'

He gathered that all this evening and weekend activity was what Nina was used to; she had done these walks and cycle trips alone. He wasn't overweight when they met and he lost half a stone in the first months. A friend commented that love makes some people sleek and others thin. Perhaps he should have read more into the fact that Nina's weight stayed the same.

It was at a campus party where Nina had sung 'La Vie en Rose' in the style of Piaf that he first noticed what he came to recognise as her mask look. It had dawned on him that Nina had no friends, just acquaintances. Her general popularity was exactly that; general, not specific to any one person. He was used to women having networks of friends but apart from when she was socialising in a group, Nina spent her time on her own. He pieced together a picture of a life lived reading, gardening and preparing lectures with frequent exercise and the odd party or theatre outing. She wouldn't go to the cinema; she couldn't stand the way it falsified life, she said, lending it a glamour it didn't deserve.

Piecing together was exactly what he had to do because

he found it difficult to form a comprehensive picture of Nina before he met her. She side-stepped those questions that lovers ask each other, confiding in return images of themselves at ten, fourteen, twenty, the problems of previous relationships, the flavour of a childhood. When he talked about his family or his first girlfriend or Angus, a close friend from university days in Warwick, Nina listened and nodded and made the odd comment, but there was no return of information. When he jokingly said that he sometimes thought she must have landed from another planet, that she was an alien sent to gather information, she laughed, replying that she was in regular contact with Mars. Nina would never give an inch when she didn't want to. The pattern of their life together was quickly established in those first months; when she was being elusive he would joke, nervously trying to conceal how frustrated he felt and, taking his cue, she would joke back. So on each occasion he set a trap for himself and provided the escape route that she used for swift avoidance. Unwittingly, he sowed the seeds of his own unhappiness.

After Nina had done her Piaf at that New Year's Eve party a young Irishman, a student, came up to them and told her how much he'd enjoyed it. He was obviously on a return trip to the sixties: his hair was long and he wore John Lennon glasses and a tie-dyed shirt.

'It's unusual to find a person singing at a party in England,' he said, 'other than drunken rugby choruses or the Birdie Song. It's more the kind of thing you get back home in Ireland.'

'Which part of Ireland are you from?' Martin asked him.

'Strabane.' He turned to Nina. 'We have a bit of a connection,' he told her.

'I'm sorry?' she said.

'My name's Conor Lally. You knew my father, Declan

Lally, at Queen's, didn't you? Look, I've a photo he dug out.'

He produced a wallet from his back pocket and found a creased black-and-white photograph. Nina didn't take it. She let him hold it in front of her and Martin peered over her arm. There was Nina with long, free-flowing hair, wearing a layered skirt and waistcoat. Her right fist was in the air in a clenched salute, her left hand curled around one pole of a banner saying, TROOPS OUT NOW! A young man whose face still held the last residues of puppy fat lifted the other pole.

Nina took a step back and sipped her drink, looking down into it. 'Declan Lally. It rings a bell. We were always demonstrating about something then.'

The young man nodded, moving closer to her. 'I was home for Christmas and I was talking about some of the lecturers, the ones worth mentioning, the ones who don't just take the money and run. Dad said he'd known a Nina Rawle. When I described you he said you must be the same person and he found this photo in an old album. The right-on sixties!'

'This is Belfast?' Martin asked, looking at that other, grainy Nina and then turning to her, touched her arm. 'I didn't know that you'd lived in Ireland.' He was puzzled, because he'd told her that his grandmother who lived in Dagenham was originally from Galway and he had once had a holiday with her there.

'No, you didn't know. I don't teach you, do I?' she asked Conor, her voice polite but tight.

'No. I'm doing Spanish and International studies.' He was pleasantly drunk and you could tell that he was one of those earnest young types who pin you to the wall at parties and give you their world view.

'Dad said that you were both into politics in a big way.

He wanted me to ask you if you still sing "The Red Flag"? He's active but he's gone soft; he's in the SDLP, refuge of the woolly middle-of-the-roader. That was the time to be a student, back then. There was real radicalism, burning-hot stuff. Look at the leaders you had: Tariq Ali, Danny Cohn-Bendit, Bernadette Devlin. Not like now – there are no real lefties, it's hard enough to find a committed feminist. People spend their time worrying about bank loans and keeping their noses clean in case they can't get a job. You've no idea how lucky you were to have been part of things then, you had the chance to make a real difference.'

Martin was looking at Nina as Conor delivered his enthusiastic monologue. Her face was freezing and setting, shutting down. He was shocked because her features were usually so expressive and the severity of her look alarmed him.

'You'll have to excuse me,' she said, putting her glass down. 'I think the pizza's disagreed with me, I must go home.'

Martin hurried after her to the car. She was accelerating away before he managed to close his door.

'Are you feeling sick? I can drive if you are.'

'I'll be okay, probably needed some air.' She was winding her window down full and an icy breeze caught in his throat.

'He was a bit of a bore, that guy. Do you remember his father?'

'Vaguely. I might have spoken to him once or twice. We all went to lots of meetings.' She turned her head towards her window, taking deep breaths. Her tone was flat, tired, her profile still expressionless.

'What did you make of Belfast?'

'It wasn't a happy time in my life. Could we drop the

subject? I think maybe I've caught that bug that's doing the rounds.'

And so the subject was dropped and they never returned to it. Martin assumed that Nina had been homesick in Ireland or experienced a bad love affair. He had nearly left Warwick after a girl jilted him. Because he never met anyone close to Nina, a confidante of any kind, he had no one to ask casual questions of, no way of filling in the gaps she left.

There were other subjects that brought on Nina's mask face. Funerals, for example; when Martin's Dagenham grandmother died Nina told him she wouldn't be going to the mass and service at the cemetery. He was astonished. She hadn't known his grandmother well but he had assumed that she would accompany him. He had loved his grandmother and felt her loss. When he heard Nina's words, spoken rigidly, the loss was heightened because he had expected to have her by him in his grief.

'What's the problem?' he asked her.

'I just don't like funerals. They're morbid, they make me feel desperate.'

'I'd like you to be there. It would help me.'

'I understand why you think that but believe me, I wouldn't be any kind of help. I'd end up having to leave during the service and that would be even more distressing for you.'

'What will I tell my family?'

'Whatever you like. Say I'm not well.'

'What about your parents? You must have gone to their funerals.'

'Actually, you're wrong, I wasn't at my mother's.'

'You didn't attend your own mother's funeral?'

'No. There's no law that says you have to, Martin.'

As he watched her the mask was taking shape, deadening her features. He knew that he was helpless in front of it and that no matter how shocked he was, how much pressure he put on her, he would get nowhere. And so, even in his grief, he made a feeble joke.

'Well, I suppose I can't expect you to come to mine, then?'

She touched his arm kindly. 'Oh, I'll probably make an exception for you.'

He stood in the church, next to his cousin and her family, aware of a space by his side. He should have been thinking about his grandmother but instead he was considering the enigma that was Nina. Kneeling, he wondered what she was doing while he was there; was she dozing in her car by a river or wandering London streets? If there was a key to Nina, he knew that he had never come near finding it. Maybe he was a fool for continuing to look but there was no one else he wanted. Glancing around the church, he reasoned that his cousin put up with her husband's occasional adulteries and his uncle closed his eyes to his wife's compulsive shopping; his dead grandmother had accepted her husband's drinking, found a way of shaping her life despite it. Perhaps that was what a successful marriage came down to; what each partner was prepared to accommodate in the other.

When he had first met Nina he was physically exhausted for weeks. There were knowing remarks from his friends but his taut, aching muscles were due to all the unaccustomed exercise as much as to the aftermath of passion. Pumped full of endorphins, he found it hard to relax at night and he slept badly, over-tired. When his eyelids drooped he sensed that he was still pedalling or striding out, arms swinging. It seemed an odd irony that this state afflicted Nina after their marriage. He would turn to see her yawning hugely, her eyes watering. In the mornings he had to shake her awake and bring her strong black coffee. Then she would move slowly, knocking into furniture and fumbling with the toothpaste. Their evenings grew shorter, with Nina often heading for bed by nine o'clock or falling asleep in the chair, her book sliding to the floor. He began to feel as if he were living with a very old person, tip-toeing around the house so as not to disturb her, catching her glasses as they dangled from her hand, turning down invitations to go out because it would be too late for Nina to stay up. Most weekends she slept until midday. It was only then, on Saturdays and Sundays, that he felt he had her full attention, that it was safe to arrange to go out. At times he would become irritated at the sight of her rubbing her eyes or closing them wearily as he was talking to her. On occasion, feeling trapped and wishing to punish her, he insisted that they go out after work but he suffered as much as she did as he witnessed her attempts to stay alert. Then he felt ashamed, as if he had been accused of brutality.

Her explanation for her exhaustion was that she wasn't sleeping well. Was it something to do with him, he asked, but she said no, she didn't understand it and as time went on he decided that it couldn't be the newness of constantly sharing a bed. She told him that she'd consulted her doctor and had been advised to try relaxing before sleep; milky drinks, soothing baths and tapes of pan pipes were recommended. Her GP didn't believe in sleeping tablets and neither did she; she couldn't bear the idea of such dependency. She swallowed herbal drinks at night and bathed in aromatherapy oils, but nothing helped. He watched, month in, month out as she stumbled somnambulistically from room to room. It became another thing he couldn't fathom. He skirted her guiltily as she applied drops to her tired eyes while he was shaving because he slept soundly, deeply, every night; he even slept through the smoke alarm when it malfunctioned. His morning and evening energy seemed unwholesome, offensive. If they referred to her fatigue they talked in those codes that married couples use to skirt around awkward subjects:

'Tired again?' he would say.

'Yes, a bit done in.'

'Patchy sleep last night?'

'Oh, you know, about the usual.'

'You could try a camomile tea.'

'Mmm, I might.'

'You need to find Rip Van Winkle's secret.'

'I wouldn't mind discovering The Seven Sleepers' den.'

Their life together was curtailed and shaped by Nina's constant exhaustion. Gradually, they saw fewer and fewer people, went out rarely. Nina said that she didn't need anyone but him and he was duly flattered, persuading himself that this was a good way to live. Other people either thought that they were unhealthily obsessed with each other or envied their exclusivity, assuming that it was the enduring and satisfying attachment of soulmates. In the evenings Nina would often sit beside him and ask him to read to her. They worked slowly through George Eliot, Tolstoy, Simenon and others, his voice trailing when he realised that she was sleeping. Then he would ease his arm from beneath her shoulders, secure a cushion under her head and slip away to garden, work on the car or sometimes, when the house was too silent, visit his friend Angus or have a drink in The Fox and Hounds. He became one of those solitary men seen in the local pub, cradling one half of lager for an hour and talking about nothing of any importance to the barman. In this way, he was almost prepared for the illness that overtook Nina. He had been living with a semi-invalid for years already. He had no huge adjustment to make. It was like effortlessly shifting gears in a car, automatically adapting to road conditions.

That night when Nina told him she was leaving him, when

he locked the bathroom door and turned the taps on so she couldn't hear him cry, he saw in the mirror the same patient, watchful eyes that used to stare back at him as he soaped his father with shaving cream. He had known the contours of cheeks and chin, the right amount of pressure to put on a razor, long before he had bristles of his own. The role he had stepped into with Nina was a reprise of his childhood. At eleven he had become part-time nurse to his father when a heart attack rendered him helpless, paralysed down one side. While his mother hurried off to her shift on the surgical ward he had dressed his father, cut up his food, played draughts and dominoes and endlessly discussed the state of the world. He enjoyed accomplishing the tasks, ticking them off mentally, anticipating his father's needs. The enforced domesticity caused him no anxiety; his witty, sociable parent invited Martin's friends in for raucous card games and let them take rides in his electric wheelchair. The secret of life, his father confided to him, was not to turn slings and arrows into tragedy. No one is truly interested in tragedy unless it's their own, Marty, he would say; there's no point in milking it for too long, it's got limited shelf-life. They played practical jokes on each other and on Martin's friends, involving whoopee cushions, plastic cat vomit, false teeth and eyeballs, which his father bought mail-order. There were times when they laughed so much they fought for breath. When an interfering teacher wrote to his home to express concern about the hours he had to spend with a sick man he felt fury at the intrusion and tore up the letter.

The shock he felt at Nina's going was similar to the loss that overwhelmed him on the morning he had brought his father's tea in and found him dead in the chair. For weeks afterwards he wandered the house, looking for things to do, distracted at being without a definite list of duties, wanting to be needed. Most of all, he missed the smell in the hollow of his father's neck which he used to inhale as he bent to trim his nostril hair; a mixture of cherry tobacco, soap and the relaxant cream he rubbed into his rigid shoulder.

On the day Nina's diagnosis was given they left the hospital and stopped for lunch at a restaurant. In Nina's haggard face he saw the shadowy features of the old woman she would probably never become. He was filled with a wish to protect her from life's cruelty. He thought of the woman he had accompanied on all those walks, the woman he had fallen for as they pored over ordnance survey maps or traced a badger sett and at that moment he loved her more than ever.

6

JOAN

Joan surveyed Nina's books with satisfaction when she had finished sorting them. They looked lovely, all standing straight and alphabetical. She dusted them every other day but she had to make sure the cloth was damp so that Nina didn't start sneezing. She never found any of them out of place and she asked Nina one morning if she read them these days. No, Nina replied, there was some writing she was doing when she had the energy; she found she didn't have much time for books now.

Nina had given her a key so that she didn't have to wait to be let in. If Nina was having a bad morning and was in the furthest end of the flat when she rang the bell, it could be a good five minutes before the door opened. Sometimes when she arrived she would see Nina out in the garden, which in Joan's opinion was much too big for someone who could do so little. It had been well tended by the previous occupants and Martin worked it at weekends. Nina would be on the patio sniffing at flowers or checking the huge terracotta tubs for dryness. If they needed watering, that was Joan's first task. On warmer days Nina would pull a canvas chair from the conservatory and place it amongst the tubs. She would sit with her dark glasses on, face raised to the sun, listening to her CD player. While Joan worked she would pinch dead buds from a camellia or from the long-lasting winter pansies.

One Friday morning about three weeks after they met Nina was looking exhausted. She asked if Joan would mind cutting her toenails.

'No, of course not,' Joan said, surprised because it was the first time she had been asked to do anything personal. 'Are you feeling worse today?'

'Yes, it's a bore. I overdid things yesterday and my joints are creaky. It goes like that sometimes. I've been trying to cut my toenails for days but my wrists are weak. I'll be developing claws if I'm not careful.' Nina smiled. 'Mind you, that would be in keeping.' She took her socks off slowly, as if she was lifting bricks.

'What did you mean, about claws?' Joan asked when she had fetched the nail clippers.

Nina replied in that level, matter-of-fact voice she used when she was talking about her illness. 'The disease I've got is called lupus. That's from the Latin for wolf. So, wolf . . . claws . . .'

Joan had never heard of it and she'd come across a fair few types of illness during the course of her job. 'That's a horrible name. Why is it called that?'

'These red marks I've got on my face are one of the symptoms. They're supposed to look a bit wolfish.' Nina touched her cheeks, moving her hair back.

The marks were more noticeable some days than others and they always flared up when she was tired. Joan had seen her rubbing them and then they would grow red and angry. Facial marks of any kind could make people self-conscious.

Joan understood that only too well; she had saved up five years previously to have an unsightly mole removed from her top lip. She was in the clinic for just half a day and it made all the difference.

'How about a bit of make-up?' she suggested 'You could buy some of that allergy-tested stuff that won't irritate your skin. A thin foundation would tone down the marks.'

Nina looked at her with an amused expression. 'I don't think so, Joan. I don't need a confidence booster. I've got the illness, that's all there is to it. I take my medicine and pace my days.'

'How did you get ill?'

'I don't know. It was supposed to be arthritis at first but then a specialist decided I was a wolf-woman. It's mainly women who get this. You can imagine that in another century I'd have been burnt at the stake.'

'There's no cure?'

'Not when it's in this advanced state. Realistically, I won't make old bones.'

Joan caught a stray piece of toenail that had escaped from the towel onto the floor. 'You've got to stay positive and not give up hope,' she said. 'There's always a bit of blue sky. Doctors are discovering cures all the time. There's even new medicines for AIDS.'

'I don't know about hope, but I am positive. I'm particularly positive about a long letter I'm writing. Is it horrible, dealing with someone else's feet?'

'Not horrible, but some are nicer than others. Yours are pretty, very soft.'

'Really? I'm not developing padded toes and hairy soles?'

Joan felt confused when Nina talked like that. Her feet were like her hands, small and well proportioned. 'Really,' she said, 'you've got good feet. When we were young me and my brother had to go to a chiropodist because we both had fallen arches. My poor gran had to fork out for expensive shoes. I still have to use arch supports sometimes, depending on the shoes I'm wearing.'

'Why did your grandmother have to buy them?'

'She brought us up when our parents died.' As Joan finished the nails she told Nina about Gran taking her and Eddie in and the house in Bromley. Then she mentioned that Gran had liked Lily of the Valley perfume too.

'Interesting,' Nina said, staring at her feet. 'And your brother, what about him?'

Joan sat back on her heels, folding the towel in. 'Eddie passed over years ago. Then Gran died not long after, so it was a case of Joan-all-alone for most of the time.'

'And have you often been lonely?'

'Well, you know, it can be difficult fending for yourself. There have been times when I'd have liked someone to lean on. That's what I missed after my divorce, even though my husband was away a lot, working. I did like being able to say, "my hubby", when I was talking to people, it gave me a warm feeling. I'd never had much success with men until I met my fiancé, Rich. It's not easy to meet single men once you reach your late twenties. They all seem to be married or pretending not to be.'

'I know what you mean. I had affairs throughout my twenties. I imagined there would always be partners available, but the supply of unattached men dries up. I stumbled over Martin in the university administration office. We were both thirty and he came, amazingly, without a complicated history; no ex-wives, no children, no current girlfriend and not unmarried because he was a closet gay.'

The way she put things, so straightforwardly, made Joan smile. 'That's why Rich has made such a difference to me.'

'Is he? Rich, I mean.'

'No, he's got to look for a job soon.' She changed the

subject, feeling uncomfortable because she had to gloss over the truth. 'I'd better stir my stumps now or I'll be running late. Was that the letterbox I heard?'

'Yes. Could you fetch the post in?'

Joan brought in a couple of brown envelopes and another of those lettercards from Ireland. This one said 'The Beauties of Clare'.

'Have you got friends in Ireland?' Joan asked.

'Sort of. Have you ever been there?' Nina had placed the card on the little table beside her and kept glancing at it as they were talking.

'No, never. It's a mess over there, I can never understand it.'

Nina nodded. 'You were never tempted to take a look at it?'

'Not me. When I can afford a holiday I go on those coach tours; they take you door to door almost and you get to know people. I've been to Bruges and the Black Forest. Last year I went to Poland for a week – it only cost a hundred and thirty pounds. It was fascinating but the food was terrible.'

'We'll have to talk some more about your eventful life. Have you got a busy weekend planned?'

'I'm decorating the bedroom and other bits and pieces. You know, all those things you don't get time for during the week. And I'll be seeing Rich. Your fridge is stocked up. Is your husband coming round?' Nina had mentioned that Martin visited at weekends and cooked meals as well as tending the garden.

'Yes, tomorrow morning. We're planning to tackle the old asparagus bed by the back wall. I must remind him to bring the hoe.'

It sounded a strange kind of separation to Joan. She wondered what this Martin was like and whether he and Nina talked to each other in that teasing tone she often used.

Maybe Martin couldn't cope with her illness and seeing that and having her own money, she'd decided to live alone. Joan couldn't imagine leaving Rich if he was ill; marriage was supposed to be for better or worse, after all.

It was at the start of the coach trip to Poland that Joan first heard Rich's name. She had taken her pocket radio and as they crawled out of Victoria a local station was doing a slot on people looking for pen-friends. Here was an unusual request, the announcer said; it was from Richard Lawson, care of Brixton Prison. Rich was a regular listener on Saturday mornings and he was feeling pretty lonely there in Brixton. Sometimes it seemed as if the world outside had gone away. He would particularly like to correspond with any ladies in the London area who'd care to write. Life just dragged some days and seemed pointless. Rich dreamed of having someone special who he could confide in.

Joan scribbled down his name and the address of the prison, not really knowing why. Maybe it was those words about being lonely that did it, they struck a chord. She often turned the key in the door to her flat wishing that there could be someone else there. It could get you down, always finding things just the way you'd left them when you came home. She had gone on a couple of coach holidays because it wasn't easy to travel as a woman on your own. You tended to find a more mature type of person on coaches and usually at least one other single lady. But even though she was used to them she had to steel herself to climb on board and see all those strange faces. Some women in couples gave her suspicious glances, registering her as single and moving closer to their husbands beside them. A proprietorial hand might be placed on a spouse's arm or knee. Joan would know that they were making a mental note to keep an eye on her. That was when she would yearn to be part of a couple herself, to have someone she could link her arm through, showing ownership and belonging. She listened to her radio at the beginning of the trips so that she had something to occupy herself with until the ice was broken with other travellers.

She thought about this Richard Lawson on and off during her holiday, particularly as the company on that trip wasn't over-friendly. She turned out to be the only single woman and 'wallflower' was the word that sprang to mind. The courier was kind but Joan caught her sympathetic glances and that made her feel worse. In the hotel in Warsaw a seedy sort of chap, a native, started talking to her, telling her in pidgin English that he worked in a butcher's shop. His front teeth were blackened and pitted. As he mimed chopping parts of an animal she assumed to be a pig from the oinking sound he made, she saw that his hands were covered in tiny nicks and cuts. He had a one-room flat in a tower block, he gave her to understand, with lovely views over the city. He suddenly grabbed her knee and asked if she would come and live with him; she wouldn't have to buy any meat, he'd bring home bits from the shop. She imagined waking up to those teeth every morning and she got up and fled to her room, locking the door. Staring in the mirror, she thought that she must look like a woman so desperate for a man, she'd settle for one with greasy hair and a rotting mouth because he could offer her scrapings from a butcher's block. Her love-life had had its downturns but she had never felt quite so bad, not even five years back when she found out that the chap she'd been seeing for a couple of months was married with three children.

She searched for the address that had been given out over the radio. She was in a prison too, she decided; a prison of loneliness. She knew about Rich's dream, she'd had it often enough. She was bothered by the fact that he must be a criminal and that she had no idea what he was in for but no harm could come from writing to him. If he wrote back something crude or sinister she could just stop contact.

She started a letter to him there and then on hotel note-paper, using the agency address. Her boldness astonished her and she looked around the small room as if to check that this untypical, incautious action wasn't being witnessed. She didn't say too much; just that she had heard his request on the radio and knew what loneliness was like. She told him that if he wanted to write back, she'd like to know a little bit about him and how long he'd been in jail. She finished off with a few Grace Ashley lines:

> Hold out your tender hand with hope
> And someone might place
> Their trust in your outstretched palm.

She posted the letter as soon as she returned to London and Rich replied in a couple of days, five pages of thin white paper. Joan was the only person who'd got in touch, he said. He'd been feeling low the morning her letter arrived, thinking he'd been mad to expect that any woman out there would want to contact a prisoner. He told her that he was thirty-eight, five feet eleven with blond hair and had been in jail for fifteen years. He did callisthenics in his cell every morning and evening to keep fit. She would probably want to know the kind of person she was writing to so he'd enclosed a photo and he could reassure her that he hadn't murdered anyone. He was in for armed robbery, holding up a security van. He'd very much like her to write back; she sounded lively and her personality had come through in her letter. She could visit if she liked, although he didn't want to impose and he'd understand if she felt she couldn't because after all, prisons weren't attractive places and it was bad enough for the wives who had to turn up. But if she wanted to, visitors were allowed on Sundays for his wing. He added that he'd liked that verse. He wasn't much of a one for poetry but if Joan was really holding her hand out, then so was he.

The small photo showed his head and shoulders. He was a good-looking chap, she thought, well set up; all that exercise had paid off. He wasn't smiling but he didn't look mean or criminal. She wrote again, describing her job and the holidays she'd had. Having someone to write to was a thrill in itself. She covered three pages that night, surprised at finding so much to say. Apart from postcards to Alice when she was on holiday and Christmas cards to a few people, she'd never had any reason to sit down with a pen. By the last page she felt daring. She said that she would visit, proposing the following Sunday. She liked the fact that he hadn't asked for a photograph in return; that made her think that he was interested in her as a person and wasn't bothered about her looks. He seemed sensitive too, understanding that going to a prison might be difficult. She appreciated that; he wasn't taking her for granted. As she sealed the envelope she was still wary. He sounded nice enough but he *was* inside. Still, she thought, if she didn't like what she found when she saw him she needn't go again and she'd be safe enough in the visitors' room. There would be no chance of an unwanted hand on her knee and a face pushed too close and it seemed unlikely that he was keeping quiet about a wife given how long he'd been inside. Once bitten, twice shy; if she had any doubts about his marital status she could always ask a warder.

She spent just an hour with Rich on that first visit and she had never known sixty minutes go so fast. There had been evenings in her flat when the hours dragged so slowly, she would check that the clock hadn't stopped. Winter nights were particularly bad, when it seemed as if the rest of the world had crept away and she was left behind the curtains listening to her own breathing.

Rich was even more nervous than her. When he walked into the room he stopped and looked, then came over very slowly and sat at the other side of the table. He had a soft voice and it was shaking. He kept pulling at his earlobe until Joan said it might drop off and they laughed and she knew that this was someone special.

The visiting room wasn't an easy place to get acquainted. It was noisy and airless but they talked non-stop until she felt lightheaded. Rich reassured her that he'd never been married and explained more about the robbery he'd gone down for. The police must have had a tip-off because they'd turned up and one of them had come at him. He'd had a gun and he'd fired it in panic; the policeman had taken a bullet in the shoulder so on top of the robbery he'd been convicted of attempted murder. He'd been a wild kid, he said, out of control since he was twelve, a string of petty offences by the time he was twenty. He wanted her to know all this, put his cards on the table right at the beginning. Prison had taught him to try and master his temper and all he wanted when he got out was to make some kind of life for himself.

They talked on. Joan told him about the man in the Warsaw hotel. Rich looked worried and said she must be more careful, there were lots of sharks in the water and if she didn't mind him saying so, she was a very attractive woman. She didn't mind at all; she thought she could put up with hearing that again. If Rich had been on that coach with her, she thought, she'd have had different looks and those disapproving women would have been giving him admiring glances. Sitting there in front of her, his broad hands resting on the table, clean-shaven in a beautifully ironed sweatshirt, he looked a cut above all the other prisoners.

As she was getting up to go he clasped his hands together and leaned forward on them.

'I'll savour every moment after you've gone,' he told her. 'Thinking about you cheers me up when I've been locked in for the night. You will come again, won't you, Joan?'

Her heart went out to him then. He looked big and sure of himself but he was so anxious. If she walked away he could do nothing about it and she knew he was on tenterhooks to hear if she'd be back.

She told him she'd come again and she did, the following Sunday and every Sunday after that. He phoned her once a week and they exchanged letters; Rich wrote on Sunday night so that it reached her by Tuesday and she sent her letter back to arrive with him on Thursday. Her grandmother used to talk critically about modern morals, people jumping into bed together as soon as they'd met. She'd had what she called an old-fashioned courtship with Joan's grandfather; hand-holding and kissing and nothing more until after the wedding. Joan now found herself conducting exactly such a courtship but without as much licence as her grandmother; kisses were swift, a quick brush of the lips. So much had to be communicated through the pressure of their hands that their palms would be glued by the end of a visit. The intensity of not being able to touch left them wrung out. They lived for their letters and each Sunday. The electricity that crackled when Joan walked into the visitors' room could have powered the London grid. When she reached home after a visit she had to dive straight into the shower.

Sometimes she trembled all Sunday evening as she imagined Rich pouring his feelings into the passionate letter he'd be writing in his cell. He wondered that those envelopes didn't scorch the postman's hands. She knew that he spent all his time thinking about her. He didn't have her distractions, the daily tasks that muffled longing. Some days she would stop in the shops or while she was vacuuming, thinking that right now he'd be picturing her; then a lovely warmth would bloom on her skin.

Never in her life had there been a man who waited patiently for her, who told her that he was jealous when he thought of her meeting any other man at all, even the wall-eyed youth in the fish shop. She knew that she could trust Rich completely; he wasn't going to be tempted by any other women, wouldn't be out on the town without her, playing the field. Many of her conversations with Alice in the wine bar had been on the subject of men's fickleness, the way you could never tell what they were up to, the money they might be spending, the affairs they might be having while your back was turned. That wasn't a problem with Rich. There was a deep security in knowing that he was secure. The last picture she saw as she closed her eyes each night was Rich in his bunk, door locked, bars at the window. Then she would give a sigh, a murmur of desire and comfort.

There were times when she couldn't believe that Rich truly existed, that those letters were going to arrive. During the long weeks she would imagine that she had dreamed him up, like a film where the hero suddenly realises that everything that has happened has been in his imagination. One of Gran's favourite films had starred Edward G. Robinson, waking up in a chair, realising that his terrible experiences of the past hour had been a fantasy. It was so unlikely that she had fallen in love with a jailbird. None of the romantic possibilities she had conjured up for herself had featured the visitors' room at Brixton Prison.

The weekend that Nina and Martin were working on the asparagus bed, she arrived at the prison on Sunday and the first thing they said when they saw each other was, 'only eight weeks to go!' They discussed the wedding and Joan brought Rich up to date on her work. She had told him about Nina the previous week and she filled him in about this illness called lupus.

'It's not contagious, is it?' he said, worried.

'No. She says it's a bit like arthritis.'

Rich was relieved. 'Oh, right. I couldn't stand it if anything happened to you, you know. If you died, I'd top myself. And if anyone harmed a hair on your head I'd swing for them.' He hit the table with his fist. One of the warders stepped forwards, holding up a warning finger. When he said things like that Joan's stomach lurched. It was frightening in a way, knowing that he loved her so much.

'I can't imagine life without you,' she told him. 'I never thought I'd have someone to say that to. I still can't believe my luck.'

He asked if she had bought her wedding outfit yet and she said that she was planning to go to Brent Cross during the week. She'd thought of asking if Nina would like to go. She needed taking out of herself; she spent too much time alone, brooding.

'Thing is, Rich, although I've mentioned you, I can't tell her you're coming out of prison because she's a client. She talks to me more about my personal life than any of the other people I go to. I suppose it's because she's only a bit older than me. It's awkward when she asks about you.'

They had talked about this before. Rich was as keen as her for people not to know his background. He scratched his head.

'Why not tell her I've been looking after my old mum in Frinton and now she's died, so I can move to London.'

'That's a good idea. It would explain me only seeing you at weekends as well and having to visit you. It's only a white lie, isn't it?'

''Course, love. Anyway, she's only buying your help, not your soul. She's got no right to know anything. You don't need to feel guilty, even if you are my soft-hearted darling.'

It was hard to make Rich understand the nature of her job. He saw it as a domestic service, just calling in to be a Mrs Mop and feed and water people. He was always advising her not to run herself ragged. She supposed that having been in prison for so long, cut off from ordinary life, he couldn't see that the personal contact with clients made the job worthwhile. She knew that Nina especially needed that bit extra; you couldn't expect a young woman to be interested only in how the bed was made and what was for dinner. But she had to bear in mind Alice's strict rule about not telling clients too many personal details, especially anything that might be upsetting or that would tarnish the agency; so details about Eddie and Rich were not for sharing.

Rich said to look out for a likely suit for him while she was at Brent Cross. He'd go and try it on the day he got out of jail. Joan had taken photos of the freshly decorated living room and they were looking at them as the end of visiting time was called.

She pointed at the sofa. 'We'll soon be sitting there together.'

'When are you doing the bedroom?'

'I made a start yesterday.'

'Bring photos of that next time. I want to imagine us in there.'

She felt heat sweep up her neck. Rich was holding a polystyrene coffee cup tight in his hand and she could see it curving inwards under the pressure, dark liquid slopping over the edge. That picture of his hand stayed with her all week, the white cup bending while his eyes were glazed with that lost look she always saw when it was time to leave.

7

NINA

'*C*arissima Majella,
     'Tonight I ache and a terrible tiredness is weighing
down my wrists, but I must press on. This disease can take
unexpected turns. When this account is read, is known, as
it inevitably must be, by a wider public, I assume there will
be many who will see my illness as a just punishment. For
religious believers, it will be the hand of God. Those who
prefer an earth-bound perspective might say that my long-
suppressed guilt made me ill, my flesh turning on me in
distaste. Others will see in my story the sign of a natural
justice, of karma; we get what is owing to us, what goes
around comes around. I can accept any of those interpret-
ations, believing none, although if I warmed to any it would
be the last. Perhaps I can sit on the fence because the lupus
is actually of little importance to me. Oh, I loathe the discomfort and the limitations, but the task I have set myself
diminishes physical annoyance. The lupus is now a means
to an end and so I embrace it.

     'The problem of the disease lies in its inevitable

---

progression. I have read that being in the blood, it can travel to the brain, causing inflammation. Memory loss might then occur and that is what concerns me most in the dark hours. The Greek philosopher Parmenides believed that memory was a mixture of heat and cold or light and dark and that if it was undisturbed it would remain perfect; if the mixture was altered, however, forgetfulness would ensue. I picture the lupus tracking through my body, weighing up where to attack next, maybe shooting upwards and altering that delicate blend cradled in my skull. We are all the sum-total of our memories, but people like me, people like us, with one stark, savage memory, must surely be prisoners of the past. Some might think that in my case the disappearance of the power of recall would be a blessing but the possibility makes me panic and strike the keys faster.

'Joan Douglas told me that she has a fiancé called Rich. I can tell from her voice when she refers to him that she's very much in love and I hope he feels the same way; I hope he's not a man frightened of emotion. I imagine Joan bustling around him, keeping him in order. I think that perhaps she has old-fashioned ways and sayings because her grandmother brought her up. She comes out with things that echo a different generation, antiquated maxims; so when she attacks her work she "improves the shining hour". Referring to a drunken neighbour, she refers to him being "half seas over". I've never known such a thorough house cleaner. The rugs are taken out and beaten every other day and my pillows plumped up so fully they are uncomfortable. She looks after me well, anticipating my needs in a way that Martin used to do but with him I grew annoyed. The wonderful liberty of paid help is that you know it will go away and you don't have to feel grateful. If that sounds calculating it is because I have reached a stage of my life where everything has to be calculated, from how far I can walk to the number of painkillers I need to stifle the aches but not my imagination.

'Joan is getting married soon. She has asked me to go and choose her outfit with her tomorrow because she thinks I've got "lovely taste". I know that's only part of it. She sees the outing as therapy for me; she wants to ferry me to the shops and take my mind off things. For Joan, activity is a panacea. If she feels lonely she heads out and eyes up clothes and furniture or engages in needlework or pops to see her friend Alice. Do I wish that I could find solace in that way now? I used to, gardening and cycling, always moving to the next thing, nifty on my feet, dodging shadows. I think the answer has to be no, because the shadows would only return but it can be consoling to find distractions. Perhaps that has been your reason for staying where you are, labouring, bandaging, listening, teaching, always having claims made on your time, stilling your thoughts in the fierce paralysing sun. I have agreed to accompany Joan because there is a part of me that wants to witness and share her happiness. Her enjoyment will soothe me and it is necessary, sometimes, to put my burden down briefly.

'Another card has arrived, from County Clare. The photographs on it show different aspects of the Burren with limestone stretching to the horizon. I considered not opening it, tearing it up and taking it to the bin but even as I was imagining ripping the shiny exterior I knew that I would unseal the gummed flap. Reading it would be easier than the hours I would otherwise spend agonising about what it contained. So I tipped a measure of brandy down my throat and slid my finger along the seal. Inside I found the third instalment of my education in Irish burial sites. My correspondent prompts me to consider the number of people culled in Ireland before their lives could run a natural course. So little violence there is truly personal and yet for such a tiny country, it contains so much anger. As I read the reference to rain I saw again the hedges glistening in the car headlights and felt the tremor of my hands on the wheel:

Dolmen or portal graves can be spectacular. From a distance, the portal here resembles a giant stone mushroom, standing massively on the skyline. People use it as a landmark, the long dead thus proving permanently useful to the living. Perhaps it is the simplest way of conveying that life, no matter how short or cruelly ended, can have lasting significance.

This awesome portal grave is at Poulnabrone, near Bally-vaughan in the Burren. The area is harsh and lovely in its wildness. Today, a heavy rain swept across it, driving fiercely at the stone.

As soon as you step across the boundaries of the Burren you feel that it is a place apart, locked in its own mysteries. Prehistoric burial chambers litter the hillsides. You can walk past them, never guessing at their existence and the secrets they have kept close over the centuries. But the walker travelling the Burren, striking out along the rough lime-stone, sees this particular massive tomb in the distance. As you approach, the huge stones grow bigger, filling the landscape. You cannot help but think that someone of great importance was buried here, someone who would have been grieved for by many and whose name would have stayed on the lips of generations afterwards: 'Fine and fairly your sword became you as you rode your slender horse, blowing your horn, with your hounds all around you. You would lift the grief from my heart, abroad on the hilltop; and my great sorrow and my woe that you died in my lifetime!'

When you touch these stones you feel their permanence and significance. No, this is not a solitary, lonely grave, even though the surrounding countryside is now deserted.

'I am more frightened by my correspondent than I care to admit, not because he or she might reveal the truth but because I might be pre-empted. My frailty dictates the pace of the task I have set myself and I so desperately want to be able to complete it, to speak to you and Martin with a freedom never allowed to me before. The sense of release and relief is enormous but I am aware of the energy and determination of the writer of these cards, an energy that reminds me so much of Finn. I envy that ease of physical movement, the ability to progress across a physical landscape. My journey can only be into my own thoughts. I know that I am now at the mercy of this traveller and it is a bitter knowledge; and I foolishly thought that I was in control of current events!

'There was a weekend, I recall, in the summer of 1970 when we thought we might see the Burren but in the end Red Dawn activities consumed all of our time. We had driven to Limerick with Finn in the old banger financed by his inheritance. It frequently broke down and on the way back the clutch went. I commented to Finn that it would make sense to buy a more reliable car but he pointed out to me that this was a typically petit-bourgeois view; how could working people take a revolutionary seriously if he had an expensive car? He deliberately drove the kind of vehicle the ordinary worker might be able to afford. I saw the logic of this; I always bowed to Finn's logic. When he explained things in his measured, serious way I could see that I had a muddled perspective, the product of too many years spent with the fat cats of Maidstone. By that time I had stopped reading bourgeois authors like P G Wodehouse and Evelyn Waugh, having absorbed Finn's admonition that they spouted class-ridden nonsense. My reading material featured Marx, Guevara, Connolly and Trotsky and the stories of Alexandra Kollontai and Rosa Luxemburg, darling of the Bolsheviks.

'We travelled to Limerick for the "National Socialist Symposium", a grand term for a meeting of tiny fringe groups. We numbered forty in all and I remember thinking even then, at the height of my interest in the cause, that it was a ludicrously small gathering to represent the nation. We certainly had a huge task if we were going to convert the country to revolutionary socialism. However, I assigned any doubts I had to my own lack of understanding. I reminded myself, as Finn never tired of pointing out, that revolutionaries had to bide their time and seize the moment when it came; I believed that Finn would know the moment.

'We met in the small upstairs room of a smoky pub in a seedy city back street. Would any of us recall now what we discussed so fiercely over pints and deep bowls of stew? Belfast had seen terrible riots that summer, fierce, bloody battles that left streets barricaded and wrecked. The fumes of petrol bombs and CS gas permeated the city. Those of us who lived there described it to the others; there was huge kudos in coming from the front line and it was apparent that comrades from Waterford and Wexford were envious of our place at the centre of the action. There would have been a dozen or more position papers, heated debates on whether the different groupings should form a federation and the perspective we should adopt on the IRA.

'Finn had sat up into the early hours of the morning for a week, tapping out statements on all these subjects, which you gathered up and sneakily duplicated in the Language department's resource room. You were red-eyed, kept awake until late and roused early but you sat by Finn's side throughout the weekend, maintaining the agreed line on core issues, emphasising important points with a *chink clink* of your bracelets. Finn never removed his black beret. He was growing a beard and looked more than ever like a home-grown Che Guevara. He drank sparingly and stayed poised on the edge of his chair, ready to pounce on weaker arguments. Young women from other groups gave him admiring glances and made a point of consulting him regularly on theories they found unclear. During the breaks he worked the room, holding people's arms, complimenting them on their hard efforts, enquiring after their families. He never tired, never looked jaded, never smoked any of the pot that circulated liberally in the evenings. People tapped into his energy; when he clasped a hand, leaning towards the comrade he was addressing, you could see their eyes brighten, their shoulders straighten. For two days the room crackled with discussion. I was hugely proud of myself because I corrected a Galway comrade when he misquoted Trotsky.

'On the Sunday afternoon, when the symposium finished, we pressed Finn to drive to the Burren but he countered that we could fit in a couple of hours newspaper selling in the city. Seeing our disappointment, he frowned and added that two members of the Revolutionary Force for the Imminent Destruction of Irish Capitalism, one of whom was heavily pregnant, were already off marketing their pamphlets in the surrounding pubs. And so we trudged rainy streets, the papers growing soggy under our arms, accepting that Finn's unflagging devotion to the cause put us to shame.

'How I wish now that you and I had gone to the Burren, abandoning our comradely duties, leaving Finn to his. It is one of Ireland's most famous areas but I never saw it, was never in that part of the country again. We might have stopped at the portal grave and been awed by it. If Finn is my correspondent did he recall that weekend as he was writing from Clare? Did he remember his tired lover and their latest recruit dragging around pubs, pushing *Workers' Struggle* at bored drinkers who bought the odd copy because they thought they were supporting the lads in the IRA? He picked up on our low spirits because he treated us to a curry and several bottles of wine afterwards, complimenting us on our hard work.

'When the car clutch gave out near the border we sat and drank the last bottle of wine while Finn fiddled under the bonnet, declared the situation hopeless and disappeared into the night to find help. We sat in the dark and you regaled me with stories of leprechauns and fairies and the sad tale of the bloody banquet of Castlegregory which you had heard from an aunt in Kerry: Black Hugh Hoare married his enemy's daughter, the beautiful Ellen, and took her to his castle at Castlegregory. When Lord Grey, Elizabeth the First's henchman, was sent to quell an Irish rebellion, Black Hugh pretended to welcome him, planning his murder all the while. Ellen, who was a staunch supporter of Irish freedom and unaware of her husband's duplicity, went to their wine cellar where she smashed all the casks rather than offer the English hospitality. Enraged by her interference, Black Hugh stabbed her but died soon after, brokenhearted. We agreed that this was a typical tale of a woman suffering at the hands of an oppressive man but at least the lovely Ellen wreaked her revenge from beyond the grave; over the centuries she was often seen haunting the spot, terrorising Black Hugh's descendants. You pulled your shirt over your head and made wailing noises in imitation of her spectral presence.

'We laughed so much we had to get out and pee, stumbling in the blackness, squealing as we encountered nettles and blackthorn. After a while we sang songs, "Scarborough Fair" and "Sloop John B", harmonising in the night. There was a sudden hailstorm which battered the roof as we passed the wine back and forth. That was a happy couple of hours, waiting for Finn to return. We were feisty and carefree with no worries other than that an essay deadline was near. The next time we were alone in the car on a wet night we had no wine or songs or stories to make us rock with laughter.

We were weighed down with a single, grim purpose. Driving on a dark, rutted road you murmured, *"siamo lontani da tutto"*, *we are far from everything* and I shivered, even though the heater was pumping out air laced with the ripe stench of cow dung.'

Nina sat still for a while, massaging her finger joints, rotating her ankles, clockwise and anti-clockwise. Then she opened the file 'Martin' on her screen.

'You have read this far, so now you know more than you ever have, perhaps more than you ever hoped to. Don't hope for too much, Martin. I am a woman who is sick in many ways and of many things. You will understand by now that Majella has always been there between us, and Finn, too.

'Do you remember how we went to buy my wedding dress and some new furniture in Bond Street? It was March and late snow fell; we ducked into a wine bar and read newspapers. I felt ordinary and comfortable. For the first time in many years I had a sense of hope. You were so sensible, so loving and enthusiastic, so *balanced*. I made you into a kind of talisman, deciding that you had been sent to rescue me. You were a sign that I was being offered a second chance. How the desperate clutch at straws!

'Majella and I made our own shopping foray for the Freshers' Ball in '69. We wore, I recall, similar kaftans that we'd bought in a patchouli-drenched hippy shop near the campus. The kaftans were cotton; mine dark green, hers orange, and they had hoods, which, when we pulled them up, made us resemble members of an arcane sect. Finn approved of them because the labels stated that they had been made in a Delhi workers' co-operative. I had the distinct impression that he would have made us take them back if they had not been politically acceptable. Majella looked a little guilty because she had not checked their provenance herself before we paid for them. As Finn fingered hers he referred to the sweatshop wages paid in the third world and talked about the comrades he had met in Madras and Calcutta. I drank in his talk of travels in India, the Soviet Union and Europe. It seemed that there was hardly a revolutionary group or underground movement around the globe that he hadn't personally encountered. My kaftan had a sweet, aromatic scent that made me think of hot skies, ornate temples and Finn eating from a plate with his fingers, his dark luxurious hair speckled with sweat. I had a photograph of Majella and me, taken that night at the ball, drunkenly clutching each other's waists, but I binned it along with everything else connected with her the night before I left Ireland for the last time.

'I visited her flat for the first time that evening. She led me along streets by the university quarter to a crescent where the steeple on the Moravian church loomed high. I didn't understand until later that Rock House, the imposing but ramshackle three-storey Victorian dwelling she took me to, belonged to Finn. From the moment I stepped through the door I was entranced because it was the antithesis of my mother's bungalow. Swooning at the pungent smell of garlic, I scanned their livingroom with deep satisfaction. The proportions were generous; a square, high-ceilinged room with crumbling plaster bulging around an imposing central chandelier. The floor was covered in a torn and faded red oriental carpet and stacks of *Workers' Struggle*. A heavy, gold-and-green striped wallpaper moistened by rising damp swayed and rippled where mildew had caused it to part company with the wall. Dozens of posters in different languages rippled with it; *Lutte Ouvrière* and *Lotta Continua* I read, absorbing the clenched fists depicted in red and black. The huge, sooty fireplace held a bright turf blaze and a collection of smooth speckled pebbles around its rim. The horsehair sofa was covered in woven cotton throws that I recognised from the hippy shop and several fraying Victorian easy chairs were piled with books. By the tall sash window, draped in gold velvet curtains which sagged with dust, stood Finn's grand piano. Amongst the disarray and camouflaged by it so effectively that it took me weeks to notice them were valuable objects, testaments to Finn's wealthy family. On the wall next to a poster of Lenin hung an original William Orpen. The tarnished candlesticks on the mantelpiece were heavy, ornate silver and the pink vases that held pens and pencils were eighteenth-century. An antique snuff box circa 1840 brimmed with the drawing pins Finn used to secure posters.

'This, I realised, was the kind of room I would have dreamt up for myself if I'd had the confidence. It was at ease with itself, not striving to make an impression, making no apology for its shabby disorder. I thought with shame of my pristine bedroom in Maidstone with its stencilled buttercups and collection of china rabbits and gave thanks that it was safely out of sight across a sea. At one end of the living room a pair of folding doors stood open, revealing their bedroom. I could see a jumble of clothes, books and more posters. The bed had a brass head and Finn's beret hung on one of the posts. I blushed at that sight, confused at the intimacy it suggested. I was still a virgin then and fascinated by the tangible, mysterious aura that surrounded couples.

'Finn made us Turkish coffee which I'd never tasted before and asked me where I came from. When I said Maidstone he grimaced. "Oh, the garden of England. Green lawns and bankers. Not much of a union tradition there."

'"Isn't there?" I asked stupidly, gulping scalding coffee.

'"No, you won't find many workers organising in Kent."

'"That's hardly Nina's fault," Majella laughed. "She can't help coming from stockbroker land."

' "No, of course. But there's no excuse for not re-educating yourself if you do. Have you read any Trotsky, Nina?"

' "No." I knew something about an ice-pick in the back of a head.

' "Here." Finn rummaged on one of the chairs. "Borrow this, it's a seminal work." He handed me a thick hardback tome with a picture of Trotsky on the cover looking sternly into the distance.

' "Leon Trotsky was a genius," Majella assured me. She was combing out her hair and she leaned over Finn, placing a swift kiss on the top of his head as if confirming that he was too.

'Finn didn't come to the ball with us. I was surprised when I realised that he was staying in to write an article for the newspaper. I suppose I had been harbouring a romantic image of the two of them dancing there but I understood as we left him hunched over his typewriter that this was due to my own lack of sophistication.

'As we flapped along the streets, our kaftans clinging to our legs Majella explained that she and Finn had met at an International Socialists rally in Rome a year previously. He was twenty-six and had just been accepted to do an MA in the Politics of Poverty at Queen's. It was great, she said, that they had got a place at the same university and as soon as she had known it was definite she'd moved in with him. Their parents disapproved but then they didn't understand the way in which love was nourished and fed by the revolutionary struggle. Isn't it wonderful, Martin, how we could utter sentiments like that back then with completely straight faces?

'She chatted on; she never tired of talking about Finn, the richness of his experiences, his fine mind. He owned the house they lived in, she told me, it had been left to him by his father. Finn's family were wealthy and he had legacies from his father and an aunt but he ploughed lots of money into Red Dawn, their revolutionary cadre which he had founded and into *Workers' Struggle* the newspaper he edited and produced. He wasn't happy being a property owner which was why he let unemployed men and their families live rent free in the top two floors of the house and took only a token payment from the student in the basement. There was a card from that grateful student on top of the piano, comparing Finn's generosity to that ancient Finn of legend: "if the brown leaves were gold that the wood lets fall, if the white wave were silver, Finn would have given it all away." I wasn't to understand for some time that Finn was generous only with that which came easily to him; he was far more guarded in dispensing his affections, they were carefully rationed. Later, I occasionally met the working-class families from upstairs on the steps or in the hallway. The men were shadowy figures who grunted unintelligible greetings from the corners of their fag-filled mouths. They took copies of *Workers' Struggle* to sell in the pubs where they whiled away most of their days. The women, who looked older than their years with their strained eyes and stiffly lacquered hair, were always struggling with wayward children and pushchairs. As they slapped a leg or stuck a dummy in a sticky mouth they gave us suspicious glances. I have no doubt that they suspected us to be members of a louche commune who might offer free love to their husbands as they reeled in from the bars.

'"Finn came back from visiting other revolutionary groups abroad and saw that Ireland needed a political party based on true socialist principles," Majella explained. "He worked for over a year to set it up. He's such a motivator, so inspiring. It's a tremendous task, educating the proletariat, but we're building all the time. It's exciting, you know, working for a cause, knowing you can make a real difference."

'I stayed at their flat that night, the first of many such

nights I spent on the sofa under musty blankets. Finn was still up when we got back at two in the morning, merry and lively. He pulled the cover carefully over his typewriter and made us delicious little herby omelettes there in the living room, holding the cast-iron frying pan over the hot turf. We opened a bottle of dark red wine and ate and drank in the soft light of the fire and a standard lamp, sitting cross-legged on the carpet. Majella urged Finn to tell me more about his trip to India and he did, licking his plate clean, as was his custom and leaning back on his elbows, his legs stretched along the hearth. I heard about Calcutta, the stark contrasts of rich and poor, his attack of dysentery in Delhi, his joining comrades in Darjeeling to protest at the tea pickers' working conditions and his night in police cells.

'"A comrade from Delhi dropped in on us a couple of weeks ago," Majella told me. "Poverty there is terrible and they're constantly spied on by the pigs. He had a dreadful chest infection but we got him to a doctor and sorted him out."

'Finn uncoiled himself, moving to the piano. "Comrades show solidarity to each other the world over, Nina. Once you are a comrade, you have a global network of friends; you're never alone. You know there will always be a roof over your head, a meal, a helping hand."

'Then he played a selection of jazz tunes, his fingers racing over the piano keys while Majella threw more turf on the fire and I let the rich wine warm my limbs. Still playing, Finn beckoned me over, shuffling along to make space for me on the stool beside him. He was composing this one for me, he told me, smiling and producing a fast, complicated tune; we'd call it "The Nina Rag". His arm brushed my breast as he reached along the keyboard and his thigh was wedged firmly against mine on the narrow seat. I felt the transfer of heat from his skin to mine. His fingernails were begrimed with typewriter ink and smuts from where he had earlier cleaned the fire grate. I imagined them against my hands and felt my breath catch. He slowed the tempo, switching suddenly to "Danny Boy" and asked me could I play at all? When I said no, he affected astonishment, saying that he'd have imagined that all fine ladies from Kent would be taught the piano. Music had played no part in my childhood; my mother regarded it as messy and intrusive. My father had liked Mantovani but my mother always made a point of switching off the radio if his orchestra came on. Taking my hands in his, Finn examined them, turning them over gently and placing them on the keys. Quite a good stretch, he said; he must give me lessons. The skin on his hands was rough, callused and warm from his exertions.

'Later Majella joined him at the piano and they both played and sang "The Internationale". Not knowing the words, I hummed along, clapping. We decided it was far too late for me to wander the streets and I couldn't face the prospect of early hymn singing so Majella fetched blankets while Finn banked the fire. She kissed me goodnight and Finn touched my shoulder, nodding.

'I savoured that kiss and touch after they had vanished to their room. I lay beneath the rough blankets, watching the flickering fire, aware of their murmured conversation and then silence. The sweetly scented turf combined with the damp odour emanating from the walls and Finn's pungent tobacco to create an aroma I have never come across since; if I smelled it now I am sure that I would weep for the girl who lay there, filled with longings and expectations. I hadn't been touched or kissed much. An only child, I had led a fairly solitary life of routine respectability and the occasional dull realisation of loneliness. I had never mixed easily, never had a boyfriend. My father had been a shy, undemonstrative man and my mother infrequently puckered her lips at the air next to my cheek. I had never considered that an omelette could be cooked over an open fire in a living room and the pan left unwashed in the grate all night; grand pianos belonged in concert halls; visitors from Delhi didn't drop in unannounced. This blurring of the accepted norms was bewitching and oddly glamorous. I craved a part in it. I reached out a hand and prodded the wallpaper, making it shiver. From outside, in distant streets, came the crackle of gunfire. As I drifted off I heard Finn's voice saying that once you're a comrade you are never alone.

'That room is as real to me still as if this bed I am propped on now was their lumpy couch. Closing my eyes, I can see the fire, the turf glowing and crumbling to a fine ash and the marshalled piles of Finn's typescripts on the table. Items of the cheap Indian jewellery Majella was always buying lay everywhere. She would discard some bangles and beads as she wandered about and pick up others, twining ropes of glass and wooden baubles around her neck, weighing her wrists down with thin brass bracelets. I could always hear her approaching before I saw her when I waited in the cafeteria. My ears would strain for the familiar jangling and clicking and the *scuff scuff* of her big boots. She confided to me one evening that Finn liked her to wear just a thin chain on her wrist when they were making love. Sometimes, as I settled on their couch, hearing faint noises from their bedroom, I saw his dark hair against her creamy throat.

'These are my ghosts, you see. They have kept close company with me all these years and kept you distanced from me as surely as any secret affair. You were always combating invisible rivals with a prior claim on me. That knowledge may comfort you or anger you. I had no right to drag you into the mired labyrinths of my life but I did love you, Martin, I do love you. It's just that when you are sick you are contagious.'

8

NINA

'*A mica mia,*
'Each time I open this computer I feel that I am challenging the lupus and its potential threat to the brain. The more I write, the more I find that I slip into memories of the life we had over two decades ago. One of my students used to praise a book which taught how to maximise brain usage and improve powers of recall with practice and concentration. As I complete each page those days we spent together grow clearer. I remember moods, looks, the soaking rain sweeping from the hills over the lough, the heady tang of lager combining with the smoky succulence of the hot frankfurters we bought at the delicatessen; the growl of army saracens in the streets, the roar of a bomb intruding on a lecture, sending quivers through our pens and up along our arms. I see your hair falling over your eyes, glowing amber in the firelight as you stretched your arm out with the toasting fork to crisp evenly a slice of floury bread. A flash of memory will come to me during the day, a snapshot of something we did together and I realise that I'm smiling,

my bones a little less leaden. Those memories are vivid, full of Parmenides' mixture of heat and light. It is as if I am simultaneously living in two time zones, in the here and now with my aching joints and then, in Belfast, with you.

'Joan Douglas and I had lunch during our shopping trip for her wedding outfit. She chose a plum crumble for pudding and as I watched her eat I saw you on the evening you broke a tooth on a plum stone. I went to casualty with you but unfortunately your accident coincided with a riot and we had to wait for hours while fractured skulls and lungs seized with CS gas were dealt with. You were in terrible pain, the nerve exposed, and I read to you from my pocket Dante, *The Divine Comedy*, to take your mind off it. It was a passage I recall exactly, from Canto 1 of the *Inferno* and I wonder now at its portent:

> Halfway on the journey of our life
> I found myself in a dark forest
> For the straight path had been lost.
> It is a hard thing to say what it was,
> This savage forest, rough and stern
> Which in the very thought renews the fear!
> So bitter it is that death is little more;
> But to deal with the good that I found
> I shall speak of other things that I noticed there
> I cannot well repeat how I entered there
> So full of slumber I was at that moment,
> When I abandoned the true way.

'Nurses scurried around us, clanging metal dishes and swishing screens as I read quietly and you rocked steadily, holding your jaw.

'"Jesus Christ and all the heavenly hosts," you said, "if

I have to wait much longer my teeth will fall out from old age.''

'Two injured soldiers were rushed in just as we thought there was a chance you would be called and you confronted a doctor, yelling that this was your country, you should get treatment before invading troops. I backed you up but of course it didn't help and we waited another long hour.

'When we got back to your flat you declared that you were ravenous and we made a huge saucepan of porridge, one of our favourite late-night winter delicacies. My mother used to cook porridge, a thin slop that lay grey and wan in the bowl; by a strange method known only to herself she managed to make it simultaneously runny and lumpy. You showed me how to produce a gloriously thick, smooth mixture, laced with double cream and demerara sugar and sometimes, when we were frozen through from standing outside pubs and restaurants trying to convert well-fed or well-soaked citizens to the revolution, a tablespoon of whisky.

'I slept in your bed with you that night, between fine white cotton sheets which had originally been hand-sewn for Finn's mother in Dublin and which carried a whiff of mildew. I was usurping Finn's place because he was away on political business in Donegal. The pillow reeked of his tobacco and there were shreds of it on the delicate lace edging of the pillowcase. I sniffed deeply, picturing him lying there, imagining that I could feel the contours of his body on the mattress. He had told me that he often practised card tricks late at night and the table on his side of the bed held the thumbed deck of cards, greasy from use. I picked them up and shuffled them, spinning them through my fingers the way I had seen him do but I lacked his expertise and they scattered. He would try his tricks out on us, expertly palming jacks and kings, leaving us baffled; his talent was much in demand socially and always drew a crowd. At parties he was often the focus of attention, either with his cards or on a piano, drawing applause. You would say, pulling a face that it was like being in the shadow of a celebrity, but you loved it, you loved watching people admire him because at the end of the night he would be going home with you.

'Just before dawn I woke, startled by the whine of a police Land-Rover. Your hair was silky against my hand and I lay for a few minutes before sleeping again, looking up at the damp patch on the ceiling by the broken window. It was the colour of weak tea and the shape of Portugal. You and Finn used it as a code when you wanted to go to bed; *let's embark for Portugal,* one of you would say meaningfully. It didn't strike me as at all odd that I knew your private codes. I failed to realise that most couples would keep those secret because I had no one to compare you to. I half-closed my eyes, making the rain-damped shape dance, thinking; now, at this moment, I am completely happy.

'In the morning I made us a hearty breakfast, what we called "the full works": white pudding, bacon, mushrooms, eggs, tomatoes and fried bread. Your fridge and cupboards were always well stocked, courtesy of Finn's legacies, the bags of booty you brought back from Pettigoe, and after I moved in, the generous trust left me by my father. We weren't at all like some of the other students who constantly penny-pinched, seeking to stretch meagre grants, loitering in the refectory at the ends of meals to collect up unused bread and cold sausages. We consumed huge quantities of rich, calorie-laden foods but never put on weight: thick slices of soda farl heaped with jam or waxy honeycomb, wedges of fruit loaf, potato bread slathered with dark yellow country butter. Finn often brought home little delicacies as surprise presents; this is just because it's a wet Thursday, he'd say, producing a box of continental lemon and almond tartines, angel food on the tongue, or crisp Dutch crackers topped with rich liver pâté. We had plenty of exercise, of course, selling papers and hurrying to demonstrations.

'In the John Lewis restaurant Joan ate her plum crumble guiltily because she had broken her sugar-free rule while I looked on pityingly, recalling how we relished meals. We devoured that breakfast in bed, listening to Bob Dylan and planning our joint birthday party. When I discovered that we shared the same birthday and were born within minutes of each other I was overjoyed. That knowledge emphasised our similarity, the feeling I had that I had found a missing part of myself. You espoused a theory that people were affected by the season of their birth. We were summery June babies and therefore likely to be easy-going. Finn had been born in November, which was why he sometimes seemed frosty and closed in on himself. Finn dismissed your idea as superstitious nonsense, saying that you gave away your Catholic upbringing by clinging to illogical claptrap.

'Joan eats carefully, with an exaggerated politeness, elbows tucked in. I can imagine that her grandmother was keen on table manners. The plums in her crumble had been de-stoned. My eyes filled unexpectedly as I observed her neat spoon movements because I suddenly sensed your presence, as strongly as if there was no more than a day's separation between us. You broke your tooth as we were writing an article for *Workers' Struggle* on the low pay of women machinists. The plums were in a brown paper bag on the table between us and when we'd lined up the stones we invented a socialist rhyme to replace the usual "tinker, tailor" refrain. We spent a lot of time in such pursuits, thinking up radical alternatives to traditional stories. So we prodded the plum stones, chanting, "chartist, comrade, anarchist, worker, freedom fighter, Fenian, suffragette, rebel."

'I am becoming fonder of Joan. She is the only woman I

have spent time with since I lost you; I have never found a female friend who matched you in any way and I have sorely missed the companionship of those days. Yesterday, when I dropped a glass I heard Joan's voice in my ears, saying, "oops! Must have dipped my fingers in butter!" and I laughed before I cursed myself for my clumsiness. Like Joan, I was essentially lonely before I married, wearing myself out with physical activity so that I wouldn't have to face too many silences. But no matter how I warm to Joan, her company is like a weak beer compared to your strong ale.

'During our shopping trip she told me about the holidays she's taken abroad and I admired her pluck. Plucky is probably the word that best sums Joan up. She gives the impression of facing adversity with her chin out. Over lunch she mentioned her brother, Eddie; he was a lovely chap, she said, he'd looked after her and Gran, nothing was too much trouble where his family was concerned. He felt a special responsibility because of his parents' death and Gran relied on him in many ways. I listened to the soft sighs that threaded Joan's memories of a loving man who drank his gran's cocoa to keep her happy, took his little sister to see West Ham and sorted out the blocked U-bend under the sink when he came back from work.

'"He was ever so nice looking," Joan said, "a bit like Montgomery Clift around the eyes. He took after our father." Then she grew distant, as if she'd said too much and excused herself to go to the Ladies'.

'While she was gone I sat amidst the buzz of shoppers, people examining their purchases and checking their credit-card receipts. I thought about men who are missed – brothers, fathers, uncles – those who leave an aching gap in a family, and I pictured Nigel Howes, the man we would have thought too poisonous to be missed by anyone – if we had thought about it at all. We didn't, of course; that kind of understanding was beyond us at the time. I recalled him in the dim bar of the Pine Trees Hotel. I'd have a hot whisky, I told him, with cloves. My head was itching under my long dark wig and when he said drink up, he'd get me another, I was thinking of his tainted money and expense account. That man, with his leather jacket and full wallet, his citrus aftershave lying sharp on the air and his nasal cockney tones ringing oddly in the ugly bar with fake oak beams, he had nothing to do with a family, people who loved him and looked forward to his return.

'"Doesn't it ever stop raining here, mate?" Nigel had asked the barman on the first night I met him and the barman had shrugged and dismissively replied that he couldn't rightly say.

'"Irish people get tired of visitors going on about the weather," I told Nigel.

'"Oh, *pardon-moi*," he said, downing a Tullamore Dew. "It's not easy finding a safe topic of conversation here, is it?"

'Maybe you shouldn't have come if you wanted safe conversation, I thought, but I smiled and asked him about the story he was working on and where he'd be visiting next, sticking to the format we'd planned. He was trying to arrange an interview with one of the IRA godfathers, he said, but he wasn't sure he'd be lucky. He wanted to get the simple truth about this "cause" they were fighting for from the horse's mouth.

'"The simple truth", I suppose that phrase summed up Nigel's tabloid mentality. I sipped my drink, feeling superior and knowledgeable.

'There had been a particularly nasty sectarian killing that day and he shook his head over it.

'"I walk around here," he said to me confidentially, one sane Brit to another, "and I look at the burnt-out buildings and the glass and the barbed wire and I tell you what, I wouldn't keep a dog in the place. Never mind the ballads and Irish freedom, they're just a bunch of murderers. If I had a family living here, I'd wash my hands of it all. I'd pack them on the boat, move over to England, start up again."

'I fed that back to you and Finn with relish. It was absolute confirmation of what we thought about Nigel Howes and so many of the other British reporters who swarmed around the streets, twisting the facts to their own purposes. We needed no further proof of their bias and arrogance. Nigel didn't get his interview with a godfather, his low-down on "the cause". I don't suppose the IRA were kindly disposed to the Tory-owned *Daily Echo*.

'I was a fervent believer in our own cause by that time. I was the kind of convert who can't understand why they have missed such an obvious truth for so long; of course a revolution was the only solution to Ireland's problems! This was so apparent that it was difficult to believe that others couldn't see it. Several years ago I was reminded of that time by a colleague who converted to Catholicism. He had acquired a pamphlet called "Catholic Apologetics", a hand-me-down from a distant relative. It provided him with responses to the arguments of scoffers and non-believers, quick-fire answers to shore up his confidence in his new faith. One of the most important texts informing my new belief back then was a booklet, "First Steps In Socialism", the Janet and John reader for new recruits. It offered fifteen answers to common questions. I can clearly recall the first two:

Q: *How come socialism hasn't worked in Russia if it's so brilliant?*
A: The revolution in Russia was undermined by western Capitalist powers and derailed by Stalinism. If the Leninist-

Trotskyist theory had been pursued, it would have succeeded.

Q: *People are naturally selfish. How will you ever get them
to share resources equally?*

A. The Capitalist system encourages individualism and per-
verts the workers' wishes to see a just social structure. Under
socialism, society will have worked through a revolutionary
process that renders individualism obsolete.

'I was no different to the primary school children I saw
through their classroom window learning their catechism or
the minister at the Presbyterian church who ran bible classes.
Every credo has its set texts; luckily, few adherents are led
by them to the dark place where mine took me. Those truths
that I studied were woven inextricably with my bonding to
you and Finn. It was an emotional and intellectual conver-
sion. I had come to view Belfast through your eyes. Instead
of poor, poky houses, grimy shops and broken pavements I
saw the little homes and workplaces of an honest, victimised
people tyrannised by a colonial power. The city developed a
glamorous patina for me; the anarchy of bombs and bullets
implied that anything was possible.

'I have received a fourth letter card and I can now see a
pattern developing. This one is from Mayo, the burial-site
pilgrim moving up the west coast. I found a map of Ireland
and I predict that soon my correspondent will travel across
country and pursue their mission northwards, across the
border. I know where this pilgrimage will end and I have
decided to enter into the spirit of it. The cards still mystify
and alarm me but I perceive that the sender and myself are
progressing along parallel lines, moving towards a certain
place. I have decided that as I cannot stop them coming, I
will journey with them, keeping pace as if our footsteps

rhyme. In the meantime, I feel a growing and awful famili-
arity with my fellow traveller and the expositions to which
I am treated:

'But I am in the west of Ireland and you in the east are all
on fire; the grazing herd crops the meadow, the meal is
ground without the miller.'

Terrible events throw everything out of kilter; it has been
the same throughout human history. The hunger that once
weakened Mayo still leaves its imprint on the landscape,
just as wickedness leaves its imprint on the soul.

This is a barren, lonely county of poor soil and stone
walls. As you walk, you have the roads to yourself, meeting
no one. Emigration as well as the famine has taken its toll
on the population and the kind of rough beauty on show
here does not attract tourists. For such a small country,
Ireland has so many spaces.

Gallery graves are set in long rectangular chambers.
The most elaborate of these are known as court graves and
they are peculiar to Mayo and the north of Ireland, where
hundreds have been found. In Mayo, the large areas of
bog land mean that well-preserved court graves have been
excavated.

There is an ornate court grave at Behy. The site overlooks
the sea and as you stand by it you find yourself thinking
that this would be a good place to end your days, with a
clear view and the Atlantic breeze bracing your bones. (By
the way, on top of a high hill in Tipperary there is a man
buried standing up, according to his last wishes. He wanted
to oversee his rich farmlands for eternity.) How fine it must
be to choose one's own grave. This Behy grave is probably
late Neolithic and had been carefully decorated and paved.
No bones were found so it seems likely that cremations were
interred here.

Behy is a high, peaceful spot, just the wind and sea birds to keep you company.

'As I write this now my hands tremble and I feel a trepidation, a sense of doom that I only wish I had felt then, when Finn made his awful suggestion to us. But then, Majella, we were both quite focused on what we had to do and why. Any fears we had were concerned with carrying out our task successfully and striking a blow for the downtrodden masses. We walked single-mindedly through the savage forest and that night, that memory, is forever cold and dark.'

Nina made her way slowly to the kitchen and bent to the fridge. She wrestled with the top of a bottle of water, wrists straining, and managed to pour some into a glass, spilling a puddle on the worktop. Cursing herself for a hopeless cripple, she drank and returned to her chair, cradling her computer.

'Martin, you must think of me as a soldier who saw terrible things on the battlefield and returned to civilian life, mentally scarred, unable ever to function normally again, to behave towards other people within the usual human parameters. Not that I am claiming a soldier's courage but in my own way I did join up, I saw myself as part of a disciplined, organised front line with a definite enemy.

'I was captivated by the rarefied world of Red Dawn. It was just us, just sixteen comrades, a close-knit group with one objective. Our lack of ambiguity was wonderful to me. I realised that what I had needed for so long was a clear and honest purpose. My Maidstone world had been clouded with hidden meanings, the discreet, muffled codes of middle-class England. I saw that I had been leading an existence which was essentially selfish. In Belfast life was raw and real, it had an electric pulse. In Mulligan's I listened to men and women my own age who had suffered cracked skulls and broken bones because they wanted civil rights. A youth appeared, pale and shivering, who had been made to stand for twenty hours in a police station, his head regularly doused in water. There were reports of army brutality, random beatings on street corners. The seriousness and importance of championing the oppressed filled me with a burning fervour which was matched by Majella's incandescence. I pictured comrades the world over selflessly striving for the same common good and all else seemed trivial.

'When I joined Red Dawn formally in January 1970 I felt that I had found my true home. Up until then I had been an observer, listening as comrades arrived at Rock House for meetings. The night, location and the times of meetings were changed frequently in case the group was being watched. When there was a gathering in Majella and Finn's room I had to sit in the kitchen with the cooker on to keep me warm while they conducted their business. I would half-heartedly write an essay or read, paying little attention to my books because I was mesmerised by their voices, knowing by the increase in volume when a fierce debate was raging. The energy of their arguments crackled through the walls, causing the hairs on the back of my neck to rise.

'As that first autumn term wore on I decided that I no longer wished to be an outsider, hearing them from a distance; I wanted to be a part of them. When the basement of Finn's house became empty in December I jumped at the chance to move in. Looking back, that decision was a milestone; by leaving hall I gave up mixing with other students, people who had interests in life beyond revolutionary politics. Arriving with my trunk, I entered an enclosed order, shutting off other influences as I slammed the front door with its tricky catch behind me.

'Inevitably, I set about making my room into a mirror image of Majella's above me, buying throws and rugs from the hippy shop. It was damp in that basement, the air always held a faint hint of gas and the filtered light was gloomy. Sometimes a noxious smell rose from the drains outside and Finn mentioned a leaking sewage pipe. Mice scratched under the floorboards and left their neat droppings in cupboards in the tiny, begrimed kitchen which I never used. Snails slunk in through cracks, leaving silvery trails across the floor; when I woke in the night needing the toilet, my bladder heavy with Mulligan's lager, I had to pick my way through their slow-moving lines. None of this mattered to me. I cheerfully ignored the rattling, ill-fitting window, the wildlife, the stinks, the dust that mysteriously floated back as soon as I shifted it, the primitive bathroom with the stained toilet and cracked claw-foot tub; the way my metal bed frame creaked and whistled every time I turned in the night. I accepted it without flinching because I was at last living the life I wanted. I bought brocade curtains for the windows from a charity shop and a *chaise longue* from an old lady who sold it for ten pounds because she liked the look of me. Once the walls had been festooned with posters the place looked homely and joss sticks helped disguise the suspect air.

'As soon as I was installed I joined Red Dawn. Although I didn't realise it at the time, I must have been seen as quite a catch. I was the only English comrade and Finn was already calculating my potential. The group had been discussing the possibility of targeting British soldiers with newspapers and leaflets. Maybe they shouldn't just be seen as oppressors, the argument went; most of them were misguided working-class boys who'd joined the army to get a job. It was decided that we would run a three-month campaign to see if soldiers could be appealed to as workers. There would be a special leaflet, explaining that they were being exploited as pawns of the state, sent to tyrannise their own class. Finn proposed that the women in the group should approach squaddies and I would be the best spokesperson, my British accent breaking the ice, reassuring them. I understood, as he smiled at me, that this would be my way of proving my commitment and I accepted eagerly. The comrades were pleased and I was exhilarated at being picked out so quickly for an important role.

'The seeds of what came after may have been planted in Finn's mind then. His subsequent suggestion to Majella and myself in front of the fire one evening was based on the small success we had achieved in engaging a couple of soldiers in conversation. The squaddies we'd spoken to had been pathetically grateful for the attentions of young women; they would probably have been as eager to converse if we had been Jehovah's witnesses. We weren't the cause of any desertions but we were shooed away by officers and we took this as proof that we had threatened the status quo. It was agreed that I had been the honey attracting the flies and Finn pondered my particular talent, waiting for a time when it could again be usefully deployed.

'It's a pity we were never together in Mulligan's in the carefree days. I don't say that because my life might have tracked a different path, but because you would have looked into my face when it was still unshuttered.'

9

MARTIN

Was it possible that after fifteen years of marriage you could know someone and yet not know them at all? Martin turned that question over in his mind a good deal, especially during the week when he was on his own, under curfew not to see Nina. The probability that the answer was yes caused him anguish. He was a man capable of deep affection and in need of it. Now, in retrospect, in his relationship with Nina he felt like a lucky individual who has found the magic lamp, been promised the services of a genie but finds that anticipated pleasures turn to ashes through his own misjudgement and tricks of fortune.

He posed the question to his friend Angus over plates of spiced lentils in the Nigerian restaurant they favoured. He was fond of Angus but sometimes he would have liked him to be a little less pragmatic. Angus went into computers after graduating from Warwick but in the early nineties he decided to become a therapist and his training encouraged him to assume a sphinx-like expression and a habit of holding his head to one side. He and Nina had met occasionally over the years but no friendship had ever been established between them. Nina's only comment about Angus was that he reminded her of a monk with his balding crown, circled by thinning hair.

Martin met Angus the week Nina announced she couldn't live with him any more but he felt as if he were talking to himself. Of course, Angus might say that that was what he should be doing; he often made obscure comments, implying the need for mysterious communion with what he referred to as 'the inner voice'. It seemed to Martin that his friend had been more humane, more easy to communicate with when he designed microchips.

'I just don't understand it,' Martin told him. 'She says she still loves me and there's no one else. But she can't stay with me, her life has to change and she must be alone. That's it. How can you end a marriage for no good reason?'

'When has Nina ever given you reasons for her behaviour?' Angus loaded dhal on to his rice.

Martin had told him about the odd disappearances over the years, the constant exhaustion. 'But this is different, this is splitting up. I would have thought that if ever Nina needed me it would be now, when she's ill.'

'Perhaps Nina doesn't know why she's doing it.'

'You think it's her illness? You think she's behaving oddly because of that?' It was an idea he had considered, that gave him some hope. A person with a progressive disease would surely be prey to mood swings and strange decisions. He liked to think that her rejection of him was caused by the rogue malady infecting her tissues, encouraging aberrant thoughts. She had never made mention of it as a reason but of course she might not even be aware of the effect the lupus was having on her, or perhaps she knew and was trying to shield him from it. 'Maybe she doesn't want to burden me,' he added. 'Maybe she thinks I won't be able to take it if she really goes under.'

Angus narrowed his eyes and said nothing.

'Well,' Martin persisted, 'what do you think?' He had ordered the fieriest dish, hoping to shock his taste buds into a response, but the food was barely registering on his palate.

'What I think isn't of much consequence. Why do you think she's doing it?'

'For God's sake, Angus, I don't know! If I understood it I wouldn't be asking you. I wouldn't be sitting here, forcing down a meal just because I know I ought to eat.'

Angus shook his head. 'I can't provide answers and certainly not to a friend. The answer lies between you and Nina.'

'Oh, right. That's so illuminating.' He threw his fork down. 'Do you know what being with Nina is like? It's like coming in here and ordering the spiced lentils because you've eaten them before and enjoyed them; you sit back and wait for the dish to arrive, anticipating their texture and flavour but when they come, looking exactly the same as last time, there is a shock; they taste different, not at all as you remembered. You check the menu, call the waiter over; no, he assures you, the recipe hasn't been changed. But you look down at your plate and you know that it has.'

'Then,' said Angus, chewing carefully, 'maybe you need to consider whether it's best to find another restaurant and choose a different meal.'

'Oh, Nina's already doing that. She's ahead of me there – as usual. Maybe my father was right after all.'

'Your father? He never knew Nina.'

'I mean he used to say that women were a closed book, that you could spend all your life trying to prise the pages open but you were doomed to failure.'

'I thought you told me your parents were happy together, even when your father was disabled.'

'They were. He just accepted that my mother was a mystery he could never fathom.'

'Quoting your father is a bad sign, Martin. Parents' apparent wisdom should never be relied on in times of crisis.'

'What else have I got to fall back on?'

'That's not a healthy outlook, is it? Retreating, modelling your ideas on a man who's dead.'

'I can't see what alternative you're offering.'

Angus sighed, blinking. 'Have you adopted your father's attitudes as an escape route?'

'Don't start psychoanalysing me.'

'Oh, well, let's have coffee.'

They talked about the theatre group Angus was involved in over their coffee, the conversation gliding easily on safe ground. Martin's voice sounded tinnily in his ears, like one of the reedy singers on the old wind-up gramophone his grandfather had left him. He didn't hold Angus to account for failing him. He knew there was little he could say. Maybe he had expected a bit more sympathy – he was being abandoned, after all.

As they left the restaurant and walked to the tube to go their separate ways Angus made the only personal remark of the evening and then it was about Nina.

'You know,' he said, rubbing his nose with his pink ticket, 'Nina has always seemed an unreachable person.' And with that he vanished, his thinning pate disappearing down the Piccadilly Line escalator.

At first Martin was angry; having wanted to hear some analysis or judgement all evening he immediately resented it when he did. No, he thought, remembering times when he had felt close to Nina, that's not fair. There was a delay on the Northern Line and he sat on a bench, recalling how she'd shown him the way she cooked some of her special sauces when they moved in together and how they would

kiss and hug in between crushing garlic and slicing vegetables. This is when you add just a pinch of cayenne or see,
just a dribble of olive oil or the secret is to add a teaspoon
of mace in the last fifteen minutes, she would instruct him.
He would watch, running his tongue on the back of her
neck, licking her fingers flavoured with peppers or the acidity
of shallots. 'The Lady of Shallots' he named her as she
knighted him with her wooden spoon. Sometimes they
became so distracted, ending up entwined on the carpet or
sofa, the food would burn or simmer down to a gluey thick-
ness but they ate it anyway, laughing, feeding their love. In
a sense, they had their honeymoon before they married,
during those six months when Nina was still full of life.
They would stay up late, playing chess or backgammon or
dancing; Nina loved to dance, especially jiving to fifties songs
and they would tilt about the living room to Bill Hailey,
Chuck Berry and Little Richard, snapping their fingers.

One hot summer night they left the curtains open, the
window thrown wide and glanced up to see a couple outside
on the pavement, watching them dance. They bowed when
'Hound Dog' finished and the couple clapped and moved on,
their faces lit up by the sheer enjoyment they had witnessed.
When they were exhausted they would lie on the floor, side
by side, watching shadows on the ceiling or making shapes
with their fingers in the lamplight.

He gazed at the platform indicator telling him the next
train was due in twelve minutes and squeezed his arms
against his chest, holding in his agony. He wanted those
days back again because that was when he had had Nina's
full attention, when he felt her love directed at him rather
than nebulously drifting around him. Unreachable; he
recalled how she would often be one stride ahead of him as
they walked, even though his legs were longer; how she
would be racing up the gears on her bike while he was still

mastering his; the way a door would shut softly in the house and looking up, he would realise she'd gone.

A man standing nearby told his companion that the delay had been caused by a chap committing suicide at Chalk Farm and Martin wondered bitterly if the figure that had toppled deliberately in front of the rushing train had just been told his marriage was finished.

By the time he could bring himself to talk to Nina about her decision to leave, he was desperate to cling on to any thread still holding them together. After they realised the seriousness of her illness, he had seen a future where he would gradually need to care for her more and more. After his childhood that held no terrors for him; he had already willingly adjusted to doing the shopping, cooking and cleaning, helping her into the shower when she was too weak to wash herself, buckling her shoes when her fingers wouldn't work. Her physical weakness and the dependency it caused opened a way back into her life for him. There was nothing he wouldn't have done for her. Perhaps that was the problem; there were times when she preferred to bite her hand in frustration rather than ask him for help. He would try not to hover around her but the role of helper came to him too easily. Before he realised what he was doing, he would be offering an arm, reaching for her tablets, pulling the table closer. Then, seeing the set of her jaw and the distance in her eyes, he would stalk away or hurriedly mention a safe topic; his work, the garden, something in the news.

The pattern set up early in their relationship flourished. He accepted Nina's terms for their separation, allowed her to dictate the pace and timing. He was to visit at weekends and she would phone him on Wednesdays. He was so relieved that their parting was not to be absolute that he took what was offered with little argument, always careful to leave as soon as he saw her becoming tired, anxious not to outstay his welcome. Secretly, he hoped that one day she would say she had changed her mind, that she would move back. He would arrive and she'd turn to him with a puzzled look, asking what on earth had come over her, deciding to part from him? I'm so sorry, Martin, she would say, I don't always think straight these days, can you fetch my cases and I'll pack them.

He was taken aback when Nina told him that she'd employed a woman to help her during the week. There were signs of this interloper in the flat when he arrived one Saturday afternoon. He sniffed lavender polish in the air and saw the well-stocked fridge and newly washed curtains. A small framed needlework picture, about four by four, was propped on the mantelpiece. He bent down to read the lines sewn in a mauve thread:

> 'In the bustle of the day
> Take a little time to look at the sun,
> Feel it lift your weary heart
> And stroke your face with its heavenly beams.'

'Hmm,' he said. 'Where on earth did you get this piece of kitsch from?'

That was when he heard about Joan Douglas, the woman from the agency. He picked up the picture. 'She brought you this?'

'Yes.' Nina smiled knowingly as he stared at her. 'Well, it doesn't do me any harm and it would hurt her feelings if I took it down.'

He set it on the shelf, his back prickly. How nice of you to consider a complete stranger's feelings, he thought.

'You didn't tell me you were going to get someone in.'

'No.'

'How long have you been thinking about it?'

'A little while.'

'You could have mentioned it.'

'I didn't think it mattered. You'll probably never meet her, she's here Monday to Friday.' Nina's voice had taken on that over-patient, strained quality that indicated he had stepped over the carefully drawn line.

I would have looked after you, he wanted to say; I could have put those shelves up and mended the lock on the bathroom window; I could come by each evening and make you a meal, I'd have given up work if necessary; you didn't have to get this poem-sewing woman in. Instead, he made a joke about just not being able to get the right type of servant these days and Nina said, oh my dear, you don't know the half of it; a lot of these gels hardly know how to dust and you can't trust them with the silver.

He did meet Joan, once at the flat and once at the hospital, outside Nina's ward. He called one Tuesday lunchtime, breaking his curfew because a letter from Nina's bank had been misdirected and he knew she was waiting to hear about some shares. As he put the envelope down on the table beside her he heard the whine of the vacuum from Nina's bedroom and a voice soaring above it:

'After the ball is over,
After the break of morn,
After the dancers leaving,
After the stars are gone,
Many a heart is aching
If you could read them all,
Many the hopes that have vanished,
After the ball.'

The intimacy of that singing in the flat made his skin tighten. Since her illness developed Nina had become intolerant of noise; when they lived together he was constantly having to turn down the radio and TV. Yet here she was, tapping on top of one of her sticks.

'Are music-hall songs a new interest?' he asked, unable to keep a hint of spite from his voice.

She raised her eyes and he saw reproach in her look. 'Joan's got a whole repertoire of them, she learned them from her grandmother. She likes to sing while she's cleaning. It's quite an education for me, I've come to know most of the lyrics: "When you're All Dressed up and No Place to Go"; "The Piccadilly Johnny with the Little Glass Eye"; "It's Nice to Get up in the Morning". Listen:

'Oh! It's nice to get up in the morning
When the sun begins to shine,
At four or five or six o'clock
In the good old summer time;
When the snow is snowing
And it's murky overhead,
Oh! It's nice to get up in the morning
But it's nicer to stay in bed.'

Nina danced her hands in the air as she sang.

Exasperation came over him. 'Very nice,' he said. 'You, we, used to listen to decent music. Remember? Schubert, Mozart. You would say that Sunday morning couldn't pass without Verdi.'

She folded her hands, lying her head back. 'Maybe we need different music at different times in our lives. I find that I don't want to hear great compositions that stir up my emotions and leave me feeling empty, craving more. I like Joan's songs because they're simple, a bit sentimental, finite. The tunes don't pretend to do anything but entertain. I can imagine that they're from a time when life was uncomplicated, more honest. You know, the good old days when you could leave your door unlocked, neighbours helped each other and you didn't have to worry about pollution and recycling.'

He couldn't tell if she was being sarcastic. 'Yes,' he replied, 'and there wouldn't have been effective painkillers for lupus.'

'Oh, now you want to spoil my imaginings. That's not nice. Don't you have to get back to work?'

Joan interrupted then, carrying a mop and one of those cleaning agents with a spray mechanism. She was wearing knee-length, light brown cotton shorts and a pink cotton T-shirt patterned with darker pink heart shapes. With her ash-blonde hair, he thought that she resembled a slice of the Neapolitan ice-cream which he hadn't tasted for years but remembered well; layers of vanilla, raspberry and chocolate. Cheap and cheerful, his mother called it, shaking her head as he and his father argued over slices. They both liked the chocolate segment best and would try to curve the knife so that they got a larger portion of that end of the block. When it had all gone they would race to scrape creamy traces from the cardboard container, clashing spoons along the edges. A perfume that pervaded the air around many women wafted from Joan and it struck him that she was wearing more make-up than he would have expected for someone who spent her days clearing up other people's mess.

Nina introduced them and Joan said, 'pleased to meet you, I'm sure,' transferring the mop so that she could hold her right hand out. Her nail varnish exactly matched the darker pink of the hearts spread on her chest. 'Now,' she said, turning to Nina, 'I've given that bathroom a good going over. I had to unscrew the shower head and get the gunge out but it's as clean as a whistle in there. Have you done the shopping list?'

'Mmm. Just salad for tonight.'

'Are you sure? That's hardly going to keep you going, a bit of rabbit food.'

'Well, maybe soup first, then. A tomato and basil.'

'Right-oh.'

'Don't forget, you're bringing your cookery books tonight so that we can think about the wedding buffet.' Nina gave him a defiant look. 'Joan's getting married soon, I'm advising her on the food.'

'That's nice for you. I must be going. You'll remember to ring tomorrow?'

'Of course.'

He let himself out, hearing their chat resume in the background, something about terrines and vol-au-vents being ideal cold foods that could be set out before the ceremony at the registry office. 'Vollyvonts', Joan said, her cockney vowels ever so slightly refined.

For a moment he stood at the front door, listening, enjoying feeling sorry for himself because he was excluded. Nina would go nowhere with him socially now. At weekends they gardened, ate a meal, watched television, read; if Nina had enough concentration they might play a game of chess. He was rarely with her after eight PM because she needed to rest by then; too much company tired her. He would find himself going to a film or driving up to the Heath for a walk, loath to go home. It was too early to write the night off but too late to make any other plans. On those evenings he felt detached, a little lost, wandering in unfamiliar territory; he was no longer a married man but neither was he divorced. His life was like a badly knitted garment, snagged, unravelling. He would watch couples strolling or sitting close in the cinema, surrounded by a benevolent glow and resolve to tell Nina that he couldn't continue like this, a part-time visitor. Then the comments of a friend who was a GP came into his mind; this disease could cause irrevocable damage, the brain could become inflamed. Nina might end up in a wheelchair. He saw his father, one side wasted, getting his motorised wheels stuck in the door frame and crying with frustration. Nina had left him but he knew he couldn't leave her.

He headed for his car, wondering why she was willing to rouse herself to help with this woman's wedding when the effort would use up precious energy. He pictured Joan in a fussy gown, one of those brightly white frothy dresses that resemble a cake decoration, a string of fake pearls around her neck and a glittery plastic tiara in her dyed hair. Why was Nina going so downmarket suddenly? Again, he thought as he drove away, it must be the lupus altering her personality. Then he felt terribly guilty that he had been snide, putting himself first. How would he cope if he had such an illness? Would he be able to command an iota of the fortitude Nina demonstrated? She hardly ever complained or talked about the disease. It was her eyes and pallor that signalled when she was particularly weak. That day when they had heard the diagnosis in the hospital, when they stopped afterwards for a meal, she had referred for the first time to her illness as 'Adolf' and that was the name they had used ever since. This lupus, she'd said, was like the Führer, invading at will, seizing territories in her joints and muscles, marching without hindrance where it pleased, making sudden, unexpected forays into new areas. So, whenever he asked how she was she would say that Adolf was sending storm troopers down her left side or around the back of her neck or that for the moment he had paused to marshal his forces and was offering a brief respite. When a stronger medication gave relief for a while Nina would declare that Adolf had been temporarily routed by those little purple and white chaps but being a skulking character bent on evil he would think of a way of countering the attack.

His guilt made him pull over to the side of the road. He sat for a few minutes with the engine idling. He had no right to judge Nina, to be sceptical about who she chose to help her, what she chose to listen to. He picked up his mobile phone, wanting to ring her and say something pleasant but he knew that there was no point. She would be cool and friendly and emphasize that he didn't need to check up on her, the last thing she wanted was fussing. 'It's all okay, Martin', she would assure him, as she had before when he rang, torn between remorse and anger; 'you go to work and enjoy the normal world', she'd said, 'that's where you deserve to be'.

And so, weighing the phone in his hand, he put it down and drove back to the university, leaving Nina to her world of medications and old-time songs and a chubby charlady who could apparently provide what he could not.

10

JOAN

The wedding outfit was hanging on her wardrobe door, covered in its clear plastic wrapping. Joan had placed it there so that when she woke in the morning, it would be the first thing she would see. It was the most expensive item of clothing she had ever bought, which was justified, because it was for one of the most important events of her life. If it hadn't been for Eddie, she would have thought *the* most important.

Nina had chosen the suit really but she hadn't told Rich that. Nina shopped in a way that was entirely foreign to Joan, who usually wandered haphazardly through Marks and Spencer, British Home Stores and C&A or, when there had been a particularly expensive month with bills and the car, Primark and Littlewoods. She would try to find ideas amongst the racks of clothes and sales bargains. Despite the numerous women's magazines she read with their advice on what to pair with what, colour matching and which styles suited the shorter, more generous figure – her own – she never managed to project herself onto the photographs of confident models. As soon as she saw similar outfits in the shops, the picture that had seemed inspirational in a magazine became clouded and doubt crept in.

On the way to Brent Cross Nina had asked what was the maximum she could spend and what kind of image she was looking for. Joan had felt vague, saying she wasn't sure; she could pay about a hundred and fifty pounds and as for image, well, something suitable for a bride, she supposed, a tasteful, flattering outfit that Rich would like too.

Nina made her laugh then by launching into a description of the different bridal types you could have: sweet and virginal in white; the dolly mixture, saucy look in peach or apricot; sophisticated woman-of-the-world in black or navy; sexy siren in red or green; fussy homemaker in stripes or checks . . .

'Stop!' Joan said, nearly missing her turning. 'You're getting me all confused!'

Nina smiled. 'Seriously, if you don't have some idea it will be a nightmare. You could end up buying exactly the wrong thing. A dress or suit, for starters?'

'Either, to be honest. I thought I'd try in M and S, they've got linen shifts. I was thinking maybe one of those with a jacket.'

'Hmm. Has Rich expressed any preferences?'

'Oh, no. He'll be happy with whatever I choose. He likes me in blues and pinks.' She glanced at Nina. 'What did you wear for your wedding?'

'A Laura Ashley dress, light blue cotton with small white flowers and a wide belt.'

'Sounds lovely. I bet it suited you, with your small waist.'

'I think we could say it was of its time. I'd advise you against linen. Looks good on a hanger but by the time you've worn it for an hour it's crumpled.' Nina was more relaxed than Joan had ever known her. She was wearing a crushed velvet hat that softened her face and a baggy cotton jacket and trousers all in the same mulberry colour that reminded Joan of a dress that Eddie had bought her in Biba a fortnight before he vanished. That type of purple and a faded brown had been popular shades then. She'd been moaning that she had nothing to wear to a friend's birthday party and he had turned up with the carrier bag, pulling it open and shaking the dress out, telling her to get into these glad rags, head out there and wow them. That dress must have been expensive. It was eyed enviously at the party but she couldn't bring herself to wear it again after he'd gone. She slept with it under her pillow, taking it out when she woke during the night and rubbing her salty eyes on its silkiness, crushing the fabric between taut fingers. She could still see him holding it up to the kitchen light, Gran mashing potatoes and telling him he was foolish with his money but smiling as she spoke and Eddie dancing the dress around, announcing, 'Joanie, you *shall* go to the ball.' Nina's clothes were smarter than the ones she usually wore and Joan was gratified that she had made an effort for their trip out; that was, after all part of the reason for inviting her, a bit of a morale booster.

Nina sat patiently in Marks and Spencer while Joan tried on a couple of dresses. When she paraded out in the final one, a blue floral number matched with a straw hat, Nina rested her chin on her hands, looking up at her.

'Presumably you've brought me because you want my opinion,' she said gravely.

'That's right. So, what do you think?'

'No.'

'None of them?'

'No, and particularly not that one. You look like minor royalty on a bad day. Get changed and I'll take you somewhere that will produce the goods.'

'It can't be too dear,' Joan warned, recalling that Nina thought nothing of flashing a gold credit card.

'No, that's all right.'

Nina led her to a small shop she'd never noticed before, perhaps because it was tucked between a bookshop and an antique furniture store, places she would never visit. Inside, Nina headed for a rack of skirts and jackets and flipped through. Joan stood by nervously, noticing a shelf of leather bags and a sale sign indicating that they were reduced from ninety-five pounds to seventy. She was about to whisper that she couldn't afford anything in here when Nina held up a couple of hangers.

'This, try this,' she said. 'Take a twelve and fourteen, it's always best to compare sizes.' She was already moving Joan towards a curtained cubicle.

The size twelve skirt wouldn't pass over Joan's hips but as soon as she had put on the fourteen she felt transformed. The lined cotton skirt and tunic top were in a deep, warm pink, beautifully cut and tailored. She looked taller, her shape more defined, like one of the women in a magazine at last. Nina came eagerly to the door of the changing booth and leaned on her stick – today she needed just the one. 'Ah yes, that's it, Joan, you look great. That shade of pink suits your colouring, brings out the brightness in your skin and hair.'

'You don't think the skirt's too long?'

'No. It's flattering. Rich will be swept off his feet.'

'I need the fourteen.'

'But the shape is slimming, the long jacket does that.' Carried away by her reflected image, Joan had only just examined the price tag. 'Oh, crumbs! It's a hundred and thirty pounds. I can't buy it, Nina, I won't have enough left for a hat and shoes.'

Nina smoothed the arms of the jacket, feeling the cloth appreciatively. 'Oh, no hats! A hat makes you look like a dowager. Have a good hairdo, pin a rose behind your ear. What size shoe do you take?'

'Five.'

'Same as me. I've got loads of shoes, flat heels which you need with that outfit. You can borrow a pair.'

'Oh, I couldn't!'

'Why not? Aren't you supposed to have something borrowed? You must; you can come back and look through when we've finished. I've no use for most of them now.' She was smiling and nodding. Her skin was flushed, the telltale rash raised. She put her hand up to scratch it.

Joan felt a lump in her throat. She wasn't used to having this kind of interest taken in her. Glancing in the mirror again, she saw how good she looked. She imagined Rich in one of the charcoal grey suits she'd spotted in Marks, standing beside her in the registry office and her hands flexed in anticipation.

'I feel like a kid, getting all dressed up for something special.'

'And you've got twenty pounds left for your hair.'

'I'm ever so glad I asked you to come. I'd never have looked in here.' Her eyes met Nina's in the mirror.

Nina shook her head abruptly, looking quickly away. 'Pleasure's all mine,' she said, moving back to her seat by the till.

They returned to Nina's flat after lunch and sorted through the dozens of shoes in the bottom of her wardrobe. There was a dark blue pair, hardly worn, soft like dancing pumps, that fitted perfectly.

'You're quite sure I can borrow these?'

'Of course. Please have them, Joan, I've been planning to give most of them to a charity collection anyway.' Nina rubbed her forehead. 'I'm tired now, I'll have a sleep. When you come back to cook later, why don't you join me for the meal? We can open a bottle, celebrate your impending nuptials.'

'Well, it's very kind but I don't know . . .' A client had never invited her to dinner before; she was nonplussed. Still, she thought, a client's never helped me choose my clothes before or given me expensive shoes. Her emotions felt very near the surface, her skin tight on her bones. She had started the morning with her thoughts full of Rich and then in the café Nina had encouraged her to talk about Eddie. There was a tingling beneath her eyelids; although the expectation of Rich was sweet and Nina's generosity warmed her, her brother's absence was unexpectedly pervading the day, edging it with heartache. However hard she tried she found it hard to recall his face now, it had receded into shadow. She could clearly remember the minty smell of his breath from the mouth spray he used constantly, convinced that he suffered from halitosis and the way he would always arrive on the dot of seven on Friday nights with fish and chips for three and a bottle of milk stout for Gran.

Nina had sunk into her chair and was pulling up a footstool. 'It's nothing to do with kindness,' she said, 'I just thought it might be pleasant.'

Joan thought of her eating alone, her tray balanced on her bony knees and of her own trip back to Leyton where she was going to make a bacon sandwich and watch television. 'I will then,' she said. 'What would you like?'

'You choose for a change. Something you'd like too and we'll toast you and Rich.'

When Joan returned it was a warm May evening, still and quiet in Nina's street. As she parked the car she heard the murmurs of voices from open windows and the deep notes of a cello resonating a couple of doors along. She leaned against the car bonnet for a few moments, appreciating the wide, clean pavements, well-proportioned houses and tall, heavy-leafed trees that purified the air, making this corner of the city so much more attractive than her own. In her part of Leyton the streets were scruffy and the paving stones overlapped. In hot weather the air was sullied with a sickly chemical smell from the plastics factory. There were few trees, just lamp-posts covered in posters advertising raves or warehouse clearances. The Chinese take-away around the corner attracted customers until late at night; cars roared up the road and emptied containers littered the gutters with evidence of bean sprouts and egg fried rice clinging to them. She hadn't managed to come far from Bromley, where the terraced houses squeezed together, she thought; of course, she owned her flat which did make a difference, but sometimes her heart sank when she saw that another daub of graffiti had been added to the wall outside her block. Then she saw Nina silhouetted in the window, inching across the room and she acknowledged that she would rather be healthy and living in Leyton than riddled with illness in prosperous Crouch End.

Joan cooked a cheese soufflé with new potatoes and runner beans for dinner, or supper as Nina called it. She could hear Nina moving around as she drained the vegetables and found that she had laid the table in the conservatory with a cream lace cloth, tall gleaming glasses, folded napkins and candles.

'It looks lovely,' Joan said, delighted, 'but you'll wear yourself out with all this bother. You really shouldn't have.'

'I slept for a couple of hours. I feel quite fresh. Are we ready?'

Nina opened champagne. It frothed into the glasses, reminding Joan of foamy wave tips. 'To you, Joan,' she said, 'and your happiness.'

'I feel like major, not minor royalty tonight!' The champagne fizzed up her nose. She laughed, patting her chest.

'Rich sounds like a good man. He must be, to have cared for his mother.'

Joan nodded. She felt on safe ground with this, having got the story straight and it was a fact that his mother had only died six months back. 'He was very fond of his mum,' she said truthfully. 'She didn't have much of a life with his father; the old man used to knock her about but at least she didn't have him around for the last ten years.'

'So does Rich have a house in Frinton?'

'No, his mum had a council place. We'll be starting from scratch together. That's why I've been doing my flat up.'

'How did the kitchen units turn out?' Nina had looked at colour charts with her during one of their outings and suggested that she painted the worn kitchen cupboards ivy green, matching sample cards to demonstrate how that would work with off-white walls. With green plants at the window, the room would have a cool, fresh look.

'They're so smart, it's amazing how much difference a bit of gloss makes.' Joan laughed. 'I feel as if I'm building a nest. I'm always on the lookout for ways of making it just right for the two of us.'

'Well, I hope it all works out as you want it, as you've planned.'

The light had dimmed outside and the candles burned steadily, wisps of smoke rising and scenting the air faintly with sandalwood. Their flames cast a glow on Nina's bony hands which lay clasped by her plate. She had put music on, something classical with slow, rich violins playing. It wasn't Joan's cup of tea but it fitted the evening and the intimacy of the small conservatory. After the tensions of the day, Joan felt soothed by the champagne and was eager to talk. Nina was looking more than ever like her grandmother; she had secured her hair in a knot at the nape of her neck and was wearing a dark dress and her shawl around her shoulders. Her Lily of the Valley scent drifted about her when she moved.

'There's only one thing I wish for that I can't have,' Joan said quietly. 'I wish that Eddie was going to be there on my wedding day to give me away. I know it's daft but, well . . .'

Her unfinished words rose up with the candle vapour. Nina poured more champagne, holding the bottle with both hands. Joan took a deep draught. 'Eddie took me to Petticoat Lane one Sunday. I'd just turned fourteen. He bought me a brooch, a silver butterfly – I was mad about butterflies for a while although it's supposed to be horses that teenage girls go for, isn't it? Anyway, I loved their colours. He got a pair of leather boots for himself, that kind with a square heel that were all the rage. They were black with ankle straps and he was so keen on them he polished them as soon as we got home. I think he fancied himself as Clint Eastwood.'

'You obviously still miss him very much,' Nina said. 'You've never said how he died.'

'No, I don't like to talk about that, I find it . . . well, too upsetting. Sorry, I hope you don't think I'm being rude.'

'Not at all. I expect there are things you'd rather forget.'

'That's right. Most of the time I don't dwell on it. I mean you can't, can you?'

'Life goes on?'

'That's right; don't rub where the shoe pinches. But then I'll see or hear something that reminds me of Eddie and I get to thinking about what might have been. I'd have been an aunty – he always said he wanted loads of kids one day. I have this dream that comes back every now and again. I had it a couple of nights ago.' She stopped because Nina was looking abstracted, rubbing a finger back and forth on the tablecloth. 'I'm not boring you, am I?'

'No, no. Please, go on.'

'Well, I'm on a big ship, like an ocean liner, and I'm

looking through a porthole and I see Eddie in a tiny dinghy, sailing away from me. The sea looks huge and there he is, rushing off on the waves. Then I start knocking on the porthole, trying to call to him, but of course the glass is so thick I don't make much noise and he can't hear me. I wake up then and I always think that I could only see the back of his head. If I could just have a dream where I saw his face or he spoke to me, it would be wonderful.'

There was a silence. A candle spluttered and the woman next door called her cat in. Nina reached for her stick and levered herself up. 'It's a pity we can't order our dreams, select one like a pull-down menu on a computer.'

'Oh, don't mind me going on, spoiling the evening! Shall I blow out the candles?'

'Please.' Nina was standing by the door into the garden, watching sparrows bicker over bread. 'We can have coffee and cheese and biscuits in the living room. You must tell me more about your plans for the big day.'

Rich was sporting a bruised eye the next time Joan visited. She exclaimed as he sat down, grabbing his arm, 'What's happened to you? Has a doctor seen that?'

'Oh, it's nothing, just a bit sore. I had a fight with a guy who stole my fags. He's worse, lost two teeth.'

She stared. How could he sound so unconcerned? 'But did you get into trouble?'

'Me? No, he started it. He's learned I don't like anything of mine being interfered with.' Rich ran his hands through his hair. 'The head screw had a bit of a rant at me, but he wasn't all that interested. There's far worse goes on here. You wouldn't want to know about it, sweetheart.'

'It won't delay you getting out?'

'No, I told you. Now don't go on about it, it's over.'

'But your eye, it's bloodshot . . .'

'Leave it, darling, it's okay.' He gripped her hands in his. 'Forget it, let's talk about something else.'

He described a funny film he'd seen on TV but she wasn't taken in, she detected that he was out of sorts. Sometimes he was like that, a little irritable. He would drum his fingers on the table and twist in his chair. She tried not to show she'd noticed, knowing that he would be apologetic in the letter she'd receive on Tuesday. He always made an effort to explain on paper when he had been bad-tempered: *it's just that I wait all week to see you and then some bastard in here starts getting on my nerves over the weekend and I get fed up. I know it's not long to go now but that doesn't help as much as it should. In fact, the days drag more than ever, as if the last one in this place will never come. Don't take this the wrong way but sometimes I almost don't want you to turn up because then I have to watch you leave. But if you didn't come, I don't know what I'd do. I think I'd get up on the roof and chuck myself off, like that bloke did last year. It's just not easy, waiting and waiting.*

So she chatted, talking about the improvements to the flat, how she'd met Martin, Nina's husband, giving him a detailed account of the trip to Brent Cross and the meal with Nina in the evening. Rich knew all about Eddie and the dream so she didn't say too much about that part, just that Nina had been nice, even though she'd run on a bit.

Rich lit a cigarette. He rolled his own, thin and wispy. He'd promised that he would try and give up once he was on the outside but he needed them in here, especially in the long hours when he'd been locked up for the night. His index and middle fingers were nicotine stained and she planned to tackle that with lemon juice and baking soda, a mixture she'd read about in the readers' tips section of a beauty magazine.

'She pokes her nose in a lot, I suppose she's got nothing better to do,' he said sharply.

'It's not like that, Rich, she's just a nice person. Fancy her giving me champagne, too! She's helping me with ideas for our buffet, by the way.'

'You haven't changed your mind, then?'

'About what?'

He was looking away, up at the clock. 'Oh, us. I thought maybe you'd gone off the idea of marrying me.'

'What on earth made you think that? I've just been telling you about buying my outfit, haven't I?'

He shrugged. 'Tony on the next block, his girlfriend called it all off a couple of days before he was due out. He reckoned she couldn't face it once it all got too real.'

'Is that what's been bugging you?'

'I don't know. You listen to blokes, you get thinking.'

'Well, you can stop thinking that. I haven't got cold feet as long as you haven't.'

'Me? No, no way!' He squeezed her fingers tight. 'We're definitely on, then?'

'Definitely.'

He looked down at their joined hands. 'And we're having a reception at the flat?'

'Yes, but I want it to be special.'

'What's this Nina suggesting then? Posh foods?'

'No. Just nice savouries.'

'Oh? I reckon sarnies and cold meat, a bit of ham and pork with some beer and wine will be fine. My brother and his lot won't expect anything swanky. Are we having a cake, marzipan and icing?'

'Nina suggested a light sponge instead, as it's a summer wedding. We found a recipe for an apricot one that looks lovely. You like apricot jam, don't you?'

'Yes. Sounds like you're getting pretty thick with this Nina, developing a taste for the high life. She likes to help you spend your money, don't she?'

'She's kind, she really is. She even told her husband about us.'

'What's he like, then?'

'Nice chap, quite good-looking, but anxious. A bit jumpy, I thought. He'd like to be there more, I'd say, but she doesn't want it. I don't understand why she won't live with him.'

'Bit pathetic, if you ask me, letting his own wife tell him when he can come round and when he can't. Hope you're not going to pick *that* idea up from Nina as well.'

She saw then that she had been indiscreet, going on about Nina and their day together. There was no champagne to be had in Brixton and she felt guilty because she had so obviously been enjoying herself while he fretted and suffered the frustration of watching the calendar. It must be terrible for him, listening to all these plans that were being made and not being able to join in. Driving to the prison along Coldharbour Lane she had thought how apt that street name was, taking her to a place where you were held in a long, chill waiting. She touched his cheek. He pressed her hand to his forehead which was tense and hot under her palm. It was just as well that she hadn't mentioned offering Nina an invitation to come to the small reception. Nina had refused, saying that she appreciated the thought but she didn't think she'd be up to it. Joan changed the subject, telling him that Alice was going to buy them a cutlery set and that she'd seen just the right curtains for the kitchen in BHS, a green to match the cupboards.

'It really won't be long, Rich,' she said, her voice unsteady. 'I know it's hard for you. Has it been bad the last few days?'

'Oh, that fight brassed me off and a couple of other blokes are getting on my nerves. One in the next cell sings bloody Elvis songs all the time. Don't mind me, tell me about the flat again, what you've done.'

She did, while he took the last puffs on his cigarette. The

paper casing shrivelled as he sucked in deeply. A red glow flared briefly. He screwed his eyes up in the smoke and stroked her bare forearms. When the bell rang for the end of visiting time he sighed, spinning his tobacco tin on the table. She thought of her dream, of Eddie vanishing in the dinghy and the mingled panic and disappointment she felt every time she woke. She told Rich that he should go first this time so that he didn't have to see her moving away from him.

11

N I N A

'*Carissima,*
    'There is a party going on across the street; a discreet
gathering – after all, one pays for the kind of discretion
practised in this neighbourhood – but now and again a phrase
of Sinatra or Eartha Kitt drifts across to me. "I've got you
under my skin," Frank was singing earlier and I thought
how true that had been of you and Finn but of course I
didn't try hard not to give in. I willingly let you fill every
corner of my life until I could hardly recall what it had been
like before I met you.
    'I savoured those mornings when I would wake in my
basement and hear the strains of traditional music coming
from your floor, The Chieftains or Planxty or maybe Lindis-
farne. Uncharacteristically, we developed a passion for
Charles Aznavour and would simultaneously put "La
Bohème" on our turntables so that his crooning lilted
between our rooms in stereo. After a perfunctory wash –
my facilities never encouraged me to linger – I would climb
the uncarpeted stairs, stopping for a moment on the fifth

step to admire the rose-tinted light glowing through the stained-glass window at the end of the long hallway, a diamond pattern that always made the sky look promising. We would breakfast together before setting off for campus, discussing in Italian the lectures to come, checking our translations, rushing so that we could buy paper cups of foaming coffee to carry to a seminar. At lunchtime we ate in the echoing refectory, usually joined by Finn and other members of Red Dawn; we proselytised for the cause amidst the hubbub, often crossing swords with Sinn Fein supporters, rival Trotskyites or Marxists as we attempted to foment student rebellion over shepherd's pie or rice strewn with pieces of stringy chicken. In the evening, back to the dusty, disorganised house with its peeling front door and the crudely made wooden plaque on the wall inside, carved by an IRA man in Crumlin Road jail which proclaimed those words from an old song:

> "Sing, oh! may England surely quake
> We'll watch till death for Erin's sake."

'The war outside came through the door with us, reflected in images on the pink-washed panelling and sagging wallpaper. There were banners and Irish flags made by internees – the tricolour and the starry plough – enlarged black and white photographs of civil rights marchers being bludgeoned by B Specials and the linen strip worked by prisoners' wives that hung the length of the hallway. It bore the wry words of an unknown seventeenth-century Irish author:

> "The world has laid low and the wind blows away like ashes Alexander, Caesar and all who were in their trust; grass-grown is Tara and see Troy now how it

is – and the English themselves, perhaps they too will pass!''

'We usually moved straight to your kitchen where Finn would have started to prepare the evening meal. I learned most of my cooking skills from him. He didn't teach me, I watched and absorbed how he mixed and blended, moving deftly between the grimy oak table and elderly cooker that smouldered when he turned it on. He used masses of garlic and had a way of crushing cloves with the blade of his knife that was as dextrous as his more complicated card tricks. The legacies of relationships stay with us in ways we never dream of. So Finn is in his own way here with me when I explain to Joan how she should grill chicken breast with a tomato and walnut sauce, coat rice with olive oil to maintain its texture or make an avocado dip with blended red pepper and lemon juice. Do you remember that dip? It's still heavenly. The first time I saw Finn making it and leaned over the bowl to sniff, he scooped some up on his finger and I licked it off. He repeated the movement, extending the same finger to you, your mouth forming an ''O'' around it. What a player he was and how we played up to him!

'We must have appeared a strange threesome to onlookers, spending so much time together. A lecturer once asked me if we were into a kinky sex triangle; from the look in his eye, I think he was interested in proposing a foursome and he was disappointed when I laughed. I did sometimes fantasise about going to bed with Finn, as, I imagine, did a lot of the women who knew him. Looking back, I realise how provocatively he often dressed. I have never known another man who wore such tight trousers. He had a particular pair of hip-hugging cotton jeans for summer that looked almost painful; the thin material bordered on transparency, displaying a riveting swell of genitals. On hot days he went bare chested so that there was a great deal of Finn on view. That sight did cause the odd flutter in the pit of my stomach but the thought of how distraught you would be if he offered and I accepted was enough to quell my imaginings. How odd and how symptomatic of my state of mind then; the offer did come and I was careful not to lose your friendship by betraying you with your lover, yet I carelessly jeopardised everything we had by joining you in a crazed act.

'The offer – oblique but a definite offer – was made at the summer party we held in '71, just before term finished. It was one of the hottest days of that year and we decided to excavate the long garden which Finn had scarcely glanced at since inheriting the house. We found a rusty scythe in the shed and Finn hacked at the thick grass while you and I cut back rioting brambles, rose bushes and a jungle of other plants which were all nameless to me then. It was hot work under the high sun. Finn wore a pair of cut-off denim shorts and we put on swimsuits and threw water from an old tin watering can over each other, shaking ourselves like puppies. Finn tossed handfuls of grass at us and we retaliated, ducking behind bushes to avoid his better aim. At one point, dizzy in the heat, I lay under an apple tree and dozed off. When I woke the two of you had vanished and I saw that your swimsuit had been abandoned by the back door. The "Spring" movement from Vivaldi's *Four Seasons* was filling the ground floor. I knew that it was music you liked to make love to so I stayed in the garden, tipping the sprinkler of the watering can over my face and eating unripe raspberries. My legs and shoulders were red from too much sun. I remember lying back under the tree, squinting at the intense sky and sensing a lightness in my limbs, as if I was a drifting feather of the thistledown that had floated around us as we disturbed the sleeping garden. I thought of the one, brief sexual encounter I had had back in February with a chemistry

student from Manchester, a disappointing experience interrupted by the return of his roommate. I wondered if anyone
would offer me the kind of pleasure I had heard echoing
behind your bedroom door.

'My mother rang that evening, before the party began, a
rare occurrence. She told me of the death of a great-aunt
whose existence I had barely been aware of. Although my
mother took no close interest in any of her family and interpreted requests for assistance or uninvited contact as unwar-
ranted intrusions into her world of bridge sessions, she was
punctilious in passing on factual details such as births, deaths
or marriages.

'"What on earth has happened to your voice?" she asked.

'"What do you mean?"

'"Your accent is peculiar. You're not becoming stage Irish,
are you?"

'Several people had remarked on my accent which
occasionally – and especially when I became intense – took
on a marked Ulster twang. Maybe it was inevitable with
someone as impressionable as me or perhaps I was unconsciously aping you as part of my enchantment; people in love
do absorb and reflect some of their loved one's attributes. I
had started to use Ulster expressions too: I said *wee* instead
of small, *wain* for child, *how about you?* instead of how are
you? During the second term I changed the spelling of my
name to the more Irish-looking "Neenagh" and asked the
university to alter official documents, causing great confusion. If my mother had seen us together she would have
noticed that I had started to dress like you, in layers and
long skirts. That night of the party we wore long-sleeved,
ankle-length tunics; they were pinched at the waist and the
bell sleeves flapped, making us look like mediaeval figures.
I was also buying bangles by then and when we moved at
the same time we set up a joint percussion, similar to that

of the Hare Krishna sect who chanted their mantras with a cymbal accompaniment. The Hare Krishna converts caused consternation as they processed, saffron-robed, amongst Belfast pedestrians who searched in vain for a way of comprehending a religion that outwitted the familiar, traditional responses of name-calling or brutality. They were the only people in Northern Ireland who could parade their beliefs on the streets in complete safety.

'I think that all the comrades came to our party, bringing bottles of beer and wine. The working class families who lived upstairs were also invited, testaments to Finn's oneness with the proletariat, and trooped down self-consciously on the dot of nine, before anyone else had arrived. They were overdressed for the occasion, their children in pretty dresses or smart shorts and sparkling white ankle socks. They stood in the kitchen, uncomfortable, the women looking with horror at the grubby surfaces. We had spent the evening making bowls of humus, garlic bread and tomato and olive salads. Finn, bearing in mind the worker guests, also provided chicken and ham sandwiches made with spongy white sliced bread, sausage rolls and bottles of cream soda and lemonade.

'As we prepared the food in the large, sparse kitchen, I asked when it had last been decorated and Finn said he thought around 1930. The square stone sink was crammed with dirty crockery which I attacked; water spouted erratically from the gasping taps and the wooden draining board was slimy from years of dripping plates. Below the sink were massed ranks of the milk and wine bottles we were always intending to clear. I detected an atmosphere between you and Finn. You rarely argued, a fact which I much appreciated after my childhood with feuding parents and so any dissent tended to be very evident.

'While he was standing at the other end of the room,

spreading slices of bread with margarine, I asked you softly in Italian if anything was wrong. Oh, you said, you wanted him to visit your home with you on Sunday but he wouldn't go, said he had too much to do. It wasn't a big thing but now and again you would like to take him so that your family would get to know him better. I wondered about the wisdom of that. I had been with you several times to the cheerful, chaotic farm in Pettigoe and I had witnessed the fixed look on your parents' faces when Finn was mentioned. In the cowshed your mother had asked me unsubtle questions about our house, what Finn spent his time doing, whether he ever saw his family. I answered vaguely, non-committal, unsure of what she already knew, not wanting to make things difficult for you. I liked your mother but my loyalties lay with you and Finn and I believed that her generation couldn't possibly understand our way of life. That was the day she put her hand on my arm, confidentially, while the rhythmic *woosh, woosh* of the milking machinery sounded in the background and said, prophetically, that there was something wanting in that young fella; she'd seen it the first time she met him. "He looks down on us even if he pretends not to," she commented, tapping her chest and adding that he had a marble heart. I wasn't listening too closely. I think I replied airily that you and Finn were in love and she prodded a cow's side, moving it along, saying, "oh sure, love is blind, it has a wild lot to answer for".

'I suppose that most of us regret not listening more carefully at certain times in our lives. We look back and realise that a word, a phrase, could have been a turning point but it missed us. Maybe if I'd paid attention to your mother that day instead of brushing aside her comments with a youthful edge of superiority – what did she, a simple if kind country-woman plodding around in apron and muddy wellingtons, know of the realities of passion and revolutionary politics?

– things might have been different. But I only half-heard her words with a casual, patronising indifference, starting to feel a twitch of boredom at her presence.

'That night you shrugged at Finn's intransigence and carried on stirring a preserving pan in which you were making a heady punch of vodka, white wine and oranges. I gathered handfuls of mint from a pot we had found wedged behind the jasmine in the garden and we threw them in. That drink was delicate, ambrosial and lethal; one glass and the world began to slant. I had a mild sunburn from the hours in the garden. My legs radiated warmth and my arms and shoulders prickled; the effects of the heat combined with alcohol made me feel as if I was charged with an electric current.

'It was a crowded, sticky, successful gathering, the kind of party which effortlessly takes shape when most people know each other. Finn drew an appreciative audience for his card tricks and then took to the piano. At one point I sat beside him and we played the simple duet arrangement of "Scarborough Fair" that he had spent weeks teaching me. I made no mistakes and his simple nod of satisfaction to me when we finished made me hugely proud of my achievement. Finn regularly praised my quick progress on the keys; what a shame, he would say, that I had never been encouraged to play as a child.

'The arrival of two Basque comrades, members of ETA, at midnight was the crowning glory. They were weary, having travelled for several months, visiting fraternal organisations in Italy, Germany and France before hitching to Scotland and catching the ferry from Stranraer to Larne where they had been pounced on by police. For two hours they had been questioned about their travels, subjected to strip searches and had their belongings ransacked. Finn was anxious to know if they had given Rock House as their destination but they assured us that they had presented themselves as casual travellers, student backpackers heading on spec for the university, hoping to crash out in the students' union. Laughing, they said that they were used to such harassment, it was nothing to them, the Spanish cops were much harder and meaner. They soon revived under the press of excited attention and glasses of punch and I talked to one of them, Pablo, for some time. His English was almost faultless which was lucky, as I spoke little Spanish and we edged close, talking ostensibly about the Irish situation and exchanging other communication with our eyes. He had glossy dark brown hair that rippled to his shoulders and a beautiful bow of a mouth; he might have seemed effeminate if he hadn't spoken in a deep, resonant voice. I found myself desiring him, needing to stroke his skin, but he was wanted by other comrades and we became separated.

'Later, at about three in the morning, when guests were vanishing, I wandered down the empty garden for some air. I was drunk, tired but wakeful in the jittery way that alcohol can cause. I was staring at the sky, my mind a blank, when Finn appeared quietly beside me and started pointing out stars, naming them. I found his mouth on mine, his hands on my shoulders and I kissed him back, listless with punch. It was a long kiss, broken off by him when he heard someone coming back into the garden. I took my hand from his neck; my bracelets clinked, making me think of you. Maybe, Finn said quietly to me, smoothing back my hair, you and I could have a party of our own some time. I remember finding that phrase, finding that way of putting it, very amorous although later I realised that he had lifted it from Jane Fonda's line in a film. I shook my head, muddled, muttering that it wasn't a good idea, you and he were as good as married. He stepped back, stony-faced; "oh, very bourgeois, very Maidstone maiden," he remarked, moving away.

'It was never mentioned again, that little scene in your garden but I sensed that Finn held it against me. He wasn't used to rejection and I imagine he thought that I would receive his attentions gratefully. It seemed to me that after that night his manner towards me became just a little chilled, but in a way that was imperceptible to you or any of the comrades. He gradually dropped my piano lessons and didn't bother to save the almonds in his packets of nuts for me. He no longer called me upstairs for a cup of his freshly ground coffee if you weren't there to shout down to me. I didn't mind too much. Although I knew he wouldn't ask me to party again, I was wary of him physically because he still elicited a response in me. I wonder why he made the offer? Was it too much punch, was it because you had argued, did he want to punish you or perhaps test me in some way or was it simple availability, a natural progression of the other tutelage he offered me?

'I did hold my own private party that night and for some nights afterwards. Pablo found me a while later and we vanished to the basement where he stayed with me for the duration of his six-day visit. I gained an in-depth knowledge of the Basque cause and Pablo's variety of sexual techniques. While mice scurried behind the skirting we produced the kinds of pleasurable sounds I had only overheard before. For the first time in my life I was overwhelmed physically, in that feverish state where you want to live and breathe another's body, where joy is so intense that you can no longer tell where your skin ends and theirs begins. I caressed the curved scar on his arm, the legacy of barbed wire when he was running from soldiers in Bilbao and drank in his stories of the guerilla warfare he had been engaged in since he was fourteen. In the dark nest of the bed he whispered to me of ethnic identity, of the right of small nations to independence. He taught me to count to five in Basque; "*bat, bi, hirur, laur, bortz,''* I repeated after him, my lips close to his and he told me that in Spain I could be arrested for speaking the language in public, just as Irish speaking used to be forbidden and punished by the British. How terrible, I thought, to deprive people of their language, of the very expression of their thoughts, and I loved Pablo for his defiant spirit as well as his beauty.

'When he had to leave I was miserable; couldn't he stay longer, I begged but he had his own cause and studies to return to. At the port we exchanged many desperate, hot kisses, swearing to write, agreeing that I would travel to see him as soon as possible.

'The recollection of that night has been prompted both by the party taking place across the street and by my latest letter card. A Latin-looking man with hippyish, shoulder-length hair like Pablo's is standing by a curve of the river Boyne, his bicycle propped beside him. My theory about my correspondent's route seems to have been correct. He or she has crossed to Meath, just a short journey to the border but that huge cultural step into the tribes of the north, in counties Armagh and Down:

The land in Meath is green and fertile, quite a contrast to stony Mayo. As I walk, the soft surface is kinder to my feet although a pilgrim should not seek comfort. An American tourist I met at Newgrange, his video camera pointing like a gun, told me that this area is just a honeycomb of graves, one of the most fantastic sites in western Europe. With the sun out, the fields look tranquil and the dark, wide Boyne flows quiet and swift. It is difficult to associate this landscape with death but perhaps its very fertility is a result of centuries of bone-enriched soil. I believe that there is a garden fertiliser containing blood and bone; it sounds a savoury mixture.

There are three burial mounds in Meath that draw many tourists with their cameras and camcorders. They are ancient, holy places, blessed by the beliefs of prehistoric peoples. An information leaflet tells you that they can be compared in age and significance to the pyramids. The meaning that their builders placed on the sanctity of burial rituals is testified to by their great labours. They hewed massive cairns from the limestone, lining roofs with stone flags or timber, carving out deep side chambers and filling them with pottery, bone ware, hammer pendants, glass and amber beads and food vessels. At Knowth, in the passage graves, these people must have sweated for weeks, months, decorating huge stones with grave art. There are spiral designs, serpents, radiating circles and zigzags, all evidence of deep respect for the bodies laid within.

In one of the sites at Tara, the mound of the hostages, there were remains of many cremations and one inhumed body, a young man lying on his side with his knees slightly bent. I looked at an illustration of him in my leaflet and these words came to me; 'Woe to her who allowed the gentle sweet-voiced lad to go into Ui Fiachrach, a land where water is plentiful and the men are unruly.' Buried with this young man was a necklace made of bronze, amber and jet. Perhaps it had been his favourite piece of decoration, given to him by a loved one or traded with him in return for pottery or an axe.

Standing on the high hill of Tara, where kings reigned and Saint Patrick preached, you breathe sweet air and think of the ringing and hammering that must have echoed as stones were pulled into place and the weeping and grieving that must have carried on the breeze down to the lowlands and the flowing river.

'Nigel Howes had a medal, a St Christopher on a silver chain. He wasn't religious, he told me one afternoon when we were out for a drive, but he had a belief in holy talismans. I never told you the details of that second evening I spent with him. I was deliberately vague because he became too real to me, revealing details of his family. We didn't want to know of any other side to Nigel; the sole point of my being with him was so that we could teach this despicable hack a lesson and so I suppressed the emotion I had witnessed, merely reporting that things were going well, he was interested and keen to see me again. So the layers of deceit and secrecy that we thought we were weaving stealthily wove themselves about us, smothering our affections, encircling and binding us so that we could no longer reach out to each other.'

12

NINA

'*Bella* Majella,

'Those words are still lovely to me. *Bellezza!* Loveliness! we used to say if we had been parted for any time at all, rushing to kiss each other on either cheek. Our affection was spontaneous; we were always touching and hugging. *Affezione;* in Italian the word means both affection and disease.

'We were hardly ever parted. I paid infrequent visits to Maidstone after the first term in Belfast and other than your occasional trips to Pettigoe and a week I spent with Pablo, we were together. Unlike our fellow students, we didn't vanish for the long summer break, backpacking around Europe or further afield to South America, India; that kind of pleasure jaunt was for the uncommitted, those who had made no political analysis of the system they lived under. Our work was there for us in Belfast, rising early to sell papers at factory gates, running through dark streets quickly to stick protest posters onto army barracks and police stations or searching carefully for information on low wages and poor working conditions. In the summer of 1971 I slaved for eight hot weeks in a biscuit factory, on a three-shift system that bewildered my brain and turned my body clock upside down. I organised a union branch while I yawned and wrapped digestives and coconut creams; you packed shirts a couple of streets away, bloodying your fingers on collar pins while you had the workers' wages scrutinised by a tribunal.

'Finn didn't join us on the factory floor because he had to organise the socialist summer school in Donegal; a week in the wet north-west spent planning the next year's strategies and renewing our dedication with readings from Larkin, Connolly and Trotsky. We stayed with the families of comrades or sympathisers who inhabited sea-sprayed cottages in small fishing villages. The air was cold and tangy, laden with the briny reek of the catch that was brought in daily. After just ten minutes outside my fingers grew numb, my cheeks scalded by whipping winds. A harassed woman with five young children, all of whom had streaming noses and barking coughs, dished us up huge portions of scorching chilli while a baby swayed on her hip. I recall four nights spent on a cold stone floor in her outhouse, surrounded by fishing nets, lobster pots and diesel-sodden parts from an outboard motor. Unseasonal Atlantic winds lashed the thatch above, moaning and tugging so that I felt as if I was at sea, hoping that the rigging would survive the storm. You, Finn and myself were lined up in our sleeping bags like the herring stacked side by side in the wooden boxes on the quay; above my head, for no purpose that I could fathom, an ironing board was wedged into the rafters. I couldn't get warm; my nylon sleeping bag was ineffectual on a bare floor in that wild climate but I didn't complain because Finn would have been unimpressed.

'In the early hours of one morning I was woken by the twitching of my cold bones and a fierce gale that made the sea sound as if it was raging up the cliffs, about to swamp us at any moment. I was terror-struck, rigid in my nylon casing. I turned to see if you were awake and saw that Finn had climbed into your sleeping bag and was moving up and down on top of you, your groans absorbed by the storm outside. I closed my eyes and tried to find a spot of warmth in my own bedding. I was reassured by your love making but it accentuated my own aching for Pablo who wrote me infrequent but passionate letters. I was due to spend a week with him as soon as our summer school was over and my thoughts kept straying to his supple limbs. Momentarily traitorous, I imagined the sun of Spain or the heat and cultural bustle of Rome, where several of our seminar group had been passing the summer. Then my imaginings switched romantically to the couple in *For Whom the Bell Tolls*, entangled in their love-nest on a war-torn mountainside. I compared their cause to ours; honourable and daring, making something worthwhile out of life and I smiled in the darkness, a kind of blessing on you and Finn, while all the time envying the heat you were generating.

'I was a hopelessly romantic character then, swept off my feet by the charms of a fascinating people and country. Romantics are dangerous because of their ability to imbue everyday situations with loaded emotional meanings. I devoured early Yeats poems and book after book of Irish legends, stories of Deirdre, Finn MacCool, the children of Lir, Cuchulain, Oisin, the Fianna; I feasted on all that Celtic myth and web spinning, loved the rousing lyrics of the songs I had learned and which I sang the loudest in Mulligan's, cheered on by people who thought it wonderful that the wee English girl with the upper-class vowels had taken to the cause. At some point in the evening the cry would rise; come on now, Nina, give us a song, give us "Follow Me up to Carlow". I would willingly oblige. Here was I, the shy little rabbit as my father used to sometimes affectionately call me, a note of disappointment in his voice; here was I, holding an audience:

"See the swords of Glen Imayle
Flashing o'er the English pale,
See all the children of the Gael
Beneath O'Byrne's banners.
Rooster of a fighting stock,
Would you let a Saxon cock
Crow out upon an Irish rock?
Fly up and teach him manners!
Curse and swear, Lord Kildare
Feagh will do what Feagh will dare
Now, Fitzwilliam, have a care,
Fallen is your star low.
Up with halbert, out with sword,
On we'll go for by the Lord,
Feagh MacHugh has given the word,
Follow me up to Carlow."

'I became more Irish than the Irish themselves, embracing all aspects of the culture. I started to teach myself the language in any spare time I had, listening to a cassette while I lay in the bath, repeating words and phrases as I soaped my skin. On Wednesdays I attended Irish dancing classes run by a woman who claimed family kinship with Charles Parnell and I was soon executing jigs and reels. You had gone to such classes as a child and we often danced along the streets, stared at by soldiers, feet nimbly scampering, heads held high, arms straight by our sides.

'I already know some of the information my correspondent is sending me; I had touched on the burial rituals of ancient Irish cultures during my extensive studies of history books. My latest card has brought with it a sense of liberation, similar to the feeling I had when I took the decision to write this history. Before then, I was trapped behind a border in my mind, a closed frontier that seemed unscaleable; I paced behind it, looking up at its heights, wondering if I would find the courage to attempt a crossing. Then the unexpected; my illness produced physical frailty but also summoned a mental strength. Now my guide has taken me across that literal border, to County Down and I find that I am grateful to him or her. Yes, I thought as I read the description of Millin Bay; this is where it has all been leading, northwards, bringing me on the road I wanted to travel, the road to which I was always destined to return.

'Restless is my sleep since Wednesday morning, troubled is my heart unless you help me, God; last night I slept on an ill bed, soon I shall grow grey, while the black-haired lad comes to mind.'

Why is it that as soon as you cross the border everything feels different? There are the obvious reasons: the British soldiers (unobtrusive these days), the larger road signs in English, the neatness, the red, white and blue kerbstones in some villages, defiant tricolours in others, the red postboxes. But it is more than that; the very air seems tense and there is a sense of life boxed in. In the south, you pass old battle sites from Cromwell's time and before or a crossroads where there was a Civil-War skirmish. In the north, placenames ring with the associations of recent explosions, murders, tortures; death that took place yesterday. But there is no north/south division when it comes to ancient places of interment; all is equal in terms of bone fragments and grave goods, just as now, the earth doesn't enquire if a Prod or Taig is being lowered down but takes them both back indifferently.

This burial site at Millin Bay, near Portaferry, is only a hundred yards or so from the sea. The defleshed bones of about fifteen bodies were found here in the 1950s. Unusually, there seems to have been carelessness with this burial because teeth had been replaced in the wrong sockets in some skulls. Perhaps for some reason it was a hurried ritual; no grave goods were discovered, which might back up this theory. There is a good deal of conjecture about all such graves. Since the nineteenth century, scholars have come up with different and conflicting ideas about meanings and customs. It is difficult, interpreting the ancient past; a long, slow process of fitting together traces of evidence.

'So, Majella, we are nearly there, nearly at the place where this all began. People who read this account might say that it began the day we met, others when I joined Red Dawn or on the August night when Finn came in, waving a copy of the *Daily Echo*, announcing that the British press was sinking to new depths. "Gobshites", he said, "gutter gobshites, twisting the facts to suit their own tabloid rags". We were drying each other's hair and I saw the newspaper through a skein of yours as I moved the hot air along its length, feeling the warm curls sweet with the scent of apple conditioner spring under my fingers. We used to brush each other's hair regularly. I would anticipate the tingle on my scalp as you swept with long deft strokes, bearing downwards, then up, lifting the curls from the nape of my neck. Goose pimples raced across my back as the brush rasped. You would pick the down of discarded fuzz from the brush and throw it into the fire where it hissed and sighed, dissolving.'

Nina smiled, whispering *'bellezza!'* into the silence of the room. The word seemed to echo, seeking corners, rustling under the skirting.

She wrote, 'Martin, this domestic scene is deceptive and yet so much of what I remember from Rock House is framed by images of cosy fires, comforting food, laughter, ease. Not at all the kind of setting for serious revolutionaries. And we were so serious, especially Finn. Although sales of *Workers' Struggle* never reached beyond a couple of hundred copies, he saw himself as a proper independent newspaper editor at the cutting edge of the Ulster scene. Occasionally he hinted that he envisaged a career as a freelance writer; he had contributed a couple of articles to local papers in the Republic, one of which had been picked up and reprinted in a Dublin national. Several left-wing journals in London had paid him for pieces about Northern Ireland and a TV crew from CBS in New York had interviewed him in the kitchen about Irish socialism. I recall peering around the door as they ran through the script; they wore jeans, hiking boots and plaid shirts and their voices were loud, jaunty. Finn, dressed in black, sat with his chair tilted back looking perfectly composed, as if he did this daily. There was great kudos for Red Dawn in the interview; he referred to the group several times as the cameras turned and featured the programme on the front page of the next edition of the paper. *Red Dawn Crosses the Atlantic*, ran the headline.

'We had often discussed the sins of the press. On Sundays Finn would buy all the British papers, hefting them on to the kitchen table as we ate breakfast; it was important to keep an eye on the lies the enemy was telling and to counter them at every available opportunity. Even the quality broadsheets didn't escape our regular censure; they were all owned by capitalist fat cats. Over bacon and eggs we examined the slant being put on the certain truths that we knew and gasped with anger at some of the distortions we read. The tabloids were the worst, trivialising, reducing every situation to trite drama. Belfast was swarming with reporters then, the British press tripping over Americans, French, Italians and Scandinavians. They were underfoot everywhere, holding microphones in front of shoppers, visiting bars to find local "colour", pointing cameras at sectarian street decorations, filming in-depth documentaries about this overwhelming resurgence of the Troubles. Children collected rubber bullets for them, demonstrated home-assembled petrol bombs and posed near British soldiers, fingers held in gestures of defiance. Passers-by became expert in offering opinions in soundbites, men who had had nothing to do with the IRA for years straightened their shoulders and talked knowledgeably about guerilla fighting, street tactics and Armalites. It seemed that there was no one in Belfast who hadn't been photographed or interviewed; the place was like a huge film set with everyone ready to speak their lines.

'There was one reporter in particular, a Nigel Howes, whose stories angered us. The *Daily Echo* had a firmly right-wing slant and all of his reports glorified the actions of the army and the RUC; why didn't he save his time and just reprint army statements verbatim, we said scornfully. He had described several demonstrations we attended as mob rule, denounced all Catholics as terrorist sympathisers and specialised in pieces about "our boys" and how much they missed all the folks back home; the accompanying pictures of smiling Tommies bore no resemblance to the half-crazed men we witnessed smashing down doors in Republican areas or screeching through the streets in jeeps, yelling abuse.

'The story exercising Finn that morning was the worst yet; Nigel Howes was reporting on the death of a young man who had once expressed interest in Red Dawn after flirting with various other organisations. In the end he had joined an anarchist group instead, an outfit even smaller than ours. Finn had met him a couple of times before deciding he wasn't a suitable recruit and thought that he had probably drifted around the edges of the IRA as well. He described him as a naive youth, a bit of a misfit. Maybe he had crossed someone, maybe he wasn't streetwise enough to deal with the circles he moved in or was dealing drugs and fell foul of a moralising gunman but he ended up dead, just one more casualty of the confusion of weapons in Belfast. Nigel Howes had sniffed out some of his background and chose to make it a "human interest" story. He focused on a young man from a poor but decent home who had been led astray by – and I recall the words exactly because they burned into our consciousness – "self-seeking, tinpot leftie groups with weird ideas and tub-thumping propaganda. They're bunches of no-hopers who have never done a day's work, live off the dole or the tax payer, have never gained anyone's vote and think they can tell the rest of us how to live." As Finn read that out to us his voice shook with an anger I'd never heard in him before.

'We were outraged. We pored over the article, jeering at the cheap sentimentality of the language but furious, too. Our mood had been positively evangelical during that month; we had returned from Donegal fired with new vigour for the struggle, filled with zeal for fighting the good fight. That August, internment had been introduced. Belfast erupted in a frenzy of gunfights and burning buildings. Going out to buy a loaf of bread was a hazardous activity. Terrified Catholics had headed for the south, convinced that genocide was imminent. Nigel's words made a mockery of their misery and were a direct challenge to us by the smug hierarchies we were pledged to oppose.

'There are two things I realise now that I couldn't see then. We took ourselves so seriously that we interpreted Nigel's report as a personal attack rather than the easily penned jibe it undoubtedly was. We had no understanding that we mattered hardly at all, that few people were aware of our existence, especially the readership of the *Daily Echo*. That article fed Finn's paranoia, a mental state that I couldn't have acknowledged or understood then. There was the whole business of altering the times and locations of Red Dawn meetings, based on Finn's belief that we were being watched by the police, the army or rival groups – perhaps all of them. There was little reason for believing that, we posed no threat to anyone, the IRA dismissed us as cranks and if the authorities took any interest in us, I'm sure it was a passing one. But the history of Irish rebellion is riddled with informers, turncoats, betrayed plans and mishaps and we lived in a city where any house might contain a band of conspirators, where the whole of society could be described as paranoid: people checked under their cars for bombs before driving to work as casually as they picked up the milk or post. There were streets you didn't walk, shops you never visited, pubs you gave a wide berth to and men you didn't tell your name to if you had any sense. At any time your neighbour a few streets away might be planning your death – maybe not a personal death if you were the haphazard casualty of a bomb or other random attack but death all the same. How can living like that not twist your perceptions?

'Finn's paranoia wasn't unusual or abnormal, just more intense than that indulged in by most of us and entangled with his overwhelming ego. And it was contagious; he infected all of us with his suspicions, exaggerating our importance in the process. He personally investigated the background and credentials of anyone who wanted to join the group because of his conviction that the security forces might try to plant someone in our midst. We must learn from what had happened in Paris in '69 and amongst anti-war groups in the States, he warned; they had been undermined by informers and secret agents. He spoke of planted evidence and malicious convictions coupled with long jail sentences. He took different routes on his journeys through the city and insisted we do the same. When letters arrived he examined them carefully, holding them up to the light, running his finger along the flap to check the seal. He often claimed to have found evidence of tampering. At times he was sure that the phone was being tapped and would instruct us to make calls from public boxes. So we were woven into his world of secrets, imagining adversaries against whom we needed to protect ourselves, genuinely fearful of entrapment.

'My recent stay with Pablo in Bilbao had bolstered our awareness of the potential enemies around us. I didn't see much of the town or of Pablo's comrades during that week because he and I took a sabbatical from active politics between his sheets. We consumed each other night and day; I was like a person who has spent years on dry rations and discovers the delights of endless, rich courses. In the brief pauses after long bouts of lovemaking I gleaned some knowledge of the cell Pablo worked with, although he was economical with information. The less I knew, he said, the better; all I needed to understand was that he was as dedicated to his cause as I was to mine. So he was willing to talk about the broad issues of Basque politics before we lay back again, hardly registering that the sun had risen and set and we hadn't left the bed. I did gather that his cell had been infiltrated the previous year by a police informer. The informer had been discovered just in time; the cell members narrowly escaped arrest and were forced to reorganise after they had dealt with him. I didn't ask what this dealing with had meant; Pablo's comrade Miguel had referred obliquely to it one evening when he dropped by and I gathered that he had carried out the punishment. He sat on the end of Pablo's bed, cleaning his handgun, drinking a can of beer. We were in the bed, naked, sharing a dish of chicken and olives and I moved closer to Pablo, conscious of the danger he faced daily. That night I dreamed that I saw him lying dead, his handsome torso bloodied by bullets and I woke and clung to him, thinking how vulnerable we are in sleep, unable to bear the thought that a traitor might have taken him from me.

'I related this story on my return, thus playing my own significant part in justifying Finn's insistence on constant vigilance.

'Finn took the most personal affront from Nigel's article. He became convinced that the reporter had discovered his name during investigations and might be thinking of mounting a campaign against us. He took the reference to propaganda as a direct attack on his creation, the newspaper he edited and produced.

'He sat there that morning, chewing his nails, chainsmoking, barely touching his food. His chair screeched on the stone-flagged floor as he twisted in it and shook the offending front page in the air. This kind of crap shouldn't be tolerated, he said, people like this shouldn't be allowed to call themselves journalists. It was a pity some of the boys didn't teach him a lesson.

'Majella and I looked at each other and then at him, startled because what he had said was so far from the policy we usually followed; we understood the armed struggle but couldn't condone it. What Finn had uttered was a kind of heresy. I asked if he really meant that and he shot me a look, saying yes, he did; the British press thought they could say what they liked, distort the facts to make a story palatable to their readership. They flew in, hung out on expense accounts at places like the Pine Trees Hotel and wrote most of their junk in a whisky-sodden haze with complete contempt for people living here. He lit another cigarette from the glowing butt in his mouth; an example needed to be made, a bit of their dirt should be thrown back at them.

'Day after day, night after night, he returned to the subject until it seemed that we talked about nothing else and we too began to see this Nigel Howes as our arch-enemy, a symbol of the rottenness that pervaded the tabloid press. Further articles by Nigel appeared, fanning our anger: an attack on a playgroup run by nationalist women, saying that it was a school for little terrorists of the future, a piece claiming that Catholic youths inserted glass and nails into spent rubber bullets and then alleged that they had been doctored by squaddies. In September came the report that brought things to a head. It barricaded Finn deeper in that fortification in his mind and helped to decide Nigel's fate. He had got hold of a copy of *Workers' Struggle*, the one which contained our manifesto, a ten-point agenda for a fairer deal for the Irish working class. Looking back, I can't recall that it made outrageous demands; it was full of rallying calls for fairer wages and working conditions and for British troops to be withdrawn, all pitched in that aggressive style we favoured, punctuated by too many angry exclamation marks. Nigel's article was set around a photo of our manifesto. The headline shouted, *The Skivers' Ten Commandments*. He had produced a sarcastic piece about the commies and Trots who were trying to stir up trouble in a war-torn city; the rent-a-leftie brigade, making political capital out of other people's misery. *Try telling the little girl who had her leg blown off in the market and was cradled in the comforting arms of a burly Tommy about your manifesto, Comrade!*

'Red Dawn was up in arms at that week's meeting. There were demands that this reporter should be made to retract, that we should launch a blistering counter-offensive via our own paper, that we should ask sister organisations in England to picket the *Daily Echo* office. Finn listened to the outcry but unusually for him, said little. He looked tense and withdrawn and kept clicking the top of his biro in and out, making a sound like the cockroaches who emerged in the kitchen at night. When people turned to him he commented that we should be cautious, think carefully about our response, but that he would certainly write a hard-hitting editorial. Maybe, he added, this Nigel Howes was a government agitator, trying to draw us out and make ourselves vulnerable. No doubt the editor of the *Echo* hobnobbed with government ministers, army top brass and MI5; the establishment lived in each other's pockets; that was how they sustained their influence. That gave us food for thought and the meeting ended sombrely.

'As we walked home that night I was warier than usual, glancing behind me, watching for anything suspicious. Majella and I had been discussing Che Guevara's writings and later, in the living room, I copied lines from *Venceremos!* that we found particularly inspiring. I wrote them in the notebook I kept for Important Revolutionary Thoughts that I gleaned or made up for myself. I still have it, with its red (of course) cover and frayed spine. I was sitting on the floor by the fire. Finn was playing the piano, one of those wandering, discordant tunes that set my teeth on edge and Majella was working on a pair of jeans, sewing v-shaped vents into the leg bottoms. There was a damp green log in the grate, making the fire hiss and spit and a Heavenly Lotus joss stick was smoking in a milk bottle. By the fender, keeping warm, was a pot of the coffee we were drinking from a set of delicate white and green bone china cups that had come from Finn's grandmother. The cream we added to it from the matching milk jug had been provided by Majella's mother's cows, those beasts that she loved and called by name, tapping their flanks affectionately.

'Half-way through the musty pages of that notebook, which still seems to have a lingering whiff of Heavenly Lotus, I find the passage that I bent over, scribbling:

"You have got to be ready to sacrifice any individual benefit for the common good. Each human grouping is more important than the individual . . . we must be inflexible in the face of error, weakness, deceit, bad faith . . . never compromise revolutionary principles."

'I read those lines out to Majella and Finn and they nodded silently. Finn broke into the "St Louis Blues" and Majella said to me that if there was ever deceit and bad faith, Nigel Howes embodied it.

'"But what can be done about people like him?" I asked. "We can't take on all of the British press and he's got a much bigger readership than we can ever attract."

'Majella lifted her hair back, absentmindedly touching her repaired tooth. Her index finger often wandered to it, especially when a hot drink had made it sensitive.

'"I don't know," she replied, echoing my feelings of frustration. "But we know the odds are stacked against us. We can only work day by day to make a difference."

'Finn shut the piano lid and came and stood by the fire, throwing another log on, securing it with his foot. He had let his hair grow longer; it was touching his shoulders and had a few white strands that contrasted starkly with his thick black curls.

'"Sometimes the revolutionary process has to take a quantum leap," he said quietly, half musingly. "The slow daily struggle isn't enough. Some of that inflexibility Guevara identified is needed."

'Majella poured more coffee, took a couple of slices of her mother's home-made ginger cake, handed one to Finn and continued sewing. I carried on scribing important thoughts. If that was when Finn started to formulate his plan, neither of us noticed. He often paced the room or stood by the fire, working ideas and strategies out aloud. So it is that the seeds of terrible things germinate, while people are going about their everyday business, enjoying their supper, mending clothes, occupied with the routines they employ to shore up their lives.

'What a story I am telling you, Martin, but not one to tell to your children. I do hope that you will have children one day but keep them safe from any knowledge of me, of the wolf-woman with the grim past.'

13

NINA

'Cara Majella,

'I am in hospital at the moment, terribly weak. They've put me on another drug and it has slowed me down even more. This morning it has taken me an hour to consume a cup of soup and a slice of bread. I didn't want the food but I have to keep something in my stomach or the drugs make me nauseous. All that energy expended for so little reason! For a fleeting moment I did feel regret for the appetite and quickness I used to possess. I'd have loved to crave "the full works" or do a few steps of a reel.

'I am afraid now, Majella, afraid that I will deteriorate rapidly before I can finish this business. They say that people who are dying always know, there's an inner wisdom telling them they're leaving. I am full of a new lassitude, a feeling of apartness. I think it is a sign that something momentous is soon to overtake me; if not death, a rapid slide to more helplessness. Last night I caught myself thinking that maybe I should abandon this plan. What good are you going to achieve after all these years? a persuasive voice whispered.

What is the point of reawakening an old tragedy? Those thoughts lulled me for a while before I saw how easy, how deceptive they were. My courage was ebbing, drained by a drug cocktail and the lifeless hospital air. So now I have bolstered my courage, forcing down food and I have a small brandy in my bag to fortify me. I am facing that last stretch of road, the one out of Belfast, heading north into dark countryside.

'I have received my last letter card from Antrim. The writer is approaching the ultimate destination.

Will you be relieved or anxious to know that this is the final one of these strange missives? Maybe by now you've become used to them, look forward to them even. It has been a fascinating pilgrimage for me, an opportunity to ponder the complex history of this island as well as a journey into the past. They say that if you want to comprehend what is to come, you should look carefully at what has gone before.

Reflect on this irony; Antrim may well have been the place where, during the Mesolithic age, the first settlers came to this part of Ireland from Scotland, via the North Channel. Archaeologists base this theory partly on the similarity between the Irish graves of this period and their Scottish and English counterparts. So death and the rituals of death have linked Ireland to her old enemies for long centuries, to a time before she viewed her nearest neighbours as foe.

Antrim is another county rich in burial chambers and more modern tales of death and the manner in which people were despatched. In the seventeenth century at Islandmagee the garrison attacked local people, killing hundreds. Bodies were thrown over the cliffs to be sucked down in the waves: 'but the sea beasts have your eyes and the crabs have your mouth and your long, soft white hands that would be fishing for salmon.' There is a Protestant graveyard in Ballycarry which bears witness to some of those who died bloodily in the 1798 rebellion. A memorial placed there by Freemasons cries, 'Erin, loved land! From age to age be thou more great, more famed and free.' I stood fascinated before this. It could have been written by any of Ireland's warring factions. The sentiments of fervent nationalism do not vary, it is the nationhood aspired to that causes spilt blood. And yet the planters who inscribed that stone held kinship with much earlier settlers, perhaps tool makers who were attracted by the flint visible on the Antrim cliffs from the Scottish shore.

There is an ideology among some in this country now that people should look forward and put the past aside. Irish dancers and theme pubs are invading Europe, in whose embrace many hope sectarian conflict will be soothed. But perhaps the way the Irish dwell on centuries of conflict, constantly picking over old scores and injustices isn't the problem at all; perhaps the real problem is that they don't go back far enough into their history.

I am writing this in a B&B near Cushendall. I am both satisfied and saddened at my journey's end. The weight of what I know hangs heavy on me; *'I too was happy for a time but ah, my figure is worn away! The world's per-secutions have come against me, there is no strength in me but sorrow.'*

Earlier this afternoon I walked to Ossian's grave, a Neo-lithic court grave which stands above a valley. Scotland can be seen in fine weather like today's. Turning, looking south, I viewed the glens rolling down towards Larne and thought, if only time could be turned back, if only wrongs could be undone!

There is a song – there is always a song about anywhere you care to name in Ireland! – with the lines, 'the green *glens of Antrim are calling to me.' Does the north, does Belfast ever beckon you? Or is it always shrouded in a bleak mist?*

There is more to do, but that is a story for another day. Tonight I am going to permit myself a trip to the cinema and reading matter other than literature about Irish antiquities.

'I have never harboured any desire to return to Ireland. I once vetoed Martin's suggestion of a holiday on the west coast of Scotland because I knew that the Antrim coast could be seen from certain places there. If this is Finn writing to me, he has changed beyond recognition in his views and sentiments, in his – reflective – tone. But of course there is no reason why he shouldn't have changed, it would be most strange if he had not. And yet, if it is him, I find that I begrudge his alteration. It doesn't seem fair that he should be allowed to represent himself as tolerant and insightful when he was so fierce and influential with his narrow credo back then.

'Finn was chewing a stick of coltsfoot on the evening when he made us an offer of doing something significant for the cause. It was the one sweet he indulged in, strolling to the corner shop where they were kept in a tall glass jar. Occasionally, when you or I called at the shop for matches or chocolate we bought him a supply. Six chalky coloured sticks for ten pence in a small white bag which exuded a smoky cinnamon scent. Since then, subject to one of those connections that stealthily criss-cross our lives without our noticing, I have always associated the aroma of cinnamon with fearful excitement.

'It was the third week of September and the weather had suddenly grown frosty. My room had lost its accumulated summer's warmth, although the gains in temperature and in the lessening of damp in July and August were offset by the heat's encouragement of rank drain smells. I was looking forward to the winter despite the chilblains I had suffered the previous year, my circulation slowing in the Arctic conditions of the basement. Belfast was a city suited to winter; harsh cold seemed a fitting backdrop to the grimness of barbed wire, forbidding security gates, streets tattered with the debris of civil disobedience, the chill edge of strife. Long, light summer nights were unkind, exposing the misery that the early dusk cloaked and softened.

'Down in my room at night I had resumed wrapping myself in a sleeping bag beneath my sheets and blankets, my vulnerable toes encased in woollen climbing socks. Your mother had seen me scratching my chilblains and shook her head over my raw red toes. She gave me two stone hot water bottles that imparted a steady heat to my sheets but I only used them when desperate because when they fell from the bed they created a crash like the aftershock of a bomb.

'After we had struck our blow for the cause I couldn't get warm at all, I was cold in a way that the hot water bottles could not touch, even when I lay with my arms around them. To my great anguish, our friendship cooled too. On the night we heard Finn's plan I turned to you and the way you regarded me had already changed. At the time I thought it your fear signalling but your eyes were never the same again; they held a cloudiness that gradually became as much of a barrier as if we had built a wall.'

The phone rang. Nina answered and conversed for a few minutes, holding the receiver under her chin while she administered her eye drops. When she had finished speaking she took two painkillers and continued writing.

'Martin, you have just rung to ask how I am and to check which bedding plants I want you to bring at the weekend.

I made my voice calm and unconcerned, continuing to be duplicitous. It would be hard to make you understand the mixture of anguish and relief I carry with me constantly now. You are coming to the dark heart of my story. Pour yourself a gin or whisky, something strong to help digest it. Now you see how our life together was scripted and circumscribed by the life I had lived before, like lingering mini tremors after the shattering earthquake.

'On the Thursday Finn drew his disciples together, Majella and I had been to an anti-internment demonstration in the city centre, a violent meeting where police had waded in with truncheons, sending the crowd fleeing. On the way home we stopped in the botanical gardens so that I could rest my ankle which I had twisted while running. Finn had been busy, vanishing for hours, looking preoccupied when he returned. I had seen him studying a map and assumed he was working out new locations for paper sales. One evening his boots were muddy and wringing wet when he had come in and Majella had complained because he'd commandeered the oven to dry them out, upsetting her plans for baked potatoes. The boots had smelt terrible as they dried, releasing fetid odours. Majella had asked where on earth he had been, a slurry pit? He hadn't replied, frowning as he'd turned chops in the pan.

'We were preoccupied ourselves, trying to fit in some of the reading we were supposed to have done for the start of our final year but which had been neglected for our political activities. We settled down to study during the evening, a pile of buttered toast between us. A stacked fire was burning in the grate, piled with chunks of wood from a rotting sycamore tree that Finn had chopped down in the garden. The velvet curtains were pulled tight against the night and we had dragged cushions off the sofa and positioned them in front of the blaze. I was making headway with Camus, registering a mild irritation with Finn who arrived back late and brought a keen chill in from the streets.

'"What route did you take home after the demonstration?" he asked.

'Majella told him, saying that we'd dodged around back streets despite my ankle. We were following the plan, varying our movements.

'"Good. And you're sure you weren't followed?"

'"As sure as we can be."

'"I kept checking every time I stopped to rub my ankle," I said. "I'm certain we weren't."

'He seemed satisfied and carried on rustling in the background, moving books. I was aware of him going to the door of the room several times, looking out, then closing it again and crossing back to the window where he glanced out from the edge of the curtain. Majella made an exasperated noise in her throat and asked could he not settle down? When he didn't respond she raised her eyebrows at me and inched her cushion forwards, resting her boots against the fender. Finally, crunching the coltsfoot, Finn fetched a third cushion and joined us in front of the fire, staring into the flames for a few minutes.

'"I must interrupt your literary studies, comrades," he said, very softly, quickly. "There's something more important than Camus and Baudelaire that we need to discuss."

'Majella looked up. "It had better be good, I'm way behind with this."

'"It's daring and risky. A lightning strike, a blow for revolutionary progress. Do you want to hear it?"

'"Go on," I said, turning down my page. Finn was pale, his eyes flinty. Some creamy coltsfoot powder had dropped on to the front of his slate-coloured polo neck and lay there disregarded. He was usually fastidious about such things.

'"What is it?" Majella asked. "A new poster campaign? Getting into police stations to hand out leaflets?" I was expecting some such suggestion, an innovative method of spreading our message.

'"No, this is something more radical. I've been considering it from all angles for a fortnight and I think it's achievable. It's to do with a certain reporter from the *Daily Echo*."

'"Howes?" Majella asked. Her firm voice carried clearly.

'Finn put a finger to his lips. "Keep it down, for God's sake, Majella. Just listen. What I'm going to say is to be heard only by the three of us. It is never to be told outside this room. It must be discussed carefully, with utmost regard to security. I can't emphasise that too much. Do you follow me?"

'"You mean the rest of the group isn't to know?" I asked. I had never heard such a thing before; our ethos was democratic centralism, full debate and action by consensus.

'"That's right. It would be too dangerous. It would be a decision and a risk run by us three alone."

'I felt a shiver of anticipation on the back of my neck. I looked at Majella, thinking that she might already have some inkling of what was in Finn's mind but she had a puzzled expression.

'He leaned towards us, the tips of his fingers pressed together, speaking rapidly. "I've been keeping an eye on Howes for a while, turning the tables, getting *my* story on *him*. He visits army HQ with great regularity, no doubt passing on whatever he thinks might be useful to their surveillance of nationalists and socialists. I'm sure it's no coincidence that after he called in there last Friday, several Sinn Féin members he'd talked to were arrested. He was viewing the demo this afternoon, parked nice and warm on the first floor of a department store. I expect he was scanning faces, waiting to finger people to the pigs."

'"I didn't know you were at the demo," Majella interrupted.

'"I took care not to be seen. I was the one doing the watching. This man is highly dangerous. Who knows when he might finger us? I keep expecting a hammering on the front door. I don't see why we should sit and wait for that bastard to make a move on us so I've taken the fight to the enemy, watched his slimy manoeuvres. To put it at its simplest, we relieve the world of the poisonous snake that is Nigel Howes. We execute him in the interests of working people and cut off his obscene libels. If he's left to carry on, workers and their organisations will suffer. He hangs about the Pine Trees Hotel early in the evenings, drinking and picking up dregs of tittle-tattle. Nina, you proved your use to us before with British soldiers, your accent was a huge asset. You could disguise yourself and engineer a meeting with him in the bar. He's fed up, probably not having the best time of his life; a sympathetic girl from back home would be just the ticket. You could go out with him a few times, gain his confidence and maybe some useful tips for us in the process. He probably knows which journalists are in the security forces' pockets and which have infiltrated left-wing groups. Information is power; we know that lesson well, I hope."

' I nodded. The base of my back felt cold where the draught from under the ill-fitting door was sidling across the room. If I had wanted to speak, I couldn't have.

'"Go on," Majella said, grasping the tips of her boots in her hands, staring into the fire.

'"I think Nina would only have to go out with him a couple of times. Then you'd suggest that a friend – that's you, Majella – would like to come along one night. You'd invite him on a visit to a little out-of-hours shebeen in the Antrim glens; his kind are suckers for that type of 'real'

Irish experience. Somewhere out in the country, at a spot we'll identify, you say you can hear a strange noise under the bonnet. You pull up and Majella shoots Howes. You bury him a bit further on. I've been to look at an ideal spot at a house that's being built there. The workmen have dug a trench about six feet deep that they're gradually filling with rubble. It's a ready-made grave; you'd only have to dig down a little way to conceal the body. The builders will do the rest for you with their debris added on top. No body will be found, there'll be nothing to link us to any of it.''

'I saw his boots, the tongues curling in the open oven, like in a still from a Chaplin comedy and the sticky clay he had scraped from them.

'"Where do we get the gun?" Majella asked.

'"I've a gun an uncle left me. It's hidden here in the house; you don't need to know where. Shooting him in the head from close range means there'll be little mess. I read it up." He leaned across and touched my arm. "I've thought of it that way, Nina, with Majella using the gun, because she's handled a shotgun in the past, on the farm. She's shot rabbits and foxes, gutted chickens and turkeys. She won't get queasy. It would be quick. The hardest bit will be burying him but Majella's strong.''

'He sat back, watching us. I wondered what kind of book he had read to inform himself of the best way to shoot a man at close range; I saw him making notes, copying a diagram. Then I thought of all the nights we had settled by the fire in similar positions, talking about pamphlets, statements, demonstrations. Wordy issues, the worst penalty for which might be a bruised head or a night in police cells. I didn't know about Majella's experience with a gun. I knew that she could milk cows, drive a tractor and wrestle a pig to staple a tag on its ear.

'"It's murder," I said indistinctly. I looked at Majella, trying to gauge her thoughts.

'She was still bent forward over her boots, flexing her feet. "It certainly is," she agreed. "A bit different to potting a bunny and taking it home for stew."

'"You're a long way from the farm in Pettigoe now,' Finn told her. 'You're a revolutionary; sometimes you must take a great leap forwards. I prefer to call it an execution, the deserved end for a traitor of the working class."

'"You really think that Howes is supplying the forces with information?" Majella asked.

'"Sure of it. He was with a guy in the Pine Trees one night who was definitely Special Branch. They had their heads together for over an hour. Nina's told us what the outcome of that kind of betrayal can be; look at Pablo's cell. We've spent so long building here, hours of hard work and persuasion. We can't let that shit ruin it all, it's up to us to take action. When it's accomplished, I'll ring the pigs and announce it. Then the other hacks will think twice about what they're committing to paper.

'"I've prepared a brief statement." He tapped his forehead. "It's in here, nothing written, no evidence, succinct and ambiguous to prevent identification: 'Nigel Howes of the *Daily Echo* has been executed by Irish freedom fighters. Let all British press scum take warning from his death.'" He stood up, putting a trembling hand on the mantelpiece. "I realise it's a lot to ask of you but I know that I can trust you both entirely. Believe me, I considered other members of the group but this plan relies on women's courage and in the end I knew it had to be kept close and true, you were the only choice. I can't guarantee that it will go smoothly or that we won't be caught. But I'm convinced that the idea I've come up with will keep the risk to a minimum. Let's face it, there are so many splinter nationalist factions, the security forces won't know where to start looking. And I'm sure they won't think of women. When you weigh up the risks, we're just as vulnerable sitting here doing nothing." He picked up the Victorian tray featuring skaters at dusk. "I'll make fresh coffee. Think it over."

'"Did you have any idea about this?" I whispered to Majella as he closed the door.

'"No. He kept it close to his chest. I can see why."

'"What do you think?"

'"Would you have the nerve?" she asked.

'At that moment there was a loud rap at the front door and we both turned, hearing Finn go to answer. I pictured the army or police out there or, even worse, a plain-clothes snatch squad. In those seconds before he reached the door I saw us beaten and mutilated, held incommunicado, forced to sign confessions. The ankle I had twisted earlier in the day as I dashed past a meaty policeman twitched with pain. The set of Majella's shoulders told me she had the same thoughts. When we heard that it was one of the upstairs tenants who'd forgotten his key we exhaled nervously.

'"Jesus!" she said. "Talk about an anti-climax!"

'"It might have been, though. It might have been them coming for us."

'"I always imagine them arriving in the early hours, when we're at our most vulnerable, dragging us from bed, laughing as they watch us dress. It happened to Annie, that woman in Andersonstown who hid the ammunition. She said it was like being raped."

'I gazed at the freckles on the bridge of her nose, remembering the evening in summer when I'd counted them while she made grass bracelets for our wrists. Her shoulders had been eggshell brown, her breath sweet as she laughed, complaining that my little finger tickled as it moved across her skin. I knew that I would do anything to defend her. The thought of anyone abusing her made me fierce. Pablo had said that despite the risks involved, there was a strong argument for striking at the enemy before they could strike at you. But to take a gun, to end a life?

'I rubbed the tops of my arms. "I don't know if I've got the nerve, I honestly don't. Couldn't we try warning him off first?"

'"I'm not sure his kind heed warnings. Anyway, Finn will have thought about that, you know he always looks at things thoroughly before reaching a decision. He must have decided it wouldn't work."

'"Yes, I suppose." I was thinking of those highly publicised killings of the last decade: Jack Kennedy, Martin Luther King and the descriptions of shattered skulls and seeping brains. Those had been done with high-powered rifles, though; a small handgun would be different. I pictured a neat wound, just one tiny dark puncture like a burn mark on cloth.

'What made me even consider what Finn suggested? What made me willing to erase the word "murder" from my mind and substitute "execution", that wonderful salve to the conscience with its hint of judicial sentence? It wasn't only the thought of what a different rap at the door might augur, I think it was that phrase of Finn's, "close and true". It made me feel wanted, important. I think I must admit to that. After all, everything that was essential to me was there in that room. I had nothing else; they were my friends, closer, more intimate than any blood tie I had ever had, the family I shared my life with.

'And then there was the heroine factor, our view of ourselves as feisty, revolutionary women, proud inheritors of Krupskaya, Kollontai, Luxemburg and all the unsung Bolsheviks in long dresses. How many times had we bemoaned the fact that women were shadowy figures in the history of the Irish struggle? Apart from Grace O'Malley in Tudor times and the bold Constance Markievicz there were no female role models. Irish history otherwise gave us only Kitty O'Shea, seen as an adulteress who led to a fine man's downfall or the fictional Kathleen Ní Houlihán, grieving mother figure. We discounted Bernadette Devlin on the basis that she had sold out, taken a seat in Westminster and become a well-meaning puppet.

'Oh, Martin, there was no grey in our construction of the world, only stark, unforgiving black and white. Oh yes, we had said as we donned our badges proclaiming, *Beneath every woman's curve there lies a muscle*, it was high time that Irish women stopped crying over their troubles and stepped into the fight, high time that they used those muscles. Majella was wearing that badge there before the fire and her reply to me was pregnant with our urge to be trail blazers for Ireland's oppressed women.

'"Finn's right, only women comrades could carry this plan out. I've always thought that I'd have to make one particular, great commitment to the revolution, something far bigger than I'd ever done before. Every revolutionary must be prepared for that and not expect to choose what it will be. This would be a positive action. We'd be safeguarding our comrades and sending the state an unequivocal message." Her voice was steady but with a charge that spoke to my own impetuosity.

'"I know, I understand what you're saying and I want to make a big commitment, too."

'"You're not sure about it though," she reflected.

'"It's so final," I whispered. "Are you sure?"

'Our excitement and fear was flowing back and forth between us but her will was strong. I felt it suck at me like a forceful tide. She nodded. "If Finn has decided it's necessary then it is, I accept the deal."

'Finn came back in then with fresh coffee, moving quietly. "Well?" he asked.

' "I'm on for it," Majella said, "but Nina's not sure. She thinks we should warn him off first."

'Finn laughed. "When have the Brits ever heeded Irish warnings? The point about being an Imperialist coloniser, Nina, is that you don't have to pay any attention to the protests of the colonised. You might as well warn the moon to stay out of the night sky."

' "I just don't know," I said, feeling feeble and distracted.

'Finn played his cards absolutely right. He didn't push or argue any further that night. "Think about it," he said. "Take two days, then let me know. If you feel you can't, then you can't. I'll only point out that you are absolutely the right person to gain Howes' trust. I could consider Ita, I suppose, she might fit the bill with encouragement."

'With the benefit of hindsight, I'm sure that Finn would never have gone to another member of the group. Extending the potential membership of the plan would have been too risky. His mention of Ita was meant to raise my anxieties because she was a newer comrade than myself, a little green and nervy. He knew that I would agonise over it, fret about her and feel ashamed that she might be willing to attempt what I would not. He was a consummate tactician and he knew me well, better than I knew myself.

'In the end, I didn't need two days to agonise. The following afternoon Majella was missing from our seminar. Another student handed me a note from her: "Finn lifted by the army this morning. Come home asap." I pretended to feel sick and tore back, my imagination ablaze with visions of Finn being beaten with rifle butts or tortured with electrodes. When I fell through the door she met me in the hall. Her eyes were red-rimmed.

' "Where is he?" I asked wildly, holding my side where I had developed a stitch.

' "In bed. They kept him for hours, then turfed him out."

' "What did they do to him? Where did they lift him?"

' "He's bruised on his back and chin where some pig sat on him in the Land-Rover. They got him outside the ship-yards; he was selling papers. Vinny saw it happen, he came and found me in the library. I went down to the barracks but they wouldn't let me in so I waited outside and then he came out through the gates. He was unsteady, pale with pain." She turned, pressing her forehead against the wall. "God, Nina, I thought I'd never see him again or he'd be paralysed or something. They've thrown people down stair-cases before."

'I placed the side of my head by hers. I could feel the damp heat of fear. "You should have come and found me straight away."

' "There wasn't time, I'd no idea where you were on cam-pus." She took a shuddering breath. "He's asleep now. They asked him all about Red Dawn and who he knew in the IRA and – oh, it's horrible, the insults . . ." She covered her face with her hands.

' "What?" I asked, "what did they say?"

' "Things about us."

' "What things, Majella?" I was impatient, I wanted to shake her. I scratched my fingernails down the wall.

' "They told him they knew about his harem, the tarts he lived with. Asked him if he paid us or did we do it for free, for a free Ireland. Said they might have to pick us up and give us a seeing to, asked him what we were like in bed."

' "Christ!" I saw their leering faces, felt as violated as if one of them had touched me. I held her around the waist and she pulled my head down to her shoulder. We were silent for a few moments. I felt completely vulnerable. Then

I thought of how shaken Finn must have been, hearing those words about the women who shared his life. "Can I see him?" I asked.

'"Don't wake him, he's exhausted and his back's killing him. I wanted him to see a doctor but he wouldn't go. I've put arnica on the sore areas but he'll feel even worse when the bruises come out."

'I peered through their bedroom door at his grey face, strained even in sleep. His right hand was shielding his face, as if from an expected blow. My own eyes watered.

'I hugged Majella then, clinging on.

'"The bastards, Majella, the rotten bastards."

'"You know who the real bastard is though, don't you? It's Nigel Howes. He fingered Finn."

'I looked up at her, pushing her hair from her face. "How do you know?"

'"Finn told me. The soldier who interrogated him more or less admitted it when Finn challenged him. He reckoned they only let him go because he kept blocking them, he wore them down and they lost interest. He reckons it was a bit of routine abuse, they didn't have anything definite. But if they lift him again we'll know who gave them information."

'I started to pace the room, unconsciously aping Finn. What would we do if Howes piled up enough intelligence for them to intern him? What on earth would Majella do? Like all women, I had thought about rape, about what I would do if it ever happened, whether I would resist or give in, hoping to keep my life if my assailant was armed; if it was a soldier with a rifle – or maybe several of them – there would be no choice. My breath was trapped deep in my ribs. I leaned against the piano, gripping the smooth, raised edge. Finn's ashtray, the top of a pickle jar, held his stubs. I knew just how his eyes crinkled when he peered through the smoke at his music.

'Majella opened the piano lid, softly picking out a few bars of "The Boys of Mullabawn". "We've got to do something about Howes now, he's left us no choice, he's turned us all into targets," she said.

'I felt relief; the decision had effectively been taken out of my hands. I was clear what I would tell Finn when he woke from his pain-filled sleep.

"I've got the nerve now, Majella," I said grimly. "Let's do it, let's execute this informer."

'She came to me, reaching out her right hand which I clasped firmly in mine. "We must seize the moment," she said urgently, lifting our arms to make a raised joint fist, that clenched symbol of protest reflected in the posters around us. I had never felt so close to her. The delirium of love and rash courage made me light-headed and the tilt of her chin told me she felt the same. I think that if Finn had come in at that moment and told us we could fly through the window, we would have believed him.

'"If anyone can do it it's us, we work well, we trust each other." I grabbed her left hand so tightly, our knuckles cracked.

'"It will be an act of terrible beauty," she said, drawing me to the fire, pulling me down. A log burst, red sparks flying. "A terrible beauty will be born."

'We sat through a significant pause and in that pause the decision was secured. We agreed to kill a man because at heart we were utopian zealots, infecting each other daily with a fabulous vision of ourselves as torch-bearers of the revolutionary flame. It was fitting that we fell back on Yeats, creating an extravagant niche for ourselves as heroic as that occupied by the 1916 rebels. Yet, when we had forever tainted our hands, hearts and minds, we could make no claim to having altered Irish history. Our action had no effect on the British press, did not impinge in any significant way on the world around us. We caused intense grief to one family and transformed our own lives into days and nights dogged by shadows. It was ourselves that we changed utterly. We would have been wiser to reflect on two other lines from "Easter 1916":

> "Too long a sacrifice
> Can make a stone of the heart."

'When Finn woke and came out to sit gingerly in a chair I placed a cushion at his back. He accepted a few aspirin which he took with a glass of whisky and raised his head so that Majella could apply more arnica to his contused chin. I made a hot water bottle and he smiled at me, holding his jaw; her majesty's forces could do with a few social pointers on entertaining guests, he said, their hospitality wasn't all it should be. To me he seemed brave and fine in his suffering. Their interrogation techniques also left a lot to be desired, he added; he'd had no trouble sidestepping their lines of enquiry, they'd got nothing from him despite their threats. Majella stood behind him, gently rubbing his temples, then kneading the tension from his shoulders. When I told him my decision he closed his eyes for a moment. Then he nodded and leaned forward to press my arm approvingly. We set about going through the plan then and there and agreed that we would refer to the undertaking in code from that night. I knew immediately what the code should be: "The Terrible Beauty."'

14

JOAN

Alice took the phonecall from Nina on a Tuesday and rang Joan immediately, catching her just before she left home.

'Nina Rawle was taken into hospital last night, so you don't need to go to her place this morning.'

Joan was standing with her wedding buffet list in her hand. Today she had planned to buy the wine, beer, gin, puff pastry and tins of asparagus, things that would keep until Friday week, the big day. Nina had told her how simple asparagus vol-au-vents were to make and how good they tasted; easy to impress guests with those, she'd said. For the last few days, Joan had felt excitement and tension mounting. She kept walking through the rooms of her flat, checking the newly painted walls and skirting for splashes or smudges, straightening the pictures she had inherited from Gran – 'The Fighting Temeraire', 'Bubbles' and 'Winter Moonlight' – plumping cushions, making sure that the new curtains in the bedroom pulled together smoothly. For two weeks she had spent every evening and Saturdays cleaning. No corner escaped her attention. As she emptied and washed the kitchen cupboards she was reminded of the Sephardic Jewish woman in Stoke Newington who had engaged her before the last Passover. Her religion decreed that her kitchen had to be scoured before the feast but she was not allowed to do it herself. The woman had worn an ugly brown acrylic wig and, despite the warmth of the day, a thick cardigan because she wasn't permitted to show her hair or arms to anyone but her husband and close family. She positioned herself at the kitchen table, giving detailed instructions about the work. Her children had drifted through as Joan laboured and she had felt odd, cleaning and polishing with an audience. As she'd reached into her top cupboard the night before, perching on a chair, she thought that she now understood better that need to prepare for an important turning point, to look around and see that everything was in a state of readiness. She had just finished cross-stitching and framing a new Grace Ashley poem which stood on the bedside table. The frame was oval and made of white fabric with a pattern of tiny red cupids holding bows and arrows:

'Love is dawn and dusk
And all things brightly glowing.
The sun rises and sets
But you shine constant in my heart.'

On Saturday Rich would come out of prison; she was going to fetch him and they were heading straight to buy his wedding suit. She had wondered if this was wise. It was so long since he had been shopping and the crowds might make him nervous. When she voiced this to him he said she wasn't to worry; he couldn't wait to get back to normal life, he wanted to dive straight in. He dreamed at night, not of quiet places, not of open countryside or empty beaches like some of the blokes inside; his mind was full of crowded pubs, crammed shopping centres, busy dog tracks, anywhere full of people who were free to be there and enjoying themselves.

She had been planning to do the shopping after her morning visit to Nina. She smoothed the list, written on the back of one of Rich's envelopes, as she spoke to Alice. 'Did Nina say what's the matter?'

'They think she's had a slight stroke, but she's all right.'

'She hasn't looked well the last few days. She seemed even more tired than usual.'

'She's in the Whittington. She said if you want to go she'd welcome the visit, but not to feel obliged.'

'Oh, I'll go and see her of course.'

She went to the supermarket first, adding a bunch of white carnations and freesias for Nina to her basket. The sweet scent of the freesias filled the car and she found herself thinking of the spray of Lily of the Valley that she'd placed on Gran's coffin in the Bromley undertakers, a small dim shop where the air was dry. Pulling up at a traffic lights, it suddenly occurred to her that Nina might die, that she might have another stroke; people often had a small one first, a precursor of the bigger shock to come. She stared at a sticker in the back window of the car in front of her: *Jesus Loves Safe Drivers.*

It was hard to imagine life without Nina now. Clients had died, but older people who she had seen deteriorating and who at least had lived full lives, 'a good innings' as many of them put it. Nina was special; there was something about her that made Joan look forward to seeing her. A few weeks previously Joan had read a magazine article which suggested that you could divide people into two types, door closers and door openers. Nina was definitely a door opener. She had introduced Joan to new foods, the names of authors and plants, which Joan had never bothered with before, not having a garden. Occasionally she had bought an African violet or a poinsettia but they always wilted and died before long. Nina had explained how it was easy to grow things inside with the right compost, degree of warmth, moisture and positioning. Joan had taken home dozens of cuttings and now her kitchen ledges boasted herbs, begonias and spider plants. There was a hanging basket of ferns and ivy in the hallway and in her living room were five tubs containing purple pelargoniums, silvery tradescantias, a dark green umbrella plant and an indoor jasmine with tiny white flowers and a heady perfume. If she had even dared to buy those plants herself she would no doubt have placed them in the wrong aspects but under Nina's instructions they were flourishing. Alice had said the flat was like Kew Gardens, a regular greenhouse.

It seemed to Joan that through Nina she was learning that there were little tricks to life, ways of doing things that brought out the best in what you had. These were the things that educated people knew about: double cream added to any sauce made it taste wonderful; a sprinkling of fresh herbs on top of a dish gave it a special touch; it was best to find two or three colours that suited you and stick to them; pictures should be hung at eye level, not stranded high up on a wall and it was quite all right to keep a rack of magazines in the bathroom, situated next to the loo.

This knowledge she had gleaned gave her confidence and made her feel all the more excited about life with Rich. They would be able to move on together, improve themselves. Of course, she wouldn't confide any of these tricks to him. She had learned that he didn't like people to have ideas beyond their station, especially if they came via Nina. He was odd like that, set in his ways like a much older man. Maybe it was one of the effects of prison; being in there must be like a time-warp, cut off from change and people with interesting things to say. He had told her that most of the blokes inside had three topics of conversation: sex, sport and sex. No, she would influence him gradually, get him to try new dishes and think again about a bidet for the bathroom, something she had always hankered after but he dismissed as foreign trash.

She had thought that Nina might be in intensive care but she was in an ordinary women's ward, lying on top of her bed in a pair of green silk pyjamas and reading a newspaper.

'I knew it was you as you came through the door,' she said, pulling herself up as Joan approached. 'I know the click of your heels.'

Joan held out the flowers. 'I brought you these.'

'How lovely. Put them on the table and I'll get one of the nurses to sort them. I didn't expect you this early. It's only about eleven, isn't it?'

'I'm not too early, am I? I was worried about you.'

'Were you? That's sweet, very sweet. No, you're fine. I'm not expecting any other visitors.'

'Isn't Martin coming?'

'Not until this evening. Then he's got to go to Amsterdam for a course he's booked on until Sunday. He started to talk about cancelling, but I insisted he mustn't. I don't want him fussing around me. There's not that much the matter.' She made an impatient movement with her hands, rustling the paper.

Joan had pulled up a chair. Nina's face was greyish, the skin parched looking, the red weals like a pattern that had been drawn on as an afterthought.

'Alice said something about a stroke.'

'Just a mild one. Who knows, maybe the drugs I take caused it. I was changing a CD and I felt odd, like I was blacking out. I phoned my doctor and I was whipped in here.'

'Will you be in long?'

'Not if I can help it. A couple of days, so they can monitor me. I hate the way they pretend things are normal, that breezy manner the nurses have. I'm on a slippery slope, I know it, they know it.'

'Maybe they have to pretend. I mean, if they didn't, they might not be able to stand the job.'

Nina nodded. 'You're pretty shrewd sometimes, Joan. What have you been doing this morning instead of looking after me?'

Joan explained about the shopping and the items she'd bought for the buffet.

'You're getting organised, then. Are you excited?'

'Not half! When I woke up this morning I could hardly believe that I've only got another four mornings of being alone and just another nine of being single.'

Nina clicked her fingers. 'Sometimes life changes, just like that, suddenly, irrevocably. You find you can never go back.'

'I won't want to go back, thank you very much,' Joan said stoutly, feeling a sudden annoyance at Nina's dull tone. 'I've waited a long time for my life to change.'

Nina smiled at her, her mouth moving into a huge yawn. 'Yes, sorry. Was I being a wet blanket?'

Ashamed at sounding snappy, Joan straightened the edge of the bedspread. Nina's neck was so thin now, it looked as fragile as a bending plant stem. It was hard to see how it supported her head. 'Don't worry, you're not exactly having a good time at the moment. I should think you're entitled to feel down. You look done in.'

'I might have a sleep. I was awake half the night.'

Joan gestured at the laptop which was on the locker beside the bed. 'You shouldn't have that in here, you're supposed to be resting.'

'You can't rest in hospital. It's important I have it.'

Joan shook her head reprovingly. 'Is there anything else I can get you?'

'A bowl of tuna salad would be good. There's plenty of stuff in my fridge if you've got time to go to the flat. Could you make one up with a dash of that French dressing? And help yourself to food, especially the soup you made and the dips; they won't stay fresh for long.'

'It'll be afternoon before I can get back, is that okay?'

'There's no rush.' Nina pulled on her dressing gown and lay back, settling pillows under her head. 'Tell me all about your flat again, everything you've done. Take me from the front door on a guided tour.'

'You've heard all that before.' She had given Nina a detailed account of the new colours and fabrics, describing the cushion covers she'd sewn and her modest collection of glass paperweights on the sideboard. The flat was so small, there wasn't much to tell; she could hardly believe that Nina had found it so interesting the first time.

'I know, I expect it's a bore for you but I'd like to hear it again. Humour me; it's soothing, like being read a story.' She closed her eyes, sighing.

Joan thought that she looked like a child, lying there on her side, slight and sleepy, her knees drawn up and a hand tucked under her cheek. A sick, weary child who needed comforting; when Eddie was bad with his asthma he used to lie on the sofa in front of the fire in his dressing gown and Gran would read him Billy Bunter stories, his wheezes punctuating her sentences. When Joan flew back from school, anxious to check on him, she would step softly into the close, warm front room, sniffing the vanilla smell of the egg custard Eddie had been tempted with. Gran would turn to her with a finger against her lips and a tired smile. Joan had been a robust child, rarely sick but she couldn't recall ever resenting Eddie's illness or the way Gran used to worry over him, taking time off work and making his favourite foods. There was something about having a brother who was older and bigger than you, who could pick you up and whirl you in the air and yet was frequently frail, that didn't permit jealousy. She and Gran had always been watching out for him, anticipating tell-tale warnings of an attack. When one started he would be irritable, telling them not to make a big thing of it but once it took hold and he became weak he accepted their help without a murmur, his breath crackling when he tried to speak. That had been one of the worst things when he vanished; it was as if they'd let down their guard, taking their eyes off him, with terrible consequences. That was ridiculous, of course; Eddie had long since grown out of the worst chest spasms and was an independent man. Still, it was hard to shake off old habits and cautiousness, hard to accept that after all that careful tending, he was gone without warning, with no tell tale signs.

Joan gave herself a shake. She didn't know what was the matter with her today, dwelling on Gran's funeral and Eddie's illness, imagining Nina dying. Touch of the glums, that's what you've got, she told herself, launching quietly into what Nina had asked to hear.

'I've got a red front door and when I step inside I'm in a small hallway. I've painted that cream emulsion over wood-chip and I've put a mirror up like you suggested, to reflect the light. The floor's just grey lino tiles but the hanging basket brightens it up. If I turn left out of the hall I'm in my living room which is now done out in a pale lemon and I made a blind for the window in deep gold; it looks lovely when the sun shines through it, like creamy butter. I'd have liked to change the brown carpet but a new one would be ever so expensive . . .'

Nina was asleep. Her bare left foot twitched, relaxing. Joan carefully hitched the bottom of the blanket over her lower legs and tiptoed away, although Nina was oblivious to the noises of the ward.

From twelve until three Joan was hurrying between clients with no time for lunch. She reached Crouch End at three-thirty to fetch Nina's food. As she pulled up, a woman in well-worn jeans and a denim jacket came down the steps of the house, looked back at the front door and walked slowly away. Joan registered that she was too old to be wearing those kind of trousers, especially as she had an ample pair of hips and a sagging bottom. Inside Nina's flat Joan checked the plants, the cooker – Nina was a terror for forgetting to turn electric rings off – and made a tuna salad, tearing the rocket leaves the way Nina liked them but leaving the cherry tomatoes whole. There was something, Nina said, about biting into a whole small tomato; it left a completely different sensation on the tongue to sliced or quartered segments. Joan laughed, thinking of this, of her particular ways. She popped a tomato in her mouth to try out this theory. It was sweet, that was the only difference she could detect and she had to be careful to keep her lips closed so the juice didn't squirt. She was terribly hungry after missing lunch and the chicken soup she'd made the day before did look inviting. She heated a large mug of it in the microwave and walked around the flat as she sipped, admiring the gleam of the honey-varnished floorboards where she'd buffed them with a soft cloth and the airy lightness imparted by the high ceilings. She thought of what it would be like if this was her place, if she was surrounded by all this warm wood and sophisticated furnishings and equipment. It would be lovely to have a conservatory to eat breakfast in, to wander in to the garden and pick a single fresh rose as Nina did in the mornings. But she couldn't see Rich here, she knew he wouldn't like it at all, the area or the house. She washed up and used the loo, eyeing the bidet next to her.

Nina was looking brighter when she arrived back at the hospital.

'They're letting me out on Saturday,' she said as Joan gave her the salad. 'Can I ask you another favour? Can you take me home and make a meal for me on Saturday night? I know you don't usually do weekends, but Martin will be away.'

Joan felt wrong-footed. 'Well, it's just that Rich is coming out . . . Rich is arriving from Frinton Saturday morning and we're going shopping for his suit.'

'Oh, I see. I'm sorry, I mustn't impose, I hadn't realised.' Her face had fallen.

Joan fiddled with a chair, thinking. 'No, I should be able to work around it. What time are you going home?'

'I expect I can negotiate that. Don't worry, I'll get a taxi.'

'Oh, you can't go home like that, alone.'

'Why not? Look, if you can make sure there's food in on Friday I'll be fine. I don't want to upset your plans.'

Joan pushed her hair back off her forehead. It was a warm day and she was perspiring from all the dashing around and the heat of the hospital. It would be impossible to agree to help Nina during the day on Saturday because Rich was getting out at ten sharp and there was no negotiating that. She could hardly ask a man who'd been in prison for years to hang on another couple of hours while she worked. Wasn't it typical, the way events bunched up together. Yet she didn't like to think of Nina at home on her own. What if the effort of getting something to eat set her back again? If she prepared a dish on Friday, she could just pop in to see that Nina was okay on Saturday night and heat the dinner through. Rich wouldn't mind that, surely; it would only take an hour.

'If you can manage during the day, I'll nip round early evening.'

'Really, it's all right. I shouldn't have asked. I was taken up with myself, I forgot how busy you must be in your own time. Sick people get selfish.'

'No, I'll come. You need an eye kept on you or you'll get up to all sorts; I know you!'

Nina laughed. 'Rich won't mind?'

''Course not. Now, are you going to eat that salad?'

'Yes, of course. I couldn't face the tired-looking chops that the kitchen here were offering.'

As Joan left the ward she saw Martin approaching. He was in a suit, carrying a briefcase and a small overnight bag. She said hallo and he nodded, unsmiling, his eyes glancing off her. She wasn't offended. Poor sod, she thought, you've got it bad and there's about as much remedy for it as there is for Nina's lupus.

She was expecting a call from Rich that evening at nine and he rang just on the hour. 'I'm packed, ready and waiting,' he said. 'It didn't take me long.'

'I'm ready and waiting too.' When he phoned she liked to sit on the floor, knees pulled up to her chest, her left arm across her stomach, hugging herself.

'I've been going through official things today. I'll have eighty-one pounds and seventy-three pence when I step through the gate on Saturday. Bloody generous of them. That won't even buy a suit these days, will it?'

'I've told you not to worry about that. I've a bit of money put by.' He sounded tired, anxious, rather like Nina had that morning.

'I'll be sponging off you right from day one.'

'Don't be like that, love, it's not sponging. You'll get work, then you'll be able to buy me things.'

'Yeah, maybe.'

'Cheer up, only a couple of days.'

'What are we doing Saturday after we get my suit?'

'I thought we'd come back here, have lunch and unpack. I want to show you what I've been doing.'

'What about the evening? Let's have a drink and go to the pictures. I've been wanting to do that for months, have a regular Saturday night instead of playing bloody ping-pong and watching game shows on the telly. What's on at the flicks?'

She had thought that she wouldn't tell him about having to call at Nina's until later on Saturday, when they'd got a bit sorted. Twisting the telephone cord around her finger, she explained about Nina's meal. There was a silence.

'Rich? I can be back by half eight, we can still get to a film if we hurry.'

'I didn't know it was like this, your job. I thought you didn't work weekends?'

'I don't usually. It's exceptional circumstances. She's had a stroke, after all.'

'Getting out of jail's pretty exceptional too. At least some people think so.' He was petulant now, sharp in a way she'd never heard before.

'I'm sorry, Rich. It's just a one-off. She'll be struggling otherwise.' She used the cajoling tone she employed with ageing clients when they were being difficult.

'What am I supposed to do while you're off being a good Samaritan?'

Her mind went blank. He was used to strict routines, of course, accustomed to having his hours organised. She thought of the couple in the flat two doors up; he went out regular as clockwork every night at six for two pints in The Lamb and Flag, returning dead on seven for dinner.

'You could always go to the pub for an hour.'

'Charming, sitting on my tod with nobody to talk to. I might as well be in here with a bit of company.' The line went dead with a loud click.

She stared at the receiver. She dialled the number, which was a payphone the prisoners had access to in the evenings but it rang and rang. In the kitchen she poured herself a vermouth and ran a finger along the herbs on the window ledge. With a slow panic rising in her chest, she suddenly couldn't imagine Rich here with her, just as she couldn't place him at Nina's. What will he do while I'm out at work, especially if he can't get a job? she thought. Picking up a tin of asparagus, she found it impossible to see a tiny vol-au-vent in his large hand. She clutched the tin against her breasts, rolling it from side to side, as if she might massage away the tension in her heart.

By Friday everything seemed back to normal. She had talked things over in the wine bar with Alice, telling her about the phonecall and Rich's previous worries about her getting cold feet. Alice was wonderfully calm, even though she'd had a hellish day with rotas that had fallen apart. She was wearing a dark red nail-varnish, weeks old, that had grown pitted and chipped around the edges. A few shreds of it had migrated to her collar. Joan longed to tackle those peeling nails with varnish remover and cotton wool. For a few moments she was distracted from what Alice was saying but when she tuned in she was reassured. It was only natural, Alice advised, that both Joan and Rich would be feeling tense, given the circumstances. Most engaged people would have had a good few tiffs by this stage, she pointed out, but the particular situation that Joan and Rich were in meant they couldn't tackle any anxieties they had. They had to bottle so much up, save it for when they saw each other that it was inevitable they'd fall out sometimes. As for Rich blowing up about Nina, that was men all over for you, getting jealous when they felt threatened; it was to do with strangers intruding on their territory, you could trace it to the fact that we're animals underneath, she said mysteriously. She was sure that it would all be okay; she even offered to make a meal for Nina herself at the weekend but Joan said no, she'd only be thinking about her if she didn't check that things were all right. She felt a peculiar responsibility for Nina, maybe because she seemed so alone in the world. Alice suggested that instead, she could call at Joan's flat early on Saturday evening and keep Rich company while Joan popped to Nina's. It would give the two of them a chance to get to know each other. Alice smiled wryly, draining her glass and ordering another; a pity she wasn't so good at giving herself advice, she said, but wasn't it always the way that you could see solutions to other people's problems while your own life baffled you.

Joan liked the idea of Alice entertaining Rich but she wasn't sure about his reaction; I don't need a bleedin' nanny, she thought she could hear him say. Then he had phoned, sounding dejected and apologetic and they had made up. His voice soft, he reiterated how sorry he was for giving her a hard time; petal, he said, my little petal, an endearment he had only used in letters before. When she mooted the plan for Alice to call he was amenable, jokingly saying that it would give him a chance to question her friend and find out Joan's terrible secrets.

Panic over, you idiot, she told herself after Rich's call. She had a shower and waited for her tinted shampoo to take. The contrast between her own clear, healthy complexion and Nina's dull skin struck her as she plucked a few straying hairs from her eyebrows, angling a lamp by her hand mirror. She had been to the hospital to see Nina each morning, taking her fruit and salads, staying for about half an hour.

They didn't have as much to say as they did in the flat or when they were out and about. There were awkward pauses which Joan filled by tidying the bedside cabinet. The silences didn't seem to bother Nina. She might not even have been aware of them. Her gaze would drift to the newspaper or she would pick up her brush and run it through her hair. Maybe it was the effect of the ward, Joan thought; what was there to talk about when nothing much happened in such a closed-off place? The stale air reminded her of Brixton. There was the same sense of claustrophobia, of time hanging heavily. When Joan stepped back into the street after visiting both places she took deep gulps of air. She would find herself driving too fast, having to take her foot off the accelerator, reminding herself that this was the normal world where she had her life and her hopes.

15

NINA

'Majella, Majella, who has been lost to me for so long, 'I thought I saw Finn in the ward here yesterday. I was convinced that it was him. I woke from a drugged doze in the late afternoon and noticed a man standing at the bottom of a bed at the far end of the room. He was wearing a dark, Mao-style jacket and the hair on the back of his head was wild, just as Finn's used to be when he had been struggling with an article and running his fingers nervously across his scalp. The woman in the bed leaned forward and gave him a cluster of purple grapes from the fruit bowl beside her. My breath caught as he raised them in the air and poised them just above his mouth, as Finn used to do, picking them neatly from the stems with his teeth. (How Finn looked after his teeth! He was forever flossing, brushing with a tartar cleansing paste and massaging his gums with a toothpick. They were handsome teeth, white and even, bearing witness to his well-nourished upbringing and childhood visits to a Dublin orthodontist.) My illusion lasted for no more than a minute; when the visitor turned to fetch a chair I saw that he was young and coarse-faced. I felt a startled disappointment, even though if it had been Finn I would probably have had another stroke on the spot.

'The Terrible Beauty stayed close and true. It was just the three of us, a tightly knit team with one objective. We kept to ourselves even more than usual. In the evenings the fire drew us near; we would lock the living-room door and check details, reiterating the stages of our mission. All those songs of protest and struggle we had sung – "glory-o, glory-o to the bold Fenian men!" – all those tales of brave guerillas that we had heard, all those classic socialist texts we had consumed, had nourished us richly and meshed us as believers. We seemed to think and move as one. I can only compare it to a religion because now, at this distance and perspective, that is what it most resembles; we were born again to the heat of revolution.

'Finn made us go out on some evenings, insisting that we visit Mulligans; it was important that we weren't seen acting out of character, he said. On the night we sealed our agreement we stayed up until one in the morning, simmering coffee by the fire as we estimated each move. Now and again Finn eased himself from his chair, his hands pressed to his back, and flexed his arms but of course he made no mention of pain, continuing to speak even as he rubbed sore muscles. I was to position myself in the bar of the Pine Trees on a chosen evening just before six-thirty, the time Nigel always appeared for what he probably called "a quick snifter". We established that I would pretend to be a secretary of some kind and that a disguise was essential. When I went to bed I lay for a long time motionless, staring into the shadows, aware of suspicious scratchings behind the disused fireplace. Unable to find a cool spot on the mattress, I threw off the bedclothes over my sleeping bag and unzipped its top. I had impressed myself with the decision I had made; its portent rang around me in the dark.

'The next day, Finn took me on what he called an orientation and identification exercise. We drove to the Pine Trees in the early evening and sat outside, waiting for Howes to arrive. While we waited Finn rehearsed me, drumming his fingers on the wheel, sometimes touching his chin and moving his jaw carefully. At one point he placed the back of his hand briefly against my right cheek, saying that his belief in me and what I had to offer the revolution had been completely justified. There had been a couple of comrades who'd been dubious about my membership of Red Dawn because of my bourgeois British Protestant origins but I was proof that socialist beliefs could cross all boundaries of nationality and creed. I was puffed with pride, my cheek pulsing where he had touched me, and a tenderness for this man who had held out for me against criticism, placing his trust in me. I felt a strong urge to kiss him then, far stronger than on that night in the garden but at that moment Nigel Howes pulled up in his car and Finn said here was the enemy. I took a good look, registering the West Ham scarf that he wore around his neck, tucked into his leather jacket.

'You and I stole a long brown wig from the Drama department and searched charity shops for shoes and a smartish suit, navy with wide lapels and a straight skirt. I hated the material, a nylon mix, but its thin, slippery texture suited my mood; I felt restless, my heart fluttery. I was constantly too warm despite the weather and I imagined my blood was overheating. Your movements slowed so that you appeared to be doing everything with great deliberation. We didn't refer to the morality of what we were about to carry out at any time; it was a given that Nigel Howes had to die as a symbol of all that was rotten in the British state and its mouthpieces. The high-speed conversation that usually went on between us diminished, our laughter dampened. We were watching our words so carefully that they thickened on our tongues. We reminded each other regularly and solemnly of how careful we had to be; our construct of ourselves as persecuted champions of the class struggle was total, bolstered by each other's fervent commitment and the rarefied air of the small world we moved in. When we heard that the FBI had gunned down a hunted comrade in New York, a young woman who had protested against slum landlords, it was confirmation that our action would strike a blow for all those who valiantly fought the system. The words "ourselves alone" kept echoing in my ears, a quiet inspiration.

'I concentrated on the image I wanted, knowing that the success of the undertaking rested on my engaging with the enemy. I bought a chiffon neck scarf like the one worn by the assistant to the Dean of Languages and after scrutinising the faces of several secretaries in the humanities block, I selected a foundation cream, eye shadow and lipstick in a chemist's. I needed a bogus identity and chose that of Amy Huntley, a girl at school who I had greatly disliked for having harmonious parents. We decided that I would meet Howes just three times to keep the risks low but to give me a chance to pump him for information.

'Finn was keen for us to proceed as soon as possible. There were five days between his proposal and my first meeting with Nigel Howes. I noticed Finn monitoring me. When I dropped a saucepan in the kitchen, scattering peas on the floor, he took it from me carefully and pointed me to a chair. It had been pure clumsiness but I supposed he suspected I was a bag of nerves. I wasn't then, I only started shaking when it was all over. Then, during the build-up and the meetings with Nigel, I entered into the rôle I had to play with astonishing ease, swept along by the momentum of my own fervour. I didn't think about the act of killing. I tucked that away at the back of my mind. You were more anxious than me because, like an actress standing in the wings, anxious to deliver her big scene, you had to wait to play your part. Finn took you to the Glens one morning early, before the builders arrived for the day, so that you could get your bearings and view the expectant grave. You came back looking pale but your mouth was set.

'I was keyed up, wanting to get the action moving on the evening I walked to the Pine Trees. I can't make any claim to having had second thoughts; Finn didn't have to push me out of the door or raise an eyebrow at me. There was a tremor in my calves and sweat on my neck under the wig but I paced steadily, unaccustomed to heeled shoes and the patent leather bag banging against my hip. My strange clothes and cosmetic-layered skin enhanced my sense of unreality; the beige cream coating my face was like a taut mask. I lived in jeans or ethnic skirts and suede desert boots, never used make-up and kept my money in my pockets. The only bag I had was a duffel which I slung across my back when my books were too heavy to clutch under my arm. The feel of the suit and tights on my legs eased the assumption of a different identity. I imitated Amy Huntley's pigeon-toed walk and pushed my wig impatiently over my shoulders in her irritating style.

'You and Finn had held a last minute run-through with me before I left. I dressed in my room and checked that the coast was clear before heading upstairs. Usually, I took the steps at a run, two or three at once, but my narrow skirt made me proceed slowly. You were both standing, waiting for me. You cradled a feather cushion against your chest, plucking at a couple of downy fragments escaping from a seam. Finn was reading a typescript, a correcting pencil stuck behind his ear. Joe Cocker was croaking "Bird on the Wire" on the stereo.

' "How do I look?" I asked, conscious of the chiffon at my neck rubbing my skin.

'You moved to either side of me like parents inspecting a daughter heading for an important social date. You touched the wig, pulling your mouth down, saying you felt you hardly knew me; I looked so weird, so straight. Finn checked that I was carrying no identification, then stood in front of me and placed his hands on my arms, going over the crucial points he'd been priming me with: I was Amy Huntley from Basingstoke, working temporarily in Belfast as personal assistant to the director of a Scandinavian drugs company. We were travelling around, looking at potential sites, never sure where we'd be from day to day. I was supposed to be meeting a date in the Pine Trees but I'd been stood up. I was to act naive, draw Nigel out through innocent-sounding questions.

'Finn patted my shoulders when I'd finished my recital. I felt as if I'd passed inspection, was judged ready to be sent into the front line of battle. The three of us stood looking at each other for a few moments, the air stiff with anticipation.

' "I'd kiss you good luck," you said, "but I don't want to smudge your make-up. God, it's awful!"

' "Howes will like it," Finn told me. Then he said something so unusual, so unexpected, I forgot to breathe. "Are you frightened?" he asked, his voice tinged with a rare concern.

'I thought for a moment. "No, I'm edgy. I want to get it done."

'He looked into my face and I thought of the night I first met him when I felt he was reading me. "Stick to one or two drinks at the most, you need to keep a clear head. If anything starts to go wrong, get away and ring us from the university. Agreed?"

' "Yes."

' "Just remember the cause," he said finally, moving away to his typewriter. "And good luck."

'You saw me to the back door, still clasping your cushion. I was to make my way out along the alley behind the houses. I felt you kiss my shoulder as I stepped out and heard you say that my suit smelled of mothballs but I was already moving into my new persona, narrowing my eyes slightly as Amy used to do when she sensed a challenge. I was inspired, aware of my own heroism and Finn's confidence in me. On my shoulders rode the safety and aspirations of all my comrades; the fact that they would never know what you and I had done for them increased the significance of the act. On a street corner I smiled at a soldier as Amy would have done. When I talk about this now it's as if I am describing another person, someone I once knew vaguely.

'Nigel came into the Pine Trees minutes after I arrived. The bar was quiet and I sat on a stool, reading the *Daily Echo*. I was sipping a tonic water and made sure I caught his eye; I smiled, remarking that it was getting colder. He brightened at hearing my accent and, gesturing at the paper, said I might have been reading his story on bombs in milk churns. I looked impressed at meeting a reporter and asked if he'd talked to any of the big names in the sectarian organisations. He touched his nose, miming secrecy, and offered me a drink. Perching on the stool beside me, he loosened his scarf and asked if I was staying in the hotel. No, I said, ruefully commenting on my failed date. We talked a little about Belfast and he asked me if I knew of a cobbler, raising his right boot to show where one of the ankle straps had come unstitched; they were lovely leather, he said, he'd got them down Petticoat Lane but the machining wasn't brilliant.

'After two drinks he asked if I fancied a meal in a little Chinese place he'd found and I agreed. He expressed surprise that any foreign companies would be interested in coming to this godforsaken country but he had read that overseas investors were interested. My father's ten years in the pharmaceutical industry proved useful; I was able to refer glibly to barbiturates and antibiotics and other companies who were competitors in the market. He remarked with a chuckle that there must be a huge demand for antidepressants in Ulster but as his main interest was himself and his job I had no need to say much more about my circumstances. I was seized by a moment of panic in the Chinese restaurant when I noticed a lecturer from the history department sitting at a corner table. He didn't know me but I thought he might have seen me around; I had forgotten my disguise but when his eyes flicked across us and away I remembered and relaxed enough to register that he was with a woman who wasn't his wife.

'I learned nothing useful, either on that night or on the evening when we drove to Donegal. There were no hot tips on the security forces or police activity. I assumed that Nigel was playing a close game, tutored by his official paymasters. A little while after the murder I came to the conclusion that he was a hack who had played up his contacts to emphasize his own importance. It wasn't until much later that I decided Finn had lied to us – but I am running ahead, that realisation dawned with the advantage of perspective and calm. There in the restaurant, munching on noodles, I heard mainly grumbles about the way other reporters fiddled expenses, the uncomfortable softness of Nigel's hotel bed and the rudeness of Belfast kids. He was polite to the point of absurdity; he would hold the car door open for me, try to assist me into my coat and apologised to me on the one occasion when he swore. I almost laughed, despising his hypocritical gallantry although it served me well because he didn't even try to kiss me. I kept glancing at him, wondering why he hadn't guessed something odd was going on. It was my Englishness that reassured him, just as Finn had envisaged; I was a comfortable confidante, possibly even a move upmarket for him. I could see that he was impressed by my refined accent and he relished having someone to boast to about his nose for a good story.

'Two days later I met him mid-afternoon, in the bar of the Pine Trees. He asked if I'd like a drive and I agreed. I assumed he meant somewhere local but he headed out of Belfast and took the road towards Derry, across the misty Sperrin mountains. He needed to get out of the city for a couple of hours, he said, all the crap that went on was wearing him down and he fancied taking a look at Donegal. I sat back in his leathery-smelling hired car and listened to his George Harrison tape, (oh, the irony of that now, George during his Zen period, singing that all things must pass away) and his talk about Provos and other hard men who made deals to meet him and then cried off. He made it sound as if they had no business of their own, nothing else to do but make themselves available for a visiting reporter and give him plenty of shocking information for his editor.

'We crossed the border and stopped for a drink in a pub near Fahan, then drove again along narrow country lanes. We saw several abandoned, ruined cottages with trees growing through their collapsed roofs and then one set back just from the road which was empty but still in reasonable condition. Nigel pulled up, saying we should have a look, see if the place was open. Dusk was falling and I felt edgy, wondering if he was looking for somewhere to have sex. I didn't want to have to pretend that kind of passion and especially not in an isolated place permeated by the damp October air. I hung back, complaining that it looked spooky but he laughed, saying come on, it would be interesting and he'd protect me from ghosts or whatever they were called here – banshees, that was it. That resonance, that cockney inflection in his voice that was so like Joan's sounded loudly in the dimming light; "baynsheeze", he said, grinning. The air felt thick against my face, water-laden. Droplets of moisture fell from bushes and the yellowing trees.

'I followed Nigel, still reluctant. Under our feet the ground was mulchy, expelling little sucking gasps as we trod below overhanging branches the sun couldn't permeate. The gate was rusty and hanging loose but the grass in front of the cottage was short, cropped by sheep whose droppings spattered the ground. I shivered; I was wearing only a thin Mac over my second-hand suit. Nigel was warmer in his leather jacket and thick black cords. His aftershave drifted back to me and I almost laughed, he was so incongruous in that setting with his King's Road clothes and gold cufflinks. The door opened easily when he pushed it and as we stepped inside a damp chill rose up to greet us. We both stared, speechless, and Nigel said, "crikey, the *Marie Celeste*!"

'The main room of the cottage was fully furnished and looked as if it had been abandoned just after a meal. Through the crepuscular shadows I made out a long square table, covered in blue oilcloth. Three willow-patterned plates and white enamel mugs stood there, salt and pepper cruets, a milk jug, a glass sugar bowl with three curved legs and an earthenware teapot. Nigel moved to the open fireplace and found a stubby candle on the mantelpiece. He lit it and placed it on one of the empty plates, making the scene look even more like a supper left by spirits.

'"I wonder what happened and when," he said, his jacket creaking as he stuck his hands in the pockets.

'"It's covered in thick dust, must have been some time ago. Maybe someone died suddenly. Maybe a son or daughter was supposed to sort it out but couldn't be bothered and emigrated." I'd heard many stories of that happening; young people keen to make their way in London or New York leaving the old house with hardly a backward glance.

'"Sad," he said, "a place like this just left to rot."

'I touched the greasy oilcloth on the table. The house had that hushed, expectant air of old, rarely visited churches. The large fireplace was choked with grey ash. One battered boot lay by its side on the fender. Over the mantelpiece hung a St Brigid's cross, a sepia-toned photograph of a solemn de Valera and one of Jack and Jackie Kennedy at Dublin airport, smiling and waving with those well-fed American good looks. Your parents had travelled to see the president and his wife when they visited Ireland; he was your mother's hero and she refused to believe the scurrilous tales of his sexual exploits that made their way even into the Irish papers after his death. You liked to tease her and make her blush by referring to his Mafia connections and insatiable appetites, remarking that it was amazing what a man could do with a bit of determination when he had a back problem. I used to listen to your banter with agitation when I first met your family; then, when I realised that it was part of a safe, ritual exchange I learned to enjoy it, astonished that you could argue yet remain on good terms. My mother had no sense of humour at all and would never have entertained badinage concerning her fixed views; oddly enough, she liked the crude, lavatorial jokes of *Carry On* films but I would never have dared to criticise her affection for Oswald Mosley or John Profumo (in her eyes respectively the greatest Prime Minister Britain never had and a dignified man brought down by a trollop and filthy Reds).

'Nigel had moved to a gloomy corner of the room where he had found a pine chest with rusted hinges. He dragged it into the candlelight and opened the lid. It made a moaning sound, like a groan of pain.

'"Look at this stuff, they left it all behind." He took out

two greying linen tablecloths, a pair of lace curtains, a black cloth cape and a small statue of the Sacred Heart, the one that took pride of place in so many Irish homes with Jesus pointing resignedly at his exposed, bleeding heart.

'I was feeling uncomfortable at this excavation of a home, even if it was an abandoned one. I said that we should leave. I was growing colder and the falling dark outside was pressing in at the dirty windows. Nigel was rubbing the statue with his arm. He took a handkerchief from his pocket and smoothed it across the face. Sitting on the edge of the table, he held it up and his voice suddenly held an emotion that startled me.

'"My mum was a Catholic," he said. "She had one of these, exactly the same, by her bed when she was dying. I don't know what happened to it afterwards. I'd forgotten it until now. Do you think . . ." He glanced at me and I saw that his eyes, which always had a moist glaze, were wetter than usual, gleaming in the low light. "Do you think," he continued, "that I was brought here for a purpose, that maybe my mum's spirit was guiding me? Do you believe in that kind of thing?"

'This was quite unlike our previous conversation. On the first evening we'd met Nigel had told me all about the world of journalism, a subject he never tired of and which I encouraged him in; I said little about myself, offering lies when he occasionally asked about my circumstances. He was a bore about his job, making much of its supposed glamour and excitement but I listened tolerantly, happy to let him run on; I breathed carefully to relieve my tension but I got a kick of pleasure from my successful deception. There in the cottage I couldn't think of anything to say. My throat was icy. He was cleaning the statue again, folding his handkerchief and running it in the creases of the plaster, along the folded red robe and dripping heart.

'"I don't know," I said finally. "I've never thought about it. I'm cold, can we go?"

'"Yeah, sure. I'd like to take this with me, I feel I should. Nobody would miss it, would they? It's not stealing, more like treasure trove."

'"You can buy one of those anywhere, Irish shops are full of them." I wished that he would just put it back in the chest and leave.

'"I know, but this is special. I think I was meant to find it. My mother – well, I still miss her, that's all. Daft, a grown man like me."

'"Okay, bring it then," I said savagely, blowing out the candle.

'He propped the statue on the back seat of the car and all the way to Belfast I was conscious of it there. I could feel the Saviour's steady gaze on my neck. His pointing finger seemed accusatory, as if he knew the plan I held in my head and was trying to warn Nigel of our intentions. His memories triggered, Nigel told me all about his mother, the lung cancer that ate her away, the way he used to bring her cold drinks – Tizer with ice cubes was her favourite – and how she used to call him her angel helper. I was sweating by the time we reached Belfast and I jumped from the car when he stopped, hurriedly agreeing that I'd ring him the following day.

'On the way back to the house I did something I had never done on my own; I stopped in a bar and asked for a brandy, a drink I hated but which I knew was given as a restorative. At first I wanted to throw up but after a few minutes I felt calmer and able to breathe properly. I could smell the damp must of the cottage on my clothes and skin; as soon as I reached home I ran a hot bath and submerged myself in scented water, washing away Nigel's sad memories and that forsaken house. In Mulligan's that night I threw myself into the conversation, sang all the rebel songs and drank far too much. I wanted the world to be warm and comforting, full of noise and sparkle.

'The night after the excursion to Donegal I rang him and suggested the trip to Antrim. You squeezed into the phone-box with me, moving up and down on the balls of your feet like someone desperate to find a toilet. We chatted briefly, Nigel telling me that he thought he had something promising on a gun-running priest just over the border and then he asked what I would like to do on Friday; what could you do in Belfast on a Friday, he added, he'd found nowhere he'd want to spend an evening. He was one of those men who injected a trace of whine into his voice when he wanted a woman to organise him. That suited me fine; anyone would think he knew the plan and was playing along with it. I had a friend, I said, a local girl who was helping my boss and me to look at locations. She knew a pub out in Antrim that opened after hours and had great music and dancing. How about it?

'"One of those sheeben places?" he asked.

'"They're called shebeens. That's right. Sounds great, better than this dreary city anyway."

'He agreed and said he'd pick us up but I quickly replied that I'd be out with my friend in the afternoon so it would be easier if we travelled in my car. We'd be outside the Pine Trees at eight.

'"It's fixed," I said to you as I put the receiver down.

'"Fixed," you echoed.

'Your patchouli scent was strong in the confined space. There was a fierce wind hurrying through the streets and your hair had been blown into a tangle, strands of it catching on your cheeks. I wanted to hold on to you, hook my thumb into your belt loop as I did sometimes when we were drunk and the pavement tilted; how well I knew the movement of your hips as you walked, your curving hips that you bemoaned, saying that you were heading for a pear-shaped middle age. But I crossed my arms instead because your frame, which had always appeared so solid and sturdy to me, seemed to have developed a certain fragility. Maybe it was the slope of your shoulders or the chapped skin on your bottom lip which you always developed at the onset of winter and had been picking; it lent you a frayed look. We glanced past each other, like strap-hangers in the tube who carefully avoid eye contact.

'"We'd better tell Finn," you said. "I need one of his fags."

'"You don't smoke."

'"I don't usually plan a shooting for a Friday either. I had one while I was in the bath last night. My mouth tastes foul."

'I thought I understood; you needed to be somehow different, just as I had by altering my appearance. We bent into the wind as we walked back to Rock House, hands dug deep in our pockets, not talking. A bomb exploded a few streets away but we didn't pause or comment, even though our eardrums reverberated. I think that we weren't in the normal world at all, we were removed, heading steadily into the half-light that would shade our lives from then on.

'Finn insisted that we attend our lectures on the Friday but I don't recall anything much about that day until the evening. He had told us that he wouldn't be around before we left for the hotel; there was a dispute on at a factory in Newtownabbey where one of the comrades worked and he was joining the evening picket to show solidarity. After breakfast he had handed you the gun. It was wrapped in a dark yellow duster. I was reminded of my mother's cleaning lady dabbing carefully at the china collection or rubbing hard at the silver fruit bowl. You opened the soft covering and took the gun out, balancing it in your hand. I reached out and touched it, our fingers brushing. You wrapped it again and took it away to your bedroom. Finn followed you and when I went to fetch my coat you were standing by your bed, locked in a long kiss, his hands on your waist.

'At five-thirty we made toast in front of the fire, for something to do. Neither of us was hungry but we took turns holding the long brass fork with the blackened tines to the flames. A crust rasped my throat, making me cough and you thumped my back. I scalded some coffee, crushing into it two of the tablets I'd bought from one of the career drug users on campus. I can't recall what they were now but he'd assured me that they gave you a kick, helped you hang loose for a good eight hours. I trusted his knowledge and experience. You see, Majella, deep down I was still anxious that we would flunk out at the last minute, turn and run; or maybe it was just myself I doubted and I decided to help us on our way. I kept the tablets hidden, knowing that Finn would be furious if he knew. I watched you down your coffee and tipped mine back in one long draught.

'We checked our list of equipment that Finn had stowed in the boot of the car: two spades from the garden shed, a blanket, several bin liners, wellingtons and two torches and waterproof walking suits he'd bought from a camping shop in Downpatrick.

'"We're ready," you said, consigning the list to the fire.

'"It's only six."

'"I know."

'"And there won't be much blood?"

'"No. Don't talk about it now. It's not good to go over it too much."

'"We'll be fine."

'"We will. We're a good team." You got up. "And we're

good dancers. Let's dance, some good old Irish jigs. We'll loosen up, hang free.''

'You looked more like my familiar Majella as you put on a record of traditional fiddle music. Your hair was scooped up in a wooden comb, marmalade coloured under the lamp on the piano and toast crumbs were trapped in the thick weave of your Arran jumper. I shoved the sofa back against a wall and we began dancing, crossing the room diagonally, passing each other in the ritual steps. We didn't pause, continuing through "Miss Walsh's Fancy", "The Foot of the Mountain", "Tatter the Road" and "Carbray's Frolics". As we grew breathless and hot and the tablets kicked in we laughed, turning towards each other and joining outstretched hands as the fast strains of "The Bantry Lasses" soared in the room. Round and round we spun, leaning backwards, the posters and paintings, the sagging wallpaper and antiques, wheeling about us in a blurred sphere. Our boots thundered fast and steady, muffled by the carpet, like a distant storm approaching. I was dizzy and dazed, intoxicated by the rushing, jaunty fiddles, feeling the high of whatever chemical was in my bloodstream. There was nothing but this lightning acceleration, your hair flying wild from the comb, your smile circling me and my own laughter catching in my chest. It was the last time in my life that I was to be free from the prison of my own insistent thoughts.

'They are allowing me to go home tomorrow. The words that the consultant omitted to say when he agreed to my discharge told me everything. I must quicken my pace, finish this business. In order to do so I must tell you that there is something I have hidden from you up till now, something more important than the pass Finn made at me or the events of the evening in Donegal with Nigel or the tablet I fed you. I'm not sure why I have kept it back; maybe I am too accustomed to dissemblance or perhaps I wasn't convinced I would have the courage to go through with this confession, take it right to the end. I was giving myself an opt-out, seeing if I actually had enough determination.

'Nigel Howes had a family, of course, as most people do, a little network of familiar faces. That was not a factor in our deliberations, we of necessity had to bar any such concerns, stifle our imaginations about the grief we might cause. I made sure that I suppressed any thoughts of his dead mother with drink and noise. But that Christmas of 1971, after our action, I came across one of those in-depth pieces so common at the time about innocent casualties of the Troubles. I was in Maidstone, licking my wounds, lying low in a haze of alcohol, picturing you and Finn escaping your own demons in Paris. My mother had left the paper on the coffee table while she went to see to the roast pork. I remember sitting on the deep, chintzy sofa, the radio playing "I Never Promised you a Rose Garden", the comforting squeak of the oven door providing the backdrop to another familiar Sunday of too much rich food followed by a soporific afternoon. Before I left home I used to hate those Sundays, dreading their inevitability, the leaden weight of lunch in my stomach and my mother's bridge cronies rolling up at four o'clock for Victoria sandwich, Darjeeling tea and endless card games. But that December I let the predictability and tedium roll over me. It made Belfast seem another world, a place so extraordinary I had come across it in a fable. The newspaper intruded briefly on my suburban hidey-hole. There was a photo of two women under the headline, "Those Left to Weep". They were standing outside a small house that fronted the pavement and they looked puzzled. The older woman wore thick National Health glasses. She had a headscarf tied under her chin and clasped a sturdy handbag in the crook of her arm. The younger woman, a girl, was wearing a calf-length shiny mac with a wide belt, very like one I had. That made me uneasy and I quickly looked at the article. The paper burned my hands as I was reading and when I finished I went to the bottom of the frosty garden and hid my face in the rushes by the pond.

'That young girl, her face smudged with horror, was Joan Douglas, the older woman her grandmother. As soon as I answered her first ring at my doorbell I knew that I had indisputably found the right person; her resemblance to her brother Nigel was unmistakable. She is not like him in stature, being short and rounded but she has his hair texture and high forehead and exactly the same vocal inflexions. Her walk resembles his too; upright, a little stiff at the hips and she has the same way of resting her right arm across her left shoulder when she is standing and talking. That was part of the difficulty of our first meeting; foolishly, perhaps, I hadn't considered that I would find a family likeness unnerving and when Joan spoke I heard Nigel ordering me a drink: "a gin and it for the lady, please".

'So I knew of Joan and I remembered from that newspaper story that Nigel had been called Eddie, his middle name, by his family. Over the years my thoughts had strayed to her and when I gave up work I decided to try and find her. By then I was aware that I had no simple disease and my studies had informed me of its interesting permutations. I had time to satisfy my need to address the past; where better place to start than with Nigel's sister, whose life I had so carelessly damaged? I contacted a private detective agency and gave them a story about wanting to find a relative. It took them just five weeks to trace Joan, despite the fact that she had kept her married name. When I discovered what she did for a living it seemed that my ill health was a gift instead of a curse. Then for some months I was too sick to take any action. Once the lupus was in remission I continued with my plans to move here and rang the agency employing Joan. As you know, Majella, it's easy to draw an unsuspecting person into your net if you have a plan.

'Now you see Joan's importance to me. I have listened to her, watched her, forced myself to grow used to her simple home truths, encouraged her to speak about her life. All this has been part expiation, part curiosity. It seems that the least I can do is let her hear what happened to her brother from my own lips; a punishment that fits the crime.

'The mapping of this story is hurting my heart. I am on a tightrope now and before I fall I will sit Joan down and tell her about us and what we did. She can read the full account if she wishes. I am going to have to believe in the kind of maxim that Joan herself would offer: *you have to be cruel to be kind.* She is due to see me tomorrow and I know that I mustn't wait any longer. It's time that Joan learned about this plot in which she has been an unwitting player even though it might mar her wedding day, even though I am not going to be in the least bit kind.'

16

JOAN AND NINA

Joan slept fitfully on the Friday night before Rich's release, waking now and again with a start, her mouth dry. At dawn she opened her eyes from the dream where Eddie was sailing away and she was pressing her face to the porthole of the ship, rubbing hopelessly at the thick, salt-misted glass to try and get a clearer view. For the first time she didn't feel the sense of desolation that usually followed the dream, didn't find herself snarled in the sheets. In the final frame, the instant before she woke, her hand had opened, fingers moving and she thought she might have been waving good-bye.

She fetched a drink of water and slid back into bed, picturing the head that would lie beside her the next night. Her thoughts flitted between Rich and Nina; was he awake too, she wondered, twisting and turning on his narrow bunk? She worried about Nina climbing into a taxi and returning to a silent, empty flat. Hopefully, the huge bunch of mixed sweet-william she had bought and left on the coffee table would act as a tonic. She was up at six, waxing her legs and cleaning the bath, stripping the bed of its daisy-patterned linen and fitting it with the crisp sheets and pillowcases she'd bought through her catalogue; Samarkand, they were called, a dusky orange with a fainter tangerine stripe. They weren't too feminine, a man should feel comfortable in them. She didn't feel like eating but made herself have a boiled egg which she consumed standing by the cooker. She had to run for the loo twice before she left the flat. Just as she was about to go she changed from her navy dress and jacket into smart jeans and a blouse; the dress was too much, she didn't want Rich feeling outdone, overshadowed in any way.

At the prison, when Rich appeared before her with a small case, she felt weak and a little timid. He looked like someone she knew vaguely, standing there out of his usual context. He seemed bigger, his shape bulkier and his shirt and trousers were wrinkled which she found disappointing but made her all the more relieved that she'd done that quick change. He put the case down and wrapped his arms around her and she knew then that all was well.

'Oh,' she said foolishly 'you're taller today.'

He laughed. 'I'm walking tall, that's all. You're looking gorgeous.'

'Am I?'

'Yeah. Let's get out of here.'

They kept touching all the way to Brent Cross, little strok-ings and pats of hair and arms, as if to reassure themselves that this was real. Rich decided on a suit within half an hour and suggested that they head back to Leyton straight away.

'Are you finding the crowds difficult?' Joan asked as they made their way to the car.

'The crowds are fine but you're even better. I want to be on my own with you. You know why, don't you?'

She grasped his hand, blushing. 'Behave, you,' she said, 'I've got to drive.'

They fell out of bed just ten minutes before Alice arrived. Joan didn't have time to wash. She hurried her jeans and shirt on, ran a comb through her hair and laughingly evaded Rich's outstretched hand as the doorbell rang. After she'd settled them both with drinks – Rich with the six-pack of lager he'd been anticipating – she confirmed that she'd be back within the hour, fetched the fish pie she'd made the night before from the fridge, kissed Rich's lips that tasted of her own skin and rattled her car keys in farewell.

At Nina's she opened the door, calling, 'only me, Joanie D,' as she always did. Nina was in the bathroom so she put the pie in the microwave and cleared away a cup and plate in the living room, tutting as she caught her foot on Nina's laptop which lay on the floor beside her chair. In the bedroom she turned down the bed and made sure the window was open slightly. A picture of her own bed from which she'd recently tumbled flashed before her eyes and she pressed her fist into the pit of her stomach. It didn't seem right to be thinking of such things in a sick woman's room; it was distracting enough that she could smell the mingled sweat of her and Rich beneath her shirt. She rested against the wall, waiting for Nina to finish in the bathroom, going back over the events of the day. In the car-park lift she had leaned into Rich, feeling a giddiness that was nothing to do with the drop through space. The sheer joy of holding his arm was hard to describe; the reassurance of that solid warmth under her fingers had made the world, just in that moment, perfectly balanced.

The microwave pinged as Nina unlocked the bathroom door, a drift of Lily of the Valley announcing her presence. Joan went forward to greet her and tell her off about leaving the computer where she might easily harm herself by tripping on it. Nina had her shawl knotted around her shoulders. Her colour was high, but not the bloom of health; her facial marks were inflamed. She was back on two sticks and walking slowly. In the dull evening shadow she looked aged, weary.

'How are you today?' Joan asked, following her through the kitchen and in to the living room. 'Is it good to be home?' There was a whiff of brandy in the air, drifting back from Nina's breath.

'Yes, yes.' She sat slowly.

'Do you like the flowers?' Joan cupped the sweet-williams, rearranging them. 'I thought they'd be nice to come back to.'

'Lovely, yes.' Her voice was muted. When Joan looked at her she averted her gaze, patting her shawl down.

'It's been quite a day, non stop. Rich and I are going to the pictures when I get back. He likes the colours in the living room, by the way, says they're very cheerful. He's not so sure about the plants. He's got some old wives' tale in his head that he heard from his mum, about too many plants using up the oxygen in a room. Funny, isn't it, the things some people believe, like catching a cold if you go out with damp hair – Gran always said that.' She was pulling the rug which had become creased, flattening it with the heel of her hand.

Nina watched her as she crouched; there was an energy, a vibrancy about her that was all wrong. Nina felt deadened, exhausted by the prospect of the task ahead which she had lain awake contemplating for most of the previous night.

'You must be hungry,' Joan said, rising. 'I've got a pie for you, I'll just pop and get it.'

'No!' Nina held a hand up, then pressed it to her forehead.

'What is it?' Joan approached and hunkered down before her when she didn't reply. The smell of alcohol was strong this close up. My goodness, she thought, I hope she's not having another stroke. 'Nina, what's the matter? Should I call the doctor?' She put a hand on Nina's arm.

Nina jerked and shook it off as if she had felt an electric shock. 'Just sit down, would you, Joan.'

'But the pie . . .'

'Forget the pie, I don't want food. Sit down, I must talk to you.'

Joan sat on the sofa. She wondered how much brandy Nina had drunk. The bottle was standing open on the table, with only an inch left in the bottom. A fresh, unopened one stood ready beside it.

Nina saw her glance. 'I've had more than I should,' she acknowledged. 'Dutch courage.'

'Well, seeing what you've got to put up with, why not?' She's had bad news at the hospital, Joan was thinking, the doctors have told her she hasn't got long to live. She trembled at the thought of the prognosis Nina was building herself up to announce.

Nina grimaced. 'Maybe you should have one, you're going to need some Dutch courage of your own.'

'No, not for me, I'm driving, aren't I. What do I need courage for? Oh, you mean for Rich? I don't need any stimulants to be with him, believe me!' She smiled but there was no response.

Nina leaned on one stick, her head bent. 'I haven't drunk so steadily for years, not since a time when I was in Ireland, a time that's got a lot to do with you. Have you ever wondered why I asked for you specially when I rang your agency?'

'I was recommended, wasn't I?'

'No. I had you traced. I wanted you for quite another reason.' She looked at Joan then and there was a warning in her eyes but it was her tone, quiet and flat, that made Joan's scalp tingle.

'What is it? What about Ireland, why is that to do with me?'

Nina reached for the bottle and took a sip of brandy. She wiped her mouth and looked out of the window. 'What I'm about to tell you – I want you to understand that I'm doing it like this, that I deliberately found you in the way I did because I wanted you to hear it from me. I know what happened to your brother, to Eddie. I know how he died.'

Joan inched forwards on the deep sofa. 'Nobody knows that, the police never caught anyone.' She couldn't begin to make out what Nina was talking about; it might be the brandy and the pills, she thought, there was a name for what it could cause, a doctor had told her once when he came to see an ailing client. She couldn't recall the word but it meant the mind got muddled.

Nina sighed. 'Yes, somebody does know, I know. I know because I was there when he died, I saw him shot and I helped to bury him.' Ah, she thought; the words are out now, released, carried in the air. She turned towards Joan who was smiling with a puzzled, nervous frown. 'It's true, I helped to plan and carry out Eddie's murder. I didn't know him as Eddie, though, I knew Nigel, the journo. I've been writing it all down, all the details will be there.'

There was a buzzing deep in Joan's ears, like the soft hum of static on a radio. 'No,' she said, gripping her knees. 'Why would you have killed my brother? It was the IRA, one of that lot.' *Scum*, Gran had spat, twisting and twisting a tea towel in the kitchen, her knotted fingers whitening with the effort; *they should all be rounded up, all the Micks, and sent packing.*

'That's what we intended the police to think. I did it with a couple of the comrades, Finn and Majella. We were a little revolutionary group and we executed your brother for the sake of Ireland.'

'But you're English,' Joan said. The glass of wine she had drunk earlier with Rich was curdling in her stomach.

Over the years she had pictured Eddie's killer as a masked man, like the ones you saw standing by coffins, ready to fire a salute, a man with a Balaclava and that horrible accent.

'Yes, that's what lured Nigel in. He had no reason not to trust me. I set him up and my friend pulled the trigger. He didn't suffer, he never knew what happened, he died instantly. We buried him in a lonely place in Antrim. I hardly knew him and I killed him.' She made a gesture with her hands, of sorrow and hopelessness.

Joan got up slowly, with the kind of effort Nina had to make. There was a constricting band around her head, pulling tighter. 'Why are you saying these things? I've been working for you, why would you want me here, why would you be a – a friend to me if you'd done this to me?'

'Exactly because I *had* done it, don't you see? All these years I've had it on my conscience and I finally found a way of telling it. Have some brandy, Joan, you're in shock.'

There was a fly circling the vase of sweet-william. Joan watched it light on a blossom, its wings flickering. The woman in the florist had said they would last for days if she mixed a special sachet in the water.

'We were about as important as that fly, our little group,' Nina said, 'but we thought we were movers and shakers and we assumed the powers of life and death. I didn't know about you then, of course; I wouldn't have wanted to know.'

She was opening another bottle of brandy, her hands shaking, fingers struggling with the top and she continued to talk but Joan couldn't hear her, her ears were full of sea noises now, the crash of waves, the hiss of spray, the moan of wind scudding across heaving waters. It made her think of Eddie in that tiny boat. She shook her head, pressed her ear lobes in to block the sounds.

'. . . drink it straight from the bottle,' Nina was saying.

'I'm sorry, Joan, so sorry, I'll never be able to tell you how much I regret what I did.' There were tears in her eyes.

Joan seized the brandy and took a deep draught. It made her gag as it scorched her throat. She walked to the window and looked at the world outside. It seemed exactly the same as it had done half an hour earlier and it shouldn't, it should have been a different colour or the pavement should have cracked open, the trees should have dropped their leaves, the sky should have fallen. This couldn't be true, that she was hearing this news in this sedate house in this handsome street from a woman whose accent sounded like the backbone of Britain. Nina was still going on, saying that she had been young and mad, saying complimentary things about her, Joan, saying that she had seen Nigel as a tool of the state, whatever that was. *He was happy one evening I spent with him in Donegal,* Joan heard, *I wanted you to know that, I don't know, it might help . . .*

Joan put the bottle down on the floor. 'You're telling me you murdered my brother.'

'Yes. We murdered him because he wrote lies about us and we buried him and I haven't had a day's peace since and I haven't deserved one. Joan, if I could only turn the clock back . . . I know exactly where the grave is, I can tell you so that you can . . .'

'Stop it!' Joan dashed for her bag, kicking the brandy over. She was sucked into the ocean now, struggling, catching her breath, desperate to keep her face above water. She ran from the room, from the house and a stream of brandy flowed around the legs of the coffee table like a sticky tide.

Nina sat motionless, weeping, her head heavy. She felt no relief, just an arid satisfaction that she had nearly completed her task. Goodbye Joan, she thought, good luck and good riddance to me from your life. Pain was tugging at her joints.

She reached for her laptop to start the instalment she had been planning before Joan's arrival:

'Majella mia; nearly there now.

'I have just told Joan and she has understandably fled from me, the wolf-woman with a tainted soul. I gave her the bare bones. All of this that I have been writing can be the flesh. You lived every moment of the next hours with me and I want you to relive it now, second by second; we were never more together or more apart, moving in unison, yet locked into our own private emotions. There have been times, making love, when I have thought of that night, the intimacy of sex resurrecting the feelings of total bonding and complete aloneness.

'We were still exhilarated from the dancing when we reached the Pine Trees. At eight-fifteen Nigel hadn't turned up. The wig was overheating my brain.

'"He definitely agreed to be here at eight?" you asked for the third, fourth, fifth time.

'"You were with me, you know he did. Maybe he's held up on one of his exclusive, impressive stories."

'"We can't sit here too long, it's not safe."

'We waited another five minutes, not talking, looking eagerly every time a car approached. It was a dismal evening, saturated by a persistent rain that oiled the windscreen. I flicked the wiper blades now and again. They needed replacing and smeared droplets across the glass. The faint, irregular screech irked me.

'"Do you think he's guessed, somehow?" I asked.

'"No way. How could he?"

'"I don't know. Maybe I said something or we were seen and he's been tipped off."

'"Then why would we be left sitting here? The pigs would have been round our necks by now."

'"Oh God!" I banged the wheel in frustration. "It's been going too smoothly, something was bound to happen."

'"He might have left a message for you inside. You'll have to go in and check."

'My hands were clammy. "What if someone sees me?"

'"You should be okay, you don't look like you."

'"What are we going to do if he can't make it?"

'"Change the plan, of course," you snapped. "Look, we've got to know, we can't go on sitting here like a pair of eejits. For Jesus' sake, go in!"

'I fumbled my way from the car, cursing Nigel under my breath. You made a flapping movement at me with your hands; *go on!* your lips formed. My heels grated on the flagstones of the hotel drive as I willed my legs on, skirting puddles. A conviction was growing in me that Nigel had rumbled our plan, that this was a set-up. I hadn't been as clever as I thought; he'd been double-bluffing me. I was going to walk into the hotel foyer and spring a trap. This might be the last rain you walk through for a while, I was thinking, the last gulps of fresh, free air that you'll take for years.

'Fear mingled with a rush of defiance in my veins; part of me craved the martyr's sacrifice. Already, I was visualising the banners the comrades would make to protest at our captivity, hearing the song that would be speedily penned and sung rousingly in all the bars along with "Kevin Barry" and "The Boys of Wexford". They were all about men, those songs of freedom, but this act of rebellion would give the nationalist people heroines as well as heroes. I didn't hesitate; if that was my destiny, so be it. I remember hoping that I'd be put in the same prison as you and my wish was granted, of course, but not by being found out. As I reached the revolving door a car horn blared and I turned to see Nigel screeching into the parking bay. He ran over to me, explaining that there had been an accident and a traffic jam. "Are we ready to party?" he asked and I laughed with relief, a kind of loud yelp, leading him to the car.

'You had already moved into the back seat and I introduced you. I had asked if you wanted to be called by a false name but you'd said why bother, he wasn't going to be repeating yours to anyone. I headed out of the city on the Larne road while Nigel blew his nose, commenting that he'd caught a stinking cold. He told us he had been in Dundalk, checking out this priest who was supposed to have connections with arms suppliers stateside; I winced at the way he said *stateside* with elaborate casualness, emphasizing his transatlantic connections. He lit a cigarette, a king-size variety and offered you one. You accepted and leaned forwards as he flicked his gold lighter. A wind rose as we reached more open countryside, slanting the rain and whipping the car aerial which emitted a plangent whine. I had to peer to see the road through the bleary screen, wishing that Finn would pay more attention to car maintenance. Nigel asked if I could turn the heater up, his cold had given him the chillywillies and I flicked it to high, the wild thought that soon he would find a permanent cure for his ailment crossing my mind.

'As we approached Larne, Nigel said that he wanted to stop and buy fish and chips; he was famished, hadn't eaten since breakfast. You should feed a cold, he said, and Friday was always his fish and chip night, ever since he was a kid. Of course I know now that *feed a cold* would have been one of Gran's sayings and I'm sure that *chillywillies* was a word she'd have used in his childhood. I glanced back at you, concerned at an unscheduled halt and caught your shrug. I could hardly refuse. We turned down his offer to get us some, saying we'd had dinner. He made a remark about ladies wanting to keep their figures although he didn't think we two lovely girls had anything to worry about. You coughed sharply. I pulled the car in away from street lights and we waited while he headed into a chip shop.

'"They might remember him in there," I said, "if the police ask."

'"Doesn't matter, they won't know who he was with. What a chauvinist geek! Reeks of aftershave, doesn't he?"

'"Yes." I didn't want to talk about him. This ordinary, humdrum business of the fish and chips was unsettling. It made me think of the condemned man's last meal. I doubted that Nigel would have chosen such plain fare, even if it was his Friday routine, if he'd known it was to be his final dish.

'"You okay?" You touched my shoulder.

'"Fine. Is he coming yet?"

'"Just on his way."

'"Are you all right?" I could feel the chemical buzz driving me, despite my fears.

'"I'm great; the adrenalin's pumping. Like you, I want to get on with it. The cigarette helped, very thoughtful of him."

'Nigel had bought plaice, a large portion of chips, a saveloy and a pickled egg. The combined aromas filled the car, circulated by the blasting heater. He loosened his scarf and removed his fleecy sheepskin gloves. He held a chip under my nose and my stomach twisted, the whiff of vinegar making my mouth smart. The egg smelled like something ancient and rotten. I knew that inside it would be a greyish hue, tough but slimy on the tongue. I tried to ignore the snuffling gasps of his chewing through his blocked nose, the crackle of batter as he tore pieces of fish, the click of his jaw. The windscreen wipers were sliding wearily in front of me and I concentrated on their *screech thump screech thump*. The car slid through sheets of water in the black, anonymous landscape. It seemed to me that I had been driving for hours. "What's this shebeen place going to be like then?" Nigel asked through a mouthful. "Will there be IRA blokes there?"

'"I shouldn't think so," you replied. "There's more to Ireland than the IRA, you know. Shebeens have music and dancing and sometimes story-telling and plenty of booze flowing."

'"The Irish certainly like their booze. Mind you, I'm not surprised, it keeps the chill out. This sodding never-ending rain! I reckon it softens people's brains." He sneezed loudly, reaching for his hanky.

'"What did you find out about this gun-running priest?" I asked, aware of you bristling behind me.

'"Well, my enquiries are still at an early stage but I'm linking up with a reporter in Boston. Most mouths were shut in Dundalk although I met one bloke who I think might prove useful if I can show him some dosh. Got to get my editor to agree that; a couple of hundred should do the trick. Either of you got any tissues? I know it's the kind of thing ladies carry in their handbags and this hanky's sopping."

'You searched your pockets. "Here," you said, "only I can't guarantee it hasn't been used." You handed him a large tissue which carried a whiff of Finn's tobacco.

'He honked into it, making me start. The inside wheels bumped the verge at the edge of the road.

'"We're nearly there," you said, giving me my signal that I should stop within a couple of miles. Nigel licked his fingers noisily and I took a deep breath, watching the road carefully. As if in anticipation of my planned action, there was a bang and the car swerved. I braked and Nigel had to catch his supper to stop it sliding from his lap.

'"What's up?" You gripped my shoulder.

'"I'm not sure, the steering went funny."

'"Burst tyre," Nigel told us. "Driver's side, front. I know

that sound well, I make a habit of getting punctures. I've probably jinxed you.'' He sounded remarkably cheerful about it.

'I stared at him, at the small crust of egg yolk at the corner of his mouth, then turned to you. I knew nothing about tyres except that they were round and made of rubber. ''Can you fix it?''

'You shrugged. ''Never have before. I've watched my brother, I'll try.'' I saw my anxiety reflected in your shadowed eyes.

'Nigel laughed. ''You girls, you shouldn't be allowed out on your own! I'll do it, I could change a tyre with my eyes closed. I suppose you have got a spare?''

'You nodded at me, your crossed fingers held up behind his back.

'''Yes,'' I told him, ''there's a spare.''

'''Well, I don't relish the idea of getting soaked but neither do I want to spend the rest of the night on a country road. Is the boot unlocked?''

'''I'll get the tyre and the jack.'' You were half-way out of your door. ''With your cold, you want to stay out of the rain as much as you can.''

'The lid of the boot went up and I offered a silent prayer to Finn; please, please have a tyre in there.

'Nigel patted my knee reassuringly. ''Don't look so worried, it's only a puncture, I'll have it fixed in no time. They call me greased lightning where tyres are concerned.''

'I nodded. ''Great, thanks.'' I realised why he was unaccountably cheerful; this was an opportunity to show off another talent to an appreciative female audience.

'You appeared by my side of the car, rolling a tyre. You ran back to the boot and returned with an item which I took to be a jack.

'''Here we go then,'' Nigel said, zipping his jacket and

tying his scarf in place, "Sir Nigel to the rescue of the damsels in distress!"

'I could still feel the pressure of his fingers on my knee. As he slammed his door raindrops flew in on me. You and he were talking out in the darkness, gesticulating at the wheel. I had a sinking sense that everything was going to go wrong, that this was all out of kilter; you shouldn't be out there chatting like friends, heads bent so that they were almost touching. Just about now, a bullet should be lodging in his skull. The torch that you were holding up for him was to illuminate his grave. Suddenly the door was yanked open and you pulled at me.

'"Get out!" you hissed.

'"What?"

'"Get out. He can't jack this thing up with your weight in it."

'"Oh." I tumbled out and wandered to the verge where my shoe heels sank into quaggy mud. A marshy smell of rotting autumnal vegetation rose. Nigel was down on his knees on the road. The car lifted into the air and he set to work with a spanner which you handed him.

'Watching the two of you, I was reminded of another, similar road in Cornwall, one with the same high hedges and worn tarmac. I had been on holiday with my parents, a break taken during the slightly better days when my father still had his lucrative job, before my mother promoted him to enemy first class. The radiator had developed a leak during the drive back from a restaurant to our hotel. The three of us had got out to look at the sizzling pipe under the bonnet and as we stood there a drizzle started. My mother took instant, personal offence when any inanimate object ceased to function efficiently and accused my father of failing to service the car properly; "and now we are stranded in this wilderness," she said, implying that we were separated from civilisation instead of five miles from Padstow. I sniggered and my father turned and winked at me, wrinkling his nose. There, on that lonely Antrim road, I missed him with a sudden, bone-deep agony and I whispered his name. Nigel sat back on his heels, sneezing half a dozen times and shaking his head. We might not have to shoot him after all, I thought wildly, he might die of pneumonia at this rate. I pictured him keeling over on the road and the two of us driving away, unable to believe our luck. Natural causes, the coroner would say; lung congestion brought about by a severe wetting. I could see the rain slant silver through the torch beam, landing on his head and I became mesmerised by it, screwing my eyes up to make the light fragment and dance. Then I realised that another light was illuminating the road; I turned and saw a van coming towards us. I had the sense to run forwards as the driver slowed and leaned down from his cab. Pulling the wig around my face, I held my hood tight, a hand across my mouth so that my voice was indistinct.

'"Have you trouble there?" he asked.

'"No, just a burst tyre."

'"Need a hand?" He was weather-beaten, grey haired. He had thick glasses, the kind that distort and enlarge the eyes.

'"No, thank you. It's nearly done."

'"Bad night for it."

'"Wet enough," I agreed.

'"I'll be on my way if you're all right."

'"Goodnight, thanks."

'He manoeuvred past the car, waving. You kept your back turned, standing in front of Nigel. I fixed my teeth together and headed towards you. You came over to me. Your eyes were strained and wide. You rested a hand against the front of my coat.

'"Nearly done," you muttered. "God, what a bastard thing to happen. I know that guy, that driver. He's called Devine.

He delivers logs to us every couple of months at the farm."

' "What's he doing here?"

' "He lives this way." You were gripping me and I couldn't see your face in the blackness. "He trades all over the place."

' "You don't think he recognised you?"

' "He can't have, I kept my back to him and my hood's up. He's got terrible eyesight, anyway; my father always says he doesn't know how he's allowed to drive. He hasn't seen me for ages, probably wouldn't remember me." Your voice was unsure.

' "We've been seen, though. If he comes forward afterwards they'll have an idea of the location."

' "Only a rough one. He didn't see that much. Anyway, we can't worry about that now. Listen, I'm going to use the gun when we get back in the car, we're almost at the spot anyway. I'll do it as you start the engine."

' "All sorted," Nigel called out, "we can pack up now."

'Inside the car, he blew his nose long and loud. His congealing, half-eaten supper lay on the dashboard. I waited for you to finish in the boot, wiping my face with my fingers.

' "Not bad, eh?" Nigel said, satisfied. "Just under a quarter of an hour. What do you think?"

' "Brilliant, really brilliant."

' "See, you've just got to have a bloke around sometimes, whatever the women's libbers say."

' "Yes, I'm sure."

'As soon as you had closed your door I reached for the keys. I looked in the rear-view mirror and saw you nod.

' "Tight nuts on there," Nigel was saying as I fired the engine; underneath the growl of the ignition turning came the sound of a sharp explosion. I swivelled around, away from him, to look at you. You wouldn't meet my gaze but busied yourself placing the gun back inside its duster.

' "Feel his pulse," you said.

'I slowly turned back to him. His head lay against the window. There was blood on his neck, flowing darkly into his scarf. His wrist was damp against my fingers. "Nothing." The unfinished egg lay in the paper below the windscreen, looking like a fixed, jaundiced eye. You leaned forward and wrapped a towel around his head, securing it in his collar.

' "Get going then," you prompted.

' "Wait a minute." I couldn't stand the smell of his supper any longer, or the sight of the cooling chips, the egg-eye and the pale, dismembered fish flesh. I bundled what was left in the paper, opened the car door and threw it over a hedge. Then I rolled down my window, inhaling. "It was making me sick," I explained. As I looked at you, at your tense jaw and burning glance, I wondered if I looked the same. I thought sudddenly of the day we had met, of the joy I had felt and a fearsome sense of dislocation startled me, an awe at what we had done and become that the drug man's tablets could not mask.'

Nina dropped her head forward and fell into a brief medicated trance full of vivid images of denuded trees, water-sodden roads, needles of wild rain dancing. She started, her mouth coated with the taste of old fear.

'Martin,' she wrote, 'see the woman you married, look at her and count yourself lucky that she removed herself from your life. This is the last stretch on the journey to perdition. I don't know what I am asking of you now; perhaps just to stay the course with me.

'I drove on through drenched, winding roads with isolated farmhouses set back behind low walls until Majella told me to take a right turn. The road became bumpy and started to climb. The engine whined in low gear. I found that I was pressing on the wheel, urging the car forwards. After half a mile the skeleton shape of a bungalow appeared in front of us, bouncing over rough stones. Whiteness caught my eye; Nigel was still holding a tissue in his right hand. I climbed into the back of the car and changed out of my wet suit into jeans and a jumper. I stuffed the wig away, scratching my scalp which had grown warm and itchy beneath it. Majella fetched the waterproofs from the boot. In silence, we pulled on the leggings, wellingtons and anoraks, securing the hoods tightly. Lastly, we encased our hands in rubber gloves. Nigel's body rocked slightly with our movements.

'We left him in the car, locking him in, and grabbed the spades. I followed Majella to the side of the house where the builders' trench lay. Our torches picked out debris: sandwich crusts, crisp packets and empty beer cans.

'She scrambled down, the top of the trench at her shoulder level. "They've filled in about a foot with junk," she said. "We'll clear it and bring him over." She gathered up some of the packets and cans, handing them to me. "We'll put those back on top when we've finished. Now, point the torches down and hop in."

'I joined her and we started digging, each of us throwing spadefuls behind us. The soil and rubble were loose but heavy, weighted by the downpour. Rain rattled on our anoraks, dripping from our hoods onto our faces. We unearthed more beer cans, pork-pie and chocolate wrappers. Some of the heavier stones defied the shovels and we had to bend to lift them, heaving them backwards.

'Majella was stronger and faster than me. She had dug her share of potato drills as she was growing up, but I tried hard to keep pace with her despite the fact that this was the first time I had held a spade; it seemed a matter of honour. After just fifteen minutes my lungs were straining and my shoulders aching but I didn't pause, not even to wipe the stinging rain from my eyes. We were silent, intent. The only sounds were of our waterproofs rustling, the spades slicing and our panting breaths.

'It took us just on an hour to clear a suitable space for a dead man of five feet ten. Majella climbed out first and hoisted me up, our trembling hands grasping. At the car, she took Nigel by the torso, her arms under his shoulders, and dragged him out. I lifted his feet in the black leather boots with side buckles that he'd proudly shown me, the ones he'd bought in Petticoat Lane when Joan was with him. I didn't look at the towel on his face, I concentrated on those buckles glinting in the beam of the torch I held wedged in my armpit. We staggered across the ground with him. When we reached the trench I looked down.

'"How do we get him in?" I knew that we could throw or roll him but I didn't want that. Some small quiver of decency must have been in me or perhaps I couldn't bear the thought of the thud he would make as he landed. Majella paused too. She stood swaying for a moment.

'"Sit him on the edge," she said, "then I'll climb in and you can ease him down to me."

'So we sat him, his boots dangling and me holding him steady while she jumped down. He still smelled of fish and vinegar. My back and calves were aching and the muscles in my upper arm throbbed from the exertion. Majella reached up for his waist and I levered him down but he toppled, slumping forwards, so that she lost her balance and sprawled under him in the space we'd dug, his legs across hers. For a moment I stood frozen. In the torchlight they looked like two ghostly lovers caught unawares in the open, the kinds of spectres that peopled some of Majella's favourite legends.

'She struggled up. "Jesus! Could you not have kept a grip on him?"

'"My hands are slippery in these gloves." There was a slide in my voice and I swallowed, willing control.

'Majella brushed herself down and pulled his limbs so that he was lying straight. I joined her. We looked through his pockets and took fifty pounds from his wallet, agreeing that it should join the coffers of Red Dawn. Around his neck was his St Cristopher medal, glinting in the torchlight. We left it with him. We shovelled again, a reversal of our previous movements, covering him with the soil we had removed. When we had shifted it all back we redistributed the rubbish and fixed heavy stones around the top. My right glove had torn at the tip of the index finger and I could feel the cloying wetness of grit under my nails. We hoisted ourselves up with the spades and torches and headed to the car without a backward glance. We stripped off our waterproofs and deposited them and the gloves in a bin liner, wrapping the spades in another and shoving the lot in the boot.

'I drove as fast as the road would allow. It was gone two in the morning and the air was cold and keen. I felt my teeth knock together, my arms tremble. I had never experienced such total, racking weariness. When I said this to Majella, she replied that I just wasn't used to physical labour; "it hardens you," she said, but I think she was unaware of any irony in her words. Other than that brief exchange, neither of us spoke. We stared ahead, she with both hands tucked in her pockets. On the other side of Larne a wavering shape materialised on the road, glimmering in the liquid light. I braked, hearing her gasp. It was a sheep; it glanced at us, then turned and shimmied away, its bottom bobbing comically in the headlights. I shook, a long shiver travelling my body. Then I started laughing, a hiccuping chuckle. Majella joined in.

'"We did it!" I crowed.

'"Yes!" She raised a clenched fist.

'I shivered again, the warmth of the car diminishing with the idling engine.

'"You 'aven't got the chillywillies, 'ave you?" she asked in a nasal cockney accent, snorting at me.

'"I think I 'ave, I think ladies like us get them too," I replied.

'"Chillywillieschillywillieschillywillies," she chanted, her eyes watering.

'I was convulsed with laughter. We sat there, hysterical in the drowning landscape. As soon as one of us calmed down the other would repeat "chillywillies" and we would start off again, our faces wet so that I couldn't tell which was the salty blurring of my eyes and which the streaming rainwater on the windows. Finally I put the car in gear and drove on. I had hiccups all the way to Belfast and Majella informed me that her mother recommended a salt cruet pressed to the back of the neck as a sure remedy.'

17

MARTIN AND NINA

Martin reached the hospital late on Monday night, catching a taxi from Heathrow. Willing the miles to go faster, he told himself he shouldn't have gone away. A detective met him in the foyer. He was given a cup of tasteless tea to wash down a tale of deception and murder. He listened to a description of a long letter and the chaos of a Saturday when lives had been fragmented. He had been in the force for ten years, the detective said, and he had never come across anything like it. His eyes mirrored Martin's own bewilderment. Nina had been well enough to speak to the police earlier in the day, he was informed. She had been told about Majella but they'd spared her the details, worried that she might relapse; perhaps Martin could tell her? Nina was in a drugged sleep. Martin sat in a side room, reading the letters, getting up now and again to pace. The hospital was quiet, a place of murmurs punctuated by the occasional whine of a lift.

At five in the morning a nurse came to tell him that Nina was showing signs of waking soon. When he entered her tiny room she was still asleep, the sheet up to her mouth. Her breathing was heavy. That was so unlike her, he thought, touching her shoulder. She had always breathed lightly; he had never been able to hear her on those rare occasions when she slept while he was awake. Once, early in their marriage, he had leaned across to check that she was actually taking breaths because she was so silent and he couldn't see her chest moving. He had been like a parent hovering anxiously over a baby in a cot. Looking down at her, he felt as if he had failed her. If he had been able to uncover her secret years ago it might not have come to this. He shouldn't have allowed her to retreat into her fearful solitude, staying alone with her demons.

He sat by the bed until she woke, staring at the wall, trying to absorb what he had read. When she opened her eyes she asked him to pour a glass of water.

'They said they'd contacted you,' she said. Her eyes were glassy from whatever they'd injected her with.

'I'd have been here sooner but it took them a while to locate me.'

'How much have they told you?'

'They gave me a copy of your letters.'

'Ah. And you're still here.'

He touched her hand. 'I see now that you've been living with demons.'

'Yes. I regret having involved you, Martin.'

'I don't regret it.'

She shook her head. 'You will, you will. I woke a little while ago and remembered; Majella's dead, she's dead and I unwittingly contributed to her dying. That's my true punishment now. What was she doing in my flat, did they tell you?'

He nodded. 'They've been in touch with her mother today, she still lives in Pettigoe.'

'Still milking her cows, I expect.' She lay back on the pillow. 'Go on. I was drugged up earlier, I couldn't stay awake when the police were here.'

'Are you sure you want to hear this now, are you well enough?'

'Oh Martin, as if that matters. Just tell me what you know.'

He tried to calm himself. 'They told you that Richard Lawson, Rich, had just got out of prison?'

'Yes. Joan had her own secret, didn't she? I was too presumptuous, thinking that I was the only one with something hidden.'

'He found your address on Joan's client list but he wasn't your first unexpected visitor of the evening. Majella got in because you'd left the doors open. Why did you do that, can you remember?'

'I'd finished printing off the section I'd been writing after Joan ran away and I felt terrible. I went to call the doctor but the phone was out of order so I decided to go to the phonebox on the corner. I must have forgotten the doors – I was too ill to care. Did I collapse in the street?'

'Yes, a motorist called an ambulance. Majella must have arrived about half an hour later. She had left Ethiopia three weeks ago on a kind of furlough; she'd been ill with a virus and it was decided she needed a complete break. Majella hadn't seen her mother for five years so she decided to visit Pettigoe. She was looked after there, built herself back up. When she felt stronger she decided to come to London and see you. She knew about lupus and guessed from what you had mentioned in your letters that you had it in an advanced state. It seems that she walked in and sat down to wait for you, assuming from the things left lying around that you'd be back shortly. She probably read the Keats anthology that was found by her feet, then fell asleep there in your chair with the expectation of seeing you when she woke up.'

'But instead of me she saw a stranger, a stranger who assaulted and killed her. He thought it was me, didn't he? Rich thought she was me. Joan went back and told him and he came after me.' She winced, closing her eyes.

'That's what he's told the police. He was angry, jealous, a bit drunk.' *Picture it,* the detective had said; *you've just got out of jail after a long stretch, spent the afternoon making love to the woman you've been waiting for after years of celibacy, sunk half a dozen cans of lager, discussed your wedding plans and you find out that this toff who's been giving your Joan big ideas killed her brother.* 'He didn't mean to kill Majella, though.' The detective had added that, when she'd screamed, Rich had punched her around the head; *he's a big bloke,* he'd explained, *if he'd wanted to finish her off he could have easily, but her heart gave way.*

Martin took a drink of water. 'The autopsy showed that she had an inflammation of the heart muscle, an undetected legacy of the virus she picked up in Africa. The shock killed her. Of course, Rich thought *he* had. He'll be charged with manslaughter.' He edited as he spoke, not mentioning that Rich had gone berserk, ripping all the plants from their containers, smashing china and pictures, tearing the bookshelves apart. The only book he hadn't damaged was the Keats, lying on the floor.

Nina kept her eyes closed. When he finished speaking she didn't respond for a while. Then she looked at him. 'I want to sleep now, Martin. I have a favour to ask you, but you can refuse if you want.'

'Go on.'

'I need to finish my account, my long letter. I know Majella will never read it now and I've given the police a statement but I can't bear the thought of leaving my written story unfinished. I haven't the strength to type it but if you brought my laptop in I could dictate it to you.'

'What have you got left to tell?'

'The aftermath of the murder, the trail of guilt that tracked me down the years.'

Looking at her, he knew that it was one of the last things he would do for her and recognised his own need to help her complete it. He would come tomorrow, he said. Her eyes were closing again as he put his coat on. When he left the room her breathing was the only sound in the stillness behind him.

The next day, on the tube, he glanced at a tabloid lying on the seat beside him; *Bloody Hungry Loony Lefties*, it said. He saw Nina's name and a photo of her from a back issue of a university journal, looking quiet and reserved. He took the paper, folded it and stuffed it in a bin on the platform.

Nina was awake when he arrived by her bed. She appeared restless, a little feverish and was anxious to press on.

'Do you know how Joan is?' she asked as he switched on the laptop.

'No. The detective I spoke to said she's gone to stay with a friend, Alice.'

'The woman who runs the agency. Well, she's got some-one, anyway.'

She spoke quickly and tonelessly as he typed, stopping now and again for a sip of water. He tried not to hear the words but simply record them; later he would read and understand them.

'On the night we left that other grave we arrived back at Rock House at around three in the morning. Finn must have been loitering by the front door because it opened before Majella could insert her key. He had a good fire burning and coffee brewing. A plate of sandwiches lay on the tray he brought in but neither of us touched them. We gave him a run down of the evening's events. He looked concerned when we told him about the van that had stopped but when Majella assured him that she had kept her back turned he relaxed. Just in case, though, he said, he'd get rid of the car straight away; one more burned-out jalopy in one of the many street barricades that smouldered in the city wouldn't draw any attention. He stretched an arm around each of us, drawing us near and kissing our heads. We'd been brilliant, he told us, overcoming setbacks and completing the mission. We were to head for bed; he would find a place to torch the car, then make his phonecall to the pigs.

'We were both yawning and subdued after our laughter on the road back. I suppose the tablets were wearing off by then, too; I felt empty. Majella was desperate for a hot bath but I'd had enough soaking for the night, I wanted only to sleep. The fire was scorching but not warming me. Majella and I hugged, as was our custom before parting for the night but even as our arms encircled each other I felt an awkwardness and we both turned away without an accompanying kiss.

'That night, and for nights to come in the months ahead, I couldn't get warm, not even in my mother's tropically heated house. A coldness had taken root deep in my bones; sometimes it seemed like the dank chill of the anonymous grave we had left Nigel in, a thing of wet earth and hard stones. Several times I dreamed that we had lost the gun, dropped it somewhere on the road or that Finn told us that it had vanished from the hiding place in which he had deposited it. Twice I had the same, technicolour nightmare that Majella and I were in a police line-up, being scrutinised by the van driver, who finally stopped pacing, took a step forwards and pointed at us. I would wake, teeth clenched, thinking that I had heard the front door shattering, kicked in by heavy army boots. Then Nigel's prized boots would come to mind; I would see them, mud-caked or recall the way he and Majella had curled together in the hollow we made.

'One Sunday morning I made tea for Finn and Majella, taking it to their bedroom and the sight of them lying close summoned up Nigel, the incessant rain, the cloying clay. I was half aware of him all the time, hidden there near the glens, gradually sinking deeper beneath the builders' detritus.

'During the rest of October and for most of November I was only dimly conscious of the world around me and of Majella and Finn. I was constantly tired, my limbs sluggish. I craved sleep. I could never get enough; I crept to bed by ten at night and dozed late into the morning, dragging myself into yesterday's stale clothes at lunchtime. The close, frozen grey of the sky outside which stayed low and leaden for weeks reinforced my desire to hibernate; just a glance through the window made my eyelids heavy. I bought another sleeping bag, inserted it inside the one I had and lay bundled tight but no warmer beneath their double weight and a heap of blankets. Guilt and remorse weren't companions in my bed; although I thought of Nigel and often pictured him when I woke briefly, I soon drifted away again. The horror of what we had done didn't start to visit me until months later. My feelings were frozen with my bones and I slept in order to anaesthetise myself. My main concern then, a selfish obsession, was the cooling of my relationship with Majella. My lassitude meant that I missed lectures and Red Dawn meetings. Finn commented that I must have 'flu and the three of us pretended to ourselves and the comrades that that was the reason for my absences. Majella appeared to be carrying on as normal but the reduction in our daily contact, although unremarked, meant that our conversation when we were together was stilted. I often felt as if she was waiting for me to say Nigel's name.

'His death made the front pages. Clergy from all denominations appealed for the whereabouts of his body to be revealed and his newspaper offered a reward for information. We scrutinised the press and particularly the *Daily Echo* which promised that it would not be deterred from printing the truth by lily-livered commies. There was a large photo of Nigel on the front page, inside a black-edged box. I remember sitting at the kitchen table while the three of us pored over it and thinking, we did that! Finn was peeling one of the tangerines which had just come into season, plucking segments and handing them to us. ''We settled his hash all right,'' he remarked, his nails shiny with juice. As I looked up Majella was biting into orange flesh but I didn't see her, I saw Nigel's mouth around his saveloy. I felt a distance, as if it was a long way around the table and wondered if it was the same for her or if she was as composed as she appeared.

'As weeks went by and nothing about the van driver was mentioned in the news we decided that even if he had associated us with the murder he had decided not to come forward, deciding that drawing down the vengeance of the killers was not a healthy option. So it was that the anarchy of street fighting with cars ablaze nightly, and the fear that lurked in every heart in the North came to our aid, keeping us safe. If the best place to hide a bean is in a can of beans, the best place to successfully conceal a murder is in a city where killings take place daily. Nobody from Red Dawn was ever questioned about the death, proving our insignificance, the pointlessness of Nigel's wasted life and, I am sure, proving also that Finn lied to us about his questioning by the army. He was lifted, of that there is no doubt and was detained for a number of hours, but I am sure that Nigel Howes was never mentioned and that the army had spotted Finn at a demonstration and decided to have a go at this head of a tin-pot group. Boredom must have been a problem for soldiers and perhaps they were having a slow day and looking for a bit of sport. No, Finn lighted on a way of making my mind up for me, via Majella. He did have his own peculiar talents.

'So our secret stayed secret, close and true, so close that it ate into us like a rogue parasite that turns on its previously compatible host. I don't know what dreams or fears visited Majella because the subject was never discussed. We referred only obliquely to what we had done and once he had finished enjoying the first flush of publicity, Finn stopped mentioning it. Our friendship, once so open and vibrant, had become like a stale marriage with no-go areas. Majella seemed to turn to Finn more than ever and I assume that she confided her anxieties in him. Suddenly, they were rarely apart and Finn was at home a lot more. On the mornings when I managed to rouse myself for lectures he accompanied us to the campus and was often present for lunch and again at the end of the day to walk us to the house, placing us on either side of him. I would see him leaning by the railings, the long beige trenchcoat he had found in the back of his father's wardrobe looking incongruous against the fluorescent yellow laces of his boots. I had the sense of a parent waiting at the end of school and half expected him to hold our hands and ask what we had done in lessons. I don't know whether he was genuinely concerned for us or, more likely, keeping a careful eye on us for any suspect reaction, any sign of guilt.

'My body decided to wake up in December. It was hard to resist the decorations going up around the city and the celebrations being organised on campus. I had assumed that I would spend that Christmas, like the previous one, with Majella and Finn, with a couple of comrades invited around for the evening. I was shocked when Finn – not Majella, not

Majella – told me in the second week of December that they were going to spend Christmas in Paris. His mother owned an apartment there, he explained, and they fancied a change. I sensed a deep, lonely fear. I remember thinking that I had known nothing about this apartment and the sudden way it was revealed to me made Finn seem a stranger.

'I hurried to find Majella. She was in the bathroom using a malodorous pink depilatory cream on her legs. I shrank back from the sulphurous smell which reminded me of Nigel's pickled egg. I stood in the doorway watching her white limb balanced on the bath rim and her deft strokes with the plastic spatula.

'"I thought we'd be spending Christmas together, like last," I said, trying to suppress the panic in my voice.

'"Oh, has Finn told you? He wants to do some work on the apartment for his mother and we get so little time. Will you go home?" She kept looking at her leg and the pink goo.

'"This is my home."

'"Well, yes but your mother might like to see you."

'I couldn't believe what I was hearing. Majella knew exactly how arid my home life had been: she had absorbed my descriptions of how agonisingly the festive season had always dragged by in Maidstone, giving as it did full rein to my mother's talent for spreading tidings of discomfort and discord.

'"You've got to be joking, Majella, you know that my mother's house is the last place I'm welcome."

'"I know, I know, but even the closest of friends need a break from each other now and again." She looked at me then, twisting her head round. Her cheeks were suffused with an embarrassed flush. "Things have been a bit fraught between Finn and myself, to be honest. We could do with some time together."

'I had never before felt like an interloper but I did then. The enquiry of a curious comrade came back to me, a question posed through the racket in Mulligan's; how come *two's company, three's a crowd* doesn't apply to your domestic set-up? she'd asked. I had shrugged, thinking smugly that she was envious or lacking understanding of the finer layers of intense friendship. Suddenly the bathroom felt crowded and uncomfortable. The intimacy of the scene, an intimacy I had shared countless times before, sitting on the bath edge while Majella wallowed in bubbles or helping her section her hair and apply a glutinous henna mixture, was all wrong. I realised that I had miscalculated something but how I had come to do this was unclear.

'"If you want to borrow the car," Majella added, "you'd be welcome in Pettigoe, I'm sure. Or maybe Declan or Vinny would like your company."

'So she had a back-up plan to farm me out to her parents or suitable comrades. I was like a difficult relative, the maiden aunt that nobody actually wants at their festive table but shoulders a reluctant duty to care for in the spirit of the season.

'I muttered that I would make my own arrangements and hastened to my room, blinking back tears that I allowed to flow as soon as I had shut my door. I cried for some time, wallowing in abandonment and self-pity, thinking back to Christmas Day the previous year, a celebration the likes of which I had never known and now knew with a terrible clarity that I never would again. I had felt the crescendo of a childish excitement which had been absent in Maidstone; it was as if I was being recompensed for all those years bereft of anticipation and sheer enjoyment.

'The week before Christmas, Majella arrived with the goose her mother had fattened and plucked for our festive dinner. She hung it by its feet in the cold bathroom where it turned in the draught, pink and pimply. I felt a twinge of pity for its limp-necked nakedness. We named it Ian, after Ian Paisley, because it glared at us with fixed eyes full of animosity. Majella would declaim to it from the bath, shaking her back brush at it, crying fiercely that Popery would be vanquished and the scarlet whore of Rome was an abomination unto the Lord.

'We started Christmas Day at eleven with champagne while we exchanged presents; I gave Finn a dark green Donegal wool jumper and Majella a silver bracelet of fine Celtic knotwork. She had bought me a fringed Connemara shawl similar to the one she had and I admired, in a beautiful weave of heathery purples. I wore it for the rest of the day, tucking it around me; I used to wrap myself in it at night too, threading the tassels through my fingers. It was the one memento I couldn't bring myself to throw away when I later cleared my room. Finn gave me a paperback on the Bolsheviks with an inscription inside: *For my comrade with fraternal greetings*.

'Light-headed with several glasses of champagne, we roasted the goose, deriving huge, tipsy amusement from enquiring of each other if Ian was crisp enough yet; made apricot and ginger stuffing, burnt a flame on top of the pudding Majella's sister had made, eased our way through six bottles of the thirty-year-old burgundy laid down by Finn's father and played backgammon before the fire, falling asleep in the late afternoon, sated and happy, with our heads on musty cushions.

'Lurking in my basement, I heard the drifting murmur of Finn and Majella talking, then their feet scuffling in the hall and the thump of the door as they went out. That Christmas just a year ago now seemed a time of innocence. I roused myself, splashed my face with water and headed to Mulligan's where I got paralytically drunk. During the night I woke to find myself in a comrade's flat, underneath blankets with a man I couldn't identify but recognised as someone I had seen at demonstrations. There was a close, unpleasant odour of stale socks and beer. A stickiness on my thighs testified to an intimacy I had no recollection of. I dressed, letting myself out into the dark cold street. I was hungover, nauseous, thick-headed. A light snow was falling and I lifted my face to it, taking gulps of air, glad of the stinging on my skin and its clean taste on my tongue. The grubby bed I had just left spoke to me of how much I had become lost to myself. I made my way along the empty pavements, moving alone and fearful through the whitening world.

'I spent five days of Christmas in Maidstone, drinking as much as I could of my mother's favourite tipples, advocaat, crème de menthe and cherry brandy. They weren't drinks I liked much but they were available in quantity and their medicinal flavours complemented my fragile feelings. My mother made no comment about the empty bottles but she eyed me curiously and a little distastefully. I had upset her plans to entertain and be entertained by members of the bridge club and I could see how glad she was when I refused invitations to accompany her to other, similarly chintzy houses for mince pies and sherry. While she was out I turned the heating up full, filled two hot water bottles and curled on the sofa with a generous glass of foaming yellow, green or syrupy red drink, watching television. Westerns, comedies, carol services, musicals and variety shows all flickered before me but I was barely aware of one programme finishing and another starting. When my mother presented me with food I ate automatically and without interest, always offering to clear away because the booze was kept in the kitchen.

'Majella was constantly in my thoughts and I was bereft, suffering from the separation. By the end of a week I knew that I couldn't stand not seeing her any longer and I booked a flight to Paris. She had given me the address there – reluctantly, I thought – when I'd said I would like to write to her during her two weeks away. I knew that I would be an unwelcome guest but I didn't care, my need for her outweighed any disapprobation I would encounter and I was without pride. I imagined that she was secretly missing me too. I argued to myself that she had had to give way to Finn, that he had been the one urging the trip and she had agreed to go for the sake of their love.

'I drank gin on the plane because it was the first item on the bar tariff. I had no idea where I was going to stay but that suited me; I had been cast adrift anyway, so hurtling through the clouds, not knowing where I would rest my head that night, was fitting.

'It was early afternoon when I arrived in a misty Paris, tight with gin and misery. I had never been there before but nothing about it interested me except that it held Majella. I stared sightlessly from the cab window. The apartment was in Montmartre, on the fourth floor of an opulent Victorian block with an old-fashioned cage lift. Majella opened the door and her face paled visibly when she saw me, hugging my duffel bag. She exuded the perfumed warmth of a recent bath and was wearing an unfamiliar red paisley dressing gown. Finn was out shopping she said, stepping back to let me in and what on earth was I doing there? As I followed her through large, immaculate and elaborately furnished rooms I saw immediately that no work had been needed on this apartment, that I had been lied to. Over the drawing room mantelpiece was a large oil portrait of a woman with a haughty face and dark hair swept up in a bun. She was so like Finn, I knew she must be his mother. I looked about at the elegant perfection surrounding me and thought how deceptive Finn was, how amazed the comrades would be if they knew that this was his background. There would be no cream soda and corned beef sandwiches served here.

'Majella stood, not inviting me to sit down, agitating her fingers in a huge bowl of potpourri. I had never liked potpourri; an ancient, decrepit great-aunt who I had been taken to visit as a child kept some by her chair. The smell of those scaly dried flowers mingled with the odour of her ulcerated legs suggested decay and loneliness. I am a trespasser, I thought, suddenly conscious of the gin on my breath and the greasy strands of the hair I hadn't bothered to wash for days clinging to my neck.

'"Why have you come?" she asked again.

'"I missed you," I said and saw her face harden with pain, I thought, as well as annoyance.

'"For goodness' sake, Nina, I've only come away for a couple of weeks."

'I swayed, drunk and tired. "Things just don't seem to be the same anymore. You're further away than Paris from me."

'She had raised a wrinkled rose petal to her nose. I could detect its faint, arid fragrance on the air between us. "Are you regretting what we did?" she asked swiftly. "You've gone peculiar, you know."

'"No, no. It's what it's done to us. I feel as if you're tired of me."

'She brushed her fingers together, a neat movement. "Don't make a mountain out of a molehill. I told you, Finn and I need time together. He's been feeling left out."

'"What do you mean, left out?"

'"Well, we did the . . . the job, didn't we? We took the action, not him."

'"But that was the way he wanted it." I was perplexed, the gin abetting my slowness. Never before had I struggled to understand Majella.

' "Look, I really didn't mean to talk about that, it's point-less." She presented a blank look to me. "Was it hell on wheels in Maidstone?"

'That was my first adult lesson in the tactic of leaving someone stranded, abandoning them to their agonies because your own guilt renders you hard and keen to hurt. As always with Majella, I was a quick student and I often reflected on that scene later and how she indicated with her voice and shoulders that we were exploring our differences no further. I didn't blame her then and I don't now. Whatever she was going through, whatever was happening between her and Finn, she was incapable of any other action. We had done a momentous thing and it had transformed us. If I was disappointed, if I thought that she was a lesser person than I had imagined – well, I was in no position to criticise. I never forgave her for walking away from me but I never once doubted that she loved me and I continued to love the person I thought I had known, or perhaps partly invented to meet my own neediness.

'Finn's key turned in the door and she moved quickly to greet him. He nodded to me, handing Majella the groceries he'd bought. I could see a chicken, wine, bread and cheeses through the string bag. He was smartly dressed in new cor-duroy trousers and a tweedy jacket. He looked older, out of reach.

' "We didn't expect you," he said.

' "I came to see Majella."

' "We're invited out, you see," he continued, as if I hadn't spoken, "out to dinner. I'd ask you to stay of course but the apartment's not mine and my mother is due to arrive at any time. We're back soon, Nina, back in Rock House. Every-thing will be the same."

'I looked again at the chicken and the red wine, pictured the coq au vin they were planning, with cheese to follow.

Afterwards, replete and content, they would make love. I felt as if my skin was being pared to the last layer. I met Majella's eyes, her green-blue eyes that were always peering slightly because she was myopic but too vain to wear glasses. I wanted to fall towards her. She gave a little hopeless shrug, pulling her dressing gown tighter. I was overwhelmed by the quick fury of the forlorn. I reached for an antique shepherdess standing on a table beside me, a pale porcelain figure with a coy expression. I smacked her down on the mahogany surface where she shattered. Then I picked up my duffel bag and walked out through their silence.

'I found a hotel near the airport, checked in, wrapped my shawl tightly about me and lay in bed watching French television, unable to comprehend a word that was said despite my fluency in the language.

'Martin told me that Majella was wearing my purple shawl when Rich found her. He must have thought that the knowledge might comfort me and in a way it did. So much of my misery had been woven into the knotted fringes but in later years, when I pulled it around my shoulders, it reminded me of that easy, joyful morning when I'd unwrapped it. I like to think that she was cradled in its fraying folds before she died.

'The day after my trip to Paris, New Year's Eve, I flew back to Belfast. Rock House was empty, the families upstairs away visiting relatives. It was freezing and my basement had the numbing chill of a vault. I could have used the upstairs sitting room, lit a fire, but I resolved not to, I couldn't trust how I would feel if I stepped in there. The fireplace in my room hadn't been swept for years. Soot occasionally dropped softly down it, puffing an ashy cloud over the grate and I didn't dare risk setting fire to the chimney, even though in my poisonous mood a Mrs Danvers gesture might have appealed. I carried a small electric fire

down from the kitchen and plugged it into a loose socket
then dragged my mattress from the bed and laid it in front
of the reddening bars.

'I had bought my full quota of duty free. I opened a
bottle of wine and climbed into my sleeping bags without
undressing. I could have gone to Mulligan's or seen what
was happening in the student union but as the company
I wanted wasn't available, I couldn't be bothered seeking
substitutes. I drank the bottle of Mosel, feeling its slow,
pleasant dulling of my thoughts. For a while I watched dust
motes drift and listened to the shiftings and creakings of the
house. At six I turned on my radio, finding Radio Éireann
and fell asleep to the stern bells of the Angelus. I woke later,
briefly, to hear the sounds of celebration and realised it must
be nearly midnight. As I uncorked another bottle there were
accordions and a jolly song:

> "If you're Irish come into the parlour,
> There's a welcome there for you.
> If your name is Timothy or Pat,
> As long as you come from Ireland
> There's a welcome on the mat.
> If you come from the mountains of Mourne
> Or Killarney's lakes so blue,
> We'll sing you a song and make a fuss,
> Whoever you are you're one of us,
> If you're Irish, this is the place for you."

'It was the kind of lyric that Majella called "old bogology".
The last lines made me think of Finn's assurance that once
you were a comrade you were never alone. I wished venom-
ously that I'd smashed more than the shepherdess. It was
from that moment that I began to blame him for my circumstances. I worked out that he was the one taking Majella

from me. It didn't occur to me that he might be subduing his own fears about Nigel's murder, seeking reassurance in Majella's arms. I was used to thinking of him as invincible. Morosely, I drank from my bottle and curled back down. At about one o'clock a knocking on the door woke me. My heart lifted; maybe Majella had followed me back, forgetting her key in the rush. I stumbled upstairs. The man I had shared a bed with a couple of weeks previously stood there, holding a bottle of champagne and smiling drunkenly at me.

'"Want to celebrate the New Year?" he invited.

'I hesitated, but only briefly. He had made use of me and now I'd return the compliment. At least his body heat would make my room less icy.

'"If you're Irish, this is the place for you," I said, pulling him in.

'On 3 January I sought out the accommodation officer on campus and requested a move back to hall. I was deadened but determined. Unused to drinking heavily, I was consuming several bottles of wine a day. It made me dull-headed and produced an amount of indulgent weeping but it took the edge off my grief and through its blanketing haze I saw what I had to do. I would continue with the cause I had made my own. The sacrifice was more than I had bargained for but Che, Leon and Rosa had made the ultimate gift of their lives. I wouldn't stay in Finn's house, however, the unwanted guest at the table. I would devote myself to my political work and my studies. I felt ennobled by my decision, more than ever the solitary, brave heroine. As long as I had a rôle to step into, as long as I could invent an interesting backcloth for my life, I could cope.

'I was satisfied with the anonymous, bare room in hall, its sobriety fitted my mood. I signed a cheque and returned to Rock House where I packed, sipped wine and left a note for Majella. It took me several attempts but I was pleased and desolated by it. I made no reference to Paris or the cooling of our friendship. I baldly stated that with finals coming up in May, I needed to concentrate on my work and I would see her around. Before my taxi arrived I went to her wardrobe and pressed my face into her dresses, hoping to keep a breathful of her with me. I will never forget the final thud of the front door and the throaty roar of the engine that carried me away from what I loved.

'Majella and Finn knocked on my door the day after their return. Finn was back in his proletarian camouflage, with beret. They had brought me Belgian chocolates, French wine and a ripe Camembert. Again, I experienced the sense of a parental presence. I saw Finn assessing the open books on my desk and the posters I had affixed to the walls; he seemed satisfied. There was only one chair which Majella sat on while Finn hunkered on the floor. I perched on the bed and opened the chocolates. I was conscious of holding myself carefully, of guarding my defences.

'"We wanted to check that you were okay," Majella said, selecting the cherry centre, as I knew she would. She coughed, a deep, chesty echo, unpleasant.

'"I'm all right. You don't sound brilliant."

'"I've had 'flu."

'"Tough." I wasn't about to offer sympathy. I was going to be as indifferent to her as she had been to me that evening in the bathroom, as she had been in Paris, even if the effort seared me.

'"We were surprised to find that you'd moved out."

'I registered that she hadn't said "disappointed" or "hurt". "As I said, I need space myself."

'"But you are okay?" Finn asked and I knew that what

he meant was, *I hope you're not going to pieces on us and thinking of blabbing.*

'I wouldn't look at him. I addressed Majella, "Yes, I am fine. Did you enjoy your break?"

'He replied, "we did, we needed it."

'I was reminded of the entertaining my mother did, where people gathered to exchange reassuringly empty phrases, content to skim the surface while nibbling canapés. I recognised how quickly intimacy can turn to distance and the awful chasm that had opened between the way we had talked and the dutiful social chat in that sterile study-bedroom made me shake my head. "We've blown it, haven't we?" I said to Majella, selecting and handing her a Turkish delight, her second-favourite centre. Neither of us had touched the nougat, which we usually fought over.

'"Just give it a bit of time," she replied but there was no belief in her voice and I laughed. I had consumed three glasses of wine for lunch.

'"You'll be coming to meetings as usual?" Finn queried.

'"Of course. Except ones held at Rock House, you'll have to make my apologies for those."

'I thought Majella was about to speak but she coughed, holding her side. I sensed Finn's shrug. "I thought maybe you were turning against us."

'"Why should I turn against a cause I've done so much for?" I presented him with more of my back view. "Do you ever think about that night?" I asked Majella, desperate to say something real.

'"I try not to. So should you. We did well, we did the right thing. That's all there is to think about."

'"You both did great work," Finn echoed. "Sterling work. If it could be made public, you'd be the toast of the left."

'Majella took a strand of hair and started to plait it. "I can't eat chips now," she said to me.

'"No, me neither."

'"Chips?" Finn asked. It was a detail we hadn't mentioned to him, the purchase of the last supper.

'We both looked at him and I think that at that moment, for the last time, we were united, realising that there were things he would never know.

'I didn't speak to Majella personally again. All that closeness, all that intimacy gone as swiftly as one of the mischievous fairies her mother swore slipped away with pats of butter from the dairy. She wasn't present at a couple of Red Dawn meetings and Finn announced at the end of January, in Declan's flat, that she had developed severe pleurisy and had gone home to Pettigoe to recover. When she reappeared, much thinner, in April, I saw her across the room at meetings or in the distance on campus. She had a faded look and the fieriness of her hair had dimmed.

'I worked on steadily, in a groove, like a walker who ploughs ahead looking to neither left nor right. I hibernated in my room, catching up on texts I had ignored for too long. I was still drinking but pacing myself, downing just enough to keep the world at arm's length, but the words on the pages in focus. I played Irish harp music, plaintive slow chords in keeping with my feelings of melancholy dignity. Sometimes in the mornings I heard hymns and a leaflet inviting me to the Evangelical brethren's Easter thanksgiving was pushed under my door. "Christ died to redeem our sins and rose again in glory", it proclaimed. There was a coloured illustration like one you would find in a child's prayer book of a tomb with the door rolled back, a hovering angel illuminated by a blazing sun and a figure draped in long white robes emerging. I shivered and crumpled it up.

'On the Tuesday after Easter I answered a knock on my door and found Pablo standing there, holding a bunch of flowers. He had written to me three times since my trip to Bilbao. I had left the last two letters, which arrived after Nigel's death, unanswered. I still liked the idea of Pablo, still found thoughts of his body enticing but I was no longer fired by lust. I was too tired, too cold inside, too keen on my self-contained state to respond to him. He was full of high spirits and I didn't contradict his assumption that my replies to his letters had gone astray. (Like all paranoid revolutionaries, he assumed that the police tracked his mail.) When he asked, while immediately starting to take his clothes off, why I had moved from Rock House I muttered that this was a better place to study for finals. I made love with him that day, and on the three subsequent nights of his stay, through embarrassment, awkwardness and the lingering residues of infatuation. The single bed, the kind that had provided delicious proximity in Rock House and Bilbao, seemed too narrow and crowded. I dreamed again of Nigel in his grave only this time the face of the lifeless body was Pablo's. When I woke, sweating, finding myself wedged uncomfortably against the wall with Pablo's heavy arm across me I felt that he was trapping me in my nightmares. I pushed away thoughts of Miguel and his handgun and the whispers of conspiracy that had passed between him and Pablo. I had little conversation; I couldn't talk about the most significant thing that had happened to me since last seeing him and therefore searched for words.

'Pablo looked at me questioningly, sensing a change in me, recognising that my eagerness had waned. On the third night he asked me if I wanted him to go and when I said yes he paled but he packed his rucksack immediately. I felt so unkind, I talked about the stress of exams causing me to feel remote, detached. It was cool, he said, these things happened; he shouldn't have arrived unexpectedly but at the door he turned and added that there had been no one else since he had met me. I felt only relief when he had gone. I got into bed and spread my limbs; that night I slept more soundly than I had done for weeks.

'As soon as my finals were over in May I packed, throwing into the waste bin my bangles, necklaces and several photos of Majella and myself. I donated the books Finn had given to me to a new Red Dawn comrade and gave curtains and throws that Majella had helped me select to a charity shop. I had contacted an old school acquaintance in London who said that I could stay with her temporarily while I looked for a job and accommodation.

'I intended to be politically active in London and I quickly joined a small leftist group but the effort of making a living distracted me. I was dismayed, too, that they wanted to make me their Irish expert, because that was a place I wished to forget. When they sought my opinion on the latest feature of the Troubles, I became impatient. The magic had gone, that was the nub of the problem. I found nothing to charm me in their humdrum meetings, nothing to excite my imagination. Without the backdrop of bombs and bullets their arguments had no immediacy. The safe London streets raised no fire in my blood. Only then I understood how much I had needed the adrenalin rush of living in a country at war; every important experience I had there was rooted in the energy of violence. I would often plunge into a severe melancholy when I left a meeting, conscious that it had only succeeded in highlighting the absence at the centre of my life. Finally, my new comrades reminded me too much of what I wanted to lock in the attic of my past.

'Six months after my return I received a letter from Majella. My hand trembled when I saw her familiar sloping handwriting on the envelope. She had taken up a temporary teaching post in Omagh and was planning to work overseas. She had split up with Finn but gave no reason. I felt curious, but a stronger emotion was the surge of satisfaction the news gave me accompanied by a hope that he was miserable. Pablo, she added, had been back in Belfast in August, enquiring after me, looking lovelorn, getting sentimental over his stout in Mulligan's. She hadn't let on that she knew where I was because she assumed I would have been in touch with him myself if I was still interested.

'My career took off, with a series of rapid promotions. London gradually sucked me into its own calmer rhythms. By the end of the seventies I could recall most of the radical arguments that had seemed important but they lacked resonance. I watched Northern Ireland continue to splinter and explode, heard the same words of anger on the same lips, saw the same streets disintegrate again and again and understood that nothing had been achieved by what I had done. Thoughts of Nigel came to me, but infrequently; it became easier to consider that night at the glen as part of another time, an act perpetrated by a person I barely recognised. When I agreed to live with Martin I believed that my marriage would be a step into a renewed, cleansed life. For the first time since I'd met Majella I experienced a jolt of the heart; here, I thought, was someone who could rescue me by letting me love him. But I merely proved to myself once more that I was adept at self-delusion, a hopeless romantic. On the day I married I set in motion the next stage of a long, inevitable cycle. Smiling optimistically in my flowered dress and with the best of intentions, I slipped a ring of grief onto Martin's finger.'

Nina put her hands over her eyes, then let them fall and looked at Martin. 'The road to hell is paved with good intentions,' she said hoarsely. 'Majella's mother was fond of that saying. I did love you, it's just that it was a defeated love from the start.'

Martin closed the computer. There was nothing he could say. He wanted to get away.

'I realised during the night that those letters weren't sent by Finn or Majella. The police confirmed that he did die in a shooting.' Nina rubbed her face, a fiery patch of skin.

Martin shrugged, rising. 'One of your other comrades must have found out, felt guilt by association.' Her eyes were closing as he spoke. He envied her the drugs that lulled her.

He walked from the hospital through a balmy early afternoon. The streets were empty but warm, like rooms that have recently been full of people and still hold their massed energy. He looked through windows at figures slumped in front of televisions or grouped at tables, eating leisurely meals. He knew that those comfortable, bland scenarios contained their own tensions but even so he was struck by the contrast between the domesticity on view and the strangeness of his own situation. He experienced an unaccustomed longing to be part of such a routine scene, surrounded by familiar expectations, grievances and small pleasures. Angus had warned him that depression might hit at any time; after all, he had suffered what his friend called a 'major life event' in his separation from Nina and to this had been added the trauma of her history and her expected death. He knew that Angus couldn't help his clinician's perspective but the way he had counted the gloomy events and dwelled on their effects only served to make Martin more despondent. How did my life come to this? he thought, breaking a leaf from a privet hedge and nibbling the dusty stem. It was the kind of thing Nina had taught him to do. He recalled the tang of her mouth when she had been chewing nasturtium leaves; quickening his pace he tried to banish the memory along with the unsummoned picture of her quick fingers searching foliage.

Back at his flat he stood under a steaming shower. During the previous night he had woken to find his eyes damp. The saltiness of his lids now reminded him of his nocturnal grief. He wondered if he would ever be able to let go of the knowledge he had, if the story he had been told would ever grow dull and uninteresting, like a yellowing book left on a shelf whose dry pages no longer entice. He doubted it. He suspected that he would haul what he knew around with him long after Nina had slipped away, Rich's trial was over and Joan had resumed whatever life she had the courage to tackle. He was like a carrier now, one of those people who unwittingly become infected with a malady and harbour it in their bloodstream.

He placed a soapy hand on his chest; his heart had been subtly, invisibly infected, just like Majella's. He knew that sometimes, in that hazy space between sleep and waking, or when he was driving or gazing into the dusty glass of a tube train, he would see Nina and Majella as they had been, carousing in Mulligan's, sunbathing in a wild garden or striding through the Belfast streets, cocky, youthful, carefree. He would try to warn them, *don't throw it away*, he'd call, *don't surrender your future*, but they wouldn't hear him or look in his direction. There in his heart, pumping deep, day in, day out, was the knowledge of all those afflicted lives; it ebbed and flowed around him, tugging at his veins, whispering through his arteries. He thought of biology lessons at school and his textbook with the lurid diagram of the circulatory system, thick black arrows pointing to chambers, valves, mapping the secret passageways that maintained cells. I may have a life to live, he thought, but I have no idea what to do with it. I don't know what meaning it can have or whether it will feel anything but a burden to me.

*   *   *

Three weeks later, Martin rang Alice on a Monday night. She had become a lifeline for him, a marker in the confusion. She'd met him for a drink after the first time he contacted her at the agency, telling him how Joan was coping. During the last call she had informed him that Joan had just discovered that she was pregnant. He thought that Alice probably pitied him and was grateful that she took care not to show it, keeping their conversations steady, factual. Joan was still staying with her. She couldn't face her flat, the home she had so eagerly prepared.

The line was busy. He waited to redial, rolling on his desk a conker that Nina had picked for him at Waltham Abbey the autumn they met. It was a little shrivelled now but still a deep burnished brown. She had reached up for it from her bike, levering herself on a pedal and polished it against her jacket, holding it out to him, saying that she wasn't in the habit of giving such expensive gifts. Anger with her seized him, bitterness at the way she had shut him out and nursed her secret as if he was incapable of understanding or forgiving. He threw the conker at the wall and watched it bounce to the floor, then cursed himself for being a fool. And what would you have done if she'd confessed all? he asked himself sarcastically. Do you honestly think you'd have been able to stay with her? Face it, the two of us were blighted from the start by something that had happened long before.

'Joan's asleep,' Alice told him when he got through. 'The doctor prescribed a sedative that won't harm the baby.'

'Is she any better?'

'Still struggling. She's planning to go back to her flat soon though and I think it would be best. The longer she leaves it, the harder it will get.'

'Yes, it's not true, is it, that things improve with time.'

'No. People say that to make life more bearable. The Irish police called yesterday. Nigel's body can be sent back next week so she's got that to get through. Maybe once she's held a proper service for him she'll feel a bit better, I don't know. I tell her she can only get through each day.'

'Has she seen Rich?'

'No, she can't bring herself to go, not back to a prison.'

'I saw Nina today. She's dying, I think.'

There was a pause on the line. 'Well, Martin, some people might say that was for the best. I know that's hard on you . . .'

'Maybe it's not. Maybe it's what I want, deep down. I think it's certainly what Nina wants.'

'I don't tell Joan about your calls, it would upset her. I'll probably tell her later, she might appreciate it in the long run.'

'There's just one thing, something Nina said. She's leaving her flat to Joan, she got a solicitor in to change her will the other day. I'll leave it up to you whether or not to tell Joan now.'

'I'll have to think about that one. I've no idea how she'd react.'

'No. Well, if there's anything I can do, any time . . .' He couldn't think what that might be but felt the need to make the offer.

'That's kind of you, I'll let you know if there is.'

He could tell from her tone that there would be no such request, that his contaminated assistance would never be required. He said goodbye and stared through the window, seeing not the hushed street but a car, rain-swept, rocking with the hysterical laughter of two young women who were trying to banish fear. He hoped that during her ill-fated wait in Nina's chair Majella might have read that letter of Keats' containing the lines, 'I am certain of nothing but of the holiness of the heart's affections.' Whatever they were guilty of, she and Nina's mutual affection had been sincere. Nina's distress at the separation from her friend had been part of her subsequent long years of punishment and the final blow was that Majella never saw her words of love, regret and longing.

He picked the conker up from where it had come to rest by the skirting, rolling it between his palms. A crack had appeared in the brown skin; soon, he knew, a mould would appear and it would rot away.

18

NINA AND JOAN

The nurse had drawn the curtains and tiptoed away.
Nina was grateful for her soft footsteps; some of them
hurried and clattered, no matter how ill they knew you were.
She was sleepy now, eyes gritty. She had little pain; the
consultant erred on the generous side with the drugs. This
is what it comes down to, she thought; hoping for a soft
footfall and a high enough dose of medicine. Still, better
than being shot or dying of shock. Joan would say: *you have
to count your blessings*. She hoped that Joan would enjoy
the flat. She would keep it beautifully. She might even hang
onto the books as objects to dust if not to read.

Martin had brought the news that Majella had been buried
in the Catholic cemetery in Pettigoe. She remembered it
well. They used to cycle past it when they had been to deliver
fresh eggs to old Mr Byrne, a distant relative of the O'Hares'.
In summer there were dog roses weaving along one wall and
crab apple trees with tart, pithy fruit that they used to pile
into the bicycle baskets and take back to Mrs O'Hare, who
would turn them into a delicious reddish-brown jelly. One

afternoon they stopped by the cemetery gate because Nina had a stitch. Majella was hankering after Finn who was in Dublin, networking with another small left-wing group. While Nina bent over her handlebars, taking deep breaths, Majella stared gloomily at the headstones, quoting; 'the grave's a fine and private place but none, I think, do there embrace.' Nina had picked a buttercup to cheer her up, tickling her chin with it, then tucked it into the band she wore around her unruly hair. If only she could have touched Majella just once more. A touch only; no words would have been needed.

Eyes closed, she was picturing Joan now, cleaning her new place, choosing paint, putting up the pictures Gran had left her and her Grace Ashley poems. There she was with a drill in her hand, installing permanent, sturdier shelving, standing back with one arm crossed diagonally over her chest to examine her handiwork. She took a break, pouring a glass of bubbly wine in the kitchen, sitting in the conservatory with one of her magazines. Nina became aware of a footfall, sensed someone approaching and reluctantly abandoned her imaginings, forcing her dull eyes open. A man was there by her bed, a man with short, receding hair, a goatee beard and wire-rimmed glasses.

'The nurse said it would be okay to see you,' he said, in slightly accented English. 'I explained I was an old friend. Hello, Nina.'

She looked, making an effort. Ah yes, there was that irregular dark brown mole by the right eyebrow, she used to feel it with her tongue, pretending it was chocolate.

'Pablo,' she said, 'how amazing.'

'May I sit down?'

'Yes.' Using her elbows, she manoeuvred herself up a little. He pulled a chair across the room. How he's changed, she thought, recalling shoulder-length hair, a shaggy goatskin waistcoat and a wide smile. He looks so conventional now, in a shirt and tie, a jacket over one arm.

He sat, resting his hands on the wooden chair frame and looked at her. 'I had no idea you were in hospital,' he said.

She was puzzled. 'How would you? We haven't been in touch for years.'

'No. It's been a long time.' He was serious, solemn even.

It was an effort to speak. She took a drink of water. 'What brought you here now?'

'I went to your flat, a neighbour told me where you were.'

'Oh.' The medication was tugging at her. She made a movement with her head, not strong enough to shake it. 'How's Spain these days?'

'I haven't lived in Spain for over twelve years. For the last nine I've been in Galway. I've studied at the university. I live in a community, a small group dedicated to spiritual growth.'

'I've always been a bit short on that.' She smiled but he stayed grave.

'This is a shock to me, Nina, finding you like this. I came to visit you because I wanted to continue the path to healing I hoped I had opened for you.'

It's his eyes that have changed the most, she realised, they're humourless. 'What are you talking about, healing? You said you didn't know I had been hospitalised.' She wondered if he was about to lay hands on her, if he had some fancy that he was a practitioner of curing through touch.

'I wanted you to find the truth in yourself,' he said earnestly, 'show you how to approach Jesus. He wants to forgive you.'

Oh no, she thought, he's come to convert me to some all-embracing faith. She turned her head away. 'Pablo, I'm really very tired. Could you come back some other day?' Her irritation reminded her of the time in her study bedroom when she wished him gone. Is this what's going to happen now, she thought; are people from the past going to keep turning up at the bedside to utter meaningful phrases, say implicit farewells? The possibility was terrible. She would be like a living exhibit in a museum.

'I won't stay much longer, Nina. But you did get my letters?'

She could hardly think through the lethargy now. 'That was all a long time ago, Pablo, let's just leave it.'

'No, no, not those, not *then*. My letters from the pilgrimage I made, the burial sites.'

Her mind cleared instantly, as if a stimulant had been injected into her veins. Her vision and hearing were sharp. 'Those were from you?'

He nodded, clearing his throat.

'I never thought of you,' she said wonderingly. She recalled the picture of the young man by the Boyne and saw how she had missed a clue. Fully alert, she sat up with a determined push, compressing her lips at the pulse of pain the movement sent through her limbs. 'But how did you know what I'd done? Was it Majella, did she tell you that time you went back to Belfast, when I'd moved away?'

'No, Finn told me. I was living in Galway and I took a trip to Belfast from a sense of nostalgia, just to look around. Finn was in Mulligan's. He got drunk – I don't touch alcohol, it's against our rules – and he told me the story. He was shot four months later.'

Her brain was racing now, piecing together. 'So was he remorseful?'

'I don't know. Maybe just too inebriated and a bit nostalgic, too. I got the impression he wasn't doing much politically any more and he'd just been made redundant from his job. I suppose he thought an old comrade from ETA would be a safe confidant.'

'He was right. You have been, up till now.'

'Up till now, yes. But Finn was wrong to think that I would see it his way. He didn't know what had been happening to me, you see, how my life had been transformed. I was jailed in Bilbao for two years in the mid seventies and I had time to rethink my existence. I met a monk, a truly holy man who helped me to see another way. It was through him that I learned of the power of pilgrimage. He believed strongly in the solace it could offer, the strengthening of the spirit that can be achieved. When I was released I made a pilgrimage to Santiago de Compostela. It was wonderful; a moving and cleansing experience. I left Spain then; the comrades would never have let me be. I spent some time in a monastery in Turin but the formal religious culture didn't suit me. I decided to return to Ireland; the country had always held an attraction for me and I read about the community. It sounded like what I was looking for. So, that's where I have been, praying, growing vegetables, studying the Bible, Irish literature and ancient Irish cultures, making a different, wholesome life.'

Now she heard that his voice had become self-satisfied, his face had a smug expression. 'I'm so pleased for you,' she said. 'So what made you decide to persecute me?'

He leaned forwards. 'No, Nina, please don't see it like that. You must understand that I had always held you in my heart. Believe me, I suffered with you on that pilgrimage through Ireland and I deserved to. Repentance should be hard. When Finn told me what you had done I experienced my own remorse. I remembered when you came to Bilbao, the things we discussed and I felt guilty that I had influenced you. I wanted you to atone and find forgiveness. So many of us did foolish things then, we were reckless, headstrong, Godless. I had discovered a way forward and I wanted to point that way to you.'

'And what made you assume I hadn't atoned, Pablo?'

'Finn was sitting there, a free man. None of you had faced the truth, that was obvious.'

He had put his hand over hers. She snatched hers away. 'How did you get my address?'

'Finn told me you were in London and Majella had gone to Africa. He gave me Majella's address. I didn't act hastily, I prayed for a long time, seeking guidance and the answer was given to me that I should draw you to repentance by taking on the burden of your sin with you. I finally wrote to Majella a couple of months ago, asking for your address. I said I had a hankering to contact you after so long. When she replied she said she didn't think you'd mind and asked if I would tell you that she hoped to see you herself before long, that she might take some time off. She mentioned that you were unwell but gave no details. Have you seen her?'

'No. One letter would have sufficed, Pablo.'

He shook his head. 'Pilgrimage is a gradual act, don't you see? By its very nature, it is a hard and demanding journey. It sanctifies as well as purges. I knew that if you weren't well, you would probably not be able to complete such a journey yourself. I saw that you would not be able to resist the meaning of the pilgrimage, no matter how deeply you had buried your memories. Those letters were a prayer, a way of helping your soul even if you resisted. I intended to come to you once I had finished, to pray with you and assist you with your burden, acknowledge my responsibility in the corruption of a young woman. But I find you here.'

She recognised that light in his eye, the intensity in his voice. It was the familiar manner of the proselytiser. 'I want you to go now.'

He stood reluctantly. 'My letters, did they prompt you to examine your past?'

'Oh yes, Pablo, in a way you could never have dreamed of. Why did you type them?'

'We don't employ our own handwriting in the community. It's too expressive of personality and character flaws. Typed thoughts are clearer and less subject to human frailty.'

'Of course, how silly of me not to have realised. I knew someone else whose beliefs made him disapprove of human frailty.' He's far gone, she mused, beyond help, poor Pablo. I wonder if it makes him happy?

'Your suffering,' he said, gesturing to the bed. 'It has meaning, you know. I can assure you of that because my own has brought me to Jesus and a purer heart. When I come back, I could pray with you. There are sweet waters of forgiveness if you are willing to let them wash over you.'

He was so earnest, so entirely consumed. She remembered the concentrated furrow on his brow when they made love and the care with which he had mixed Sangria and lime juice while explaining the ancient origins of Euskara, the Basque language, whose roots remained mysterious.

She smiled at him, holding out her hand. 'I'm glad you came, but now please go.' He touched her fingers and moved away. She heard the door squeak. When she was sure he had gone she laughed, a light chuckle of pleasure. How apt, she thought; here I am, back where I started, faced with aggressive Christianity. Should I have joined the Evangelicals then, would I have been a better person, saved, safe, no blood on my hands? If I could go back, would that be my choice? She tried to imagine wearing the uniform of the devout, scrubbing her face until the skin shone, tying her hair back with barrettes, lacing up sensible shoes, and failed, was repulsed by the image. Now, when she thought of the last few months, she was reminded of a formal dance, one where the partners break away, circle the room and return to meet at the same spot.

A nurse arrived, drawn by the laughter. 'Are you all right?'

'Yes, thank you.'

'I've not heard you laugh before. Was it the fellah who visited that cheered you up?' She had a Kerry accent, rich, creamy, like the butter they used to cram on the soda farls.

'He did.'

'He's a good looker. Is he continental?'

'Spanish. Did you fancy him?' The nurse was young, dark haired with lively eyes.

'A bit old for me, maybe.'

'I suspect he might be devoted to a life of celibacy, but I'm not sure. He said he'll be back. Once upon a time he was great fun but I think that's changed now. He liked wine and food and he was talented between the sheets; we did it oh, five, six times a night and it was heavenly, delicious, almost like being near Jesus, I should think. I certainly felt like shouting Hallelujah!' The nurse frowned and checked her pulse. A bell rang and she darted away, her flat shoes sliding on the smooth floor.

A Dublin accent sounded in the corridor, nasal and lazy. At the end she was surrounded by Irish nurses from a dozen different counties. They had all started to sound like Majella. Sometimes she was alarmed when she heard them, but mainly she was amused at the irony. The adrenalin brought on by Pablo had vanished as quickly as it had come. She could feel sleep coming closer, stealing across the pillow.

There was a snatch of a song in her head, one that Majella had taught her while they stood selling papers outside a sweet factory just after dawn on a March morning, misty and mild. In the jumbled hurry from bed she had put her jumper on back to front; the misplaced seam pinching her neck. She tried to hum the tune now, but her throat was dry:

Sleep is a river,
Flow on forever,
And for your boatman choose old John O'Dreams.

A man coming from the factory, yawning after his shift, had overheard them and said he'd buy two papers and give them an extra fifty pence if they'd sing it for him. They'd obliged and he had smiled, saying 'you wild wee girls need your heads examined, you should be safe at home tucked up in your beds.'

The central heating groaned softly, *tock tock*. She had asked the nurse to turn her radiator off. All her partners had now returned to their places and accounted for themselves. She was satisfied. Soon, she thought without alarm, I shall have a true marble heart of my own. That was all she craved now; a still heart, a still mind. As she drifted, turning on her side, the regular click of the cooling heater marked the time of a jig, 'The Wren in the Hedge', and she felt the lightness of the dance start to travel from the soles of her feet, along her calves and thighs and up through her body.

Joan sat in her pink suit at the kitchen table, listening to the fridge hum. The waistband of her skirt was tight; another week and she wouldn't have been able to get into it. Alice had just left, saying that she'd call back later in the evening, reminding Joan to eat something. *Don't forget you're eating for two*, Gran used to remind the pregnant girls she worked with. She always knew when a woman was expecting, often before the mother-to-be had realised herself. It was in the eyes, she said.

They had cremated Eddie that afternoon. Whatever remained of him had come back from Ireland in a dark wood coffin. Some unknown, kind person had fixed a small posy of flowers to the lid. Gran had been buried but Joan knew that her brother should be cremated. It seemed more final and his cold abandoned bones deserved warming at last. The police had said that if she wanted she could go and look at the spot where he had lain for all those years. The house owners who had unknowingly walked regularly across his grave to get to their garage sent her a note, expressing condolences, saying that she would be welcome to visit. Alice read it with her and asked if she would like to go. She had refused vehemently; it was a place she never wanted to see.

It had been just herself and Alice in the crematorium, a brief service with an anonymous minister saying a few prayers. As Joan didn't have a garden, Alice had suggested that she place Eddie's ashes in hers; that way Joan could visit him any time she liked and he would be amongst friends. They had interred the small urn together in the small space that Alice had prepared near a magnolia.

It seemed right to return to her own place after laying Eddie to rest. Stepping back in, she had moved tautly and slowly. Standing in the living room was like meeting someone you had been close to but hadn't seen for a long time. She sensed that she had to find a way to make the flat hers again and thought that maybe, if she could summon the energy, a thorough clean would be the best option. She was pacing herself, though; she hadn't looked in the bedroom yet, she was saving that until the kitchen and living room had grown on her a bit and she was breathing properly.

She thought that Alice had been shocked when she chose to wear her wedding suit for the funeral, especially when she considered who had helped her buy it but she was determined. Eddie would have approved of its quality and style and she would never wear it to get married now. She unbuttoned the jacket and went to the window ledge where she ran her fingers over the drying plants. They evoked

Nina, a figure bending over a pile of cuttings, trowel in hand. All those months, she thought, all those months she was playing me on a line, giving me bait. She turned on the cold tap and splashed her face, then rubbed hard with a towel, holding it still over her eyes for a moment when her skin was dry and tingling.

It was a day for finishing things. She opened the kitchen cupboards, emptying them of the alcohol and foods she had bought for the wedding party, piling tins and bottles into carrier bags. She took a couple of cardboard boxes and stacked all the plants in them, clearing every trace of greenery. As she moved the bags and boxes to the hall she built up momentum for the bedroom. Pushing the door open, she walked in pretending that this was a client's place that needed sorting. If she kept on the move, steady, working to the kind of rhythm she used in her job, she would manage. She swiftly stripped the bed of the Samarkand linen, dumped it in the middle of the floor and added Rich's suit, the blue shoes Nina had given her and the Grace Ashley tapestry from the bedside table. Then she took her pink suit off, threw it on the heap and dressed in an old shirt and trousers. She bundled the lot into a plastic sack and carried all the cleared items down to her car, bumping the bags on the stairs, kicking the sack before her.

She dropped the food and drink off at the night shelter in Haringey and drove on to the Misses Baxter, twin sisters in their eighties who had been customers of the agency for years. They had a huge tangled garden and loved bonfires; every fortnight, when she called to vacuum and do the laundry, they got her to burn cardboard boxes, newspapers, kitchen refuse and lawn trimmings in the rank, weedy area past the garden shed. While she lit the match they would stand, frail and excited, inside the curtain at the French window, holding hands and watching intently. There was a little ritual; each time, when the first flame licked, Joan turned and waved to them and they waved back, right hands fluttering, the long lacy curtain of the window floating behind them.

This wasn't her scheduled day to visit, but she didn't think that they would mind an extra burn-up and she was proved right. Their eyes shone when she explained that she needed to get rid of some rubbish and not having a garden of her own, wondered if she might borrow theirs. She took some of the newspapers they had been saving and carried her sack to the singed area. There, she turned out the evidence of unfulfilled hopes, raking it into a tidy pile and put a match to the papers.

As the flames took hold she turned and waved, then looked back at the charring materials, pushing them down with the special stout metal prong that the Misses Baxter provided. Smoke rose in a grey spiral. A button melted on Rich's jacket, the dark orange of a pillowcase blended with the rose hem of her skirt. As the plants smouldered, they smelled like autumn. She struck at protruding leaves until they crumpled, melting away. She thought of all those hours in Brixton, the endearments she had murmured; she saw herself standing in front of a mirror, impressed with her image, Nina nodding at her shoulder. Rich had said the sheets were handsome; in prison he'd had nylon rubbish.

She had no memory of the drive back to Leyton that Saturday night. She could recall hearing Rich and Alice's laughter as she fumbled the door open; when she stumbled into the sitting room Rich had been draining a can of lager, his legs swinging over the side of the armchair. Alice had looked up first and came towards her. As soon as Alice's hand touched her she had started wailing, a cry of misery from an Eastern funeral, the high keening of women garbed in dusty black. 'I don't know how to tell you this,' she'd heard Alice say when she woke from the drugged sleep the doctor's injection had induced, a large needle quelling her hysteria, 'I'm afraid it's bad news about Rich'. In her confusion she imagined that Alice was talking about an accident; 'What was he doing in a taxi?' she asked. 'Where did it crash?' Then she heard the name Majella, that odd name she'd never heard of before Nina said it and remembered a denim-clad woman leaving Nina's house. There were names now that would remain significant for the rest of her life whereas hers had meant nothing to them when they had played judge and jury on her brother.

As the blaze intensified she held her hands out to the flames, then raised them to her face, pressing some of that consuming heat into her cheeks.

She stood there until the fire had burned out and she was sure that only blackened fragments remained. The Misses Baxter saw her to the door and she walked to her car, weary, smelling the cindery reek of her clothes, knowing that she would ask Alice to take these clients off her rota.

In her flat she had a bath and opened a tin of soup. 'Petal,' Rich had said that Saturday, when they had made love, 'I could eat a horse', and she had run in here naked to the kitchen, grabbing a packet of ham and bread rolls, making a quick bed picnic. Alice had brought her a letter from Rich, expressing his sorrow, explaining that he'd lost control and that it had been his anger on her behalf that had made him go for that woman he thought was Nina Rawle. He made it sound as if taking a life wasn't so bad if it was a mistake. 'I get mad now, thinking she's still alive,' he'd added. He wanted to marry her more than ever; the baby needed its father, but Joan was unmoved by his words, knowing that she had to cut him out of her life. She'd had enough of people doing things on her behalf. First Nina, then Rich; she wanted to put a stop to it, know that there was no other hand steering her days. That couple of hours that she and Rich had spent in bed together seemed far in the past, like something she had longed for and dreamed, waking to find that it was wishful thinking. If she married Rich she would always be linked to violence, there would be a direct connection between the deaths that had occurred and her baby. Someone had to start anew, shaking off the past and it was going to be this child.

As she drank her soup she took Eddie's St Christopher medal from her bag, rubbing her thumb gently over the saint's profile. It had been returned to her as clean as on the day Gran gave it to him. 'To keep you safe,' she'd said, worried about the terrible place he was going to. Joan was glad that it had been with him down in the earth. She tried not to think about Nina but she reckoned that if any mercy was shown to her when she passed over, it would be because that medal had been left with him. Of course she did think about Nina. She would see her face that last night, the nose grown beaky, hair still damp, scraped back. 'I hadn't counted on getting so fond of you,' she'd said apologetically during one of the pauses, when Joan had been staring at her. She had stared so hard that at one point she had seen two Nina faces swimming side by side and she had been reminded of the Misses Baxter at the window. And again Nina had whispered, 'you must believe me, I genuinely enjoyed your company, it wasn't pretence, once I got to know you.' Strange, how people tried to excuse turning a knife in you.

She had no idea whether Nina had liked her or not but at times she missed her. In the mornings she caught herself glancing at the clock, thinking; just about now I'd be cutting her grapefruit or it would be time to mop the kitchen floor. Alice lived on things on toast: eggs, cheese or mushrooms piled on sliced bread. Sometimes, when she had presented another plate of Welsh rarebit or scrambled egg Joan would visualise asparagus with a hollandaise sauce, pasta lightly dressed with pine nuts and basil. She would recall the dusky evening in the conservatory when the candle had been glimmering and she had talked about Eddie, describing her dream. There, with Nina, she had experienced a mixture of sadness and contentment that had never happened before. She didn't reveal any of these thoughts to Alice because it would have sounded so odd and ungrateful.

Knowing how Eddie had met his death had reawoken thoughts of how things might have been if he had lived, if he had achieved the success he had often anticipated over supper in the kitchen. She recalled his excitement at his posting to Belfast; Gran had been a bit disappointed at his news, despite the promotion it involved, because she was a great fan of Max Bygraves and Eddie had been about to take her to one of his concerts. He planned to use his press pass at the stage door and introduce Gran to her hero. Mixing dark cocoa powder with sugar and a drop of milk, combining it to a smooth paste before adding hot water, he promised to arrange it as soon as he returned. Belfast would be full of human interest stories, he had said eagerly, packed with the dramatic possibilities that made great news; love, hate, rivalry, bitterness and little acts of ordinary kindness in extraordinary circumstances, all in one small province.

She traced a pattern in the skim of soup left in the bowl, wondering if she would have gone to college if Eddie had come back, picturing the house he would have bought for Gran, the children he might have had. But he had met a woman in a dark wig who scorned him.

It was the same time of evening as when she had sat over dinner with Nina, the shadows lengthening. At this hour every night she felt panic, a sense of the old loneliness but with an added twist of desperation. She would try to concentrate on the baby, knowing from the magazine articles she had scanned that her anxiety could be transmitted to it. Alice had brought her a supply of such magazines, hoping no doubt to focus her mind on happy thoughts but it was a daily crossword that afforded her most solace. She remembered that Gran used to turn to crosswords when she was fretting: *best to keep occupied*, she'd say, *no good crying over spilt milk*. When money was low or an insurance premium due she'd sit at the kitchen table with a bumper puzzle book. Eddie had always been quick at working out clues, even the hardest ones didn't take him long. Not that being swift with words had done him much good in the long run; he had wanted to report the news, but instead he'd become it. Journalists had been contacting Alice, asking to get an interview; one paper had mentioned that it would pay a large sum of money for Joan's story. So far, Alice had kept them at bay but now she was back in her own place they would probably come knocking. Maybe she would sell her story, tell her side of things, the cash would certainly be useful.

The idea of buying a crossword book had motivated Joan to take her first trip out alone a week before. She had walked to the corner shop feeling as feeble as an invalid, her legs unsteady, the air startlingly fresh. Although the sun wasn't bright she shielded her eyes. Once, at school, she had tried on her friend's glasses and had stepped back, hands out defensively, as the magnified playground reared up at her. Out in the street near Alice's house the pavement and trees loomed hugely, too much in focus. She had leaned against a bus stop half way, placing her hand against the concrete post for reassurance. In the shop she chose simple puzzles. While she was completing them she forgot her cares, lost in the pattern of clues and the satisfaction of fitting letters together.

She reached for the book now to pass the time until Alice

returned. As she scanned the list of clues she recalled an evening in the kitchen in Bromley when she had been trying to master playing with a yo-yo. She must have been about seven at the time. Eddie had breezed in from playing football and immediately solved a clue that had been bothering Gran for over an hour. 'You're so sharp you'll cut yourself,' Gran had said, but with ill-concealed pride. Eddie had winked at Gran, then turned to his sister and held her hand, showing her how to control the yo-yo: 'you've got to get a rhythm going, Joanie.' She could see the yo-yo now, its red and yellow spool with the Mickey Mouse face spinning and her brother's hand on hers moving up and down, up and down and Gran's head bent over her book. Eddie had smelled of damp grass and evening air; his fingers covering hers had been muddy, warm with sweat.

She slipped his St Christopher medal around her neck. It lay just above the rise of her breasts, which were tender, adjusting to the life she carried. Lifting her pen, she completed One Down and crossed off the clue.